Only The Dead

Only The Dead

James Cooke

Copyright

Copyright © 2019 James Cooke

All rights reserved.

This book is a work of fiction. Names, characters, places and incidents are either a product of the author's imagination or are used fictitiously. Any resemblance to actual people living or dead, events or locales is entirely coincidental.

Dedication

For my family whose love, presence
and patience mean everything.

Acknowledgement

Cover Photo by Matteo Catanese on Unsplash
Thanks Matteo.

Part One

Torture the data and it will confess to anything.

Ronald Coas

Chapter 1

MOORHOUSE CAME IN through the glass doors of the restaurant and paused, his face empty behind a pair of old Rayburns. Mid-forties, muscled, lithe and athletic he was made for endurance. He wore weathered denims and crumpled camo jacket, check fleece shirt open at his tawny neck and ancient desert boots. With his bloodless complexion, shaven head and five-day beard, he looked a cross between a cage fighter and a street bum. Hardly a conventional breakfast guest for a grand old hotel like the Prishtina. Disdainful patrons turned to stare at this frayed man, making plain their disapproval, but they quickly turned away as if to be seen looking might invite trouble.

Shimmon was seated at a table towards the back of the room. He sipped his coffee with feigned detachment and waited. He couldn't see the eyes behind the shades but he knew that they were scanning the room for him. His nerves jangled with anticipation and a cold, fat drop of sweat crawled down his spine. Moorhouse spotted him, gave him a barely perceptible twitch of recognition then turned abruptly on his heel. The impulse to scurry after him was strong but Shimmon controlled it. He took a last mouthful of pastry, washed it down with a slug of coffee and carefully folded his overnight edition of the Guardian. Only then did he ease back his chair and pick up his coat and laptop.

Outside, cold front rain chilled Prishtina's streets, driving morning commuters and beggars alike to shelter. Moorhouse was waiting under the hotel's portico, sharing a cigarette and comfortable silence with another man. On seeing Shimmon, he flipped the cigarette into a flowerbox and flexed his shoulders. Close to, he seemed time-stretched and etoliated, like someone living too close to his bones. His razored skull framed a thin, icy smile, and there were holes in his beard, as though he had beamed down a few molecules short. Shimmon sensed similar, menacing scars in his psyche and was glad to be on the same side.

Moorhouse tilted his head towards his companion. 'This is Sken. The best fixer I know.' He spoke with the clipped, off-beat notes of a man who spent too much time in his own world. 'The source we're going to see is Turkish. I run to Serbian and Albanian, so Sken's going to translate.'

Sken was diminutive, with black hair, olive skin and limbs that were too stumpy for his fake Gap jeans. His dark eyes flickered Shimmon's way and they exchanged perfunctory nods.

'He's an Albanian Kosovar but he's secure,' Moorhouse added unnecessarily. 'I can vouch for him.'

Shimmon concealed his indifference with a nod. 'That's good enough for me.'

An investigative journalist, Shimmon had come to Prishtina to interview Andri Boletini, a middle-ranking Kosovan mobster. It was not an assignment for the faint-hearted. Kosovo might have been cleansed but the ground was constantly in play. Ethnicity, religion or criminality - whatever the cause, for some this area of the Balkans remained a war zone in all but name. NATO had put the slaughter on hold but Shimmon knew that the killing could return at any time. He had scheduled a fast return on his fear, arriving last evening and flying out later this afternoon, but half a day contained more than enough time for this place to turn into the wrong place. Perhaps even the final place. Moorhouse had been retained as his security advisor, and Shimmon liked what he saw. The understated power. The self-assuredness. The readiness to do whatever was required.

Sken walked quickly through the puddles and climbed behind the wheel of a battered Fiat Uno. Moorhouse folded himself into the front passenger seat, leaving Shimmon to squeeze into the rear. The journalist had to sit sideways to fit and, as he struggled with the seatbelt, he caught himself in the mirror. It was an unedifying sight. A man older than his years, breathless, grey and bulky, eyes dull and lifeless beneath unkempt brows, and a two-day stubble that looked greasy, as if it had been painted on.

They drove past the Ramiz Sports Centre, turned north onto Vidovdanska then exited onto the Jug Bogdanova. The city opened out into scrubby parkland which soon gave way to mixed farming country that undulated into steep scarps and woodland. This was Pozderka, gateway to a lost eighteenth century world of isolated hamlets and hill farms. On Google Earth, it had looked like a modern suburb reaching out into the countryside, but the only hint of the twenty-first century was a scattering of modern mansions and hotels.

They carried on for a further forty minutes before turning off onto a dirt road that was wet and sticky but passable. It had stopped raining and a curious mist coated the hillside, bringing shifting patterns of light that flitted through the beeches and mulberries like wraiths.

Moorhouse was more animated now, his head darting left and right, but still he communicated nothing to the man sitting behind him. The security advisor hadn't broken silence since leaving the hotel, an intimidating freeze-out that Shimmon was not prepared to challenge. Words seemed more precious to this gun-for-hire than bodily fluids to a priest, to be exchanged only for enlightenment.

They pulled up outside a two storey house. The whitewashed walls and red tiled roof awakened in Shimmon memories of Tuscany and childhood vacations. He could almost taste the vineyards. But there was no time to dwell on the past. Riding a wave of adrenaline, he was first out of the car, first to the house. The front door was yawning a welcome and he stepped inside. Only then did it hit him that something was wrong. No-one came to meet him, no one answered his shouted greeting, no-one demanded to know what he was doing there. The stillness in this house was the stillness of death.

Fear stirred from the pit of his stomach and it continued to rise even when his companions came to stand by him. The sight of Moorhouse gripping a

Heckler & Koch P9S pistol, far from reassuring him, brought the bile to his throat.

'Next time, fucknucks,' the BG hissed fiercely, 'you wait until I've scoped the place.'

Shimmon nodded foolishly. His chest had seized with fear and a reluctance to breathe in the putrescent air. The smell was indistinct, mingling as it did with the aromas of the countryside they had brought in with them, but it was there nonetheless. The miasma of the slaughterhouse. He knew that he should run away but his body wouldn't react. Instead, with slow-mo reluctance, he followed the others as they edged towards the lounge.

The stench was stronger here, and it was accompanied by a curious droning sound, like an untuned radio. The curtains were closed and it was difficult to make sense of the shadowy shapes in the gloom. The light switch wasn't working, so Moorhouse crossed the room and swept back the drapes.

A fury of flies filled the air but Shimmon hardly noticed. His eyes were drawn inexorably to the man and woman. Both were naked and both were dead, their faces compressed and leathery, their bodies beginning to swell and their veins standing out green and red. Even as he watched, the blowflies swarmed back over them, feverish in their anticipation.

Don't look at the eyes! He recalled the advice of a young Guards Captain when he had covered the early Bosnian massacres. *The eyes stay with you. You're forever wondering about their dying moments.*

The woman was sprawled half-in, half-out of an armchair as though she had been flung into it. There were two entry wounds in the middle of her forehead. Tap-tap, you're dead. The bullet holes were surprisingly small, though the surrounding skin was bruised and split, the abrasion collars indicating how close her killer had stood.

The man's dying had been less merciful. He had been taped to an upright chair and tortured. His face was masked with layer upon layer of agony. His fingers and toes were bloodied, torn and splintered. His tongue had been cut out, blood congealing where it had flowed over his chin and chest, the tongue discarded on the floor amid the blood and excrement. And, as if that message wasn't clear enough, patches of the man's torso had been crudely flayed, stripped to the muscle to spell out the word TRATER. There was no sign of a bullet or knife wound that might have ended the man's torment. He had simply died of the suffering.

'Sweet Jesus!' Shimmon had seen plenty of death in his time but nothing quite like this. He turned away, struggling for breath, and dry-heaved.

'They broke him,' Moorhouse said tersely. 'Fuckers know we're coming.'

The taut edge of contact in his BG's voice quelled Shimmon's retching shock. Moorhouse was poised, senses probing through the buzzing of the flies, alert for a footfall, a heavy breath, or a drift of deodorant, obsessively caressing his pistol and taking reassurance from the chambered round. Sken had shrunk into himself, goose-pimpled and pallid, with a dark circle of fear about his eyes. A pistol had appeared in his hand, an old Czech CZ 75.

There was a sound out back. Someone, or something. Motioning them to stay put, Moorhouse moved swiftly to the door. A brief listening pause, then he drifted towards the rear of the house. Moments later, there was the unmistakable purr of a mini machine pistol, a deep, slapping grunt, and the sound of a body hitting the floor.

There had been no answering bark from Moorhouse's P9S.

Sken reacted with the startle reflex of a cat. Uttering a sound somewhere between a scream and a curse, he flew off towards the front door. Flew into another burst of gunfire.

There was a shocked interlude, as though someone had accidentally hit the pause button, then panic kicked in. Shimmon wasn't hurt, but that only left more space for the terror. He was trapped and alone. If he stayed inside, they would take him with ease. If he went through that door, a bullet storm would tear him apart. Death faced him at every turn. His heart lodged in his throat, his head pounded erratically. Maybe - the thought leaped unwanted into his mind - maybe he deserved to die. But not here. Not like this. And, suppose they didn't want to kill him? What if they intended to send *him* into Purgatory and cut out *his* tongue?

The sheer terror of his situation supplanted his fear. He went for it, a power-breaking surge of energy that drove him to smash open the French windows with a chair and race through into the garden. Without a backward glance, he sprinted across flower bed and lawn, leaped over a ditch and crashed into the dense barrier of thorn and branch. The hedge had been designed to keep animals out, not people in, and for an instant he thought that his momentum was taking him through. But the thicket snagged his shoulder bag and brought him down.

Winded, he tried to make himself invisible, pressing himself deeper into the soggy ground. But the alarm calls of strange birds assailed him, letting him know that this was no hiding place. Oblivious to his torn and bruised skin, he struggled to his feet, only for the hedge to come alive, reach out and drag him back down.

Then the pain struck, stabbing and twisting like a hot knife from his back to his chest and squeezing his eyes shut. He thought that he had impaled himself on a branch, but the pain leaked through the rest of his body and he knew that he had been shot. With that realisation came a deathly hush, like all the transmitters had gone down. Even the bird alarms were off.

Instinctively, he closed his eyes on coming death.

Strong hands seized him, dragging him from the clutches of the hedge and flipping him onto his back. Surprisingly, he no longer felt pain. It was as though he had been wrapped in a fire blanket. The face of a man stared down at him, his eyes dark and hateful, reflecting only torment and death. He had an Uzi in one hand, a razored blade in the other.

'You English! You think you own the world!' He spat the words, as though they were the reason for his assault. 'Your time is finished. The devil is coming and he is going to fuck all you people to death!'

Shimmon was a dead man. He knew that. And yet, the fear that gripped him went beyond his own dying.

He had failed. He had uncovered a powerful and terrible secret but he had shared it with no one. Afraid of being scooped, he had kept it to himself, and now the secret would die with him.

His last thought, as his world faded through a red haze, was the bitter futility of it all. He could summon no clever riposte for his killer, no grand words for the reaper, only the most trite and terrible of observations:

No one will ever know!

Chapter 2

ALI FEYSOR WAS deep in delta sleep when the call came. Disorientated, she sat bolt upright. A wash of iridescent light filtered through the curtains, bringing with it the drone of early morning traffic from the Edgware Road. She fumbled for her cell phone then winced as the vodka kicked back. Another night out with the girls. Before she had time to regret, or to reflect on the growing frequency of her drinking bouts, the drummer in her skull started up with a quick, heavy beat then slipped into perfect time with the ring tone. Eyes squinting against the pain, she focused on the caller ID. It was John Irvine, her Editor at the Sunday Echo.

'Sorry to wake you, kiddo,' he said. 'I need you in the office.'

Ali glanced at the clock; it glowed six-five. 'Why me? I'm not one of your bloody nighthawks.'

'This is personal. It's about Steven. Steven Shimmon.'

Steven Shimmon! A real blast from the past. He had been her mentor when she had first joined the investigations team on the Echo. They had actually been quite close for a while, in a gruff big brother-sassy kid sister kind of way, but that had been a lifetime ago. A lifetime in which he had left the Echo to go freelance, she had inherited his role as senior investigative reporter and they had all but lost touch.

'Don't tell me,' she grunted, easing her throbbing head back onto the pillow. 'He wants his old job back. Give it to him. Just let me sleep.'

'He's dead.' Irvine hesitated, a catch in his throat. 'Steven has been murdered.'

'Murdered!' Ali swung her legs out of bed. The drumming in her head was miraculously gone. 'How? What happened?'

'I don't have the details. I've only just heard, myself. Apparently, some vermin tried to mug him and he fought back. It's the kind of holier-than-thou reaction you'd expect from Steven. He can't just bite his tongue like the rest of us. Let's say, seven-thirty.'

With that, he was gone. But the distress in his voice lingered. It penetrated her disconnection like an unwanted touch, caressing her with its desolation. No tears passed her eyes but they weren't far away. Unwilling to confront her swelling emotion, she shrugged off Shimmon's dead hand, pulled her nightshirt over her head and made for the shower.

THE SUNDAY ECHO occupied the fourth floor of the six storey Echo House in Wapping. Most of its space was taken up by the open plan newsroom, with its ergonomic grid of cubicles, tables and computer terminals set on sound absorbing carpet. TV screens tuned to 24-hour news channels decorated the walls and there were vending machines for drinks and snacks.

Ali went straight to her cube, deposited her laptop case - a sports messenger bag that held her MacBook, iPhone, purse, papers and everyday junk - then booted her terminal. Still standing, she surveyed the empty office with real curiosity. At this time of day, it was a parallel, alien world: same physical space but none of the manic activity, camaraderie and graveyard wit that characterised the business end of the week. She spied Irvine alone in his den and marched in without knocking.

The main feature of his office, the one guaranteed to distract even the most focused of visitors, was a picture window that looked out over Docklands' condo canyon: a breath-taking vision of futurism rooted in some sentimental past. A sound-proofed glass wall faced the other way into the newsroom. The office itself was split into two. Irvine occupied one half, with his rosewood desk, family photos, multi-media systems, coffee machine and water dispenser. A conference table took up the rest of the room, an array of upright chairs tucked neatly beneath it. There were no pictures on the wall, just more multi-media, a smart whiteboard and a single, framed cartoon – a close up of a woman's genitalia over-drawn to resemble a man's face, with the caption:

I've seen the man in the street and he's a twat.

Irvine was sitting at his desk, gazing out over the old Docklands, but his face showed no pleasure in the view. Fair-haired, foppish and rounded, he was in his mid-forties and favoured a timeless style of striped shirt, grey trousers and grey-blue wool jacket. A punkish white scar bisected his left brow, memento of a childhood tumble from a tree. It made Ali wonder if he wore studs and chains at night. His jacket was slung over his chair.

He glanced up as she came in. Even dressed simply, in a charcoal wool crepe trouser suit over a white pleat shirt and black shoes, she was good to look at. A willowy five-seven without her heels, she had a long face that was sensuous and warm. The little make-up she used – just a hint of mascara – lightly framed her hazel eyes. Her burnt umber hair was cut into a neat bob.

'Well, buggar me,' he exclaimed, all mock gravitas. 'Feysor in the office before midday! We'll have to bump the climate summit off the front page.'

'Savour the moment, John.' She helped herself to coffee, slumped into a seat and squinted across the desk. Her eyes, usually so sparkling and watchful, were vodka dull. 'Just tell me what's on your mind and I'll be back to my bed.'

He smiled, but a sadness had entered his eyes. 'Steven was very fond of you, you know. He followed your career with great interest.'

She hadn't known. A knot tightened in her stomach and her head started throbbing again, but she allowed no grief into her heart. For Ali, everything hurt or nothing hurt. If she opened herself up to Shimmon's death, she would be swept away on a flood of her own bad memories that were too painful to relive. Irvine's wake-up call had put her emotions into shutdown and she intended keeping them that way.

'I'm sorry about Steven,' she said quietly. 'I know how close you were.'

'He was killed in Prishtina, Kosovo,' he told her, his voice harsh with suppressed emotion. 'To be frank, I can't make sense of it. He had a bodyguard. Ex-special forces. A real top gun, by all accounts. Came highly recommended.' He paused. 'He's dead, too. Taking out a guy like that doesn't sound like your average street mugger at work.'

'I guess that's Kosovo for you.'

He fixed his gaze on her, sat back and steepled his fingers. 'I've got a problem.'

'That's not uncommon in a man your age.'

Another smile, this one amused. 'How do you feel about big-footing Steven's story?'

'How do I feel? . . . ' She hesitated. Shimmon had once been a mentor and friend. He was a two time winner of *Journalist of the Year*, a reporter whose work had put one-time Home Secretary Paul Bates behind bars for corruption and perjury, and exposed bribery by British armaments firms. Earlier in her career, she would have been flattered to be asked to take over a story of his. But experience had diminished her awe. It had taken her years to banish the spectre of his brilliance and build her own reputation and, now that his ghost was stalking her again, she felt oppressed, insulted, and not a little resentful. 'Is that what you dragged me in for? To finish someone else's story? I've got my own investigations running. Serious stuff.'

He shuffled some papers on his desk, though he didn't look at them. 'Your piece about political corruption in the Met is all but wrapped up. As for your investigation into Irish Organised Crime: put it into snooze. It'll still be there when the world has rotated. Is there anything else in the pipeline? Any more *serious* stuff?'

She eyed him balefully. 'Have you discussed this with Jack?'

Jack Bradley was the paper's investigations editor. He was currently trekking the Peruvian Andes.

'Jack's on board.'

Her eyes burrowed into him. She seemed to be searching for something hidden, a secret agenda perhaps, something she wanted to know yet couldn't define. Eventually, she tilted her head and regarded him with curiosity.

'What kind of story are we talking about?'

'Corruption in high places.' He saw her grimace and chuckled. 'Steven was investigating the assassination of Mergim Lucca, the guy who led the Serb Volunteer Force in the Yugoslav wars. Lucca was cited by the war crimes commission for ethnic cleansing. He was also a Kosovan mafia boss.'

She nodded. 'He was killed by his own people, as I remember it. What's to investigate?'

Irvine was silent for a moment, her question tangling his thoughts. 'Steven had information that the SAS was complicit in the killing. Acting on behalf of HMG.'

'Lucca was pure evil.' She spoke slowly, as if she was forming her thoughts out loud. 'The kind of man for whom killing was a benediction.' She shrugged. 'So our heroes-in-camo rid the world of a mass murderer and saved the cost of his trial and imprisonment. That's a good news clip, John. Maybe a few lines below the fold on page six. Why would Steven be interested?'

'You know Steven: two wrongs can't make it right. *This is a crime against humanity. There are issues of human rights and justice involved.* He had a point. You can't have government kill squads executing people without a trial. If we allow governments that kind of free rein, unexposed, where does it end?'

An affectionate smile touched her lips. 'Bloody Steven. Even dead, he has to have the last word.'

'He had a passion for justice.' Irvine was staring at her, his face locked into a rare intensity. 'If he took on an investigation, it became more than an exposé, much more. He couldn't help himself. His hatred of immorality and injustice consumed him. It turned him from a journalist into a crusader. It's why he went freelance. The system simply couldn't accommodate him.' He paused, his face colouring at his unexpected airing of emotion. 'You're two of a kind, you and he.'

The silence that followed was one neither of them would have chosen. Irvine sucked in his cheeks and studied a dead space between them. Ali had never seen him wrapped so tight, just didn't know how to react. She took a moment to pour another coffee.

'Okay,' she said at last. 'So HMG was complicit in Lucca's death. Why?'

'The official line is that the SAS weren't even there. The unofficial official line is that they were there on a watching brief. In other words, they were silent witnesses. However, Steven believed that they had a more hands-on role. He was convinced that Lucca was killed to cover up links between HMG and the Kosovan mafia, and that our guys pulled the trigger. Naturally, this theory has been ridiculed by all branches of government.'

She nodded: *naturally*. 'What kind of links?'

'Steven pitched me on political assassination and organized crime, said it was still going on.'

'He had proof of this?'

Irvine didn't answer. She stared long and hard at him, then the resolution seemed to go out of his eyes and his gaze shifted to somewhere over her shoulder.

She shook her head. 'You don't have corroboration, do you. He kept you out of the loop.'

He grinned contritely. 'This is Steven we're talking about.' He gave her an expansive shrug. 'He claimed it was for my own benefit. If I don't know his source then I can't be compromised. It's his biggest story yet. That's what he says, and, since Steven isn't prone to hyperbole, that's good enough for me. Problem is, he hasn't reached the sharing stage. You know what he's like. The more important the story, the more you press him, the tighter he gets.' Irvine caught himself using the present tense and paused. 'What can I say? He was the most moral person I've ever known and that made him a law unto himself. If I'd pushed him, he would have walked out. He'd have taken his story to one of our rivals and to hell with friendship and loyalty. Maybe I should have kept closer tabs but I never envisaged this mess.'

She nodded thoughtfully. There was a ring of truth to what Irvine was saying. Shimmon *had* been paranoid about snoops - rival journos and government spooks who might scoop or spike his stories. Even when working in-house, he had never disclosed information, never shared sources. He had convinced himself that his calls were being monitored, his emails intercepted, his conversations bugged and his junk mail steamed. He had even refused to use the Echo's computers, keeping everything on his own laptop, and he had treated that like a duplicitous lover, never letting it out of his sight. Nonetheless, she didn't quite believe Irvine's denial of knowledge.

She gave him sceptical. 'It's thin, John. You've given me nothing to go on. How do I even know there is a story?'

'You know because I say there is.'

She arched her eyebrows. 'Because you say there is. That's proof enough for me.'

He ignored her sarcasm. 'There's a big story in there, Ali. Do you think I called you in for the pleasure of your company?' That brought a tired smile; he smiled back at her. 'I need a good investigator, someone with your flair.'

'Flair?'

'You sniff out real stories, dig up information that no one else can find. You're a natural investigator.'

'Is this the time to bring up that pay hike?'

'Ah,' he grunted, thrusting his hands out like a pair of balancing scales, 'a salary review. That would bring your downside into play. Your tendency to work outside the box, to flout the Echo's working practices, to operate like a freelance. You're Steven's spiritual heir, all right.'

'Sure. Sole heir to his scut work.' She took a deep breath and released it as if she was blowing a smoke ring. 'So this story, is it the reason he was in Kosovo?'

'Prishtina's not what you'd call a prime holiday destination.'

They were interrupted by the noise of a Sikorsky S76 dropping onto the helipad outside. Momentarily distracted, they watched in fascination as the pilot lost then regained his line, crunching onto the roundel as if it was the pad of a warship pitching in a storm.

'Executive Board dropping in for the monthly chinwag,' Irvine chuckled. 'That'll have them reaching for their sick bags!' He paused. Compassion rested uneasily on his features but it was no less genuine for that. 'I'm giving you a choice in this, Ali. Turn it down if you're not comfortable with it.'

She drained the last of her coffee in a single mouthful. 'What's the nature of this choice?'

He considered for a moment. 'Cover Steven or take over the motoring blog.'

She laughed, a light, girlish giggle. 'Okay. I'll pick it up. But when I've dug it over, when I have some substance, whether I run with it or drop it, the decision is mine.'

He nodded, relieved and grateful, and perhaps a little smug at getting the answer he had expected. 'There's another problem.'

'No kidding!'

'His notes and files are in his apartment. I'd go myself but I've got the Board. Anyway, you're the person to judge what's useful.' He pushed a key across the desk. 'After, I want you in Prishtina. Find out why he was there. Retrieve his laptop and anything else of interest.'

'Retrieve his laptop?' she echoed, all mock gravity. 'Not a job for an intern, then.'

'I hesitate to ask you, Ali,' he said, matching irony with irony, 'but there's no one else I can trust.'

She smiled bleakly, dismissing flattery and optimism both. 'His laptop will be long gone. It's a cash converter to a thief.'

'Buy it back.'

'How am I supposed to manage that? Run an ad in the Prishtina Times?'

'You're the investigator, Ali.'

She shook her head in disbelief. 'What's the budget line on this?'

'Just bring in the story.'

She stared at him long and shrewd, as though pondering her options. Eventually, she picked up the key. 'Before I go rummaging through his flat, is there anything in his private life you should warn me about?'

'Nothing that would put you in therapy.' He paused. 'Talking of your delicate sensibilities, there's the question of formal identification. In Prishtina. Are you up for that?'

She gave him surprised. 'There must be someone else, someone close to him.'

'He has a mother and sister in New Zealand. Dunedin, wherever that is. When I called this morning, his mother refused to believe what I was saying. She didn't take it in until her daughter came to the phone. It was not a pleasant experience, I can tell you. His mother is too old to travel. His sister can't leave her children.'

Still Ali hesitated. 'This doesn't feel right. I didn't know him that well.'

'But you would recognise him? Yes, of course you would. Look, if you can't cope with the ID, just say.' He waited for her reluctant nod. 'Good for you. You'd better crack on. You're booked on this afternoon's flight.'

'Booked! . . . Jesus, John! What if I'd said no!'

He spread his hands, the picture of innocence. 'This is no time to be fucking around, Ali. God knows who's going through his hotel room even as we speak.'

'You played me, you bastard!' She came angrily to her feet. 'No wonder everybody despises you!'

He beamed mock contrition at her.

Ali turned and left without another word.

Chapter 3

ALI SLIPPED INTO Shimmon's Maida Vale apartment, went directly to the security pad and punched in the code. The pre-alarm fell silent and she took a moment to regain her bearings. It was several years since she had been here but nothing had changed to disturb the familiarity. The entrance hall still offered up five glass-paneled doors, all closed. There was the same polished oak floor, pastel décor and limited edition Ackermans on the walls. Yet, there was a tangible difference. A curious stillness. A whiff of decay and stale cigarette smoke that hung in the air and caused her chest to tighten. This was no longer Shimmon's home, it was his mausoleum.

That thought spurred her into action. Find what she had come for and get out of here!

She flipped through the mail on the floor, found nothing but junk and bills, then turned to the converted bedroom that he used as his office. It was a room torn apart. Papers, books and sundries were scattered on the floor. The Mac was open, its drive removed. Gone, too, were his external HDs, fireproof disk safe and USB sticks. Even the shredder bin was empty.

The room had been spun hard, that much was obvious, but why, and by whom?

She recorded the mess on her phone camera, then began rooting through the debris. Empty folders, insurance policies, newspaper clippings, receipts, bank statements, warranties and other minutiae. A whole life meticulously saved, filed and now dumped. A whole life, that is, minus his coveted research notes, drafts and polished pieces

Hoping that they might prove useful, she folded his bank statements into her bag then moved on to the bedroom. Here, the signs of invasion were less obvious. She rummaged through drawers, searched wardrobes, felt under the mattress and patted down clothing. But she did so with the growing realisation that someone had beaten her to it, someone who knew better than she how to spin a home. Someone with the skills to break into this apartment without setting off the alarm. Someone who had ignored goodies like Shimmon's top of the range Nikon D3 and a wad of bank notes.

She didn't have to go into the bathroom. A passing glance was enough to confirm that the room had been laid to waste. Even the bath panel was off. Her mood spiraling downwards, she went on through to the kitchen. Cereals and other dried foodstuffs scrunched underfoot, their empty containers discarded randomly. These people were nothing if not thorough. The fridge was barely stocked, apart from a few bottles of wine, and the freezer was filled with ready meals. An image popped into her head - Shimmon alone with a glass of wine and TV dinner - and she found herself brushing away a tear.

Slowly, as if by osmosis, she became aware of the traffic on the Edgware Road, a noise that seemed to intensify the dead silence inside the apartment. She stirred herself, opened cupboards, looked into storage jars, leafed through papers on the counter. Dirty crocks littered the worktops. Absently, she started to gather them to the dishwasher.

She stopped herself. *What are you doing? Focus, girl! Try to think like Shimmon!*

Think like Shimmon! What was that supposed to mean?

She moved on through the dining area – just a table and chairs - to the lounge. More wreckage. Shelves swept bare. Floor ankle-deep in discarded books, shattered ornaments and broken picture frames. Even the casings had been stripped from the TV and AV boxes.

Diligently, she videoed the room with her phone, though she knew that there was nothing for her here.

She picked her way through to Shimmon's leather recliner and plonked herself down. On the window sill stood a potted plant with brown, withered leaves. That seemed to say it all. She used her cell phone to call the police. The impersonal voice took her details and told her to expect officers within thirty to sixty minutes. The delay didn't faze her. She knew that this kind of crime didn't rate a blue-light response, not with the homeowner dead abroad and intruders long gone.

She swivelled the chair back and forth. Both instinct and experience told her that this mess was connected to his murder. *Never believe in coincidence*, Shimmon had told her again and again. *It's God's way of saying you don't have all the information.* If the two events *were* connected - his murder and this break-in - she could rule out a chance mugging in Kosovo. Shimmon had been deliberately targeted. But why? And by whom? What on earth had he got himself into?

She didn't hear the creaking of the front door or anyone coming in, but suddenly a draught of cool air touched the back of her neck, making her hairs stand up. Thinking that the police had arrived, she got up to meet them. But the front door was closed, the flat as silent and empty as before.

Feeling foolish, she returned to the lounge. She sat down and reached for her bag, only for the breeze to touch her again. It was as if someone was moving around her, as if a little piece of Shimmon had survived the slaughter and come home to visit. She shivered. His spirit was keeping her company and that should have spooked her. Curiously, the thought made her feel safe and protected. Man or wraith, Steven Shimmon would never harm her.

She smiled as she recalled their off-beat friendship. She had arrived in Wapping, fresh from her success at the Birmingham Post, a rookie pumped up with raw talent and bravado but lacking in survival technique. This was an age when employer duty of care was no more than a lawyer's wet dream and the Echo's induction policy had been to hurl the neophytes into the deep end. Yet Shimmon - a man who had enjoyed a rep as a lone operator who suffered neither fools nor the wise - had inducted her into his world, the sorcerer passing on the knowledge to his chosen apprentice. Without his support and guidance, she doubted whether she would have survived a tabloid world that was harder, meaner and more ruthless than she had ever imagined.

They had never been close friends. They had rarely drank together or met up outside of work. At best, she had been a kind of mischievous muse to his cynical old pro. Yet he had touched her deeply. Even though he had left the Echo five years ago, she couldn't think of him without feelings of affection and protectiveness and indebtedness.

Right now, it was the indebtedness that mattered most.

ALI LIVED IN what they used to call a maisonette, a two-up, two-down apartment above a row of shops in Colindale. When she had bought the place five years ago, its interior had been styled after a TV makeover - modern, cold and minimalist. Now it was snug and warm, and cluttered with comfortable furniture and a lifetime's collection of books, music, movies and keepsakes. The perfect sanctuary for someone who worked crazy hours and wasted too much of her life peeping into society's darkside.

It was late morning when she arrived home, just a couple of hours before she would have to leave for the airport. She discarded her bag, flicked on the muted TV for company and filled the void with *Evanescence*, the *Fallen* CD. She checked her messages and emails. Nothing demanded her immediate attention. She made coffee then called Irvine.

'I've just got back from Steven's apartment. Someone broke in and ransacked the place.'

'Buggar me! It rains then it pours. What's the damage?'

'Hard to tell. They ripped the place apart but they didn't crap on the carpet. They left a couple of grand's worth of photographic equipment, and pile of cash, but they took his disks and files. They even removed the hard drive from his computer. These guys were after information, John. They snagged it all.'

He gave her sceptical. 'What do the police say?'

'As soon as they knew he was dead, the robbery became a victimless crime. There wasn't much they could do, to be fair. They promised a detective and a forensics officer sometime never, gave me a business card and left.'

'Lazy bastards!' Irvine snapped. 'I'll get on to them and kick some arse.'

'You're missing the point!' She realised that her voice was rising with exasperation and she stopped herself. 'Someone murdered Steven then gutted his flat. It wasn't some random happening. Whoever did this targeted Steven specifically. They neutralised his alarm system and switched it back on as they left. They ignored his valuables and cleaned out his data. They were pros, John.'

'What are you suggesting? Someone mugged him in Prishtina, stole his keys then flew straight to London and turned over his flat? Come on, kiddo. You're twisting a mild case of serendipity into a full-blown conspiracy.' He offered her a droopy, kindly tone that reminded her of her old Maths teacher trying to get her to understand the rudiments of algebra. 'The Prishtina police are investigating his death as a robbery gone wrong, and my Foreign Office contacts concur. Steven was murdered for small change and his flat was broken into by feral beings. If I thought otherwise, if I thought for one moment that this assignment was dangerous, I wouldn't be asking you to take it on.'

She grunted, not quite convinced. She knew well enough that Redtop sales were sliding exponentially and that the desperation for scoops had brought the black angel to Wapping. Irvine would never knowingly set her up but he might skimp on the risk assessment.

He misread her silence. 'If you're not happy, Ali, you don't have to do this.'

She injected a note of false alarm. 'The motoring blog, right?'

He chuckled, said nothing.

She sniffed. 'I'm good.'

'You're better than that!' he told her without a hint of irony. 'Keep me posted.'

He rang off.

Ali didn't like the idea of travelling blind to Kosovo. She needed a quick fix on this *story of stories*, but where from? Shimmon's files were gone. All she had to go on was some notion that the government had conspired to assassinate Lucca to cover up its dealings with the Kosovan mafia.

A notion, no more. But it was somewhere to start.

It was a straightforward matter to find details on Lucca. She merely had to log on to the Echo's morgue to learn that the Kosovan Serb had been a career criminal since his early teens. Long before the outbreak of the Yugoslav wars, he had been wanted on charges of murder and armed robbery. Come the war, he had formed and led the notorious Serb Volunteer Force, using it to slaughter his rival gang leaders, crown himself King of the crime lords and form cartels with the Albanians, Bulgarians and others. He had trafficked in anything that turned a profit - drugs, porn, people, gambling, sex, protection, cars, counterfeit goods, weapons - turning Prishtina into the Ebay of mayhem. He had smuggled and pimped white slaves to the west. He had supplied much of the heroin sold in Europe and North America. And he had broken arms embargoes worldwide to sell to the most black-hearted of regimes.

Away from business, he had led his SVF on an ethnic cleansing binge, bathing himself in the blood of Muslims. He was instrumental in the rape camps, the systematic slaughter of male civilians and, a particular favourite of his, the corralling of civilians into barns and setting them afire.

By nineties-end, he had become a Serb folk hero. He had also achieved the status of international war criminal, and it was this that had ultimately sealed his fate. He had gone on the run but the Hague War Crimes Tribunal had indicted him in absentia on multiple counts of murder, rape and callous inhumanity.

Ali paused, resting her strained eyes from the on-screen tales of barbarism. She stretched her back, the coffee flowed and the screen came back into focus.

At the time of his assassination in 1999, Lucca had still been living free, protected by the Serbian police. His murder had been covered by all the British and European newspapers. There was general agreement that he had been killed by his own lieutenants in a leadership coup. His wife and children had been killed with him, thus wiping out his blood line and precluding vendettas. The motivation had been straightforward enough: greed and power, and the need to deflect the attention of the international community from the everyday criminal activities of the Kosovan mafia. There was no hint of British involvement.

In search of alternative theories, Ali Googled the net's conspiracy sites. This was a virtual realm where snippets of incredible truth intermingled with even more incredible fantasy, paranoia and alternative facts, featuring alien visits, Machiavellian governments, multinational machinations, black economies and all-powerful deep states. There were hundreds of sites on Roswell, JFK and 9/11 alone. Most theories on the Lucca killing put it down to an internal mafia coup. The Bulgarian mafia and the UDBA, that most feared of Serb secret police operations, gained honourable mentions. As did Allah's avenging angel. But not even the most twisted conspiracist was suggesting that the British government had had anything to do with it.

That made sense. With the end of overt hostilities in Kosovo, the Hague Tribunal had been preparing a case against Lucca for genocide. A high profile arrest and trial was the order of the day, not covert assassination. Why would the government, any government, send in a wet team?

If anyone knew the answer to that question, it would be Shimmon's old friend and confidante, Malci Macleod. Macleod was a political commentator who had blazoned his Middle England values in his column for his 'middle-brow' tabloid. He was a master juggler of contacts who knew everyone who mattered and everything that went on. Known in some circles as 'rumour-central', he had for years been the conduit for the kind of leak that government and security services thought too sensitive for official dissemination. Ali knew that he had provided Shimmon with many a story. On occasions, as a favour to Shimmon, he had even supplied leads for Ali. Now in his late seventies, he dabbled only occasionally, like an ex-smoker treating himself to a cigar at Christmas, but Ali knew that Shimmon had still routinely consulted him.

She caught him at home.

'I can't believe it,' he said. 'Steven dead. You just can't take it in, can you?'

'No, you can't.' Ali felt herself thickening up. 'What was he doing in Kosovo?'

'Now, why would you want to know that?'

She felt her heart quicken as she heard his tone: *he knows!* 'Irvine's asked me to finish his story about Lucca. That's your territory, Malci. Steven would have come to you.'

A pause. She listened to the rasping of his breathing, found it unsettling.

Eventually, he said, 'Let me think about it.'

'What do you mean, *think about it*? What's to think about?'

'There are too many ramifications.'

'What kind of ramifications?'

His shrug was almost audible. 'Steven delved too deep and woke the monster that killed him. Now you're asking me to help you do the same.' More rasping. 'To be quite frank, young Ali, I don't think you're up to the realpolitik.'

Chapter 4

AT ABOUT THE same time as Ali was leaving for the airport, David Sandford was making his way into the Gower Street HQ of Alphaplus Research. He exchanged pleasantries with the woman on reception then touched his ID card to the reader and was beeped through to the inner lobby. To his right were the business offices, dominated by a large, open-plan room that was designed as a creative work environment – all glass, laminate, brushed steel, ostentatious technology and casually-dressed staff. Sandford never went right. He had oversight of the research company but he took no part in its day-to-day running. Alphaplus was the front for a covert, direct action MI5 unit, and Sandford's only interest in it was to maintain the air-gap.

There was a lift door on his left. No buttons, just a keypad. He tapped in the code and the door slid open to reveal a short passageway. This was the Mantrap. Designed like an airlock, it had two steel-reinforced portals that could not be opened simultaneously. Once the door closed behind him, the only way out of the trap was to stare into the iris scanner and enter the day's code. Failing that, he would have to wait on the discretion of whoever happened to be on duty. For someone without authorization, the Mantrap could prove a long wait.

Sandford was authorized. He exited the Mantrap and entered the *Opaque Zone*. This was an ultra-secure area protected by state-of-the-art access control and an anti-surveillance shield that was built into the fabric of the building. Within the Zone was yet another layer of security, the *Cage*, a fully-equipped conference room set inside a Faraday Cage that suppressed all electromagnetic and kinetic signals. It was a windowless space that contained a conference table, chairs, computer, smart board and multimedia system. All of the electronics were stand-alone.

Sandford unlocked his office, deposited his coat and bag, then went to the bathroom. An outwardly friendly man in his mid-fifties, he retained the youthful tautness and energy of an athlete, and his artificial tan, close trimmed ash-grey hair and snappy suit put him at home with the commuters. But he was no City Boy. He had served all his working life as an officer in the Security Service, also known as MI5. An expert in bugging, break-ins, surveillance and dirty tricks, he had cut his teeth on the unions and other enemies within and gone on to make a fearsome rep in special ops. He was a patriot and proud of it, a man who saw security threats everywhere and would cross any red line to safeguard his homeland.

He wasn't the only operative with that mindset, of course. When Parliament began pushing for transparency and public accountability for the security services, Sandford was one of a small cadre of MI5 insiders who resolved to push back. In 1995, when Five collocated its scattered directorates into its new

Thames House HQ, Sandford and his fellow partisans turned their covert skills on their own people to form the ghost unit known as Alpha. Operating under the maxim, *Power always adapts,* they exploited the Kafkaesque upheaval of Five's reorganisation to draw a veil over their own activities. They buried Alpha under so many layers of bureaucracy and budget laundering that no outsider – MI5 spook, JIC *[Joint Intelligence Committee]* member or Jo Public – had ever been aware of its existence. They had even misappropriated Five's Gower Street facility, redacting the building records when K Branch and SIS Liaison moved out and stealing this prime slice of London real estate for their own use.

Now, as Alpha's Head of Operations, Sandford led a hand-picked team of ex-MI5 officers, recruited for their blind allegiance to the Service and their expertise in counter-intelligence and subversion. Most of their time was taken up sabotaging investigations into the security services and running black ops to plug the holes left by politically correct oversight.

Sandford held his hands under the dryer, then proceeded to the Cage. Inside, two men were waiting for him. Seymour and Burns, Neither was the kind of man who was used to waiting but he fielded their antipathy with quiet confidence.

Seymour was Alpha's executive head. He was also Director of Five's A Branch and one of only two current Security Service staffers who knew of Alpha's existence. The other in the know was DG Leslie Housley who. despite his position as the head of Five, had no direct involvement in Alpha, no strategic or budgetary control and no knowledge of its day-to-day deliberated for a long moment before asking, 'What's our exposure?'

'The Kosovars killed Shimmon and Boletini. They trashed Shimmon's laptop, phone and other hardware. We found no reference to Boletini or any other source when we cleaned Shimmon's apartment and hotel room. Shimmon departed this world leaving no discernible footprint.' He raised a Gallic eyebrow. 'A freelance hack is robbed and killed in Kosovo. Quelle surprise! No one knows what he was up to. Nobody cares. Dead trail. That fact alone more or less guarantees that his story died with him.'

'More or less?' Burns' practiced reasonableness had developed an icy core. 'You've already told me that you don't know what took Shimmon to Kosovo. Can you *guarantee* me that he was working alone? Or that no-one will step forward in his place? Or that Boletini was a lone voice? Of course not. You offer me false hope when I require certainty. Perhaps you should consider the priesthood.'

'We had all the bases covered,' Sandford informed him confidently. 'We were tracking Shimmon's movements, monitoring his comms, keystroking his computer. He was definitely working alone.'

'Working alone,' Burns echoed. 'But with whose help?'

'Help? The man was a misanthrope. He would rather trash a story than collaborate with another human being.'

'I'm talking about his source at Operation Analytics.'

Sandford hesitated. 'We haven't established that there is one.'

'Of course we have.' Burns was caustic, impatient. 'Analytics is an ultra-secret operation involving intelligence analysts from Five and the National Crime Agency. All with high level clearance - Enhanced Security Check or Developed Vetting. No-one outside of their operation – apart from us, that is - knows of its existence. Have either of you talked to Shimmon? Of course not. Then how did he know? Take my word for it, Analytics might not know it yet but they have a mole.'

Sandford was far too experienced to accept Burns at face value. It was a given that intelligence chiefs kept things from their own people. Slyly, he decided to call his bluff. 'Perhaps we should apprise them, let them deal with the leak.'

'It would best serve us to deal with this mole ourselves.'

'Why?'

'Analytics have just identified two men whom they see as key figures in a major international crime organisation with links to terrorism. These men happen to be close associates of our old friend Griffin.'

At the mention of Griffin, Seymour frowned. Back in the late nineties, the MI5 man had acted as case officer for several key players in the Balkans Shadow Protection Programme, a kind of black ops witness protection programme for Balkan war criminals. Another secret within a secret. Only one of those clients had survived this long, a man known by the code name Griffin. Seymour had long regarded Griffin as his nemesis.

'Analytics is a data mining op,' Burns continued. 'It is only a matter of time before they dig through to

Griffin, crack his ID then work back to Alpha. If they do that, Alpha will be exposed and rendered inoperative.'

Sandford was still thinking about Analytics. 'These analysts are our own people. They won't betray us.'

'Our people be damned!' Burns was contemptuous. 'This new generation is nothing like us. They lack the commitment and stomach for the struggle. They're a bunch of bleeding heart functionaries who see nothing wrong with public accountability, open recruitment and DGs outed like movie stars. They would see it as their duty to expose Alpha's activities to the world. These people are the future of our security services, God help us. '

'They might dig up Griffin,' Seymour said, 'but that won't lead them to us. Griffin is a relic. Outside of this room, there is only one person who can decrypt him and that's the man who recruited him. Lord Figgis. His Lordship won't talk. The archives were cleansed years ago, The only connection to Griffin is Griffin himself.'

Burns said, 'Therein lies the problem.'

'It won't be a problem if we cut him loose.' Sandford puffed his cheeks out, a contrived concession of regret at saying the unthinkable. 'Protecting him conflicts with our prime objective, to bury snafus and insulate the Service. Griffin was a big mistake. We should get rid of him now, before Analytics get close.'

'We can't do that,' Burns told him. 'Truth will out but this kind of truth is especially dangerous if spoken before time. Our interests intertwine. Griffin has us by the balls. Either we continue to protect him or he cracks Alpha wide open. Our time will come but, for the moment, he is untouchable.'

Sandford wasn't convinced. 'Even if he were to surface, who would believe him. He is certified dead. He no longer fits his former ID and appearance. The old Griffin is gone.'

Seymour was less sanguine. 'He is sure to have some way of authenticating who he is. A man like that will have deposited his DNA all over, like a dog scent-marking its territory. We declared him dead and, hey presto, here he is. People will believe him. *I* would believe him. That's the problem when you bury the truth. Any subsequent exhumation becomes proof of guilt.'

'If they expose Alpha,' Burns cautioned them, 'the entire security system will come crashing down. People will ask why they need the security services when we consistently get things wrong – the cold war, the IRA, the 7/7 bombings, WMD, ISIS. We've taken so much heat from the Iraq and rendition enquiries, I doubt we could weather another crisis. The security services – MI5 and MI6 both - would be hobbled by our enemies in parliament. And as for you? My guess is you would go to prison.'

Sandford scowled. 'For doing our job?'

Burns curled his lip. 'Alpha is so far off the books you're just a deniable cabal of rogue officers.' He paused, staring from one to the other in a way that was unsettling. 'To survive, we must deal with this. Our priority is to kill the leak, hold off Analytics, and make Griffin deniable before Analytics get to him. It is essential that we retain the freedom to deal with Griffin in a time and manner of our choosing.'

The silence closed in around them, telling, claustrophobic and unsettling.

'Shimmon still worries me,' Burns said at last. 'He was close to exposing Alpha. He was no fool. If he went to Prishtina, there must have been a good reason for it. What was he doing there?'

'Does it matter?' Seymour said. 'The man is dead. His story died with him.'

'We don't know his source, and that represents a rather big loose end.' Burns' stare was a reproof; as hard as a punch. 'Shimmon was shooting very close to the mark. He was making the right links. He knew about Kosovo and Griffin and our efforts to keep it secret. He knew far too much.'

'To an outsider, what he knew would look like the insane meanderings of a confirmed conspiracy theorist.'

'Nevertheless,' said Burns, 'there remains a crack in the edifice. Shimmon crawled through and others will follow. We have to assume that it's only a question of time before his mole finds another messenger. In six months' time, or six years', someone will tug on the loose end and who knows what will unravel. If he gets away with this, the mole will want to spill other secrets. It's the nature of the beast. We have to seal that crack, cut off the loose end, find and eliminate the mole. Lest we forget, our little operation was brought into being precisely because someone in the past couldn't be bothered to tie everything off.' Burns took a moment to consolidate his thoughts. 'The Echo was bankrolling Shimmon. The editor, Irvine, qualifies as a loose end. We need to know what he knows.'

'According to my sources,' Seymour said, 'Irvine has only the sketchiest of knowledge. Shimmon was a loner and Irvine was fool enough to trust him.'

'We must cover all eventualities. Ratchet up the surveillance on Irvine. Hack, tap and trace - the full works. Call in favours with Menwith Hill. And prime Echelon.'

[Menwith Hill was the United States' top-secret listening-post near Harrogate. Under US law, the phone-tapping of foreign nationals in a foreign country was permissible. British intelligence agencies used Menwith to circumvent their own legal requirement to obtain Home Office warrants for tapping.

As for Echelon, this was the system controlling the collection and distribution of civilian telecommunications traffic. Using the latest Random Frequency Tracking System, it captured data from communication satellites, public telephone networks and microwave links. Its system of groundstations could intercept and interrogate telephone calls, e-mails and other data traffic. Its computers monitored the traffic for key words which, when flagged up, triggered operators to dip in and assess its importance. Echelon was part of GCHQ's MTI [Mastering the Internet] programme.]

Sandford had serious objections. 'I've been involved in every major Alpha op since it formed. Add to that, my work in special ops and A Branch, and there's one thing I can say with absolute certainty: we can't trust the Americans with information this sensitive. We're trying to contain the leak, not disseminate it worldwide.'

'We give them the what, not the why.'

'What's the difference?' Sandford was unconvinced. 'These people are not amateurs.'

'Quite. Without them we'll never be up on the wire. Our priority is to resolve this matter, whatever it takes.

That means rooting out the bodies and re-burying them where they will never be found.'

Chapter 5

IT WAS EARLY evening when Ali flew into Prishtina International Airport. She passed through Arrivals and collected her luggage, a single case to add to the shoulder bag she had carried on. PIA was a modern airport, designed with the sparkling facilities of a regional hub, yet it was strangely quiet that day. There were no cheap-flight sun seekers, no business types clutching notebooks, no hen parties incontinent with booze. Even the beggars had been cleaned away. It felt like a retail mall that no-one shopped at any more.

Irvine had arranged for a local fixer-cum-interpreter to meet her and Donylla was waiting with a smile that was warm and eager and conversation to match. Ali found her instantly likeable. Mid-twenties, she had butter oil complexion, a pencil thin body that owed more to nature than Belson chic, and long black hair that framed a beauty whose origins were both Slav and Arab. She picked up Ali's case and led the way to her car, an ancient VW Golf.

It took them twenty minutes to cover the 16k to the city. In that time, Ali learned that Donylla possessed a Maths degree, had studied English at North London University and had returned to Kosovo to work for UNMIK, the UN administrative function. In exchange,

Ali revealed that she was in-country to retrieve the body of her friend and colleague, Steven Shimmon. It was a half-truth, the half that she didn't mind sharing.

Ali checked in to The Prishtina Hotel, acutely aware that Shimmon had done the same only days before. Boasting aircon luxury, airport-level security and the kind of service that went out of fashion with monochrome TV, the hotel was a favourite with the international press and business corps. It was a little Switzerland, a place where Muslim and Christian could escape the ethnic hatred and meet for lunch.

Leaving Donylla to park the car, Ali went up to her room. It was an inviting place, with its modern lounge design, plush armchairs and elegant marble en-suite, but this was no time to linger. She dumped her bags and returned to reception, where she showed her paperwork and asked about Shimmon's personal effects.

The Manager took it upon himself to look after her, a duty and a courtesy. He spoke good English but he used it with restraint as he led her to Shimmon's room. She was surprised to find that it hadn't been re-let. He opened the door then waited outside in the corridor.

Ali could see no obvious sign that the suite had been tossed. The odour of cigarette smoke still clung to the air but the room was clean and tidy. Shimmon hadn't brought much to Kosovo, would be taking even less home. A single case stood on the floor by the bed but there was no laptop, and that was a real blow. Conscious of the waiting Manager, she quickly searched the room, checking drawers, feeling under the mattress, looking in every place where Shimmon might have hidden a data back up. She drew a blank.

Back outside, the Manager insisted on carrying Shimmon's case to her room.

She asked, 'Did Mr Shimmon store anything in your safe?'

'No. Nothing.'

'Did he give you anything to look after? His computer, perhaps? A letter, or a package?'

'No.' The Manager shot her a look of mild distress. 'Is something missing?'

She shook her head. 'I'm just making sure I have everything.'

When he had gone, she heaved the case onto her bed and rifled through it like a thief. She unfolded shirts, looked in pockets, inspected his socks and shoes. No phone, computer, camera or recorder. Just clothing and toiletries, the former suffused with the odour of cigarette tobacco and Lynx. Without expectation, she opened the pocket hidden in the side wall of the case. Irvine had told her about that one, mocking his old friend for his conceit in thinking that he needed it. But when she eased up the seam and pulled apart the Velcro, she found a USB flash drive and two tightly folded wads of A4.

'Nice one, Steven,' she murmured. 'Chalk One to paranoia.'

With exaggerated care, as though removing the detonator from a nuke, she extracted the flash drive. Eyes bright with anticipation, she booted her computer, only to discover that the drive was password protected. Fearful that she might trigger a booby trap, she didn't try to break the code. Instead, she turned to the papers.

The first was a printout of an article from Agence France Press, dated October 2000. Entitled, *An Aristo for the New Millennium?*, it had been downloaded from kosovopeace.org. It was a feature on Lord Harry Figgis, though why Shimmon would have been interested in him Ali had no idea. Reading it, she learned less than she already knew of his Lordship's life. An aristocrat with a lineage that went back centuries, Figgis was one of the richest men in Britain and modern enough to be a close advisor to both Labour and Tory governments. Several paragraphs were covered with orange highlighter and scribbled annotations. These related to the nineties, when Figgis had been deployed to Kosovo as a Diplomat and Administrator. Whilst there, his remit had been to forge contacts with all parties, including paramilitary groups. Based on the premise that if Shimmon was interested so was she, she put the article in her bag.

She opened up the second document and suddenly all sounds faded and the room was very still. In her hand she was holding the summary report of the debriefing of an SAS mission. It was speckled with coffee stains and scribbles but easy enough to read.

Summary Debrief: Operation Mammon: CTR, Goljak Kosovo, Wednesday November 17, 1999
Alpha One Five: *PC, BP, KM, HD*

Mission: *CTR* [Close Target Recce] *of isolated farmhouse where, according to int* [intelligence], *Lucca was hiding out with his family.*

Debrief: *Team inserted 12k to north of target and tabbed in under darkness. Established LUPs*

[Lying Up Points] *just below the ridge-line, 900m from farmhouse. Observed farmhouse using NVAs* [Night Viewing Aids]. *Noted armed guards patrolling inner and outer perimeters. Discussed and rejected infil* [infiltration] *of the farmhouse to insert LDs* [listening devices] *as the chances of contact were too high.*

Lucca emerged from the house at 7.13 am, called the guards to him then went back inside, leaving the guards in the yard. Having confirmed Lucca's presence, the team used burst transmission to contact Hereford for permission to snatch him. They were told: 'Hands off. CTR takes preference.'

Lucca re-emerged at 8.22 am. Accompanied by three men, he went into the barn. They re-emerged in a car. As it accelerated through the yard, it exploded. Such was the force, the team initially thought it had been struck by a missile. On later inspection, they concluded it had been a massive car bomb.

The gunmen who had been standing in the farmyard were dead, wounded or stunned. Two men emerged from the farmhouse and one man from the barn. All three wore balaclavas. They went from man to man in the yard and shot each one in the head, execution style. Then two of the three turned their guns on the third man and killed him, too.

The two survivors went to the barn, drove out in a second car, and sped off down the track towards the main road.

At the farm, the team found a huge crater. The car was reduced to shrapnel. The bodies inside the vehicle had been all but vaporised. In the house, they found Lucca's wife and two of his children. All three were dead, their throats cut. There was no sign of a struggle.

The team concluded that Lucca and his family had been assassinated by his own men.

The team took photos and exfiltrated to the north and their EP [Extraction Point].

Ali allowed her gaze to drift to the window and beyond. If genuine, this report was proof that the SAS had been on scene at the assassination, but as witnesses rather than participants. The key phrase was *If genuine*. Anyone with a computer could fake a report. Shimmon was the most unlikely dupe - he was compulsive in the way he checked every bit of information, obsessive in his double-checking - but she had no way of knowing if he had had the opportunity to check, re-check and accept the authenticity of this particular paper.

Desperate for something more, she looked again at the Figgis article. It wasn't easy interpreting Shimmon's scrawl, but his notes seemed to be aide memoires, emphasising the need to cross-check sources. The name Laughton cropped up twice. There was a second name, Griffin, as in: *is this Griffin?* A note in the right margin to *follow the money*, with a single string of digits that she interpreted as a cell phone number. It was answered after four rings.

'Connolly.' The guy sounded like everyman's friend, soft Dublin Irish, bubbling over with blarney-lite patter.

Ali asked, 'John Connolly?'

'Brett.'

'That's it, Brett. I'm sorry, the writing on this note is indecipherable. I'm Ali Feysor, a colleague of Steven Shimmon in London. Steven told me to call....'

'I can't talk about that.' His tone dropped a notch. 'Not on the phone.'

'Wait a minute. You don't know ...'

The line was already dead.

She hit redial but Connolly had turned off his phone. For Ali, however, his reaction confirmed that he was a lead.

She Googled Operation Mammon on her phone, found no reference, so she punched in her preset for Irvine. 'It's me. There's no laptop or phone amongst his belongings at the hotel, but I've found a memory stick and some papers. Did Steven ever mention an Operation Mammon?'

'Mammon? No, never. What have you found?'

'I don't know yet.'

'Well, find someone who does!'

ELEVEN HUNDRED MILES away, a GCHQ operative turned from her screen and called her supervisor.

'I've got a hit on Echelon. Key word *Mammon*. It's from a cell phone located in South East Europe.'

The supervisor checked his own screen.

'Okay, forward it to Curzon Street.'

Chapter 6

ALI TOSSED HER phone onto the bed, sucked in a long breath and silently cursed Irvine. Did the man actually expect her to retrieve Shimmon's laptop? How was she supposed to do that? *You're a natural investigator,* he had fawned, *you dig up information that no one else can find.* Fuck Irvine and his flattery. She had no idea where to start looking, no clue as to who or what she was looking for. And even if she had known, Shimmon's killers would have disappeared by now, footprints in a blizzard, his computer vanished forever into Prishtina's black economy.

She would try, of course. She was no pay-packet journalist, content to ask questions she knew the answers to and bail at the first hint of trouble. She was an investigator, the nosiest of nosey bastards, and her curiosity was already turning in her chest like a worm. She couldn't leave Kosovo without knowing what had brought Shimmon here. She had to know what connected Lucca's death with Lord Figgis and the murder of Shimmon. If she gave up now, the conundrum would prowl her dreams for years to come. At the very least, she should pick up Shimmon's trail, see where and to whom it led.

Without further consideration, she returned to the hotel lobby. Donylla was in conversation with the receptionist. Like so many of his countrymen, the receptionist was wiry in the way Brits had been before the fast food plague. His eyes danced with fun, his hair was black flecked with grey and, when he spoke, his tone was civil.

'I am Miro,' he informed her in English that was almost as good as Donylla's. 'I remember your friend.'

'Did you talk to him?'

'Mr Shimmon?' Miro's face acquired a sudden gravity. 'I am thinking he is tourist but now I know he is reporter. He is collected by another Englishman. This man I do not know. He is bodyguard, I think. Many men like him work here since the war. He has driver with him. Enver. Enver I know. He is local. Both men, security man and Enver, they disappear after murder. Police believe they rob Mr Shimmon. Kill him.'

Ali stiffened at that, and her heart beat faster. Irvine had told her that Shimmon's companions had been murdered with him. Something in Miro's tone prompted her to say:

'But you don't think so.'

'Enver is man to find you contacts, girls, clubs, maybe drugs. He is not violent man. I think your Mr Shimmon asks too many questions. Journalists are not welcome in some parts.'

'Are you saying that he provoked someone here, in Prishtina?'

'Someone.' Miro shrugged. 'Maybe your friend doesn't answer *their* questions and is killed. Maybe he gives wrong answer and is killed.'

'But the police disagree.' Ali frowned. 'He was killed here, in Prishtina. Can you tell me where?'

'He is found in city. Decani Hotel. He dies elsewhere.'

'What do you mean?'

Ali waited, but he had no intention of elaborating.

She asked, 'Do you know where this *elsewhere* is?'

Miro smiled, but the spark had momentarily deserted him. 'Enver tells me they go to house in Tregu. He is not happy about this.'

'Do you have the address?'

'There is no address.'

With that, he gave her the sort of regretful nod that terminates a casual conversation and turned to some paperwork.

ALI AND DONYLLA had dinner in the hotel restaurant. It was a long, narrow room with sculpted ceiling and walls broken up by shallow recesses hung with Gall paintings. There was a handful of other diners, businessmen mostly. Both women ordered beef, vegetable soup and bread. Donylla made do with fresh fruit juice, while Ali had a vodka Red Bull. She needed it. The drink was drained from her glass before she broke their silence.

'Everyone here seems to have good English.'

Donylla grinned. 'There are so many languages - Albanian, Serbian, Turkish, and the UNMIK languages. English is the common tongue.' She paused as she saw another meaning to Ali's remark. 'Perhaps you think you don't need me?' She shrugged. 'Not everyone has English. I will be useful to you.'

Ali offered a reassuring smile; if nothing else, she was glad of the company. 'So what do you do when you're not picking up strangers at airports?'

'Mainly, I translate documents at UNMIK. It is a good job, with lots of benefits. At least, that is what they tell me. It is not so interesting.'

'What would you like to do?'

'Travel the world. It is my dream. There are so many places I have seen only in books and on television.'

'So do it.'

'I don't have the money. Perhaps I should go into journalism. Journalists are the freest people in the world.'

'If I were that free,' Ali told her bluntly, 'I wouldn't be sitting here.'

Their food arrived and they chatted while they ate. At first, Ali just listened and prompted, steering the conversation away from herself towards Donylla. But, when Donylla began speaking of her time in London, Ali started to relax and, by the time they had moved on to alcohol, music and men, they were sparkling like old friends.

'This night,' Donylla announced between mouthfuls of beef, 'I will show you Kurrizi and the Qafa. There is a big music scene in the bars and cafes, and in the tunnels, of course. I will introduce you to kenge. And anatolian rock.'

Another time, Ali would have booked in for the full tour. But this was the town where Steven Shimmon had so recently been murdered. It would feel disrespectful. 'A quiet bar will do me. As long as the vodka's good. Tomorrow, I must talk to the police.

And visit this Decani Hotel. Afterwards, you can drive me to Tregu.'

Donylla's smile disappeared, though a kind of sympathetic understanding stayed in her eyes. 'That is not such a good idea. Tregu is in Western Goljak and is not on the tourist trail. The people in those parts, they do not welcome strangers. It can be a dangerous place.'

'How dangerous?'

'It is not a good place to visit. You could be a month there and still you would learn nothing. What is the point?' She had meant the question to be rhetorical but it didn't come out that way. She read the conflicting emotions in Ali's eyes as the journalist juggled curiosity, disappointment and anger. 'I understand. He was your friend. If you must go, I will take you. But I advise against it.'

It was good advice and Ali knew it. But how else was she to find out why Shimmon had come here?

'And the Decani?'

An involuntary scowl crossed Donylla's features. 'It is better to visit when it is busy. It is safer that way. Now it is busy.'

THE DECANI HOTEL was in a narrow street in the historic old town. Once touted as a tourist Mecca, this ancient district was in fast decay, blighted by the ever-encroaching cranes and concrete blocks that towered over its fourteenth century mosques. Cities were like that, of course. Buildings were cut down and others planted in their place; streets died and were resurrected; shops mutated into bars; churches became night clubs; hypocrisy begat sin. These changes were brutal and irreversible. But Prishtina was its people, not its fabric. It had a survivors' soul and, even as its historic core was being eaten away by the spider cancer of unplanned and illegal high rise, its inhabitants continued to thrive, multiply and emigrate.

The Decani itself was crumbling, with flaking white stucco and malfunctioning neon, and it was crowded by seedy-looking bars and clubs. Donylla manoeuvred into a kerbside space and immediately a young girl with cheap, skimpy clothes bobbed down. Confronted by the scowling rejection of two women, she said something unintelligible and tottered off on high heels that were too big for her. A large, scantily-dressed woman leaned against the doorpost of a lap-dancing club and glared at them. Not wanting a scene, Ali averted her eyes and followed Donylla to the Decani.

Inside, Ali stalled, shocked to think that the urbane Steven Shimmon would have come here. It was the kind of place where lost souls made their home and working girls rented rooms by the hour. A roach-infested sweatbox that reeked of boiled cabbage, human waste and stale sex. The décor was nicotine brown, with scuffed and dirty wallpaper, and a carpet decorated with spill stains and the butts of assorted smokes. Posters adorned the walls. They had been put up to add a splash of colour but, curled and torn, they merely reinforced the sense of decrepitude.

The concierge was a small, skinny runt of a man with curious teeth. Donylla spoke with him then informed Ali that she would have to hire the room where Shimmon had died in order to see it. Every instinct that Ali possessed screamed, *Danger ahead! Get out of here!* Nevertheless, she paid up and the two women followed the runt down a murky ground floor corridor.

The room was tiny, with shabby blue walls, an ancient iron bed, rumpled sheets and an armchair that was shedding its horsehair. The street girls were on overtime, and the sound of clacking heels, rocking beds and banging doors reverberated overhead. Ali stared at the bed in front of her and shuddered. She could imagine it creaking and groaning, running with wildlife, the mattress lumpy, the pillow flattened by a thousand greasy heads.

Through Donylla, the concierge told her that Shimmon had been murdered and robbed in this room by a prostitute and her pimp who had since vanished. Turks, he added, as if that explained it all. He left them.

Ali glanced around but there was nothing to see. What had she expected? She offered Donylla a sad, wry smile and they walked back to the lobby in silence. On the way out, Donylla exchanged harsh words with the concierge but Ali was too desponding to care.

They were a couple of strides short of the hotel entrance when a hard-faced man appeared in the doorway. He fixed Ali with an abusive stare and a cold knot of fear seized her. It was a pimp's appraisal rather than a punter's. She steeled herself to pass him but he shifted across to block her and her heart started thumping out of control. He wasn't particularly big or powerful, but his eyes flickered to unsheath centuries of hatred. He leaned into her, all rancid breath, and gave her a little slash of a smile. She braced herself for his touch.

'You don't belong here, English,' he said, his voice light yet guttural. 'Go home while you still can.'

Donylla snapped out a few sharp words in Albanian. He leered at her and Donylla countered with a stream of invective, her language peppered with universal Anglo-Saxon. The guy stood rock-still, blocking them for long enough to show who had the power, then he inched aside. They had to brush against him to get out.

'These people are dogs!' Donylla muttered as they walked swiftly away. 'Why would your friend go into such a place?'

Ali shrugged, nonplussed. She could have named a few colleagues who might have been seduced by the Decani's attractions, but she kept that shaming knowledge to herself. One thing she did know for certain: Steven Shimmon was not one of them. True, the man had a fascination for the low life but - a deeper truth this - he lacked the heart to live it. He was brave enough, physically. He would have charged, alone and unarmed, into the valley of death. But he loathed filth and he was terrified of disease. As for the pleasures of the flesh: fake blondes from Eastern Europe could not have tempted him. He was, to quote his favoured phrase, as queer as a fruit bat and chaste as a fairy.

He was no more likely to have come here than she was.

Which brought her to another truth: the meaning of Miro's words: Shimmon hadn't died here, his body had been brought from the killing zone.

Why?

Chapter 7

ALI IGNORED THE breakfast menu of pastries and preserves and settled for coffee. She flipped through the early editions of the London papers but they couldn't hold her interest. Despite the ugly encounter at the Decani, she had slept soundly and she was impatient for Donylla to arrive so that she could punch the clock.

Like a paparazzo on vacation, she began snapping mental images of the people in the room. The German couple, trim and self-contained, descended on this bargain basement country in search of property investments. The middle-aged lawyer, close and intimate with his attractive secretary. The young businessman with sun-bed tan, sombre suit and silk tie, absently spooning blueberries and cream while he ran over his PowerPoint presentation.

A woman walked into the room, looked around for someone, couldn't find him and left. A man entered and immediately fixed on Ali. Late-thirties, tall, lithe and Anglo, with straw coloured hair and azure eyes set in a wide, handsome face, he was dressed like a banker on a short-notice trip. A smile creased his face as he approached.

'Ms Feysor? I'm Mike Jones, from the British Embassy in Belgrade.'

'Belgrade?' She frowned, immediately on her guard. 'What are you doing here? And how do you know my name?'

He selected the chair nearest to her and sat down. 'I've been asked to ensure that the natives are co-operative. And to assist you in the formal identification of Steven Shimmon.'

'Asked by whom? Irvine? The Sunday Echo?' She took in his easy, negative smile, and her suspicion increased, 'I assume you have some ID?'

'Of course.'

She studied his photocard carefully. It appeared to be genuine, but what did she know?

'Fine,' she said. 'Now you can tell me what you're really doing here.'

'I'm sorry. I don't understand.'

'Why come all the way from Belgrade when there's a British Council, here, in Prishtina.'

'They're not equipped to handle this.'

'Handle what? Repatriating bodies is their job.' She took in his mute smile and fixed him with open scepticism. 'I haven't informed you, or the British Council, or any other of your precious apparatchiks that I'm in-country. How did you know I'm in Prishtina?'

'You came through immigration.'

She concealed her surprise by turning it into indignation. 'Do they flag every Brit, or just journalists?'

'I'm not at liberty to answer that.' He parried her antipathy with an easy smile. 'Security considerations, you understand.'

She understood all right. 'What do you know about the investigation into Steven's death? Are the local police competent? Will they take it seriously?'

'I can assure you, Ms Feysor, that the local law enforcement authorities are perfectly competent. They are keeping us fully informed of their progress.'

'I hope so! But just to be sure, I'm going to sink my teeth into this until we get the vermin who killed him.'

'We can't have you sinking your fangs into anything.' The easy smile remained but a hard edge had crept into his voice. 'Our relations with the Kosovan authorities are very sensitive. It has taken years of careful diplomacy to build them. I must insist that you leave these matters to us.'

'I thought you were here to help me.'

'I am. To smooth the process at the mortuary. To offer you the moral support of the British government.'

Ali noticed that Donylla had appeared. She was hovering by the door, eyes fixed tactfully on a painting somewhere to Ali's right.

She said, 'And you'll keep the pressure on?'

'Of course.' Sensing her resistance, he slid his chair close enough to encroach on her personal space. 'Don't be fooled by the comfort and safety of your hotel, Ms Feysor. The Prishtina is the civilized face of a land dipped in blood. Think of it as your Green Zone. A safe haven in a country built on centuries of vendetta and butchery. Believe you me, you don't want to go walkabout in this neck of the woods.'

Ali nodded. Last night's visit to the Decani had already given her a flavour of the world outside Jones' *Green Zone*. But the man wasn't concerned for her safety. She understood that, just as she knew that she was being leaned on. Not that she was intimidated. As a journalist, she was used to people - police, criminals, politicos - trying to pull the shades. As it happened, it was the worst attitude anyone could adopt. It just made her more bloody-minded than ever.

JONES OFFERED HER a lift to the mortuary but she preferred to travel with Donylla. The interpreter was uncharacteristically tight-lipped as they made their way to her Golf. She didn't break silence until they were in the vehicle, and even then she held her voice under, as though afraid of being overheard.

'The police officer in charge of the investigation will not see you.'

'Why not?'

'He would not say. He did confirm that they found no laptop or phone with Mr Shimmon.'

Ali set her jaw, an involuntary gesture of determination. 'As soon as we finish at the mortuary, you can take me to police headquarters.

'Of course.' Donylla nodded gravely then started the car. 'There is more. Miro thinks your friend was murdered in Tregu. The killers dumped him at the Decani, disposed of the other two men and paid off the police.'

'Oh God!' Ali's world lurched then steadied. She felt nauseous. When she swallowed, her throat hurt. 'When did he say that?'

'Just now. At the hotel. It is why I am late.'

'So the concierge at the Decani was lying.'

'His kind will always lie.'

'Does Miro have proof? Anything I can confront the police with?'

'Nothing he can give to you. And please, do not mention his name, not to the police, not to anyone. You would place his life in great danger.'

PRISHTINA HOSPITAL WAS a sprawling mess of drabness on the edge of the Kodra e Diellit district, dilapidated old buildings interspersed with the spanking new. Jones had beaten them to it and was waiting with a local official by the mortuary entrance. Ali passed her iPhone to Donylla.

'I need a picture of Jones. But only if you can get it without his knowledge.'

Donylla flashed her a mischievous smile. 'Leave it to me.'

Inside, the official produced two trays of Shimmon's effects. The first held clothing: brown slacks, red sweater, grey coat, nothing but fluff in the pockets. The other contained a battered cigarette packet, keys and some tissues. Not much of a legacy. Ali pocketed the keys and left the rest.

None of them said a word during the short walk to the chapel. At the threshold, Ali hesitated. She hadn't anticipated a problem but now her confidence all but deserted her. She took a deep breath and reminded herself that all she had to do was peep at Steven and affirm his identity. Irvine had recruited a funeral firm to take care of the paperwork and air freight the body back to the UK. There was no need for her to linger, or grieve, or shrink from her task. Just say yes. Get the hell out. Job done.

The room itself was soft-lit. Pastel drapes, hung from ceiling to floor, covered three walls. The place might have been designated a chapel, but there were no religious artefacts in sight: no relics for Christian, Moslem, Jew, Hindu, soccer fan or Elvis freak. This was a place for death, not after-life.

Centre-piece was a gurney camouflaged with purple cloth. On top, wrapped in a simple shroud and part-covered with a white sheet, lay Steven Shimmon. Dusted off, repaired and made over, he looked like a stage prop. An empty shell, the life sucked out, the light extinguished.

The sight overwhelmed Ali, not with grief but with pity. Steven Shimmon would have been so humiliated to be on show like this. A private person, he had never revealed his inner self to anyone, yet here he was, his vulnerability and aloneness exposed for all to see.

Shimmon had left behind no lasting legacy, no wife or child, only the kind of chattering-class friends who would quickly expunge him from their memories. Even his life's work would count for nothing in a world grown so cynical that it would accuse Saint Francis of bestiality. Not that Steven Shimmon had been a saint. But he had cared deeply about injustice. The times when the wrong man was convicted, or the punishment didn't fit the crime, or there was crime without punishment, or punishment without crime. His had been a black and white view of right and wrong, almost child-like in its intensity, and he had been totally committed to fairness as the backbone of the judicial system. A system, he had been fond of telling her, that had fallen between the twin pillars of justice and rights, fracturing its spine in the process.

A good man had been murdered and few would mourn. It was a miserable thought, and Ali found herself fighting back hot tears.

Beside her, Donylla crossed herself and muttered a prayer for the soul of Steven Shimmon.

Ali shuddered as a surge of bitter contempt swept through her. She wanted to ask Donylla why her God had endorsed such a terrible death for Shimmon, why He had turned away from the disaster of his Balkan creation, how He could have allowed the region to suffer so much at the hands of rapacious, greedy and evil men. Above all, she wanted to know how an intelligent and sensitive woman like Donylla could believe in a deity who was such a sadist.

Donylla sensed her change in mood. 'You are thinking, where is God?' she said softly. 'He is looking down from above, wondering what His children have done.'

Ali nodded, unexpectedly choked and unable to give voice to her venom. Her anger receded as swiftly as it had come and she found herself envying her companion her blind faith. Ali had been brought up a Catholic but, since the untimely and cruel death of her mother, she had stopped believing in the mirror world, the place where God makes everything okay again. Forever faithless but not lacking in faith, her own religious belief now boiled down to death as nothingness and, at times like this, it was a belief that offered precious little comfort.

And yet, her anger and pity were not impotent. They re-ignited a flame within her, the burning desire for justice and retribution that had brought her into journalism in the first place. Now she had more than curiosity to drive her. With the flame had come the resolve, not just to finish Shimmon's story, but to find out who had killed him and why.

BACK IN THE car park, Jones cut Ali away from Donylla. 'You handled that well.'

She gave him diffidence. 'It's not like he was blood.'

'Nevertheless. . . .' He offered her a friendly smile. 'Can I drive you to the airport?'

'I don't have my luggage with me.'

'I can arrange that.'

She realised that he was railroading her. 'I'm booked for another night at the Prishtina.'

He stared at her like she was the biggest disappointment of his life. 'You're done, here. The funeral company will get Shimmon's body home. What else is there for you?'

'You're here to help me,' she reminded him mildly. 'So help me. Let you and me go to the police together.'

'There is no *you and me*, Ms Feysor. The Embassy is handling this matter. You, I'm afraid, are out.'

'What the hell does that mean?'

'What the hell does it sound like?' His smile had turned ugly. 'The local police will not speak with you. They have issued instructions that you are not to approach them. They will brook no interference from the British press. The matter is off limits.'

'I'm here as a private citizen, not a journalist.'

'You go near them and I'll yank your passport and have you deported. You got that?'

'You can't do that.'

'By the time your lawyers have exhausted due process you'll have been home a year.'

'What's going on?' she demanded, her voice soft with fury. 'What possible reason could HMG have for covering up the murder of one of its own citizens?'

'Nothing is being covered up. Other people are handling it, that's all.'

'Bullshit!'

Jones lost patience, took her by the arm and turned her towards his car. 'Get in the vehicle.'

She tried to jerk her arm free, failed, then began to struggle against him. Donylla started towards them but Ali stopped her with a sharp look. None of them noticed the SUV parked across the way, or the discreet interest of the two men inside.

Breathing heavily, Ali asked, 'Do you want me to scream the place down?'

Suddenly conscious of the world around them, Jones let go. His eyes had become small and hard and his fingers worked against each other with no purpose. 'Would you get in the car, Ms Feysor. Please.'

'I'll bet you can't get it up, can you?'

He smiled at that, genuinely amused. 'The Kosovan authorities would like you gone.'

'Really?' She stepped out of reach. 'Well, you tell them I'm a tourist who intends to sample the night life.'

'I don't think that's a good idea, do you?'

'Don't worry,' she said, deliberately misunderstanding his meaning. 'I might resemble the Great Brit Abroad but I have no intention of flashing my tits and puking in the gutter.'

Chapter 8

'GCHQ INTERCEPTED A phone call containing the key word *Mammon*,' Ryman said. 'From a cell phone located in Kosovo. The call was made to the Sunday Echo. The phone is registered to an investigative reporter, Ali Feysor.'

Ryman paused, suddenly aware of a toxic atmosphere in the room. Sandford and Seymour were staring at him as if he had just thrown shit on the table. The three men were in the Gower Street Cage, Ryman took a breath to compose himself. No blame could attach to him. He was just the messenger here, a surveillance and counter-espionage expert who had been called to this crisis meet to deliver the overnight intel.

'Ostensibly,' he continued, 'Feysor is in Kosovo to repatriate the remains of Steven Shimmon. However, given that she knows about Mammon, we have to assume that she's not there merely to save on undertaker's fees.'

Seymour frowned. 'Feysor is the Sunday Echo's star investigator. Shimmon was contracted to The Echo.' He stared accusingly at Sandford. 'The Sunday Echo!

You told me this would go away. Now I find it's getting out of hand.'

'We're on top of it,' Sandford assured him calmly. 'We're monitoring her phone and emails, I've got a man dogging her in Kosovo and a sneak-and-peek on the way to her flat. Shimmon was working alone. We are sure of that. Worst case scenario, Feysor is following up on Shimmon's story. She will find nothing. Prishtina is sterile ground. Shimmon and his contact are dead, their information destroyed. As for Shimmon's apartment, all data sources have been cleaned, digital and paper. She will have to start over and she's not in Shimmon's league as an investigator. I see her as a non-issue.'

Seymour snorted derisively. 'Feysor is a high profile journalist with the clout to create real complications. Too many people have underestimated that bitch. She's good at what she does. Too damn good. And you're telling me that someone like that knows about Mammon! . . .' He glared at Ryman. 'What does her psych evaluation tell us?'

Ryman fidgeted with the thin file on the table in front of him. He was mid-forties, though his baby face and designer clothes made him look years younger. His intelligence career had been mostly in F Branch, involving the surveillance of subversives, political groups and terrorists. He had been recruited to Alpha some three years ago but had quickly come to regret the move. On first sight, it had seemed the perfect opportunity. With the Security Service increasingly hidebound by new laws and regulations, he had long dreamed of a utopian organization with the ability to initiate any investigation it chose without the necessity to explain its actions to anyone. But Alpha had turned out to be a dystopian nightmare. It was the old story. To live above the law you had to be morally incorruptible. Sadly for Ryman, people like that just didn't exist.

'Feysor graduated Birmingham with a first class honours in Law,' he intoned, 'then interned on the Birmingham Post. After breaking a couple of big corruption stories, she was head-hunted by the Sunday Echo. That was eight years ago. She and Shimmon were at the Echo together for just a few months. He was her mentor but there's no evidence that they were particularly close. Since then, she has made a name for herself as an investigative reporter, specialising in stories about corruption – politics, big business, organised crime.' He paused momentarily. 'Bottom line, she's a first rate investigator with the nose for a scandal and the skills to uncover it. She has the guts and bloody-mindedness to go for anyone. It doesn't matter how powerful they are. Once she gets her teeth into a story she doesn't let go. She burns on a slow fuse. Inextinguishable. She won't quit until she has what she wants.'

Seymour frowned. 'Are you saying you can't stop one woman?'

Ryman answered indirectly. 'She refuses to be intimidated. Plenty have tried. Anonymous phone calls, texts, emails, personal abuse and attacks on social media. She ignores them all. Threatened with defamation suits, she just calls their bluff; none have ever reached the courts.'

'So find her price,' Seymour said. 'Buy her off.'

'In my judgement,' Ryman said patiently, 'any such offer would strengthen her resolve. For her, money is not a driver. She has a good salary, no debt, money in the bank and a savings account. She owns a flat in Colindale, which has no mortgage. Apparently an uncle left it her in his will.'

'She's a journalist,' Sandford pointed out. 'She bribes sources, fiddles expenses.'

'Apparently not.'

'Some other weakness, then. Drink? Drugs? Gambling? Sex?'

Another shake of the head.

'How can you be so sure?'

'Her habit of digging in awkward places has earned her a place on Five's watch list. Over the years, we have investigated her in some depth.' Ryman dropped his gaze to the file in front of him. 'She is thirty-four years old, an only child. She was born in Southampton but her family moved to Winchester when she was six. Her father is a GP, her mother is dead. Killed in a car crash when Feysor was twenty. Apparently, that sent her off the rails for a time. She went through a year of heavy drinking and serial relationships. Nothing too dramatic, and certainly nothing that could damage her in today's moral climate. She pulled herself together.'

Sandford again. 'Long-term relationships?'

'Nothing documented. She keeps people at arm's length.'

'Everyone has their Achilles heel,' Sandford protested. 'It's just a question of looking for it.'

'If she has one,' Ryman answered cautiously, 'we've not been able to find it.'

'Then create it,' Sandford said.

The three men dwelt on that for a long, fruitless moment.

'She has a reputation for being political,' Seymour said at length. 'A leftie. Can we use that against her?'

'The rumours don't pan out.' There was a hint of impatience in Ryman's tone, as though he was weary of explaining the obvious. 'There is no evidence of political activity, not even from her student days. She has no discernible loyalties to any cause, no links to political parties or special interest groups. The political tag probably stems from her penchant for investigating corruption in high places. She has caused the downfall of politicians all right, but from across the spectrum. She might be a bitch but she's an equal opportunities bitch.'

Sandford scowled. 'Sounds to me like you're in love with her.'

Ryman reddened, though whether with anger or embarrassment it was impossible to tell from his tight-lipped features.

Seymour sat back and folded his arms. 'You're an analyst. Analyse. How *do* we spike this woman?'

Ryman considered for a moment.

'Our greatest chance of success lies in putting Shimmon's story out there ourselves. We plant it with our friends, lace it with just enough truth to be believable, and get them to spin it in such a way as to discredit Shimmon's – and by default, Feysor's - version.'

Seymour nodded cautiously. 'Are you sure our *friends* won't sit on it? Try to verify what we give them only to stumble on the real story.'

'Verify?' Ryman was quietly amused. 'No-one verifies any more. This is the age of self-gratification. Whoever writes the story first defines the truth. *That's* the modern verification. All we have to do is get there first.'

Seymour scowled. 'That sounds like a wish and a prayer.'

'Most people get their news from social media. That way, they get the version that conforms to their own world view. These sites use algorithms to lock people into partisan silos and filter bubbles that exclude anything and everything they don't like. It's a way of creating their own virtual utopias.' Ryman paused. 'And here's the good part. There are human curators behind the algorithms who can direct people to faux stories. We happen to own a curator or two. We set up plausible news stories then use click-baiting techniques to draw in the clickers, sharers and commenters. These people aren't known for checking the authenticity of stories before they share them. By using a full range of algorithms, we can ensure that our version of events becomes the accepted version.'

Seymour paused, his face conflicted with thought. 'And if the story isn't picked up? Or if it attracts the attention of real journalists?' He shook his head. 'No. The power of personalisation filters is unproven. We can't rely on them. Lies can be exposed just as swiftly as they are spread.'

Sandford reached for Feysor's file, though he didn't open it. 'We need to convince the woman that there is no story. If she comes to see Shimmon as some kind of conspiracy nut, chasing a fiction of his own paranoia, she would abandon the story of her own accord. At the same time, we could drop another story into her lap. Something big enough to divert her but one that can't turn round and bite us. We have plenty of those on file.'

Seymour looked from one to the other, giving them a chance to speak that neither took.

'Okay,' he said. 'Hope for the best, plan for the worst. Prepare a story for our media friends but sit on it for now. No need to stir the nest just yet. But we cover ourselves. Treat Feysor as a serious threat. Maintain a watching brief. I need to know everything she knows. Who is she talking to? How does she know about Mammon? How much does she know? Where does she go from here?' He paused, a heartbeat. 'Let's be proactive. It might even lead us to the Analytics mole. We're already on Irvine, I take it?'

Sandford nodded. 'Our American cousins are co-operating.'

'What about our brothers across the river? Are MI6 on board with this? We can't afford to have them running interference.'

'They've as much to lose as we do. Kosovo was a joint venture, remember?'

'Don't take them for granted,' Seymour grunted. 'Give them an opportunity to fuck us over and they will take it.' He paused. 'If we have to call in a favour or two, then so be it. Our masters will not be happy that Feysor is still in the game. They wanted this threat killed off, not running on fresh legs.'

'Feysor is still in Kosovo,' Sandford said. 'It would be a good place to distract her, perhaps even discourage her.'

'Are we set up for that?'

'I have a man on scene.' Sandford hesitated. 'On past form, Feysor won't bed down early. She'll hit the bars. There could be an incident.'

That brought an ominous silence to the room. The two men, Sandford and Ryman, watched Seymour's face and waited quietly for a response. He surprised them by changing tack,

'There is another matter. Griffin has asked us to find a girl. She goes by the name of Sarah York, Apparently, she disappeared a few days ago. No warning, no explanation.'

'Who is she?'

'She belongs to Griffin's inner circle, I'm told. Family, I would guess, but his people are not very forthcoming on personal detail.'

Sandford's eyes clouded, 'Since when do we do Griffin's bidding? He has an army of operatives. Half the police forces in the world are in his pocket. Why would he need our help?'

'Griffin can't trust his own people with this.' Seymour permitted himself to smile at the irony: *all that wealth and he can't trust his own people!* 'One of them helped the girl disappear. A minder name of Jackson. He vanished at the same time as the girl. They think he might even be with her.'

Sandford wasn't happy. 'What do we care if some girl disappears? Let him get another one.'

Seymour offered him a humourless smile. 'She stole a USB data stick before she left. According to Griffin, that puts her in possession of unknown quantities of ultra-sensitive information that could expose him and blow us all out of the water.'

Sandford asked, 'Is she likely to use it?'

'In the absence of assurances to the contrary, we have to assume yes.'

'Then we're in trouble,' Sandford said. 'It's not like the old days, when whistleblowers took their grievances to Fleet Street who then invited us to issue a D notice. Once your secret has entered cyberspace, it is de facto declassified.'

Seymour shrugged. 'Griffin has an IT army monitoring for leaks. He'll hack, delete and destroy the whole damn web if he has to.'

'Good luck with that.' Ryman gave him sceptical. 'What kind of ultra-sensitive information is on this drive?'

'He won't say. I would surmise details of his illegal business operations, his money laundering activities, his dealings with us. Whatever, it's enough to have Griffin shitting blood. He is adamant that we retrieve the data stick without looking at it. Which makes it a must see. We need to acquire the contents of her memory stick without Griffin knowing. That means without the girl knowing.' Pause. 'We have a profile of sorts.'

He produced a thin file and passed it over. Sandford scanned it quickly, learning that Sarah York was twenty-years-old, a UK citizen who was born in South Africa, resident in the US and studying in London. There was a photograph, showing a slight girl with an attractive round-faced smile, dark brown eyes and dyed straw blonde hair, but there was little in the way of an actual bio. Just sketchy personal data, including cell phone and bank details. She was into her second year at Imperial College, reading Ecology and Environmental Biology. There was a list of her university activities.

'It says here,' Sandford said, 'that she's a member of an environmental group called *Scorched Earth Information Exchange*. They sound very cataclysmic. I'm not familiar with them.'

'You wouldn't be,' Seymour told him. 'They're nontoxic. They set up as a campaigning group but they're just a talking shop. There's not much to them – amateurish website, blogs and tweets. Very few followers. Their stated aim is to increase awareness of global warming. There are no hidden layers. It's kids' stuff. They are not a threat. You can discount that angle. The girl's not political. She's indulging in some adolescent rebellion.'

Sandford was skeptical. 'Do we silence her?'

'No. Griffin wants her, the data stick and the minder all untouched. He is very specific about that.'

'Griffin is very specific!' Sandford all but spat the words. 'It's time we tackled the Griffin problem head on.' He hesitated, then let his anger flow. 'I've done everything to keep this country safe – psy-ops, wet ops, black ops, even running rendition before it became extraordinary – and I take pride in the fact. I haven't done all that so I can take on a misper for a man like Griffin. Griffin is a liability. First Shimmon gets close to exposing him, then Feysor comes sniffing around, now some kid steals his secrets. I say again, we should eliminate him before it's too late.

'And I say again,' said Seymour, 'the moment is not opportune. We must get to the girl before he does. Finding her is our top priority. She represents our best chance of shutting this down cleanly. We need that data drive.'

Sandford's eyes shifted momentarily to the door, then cut sideways at the other man. For a moment, he seemed on the point of rebellion. But he let the matter hang.

Seymour said, 'We should have identified Shimmon as a threat much earlier, before it got this far. Our radar failed and that's a concern. We have to go back over the ground. Spin Shimmon's life. This time be thorough. Take it apart, piece by piece. See where we went wrong.'

Sandford nodded. 'And Feysor?'

Seymour considered for a moment. 'We are approaching critical point, gentlemen. Bottom line, we represent the country's last line of defence. It is left to us to make the tough decisions that nobody else will make.' Another pause. 'Two Echo hacks dying in Prishtina within days of each other. . . . We don't need that kind of attention.' A further moment's thought. 'Push her hard. Let's find out how committed she is.'

Chapter 9

AS THEY DROVE north from the city, Ali subdued her anger by plugging in her earphones, shuffling her music and trying to piece together what was happening.

She could disregard the official account of Shimmon's death as a mugging gone wrong. There was no doubt in her mind that he had been murdered in pursuit of his story. According to Miro at the hotel, he had asked too many questions, or asked the wrong people, and had been killed for his curiosity. His computer had been stolen, his body dumped at the Decani Hotel, his companions disappeared and the cops paid off. If that was the case - and she had no reason to doubt Miro - she could expect no help from the local police. More to the point, the murder enquiry was going to be less than rigorous.

From what little she knew, it seemed reasonable to infer that Shimmon had come to Kosovo to investigate the claim of SAS involvement in the killing of Lucca. A killing, according to Irvine, that had been designed to cover up government involvement with the Kosovan mafia. But why would HMG be involved with a criminal organization whose product portfolio included drugs, gambling and sex slaves?

Tregu held the key. She knew that as if Shimmon had risen from the gurney to tell her himself. It would unlock the code to his murder and story both. She could dismiss out of hand the possibility that he had gone there on some kind of covert op. The image of the urbane and sedentary Steven Shimmon stealing through the badlands on some Heart of Darkness trip didn't hold up. He might have been searching out the farmhouse mentioned in the SAS debrief, or looking to interview a witness, but he would have traveled ostentatiously, the quintessential Antipodean on a world tour. Someone would have seen him there and finding that someone was the jump-off point for her own investigation.

The attempts to keep her away from the story pointed to another part of the puzzle. The local police and FCO both wanted her gone from Kosovo. Why was the FCO so keen to snag her interest? What kind of accord had HMG enjoyed with the Kosovan mafia?

This was shaping up to be a real story. Government corruption and government kill squads. The thought of a white knuckle ride through that scene was enough to set her juices running. Editors go to war over stories like this. People like her prospect deep for them. And this had been handed to her on a golden platter!

Or had it?

Donylla tapped her thigh and Ali detached her earphones.

'We have arrived.'

Tregu turned out to be little more than a sprawling farmstead. It was a tourist's wet dream, the kind of place where peasants scythed hay in warm sunshine, wild life teemed and extended families shared their bucolic homes with their cattle and goats. Bitter wood smoke mixed with the pungent smell of livestock and the sweet aroma of fruit and hay. The city rain hadn't reached this far and the sun baked down on the patched and dusty blacktop, playing up to this impersonation of a rural idyll.

Ali was no tourist. She was a city girl for whom the countryside was a place of unchecked filth and disease. Staring out at the mangy dogs and chickens scratching in the dirt, she couldn't help hankering after the piss-stained housing barracks they had left behind in Prishtina. It took the reassuring quakes of passing trucks to remind her that the civilized world hadn't yet fallen.

An old man was sitting torpid on his doorstep, as he had the day before and the day before that. His face was cracked and pitted like a dried up river bed. Keeping his eye on the two women in the car, he half-turned into the house and exchanged words with someone inside.

Ali stretched her neck, stiff with traveling, then nodded in his direction. 'Looks like we're attracting attention.'

Donylla watched him for a moment then took Ali's phone with its picture of Shimmon and got out of the car. The old man offered her a toothless smile, which was promising, but a curt reply to her enquiry, which wasn't. The interpreter returned with a frustrated shrug.

'He says no westerners came this way and none have died here.'

'Do you believe him?'

Donylla's face twisted in contempt. 'He would lie to us as a matter of course. But there is something else. He is frightened. I can see it in his eyes. He does not want to be seen talking to a western journalist.'

'So what's new?' Ali responded, unabashed. 'I've been the leper in the nudist colony all my working life. It's a good sign when people try to shut you out. It means they have something to hide. And where there's a secret, there's always someone bursting to share it.'

'Not here, Ali. There is too much fear. These people are scared. Scared of you, scared of me, scared of who might be watching.' Donylla held Ali's gaze with an intensity that was just short of disturbing. 'It is as I warned you, this place is dangerous. Life here is based on the clan structure - they call it the Fic, a kind of brotherhood - and it is impossible for outsiders to penetrate. Everything is secondary to the ancient honour of the family. They have a code of retribution, the Hammurabi, that goes back over two thousand years. There are men here who never leave their home because of it. They fear being murdered over some ancient family feud. Always, the ghosts of the slaughtered demand revenge. These people, they cannot escape their history. They are forever *in blood*. They never forget and they never let anything go.'

'Well, nor do I.' Ali stared back with equal passion. 'Something happened to Steven here and I mean to find out what.'

Donylla offered a wry shrug. 'This is a dark maze, Ali. They say only a fool or madman will enter such a place.'

'A madman and a fool!' Ali grinned. 'I think we're well qualified, don't you?'

The interpreter smiled. 'Yes, I think so!'

But where to start? Ali had engaged in plenty of door-knocking in her time but this was door-to-door with a difference, the trick being to find a door - any door - in a sparsely populated area that stretched over countless square kilometres. She understood now what Miro had meant by claiming *There is no address*. The only map she had was a sparse image on her iPhone. She had GPS, which told her where she was, but it couldn't tell her what she was looking for or if she was looking in the right place.

Talk about a needle in a haystack!

They concocted a plan of sorts. Drive along Route 25, starting northward from Tregu, and systematically check out each building and turnoff. They found little to encourage them. Whenever they left behind the national route, they entered territory that was dark, forsaken and watchful. Ali sensed her companion's unease and a chilling sense of foreboding insinuated itself. She would never find Shimmon's killers but there was a real danger that the killers would find her. What then? This was a damaged land. A dark place, steeped in blood and monstrous secrets, where generation after generation had been cleansed on tribal, religious or ethnic grounds. A land where women and children could have their throats cut to sever a blood line and a visiting journalist could be murdered for a few Euros.

They negotiated narrow, tree-lined lanes that threatened to rip the heart out of Donylla's VW. Some were dead ends, leading to farmhouse or field. Others continued for miles before deteriorating into rutted dirt tracks that petered out in the passes and forests of the higher valleys. None carried any traffic. Brown bears and wolves roamed these hills but they saw only rabbits, wildfowl and corbies. Now and then they paused to turn the car, or to stoop in hedgerow or copse. The bread, cheese and bottled water that Donylla had brought along, they consumed on the move.

They came across isolated hamlets and houses, places with no names and names without places, many abandoned to disrepair as their inhabitants relocated to Prishtina and beyond. There were modern houses, too, some complete, others with roofs and windows not yet in place, each one as derelict as the deserted hovels.

As for the people, they were identikit peasants, clad in layers of clothing and distinctive headdress, their ancient, hostile faces so deeply etched by the weather that they could have been part of the landscape. They interrupted their labours to gaze dolefully at the car passing by. If approached, they were tight-lipped. Always tight-lipped. They were poor, yet they were better off than many of their kinsfolk whose lives had begun here and ended in other places. The ones who had become drug mules, or prostitutes, or worse.

To Ali, it seemed that they were caught in a loop: same old hamlet, same old questions, same old negative reaction to Shimmon's photo, same old denial of knowledge. She sighed. This wasn't the first time her blind stubbornness had led her into such futile tautology.

The colours were beginning to fade on the hills when they reached the rough gravel drive to yet another modern house. This was someone's dream home, a pink Italianate villa with balconies, terraces, Bavarian turrets and Grecian porticos, an architectural paroxysm with extensive views west to the hills of Mokra Gora. It was uninhabited but there was activity. A builder's truck in the yard.

A young man in overalls appeared as they got out of the car. He greeted them with a friendly word and a smile that stopped just short of a leer.

Donylla engaged him in animated conversation. At length, she turned to Ali with a summary.

'He says this house was built by a local boss without planning consent. There are no services – no water, no sewage, no electricity – so the house has been abandoned. He has been employed to board it up, to keep it safe from the weather and the gypsies. This, and other places like it.' She paused, her eyes aglow with triumph. 'He says that yesterday he was called off the job to go to another house. This other house is lived in. He had to make a temporary repair to some windows that had been smashed in a fight. There are rumours that people were shot there. I think this is what we are looking for.'

A shiver of fearful anticipation rolled down Ali's spine. 'Did he say where?'

'He requires a finder's fee.'

Without demur, Ali went into a huddle with Donylla and dug some notes from her satchel. The interpreter took twenty Euros.

'Don't look so eager or he will demand more.' Donylla paused, a broad grin on her face. 'We are lucky at last.'

'That Lady Luck,' Ali smiled cynically. 'She's a sucker for a lost hack with a slush fund.'

Chapter 10

THEY CONTINUED NORTH on the Glavnik Road until they reached their landmark, a silver birch thrusting through the roof of an abandoned house. Another hundred metres and they turned onto a track that cut deep into a fossilised landscape of meadow and woodland. Grey-green pasture clung to the hillside and there were glimpses of flaxen fields through the twisted hedgerows. The way was pitted with potholes and erosion cuts, and, in their little car, it seemed a bruising eternity before they reached the two storey house where Shimmon had stopped only days before.

With its whitewashed walls, russet tiles and satellite dish, the place came across as an Elysian retreat. But closer inspection revealed peeling paint, broken roof tiles, lawn and hedge left wild and garden furniture scattered to the winds. There was no evidence of police activity, no coloured tape fluttering in the breeze, no sign at all that this was a crime scene.

Ali hammered on the door. There was no response. Donylla tried, with the same result. Ali's heart sank with impending failure. Her presence here was futile. Whatever Shimmon had been seeking, she would not find it here.

They were returning to the car when an old woman appeared on the porch. She was tiny, under five feet, and her sharp, censorious splinter of a face glared out at them from beneath a hoodie of a headscarf. Clearly agitated by their presence, she spat something in an incomprehensible language and Ali was glad of Donylla's presence. The interpreter entered into an animated discussion that was clearly centred on Ali. Gradually, the old woman's tone mellowed and she started glancing at Ali with what, in a wolf, might have passed for sympathy.

Donylla turned to Ali. 'Two Englishman were killed here, last week.' She said it with a dying fall in her voice, as though she was referring to a tragedy in her own life. 'And their Albanian guide. The couple who lived here were also murdered. They were ethnic Turks.'

Ali felt the blood drain from her cheeks and her eyes glittered with an unexpected mascara of tears. 'This is the place?'

The woman placed her hand on Ali's arm and spoke directly to her. They locked eyes while Donylla translated with a grey smile.

'She says she is sorry for your loss. I told her that you are looking for your husband. A small liberty, but that is something they understand in these parts.' The old woman spoke again, briefly. Donylla listened, then said, 'She asks if you would like some tea.'

Ali nodded at the old woman. 'Thank you.'

They followed her into a snug hallway. A fox red rug covered the centre of the wooden floor and an oak balustraded staircase wound upwards to the next storey. In the corner by the front door, an upright piano groaned under stacks of sheet music. An old bike was propped against a wall. There was a pervasive smell of polish, carbolic and sickly-sweet hyacinths that reminded Ali of hospitals and death.

The old woman showed them into the lounge and went off towards the kitchen. The room in which they stood was surprisingly modern There were black leather chairs, white rugs and smoked glass coffee tables. In a console by the wall was a smart TV and Blu-ray player. Shelves were stacked with books, films and antiquities - statues and pottery, mostly. The room was suffused with a soft orange glow from the late afternoon sun, and there was a stunning view across the downward sloping lawn, over a hedge to the river valley below.

So far so normal. But two sheets of timber sealed the shattered French windows and the stench and paraphernalia of the cleaner's art - buckets, cleaning fluids, cloths and sponges - were everywhere. They were in the killing room, that much was obvious, and Ali sensed that the old woman would never exorcise the butchery from this house. The harder she scrubbed, the deeper the viscera would penetrate the building's fabric. Better to torch the place than let it become a memorial to slaughter.

The old woman returned with cups on a tray. She seemed even tinier than before. There was an ancient beauty there, one that years of weather and toil had not worn away, and bright eyes that told of a lifetime of kindness and compassion.

Ali took the proffered herbal concoction and sipped it slowly. She asked, 'Did she meet my *husband*?'

Donylla put the question. The old woman shook her head and, even before Donylla translated, Ali knew the answer.

'Why did he come here?'

'To meet the people of the house.'

'Does she know who killed them?'

'Everybody knows.' Donylla was frowning with concentration as she became the human conduit for a snappy Q&A session.

'Who was it?'

'It was the Fic. That is what she says. But Fic is a very general term. It could mean anyone.'

'Ask her for names.'

'She won't be more specific. She is too frightened.'

Ali nodded. 'Why were they killed?'

'The journalist because he asked questions. The people of the house because they were giving answers.'

'What were these questions?'

Another shake of the head.

'Had they met him before?'

'She does not know.'

'Does she know who moved the bodies?'

'She cannot say.'

'What did the people of the house do for a living?'

'She would rather not say.'

Ali was stumped into silence. She was looking for somewhere to plant her cup when her eyes fell on a smear of blood on the wallpaper. Someone had slithered down the wall. Below it, was a small pool of blood, coagulated and oxidised, where that someone had come to rest against the skirting board. Ali had a flashing image of Shimmon sprawling there and felt a burning in her throat.

The old woman followed her gaze and spoke softly. Donylla's literal translation sounded strangely stilted.

'The god lives in silence who has scourged this land with blood.'

Ali had nothing to say to that.

'She hasn't finished with the cleaning, yet.' Donylla continued. 'The house must be cleaned before it can be sold. The blood belonged to the man of the house. They tortured him and killed his wife. Your friend they killed in the garden. She thinks he was trying to run away. His companions they killed in the house. She asks if you would like to see where your friend died?'

Ali hesitated, a fraction of a second that seemed a lifetime. She nodded, though she didn't know why.

As she was led into the garden, she experienced the strange sensation that she was moving away from as well as towards something, though she didn't know what. They trooped through the overgrown lawn to the hedge. The late afternoon sunshine reflected off the foliage and deepened colour and shadow everywhere. Something rustled through the hedge to her left and glided into the flower-choked meadow beyond. She could smell rotting vegetation and the faint aroma of wood smoke. Tits and sparrows flitted through the branches and the air was filled with unidentifiable bird song.

She tried to map the tranquility of this garden onto the savage imagery of murder, but it was impossible. She was desperate to feel Shimmon's presence here but there was only numbness. To an aboriginal tracker, the signs left by Shimmon's dying would have been as clear as blood on a white carpet, but not to Ali. Broken branches meant no more to her than trampled flowers, and rain had washed his life-blood into the soil.

She shivered, though the air was mild, and suddenly this place felt desolate and hostile, almost primeval in its savagery. The warmth and comfort of the hotel beckoned like an oasis in the desert and she turned to go. As she did so, she caught a double flash in the hedgerow, gold then black. The goldcrest disappeared in a blink, but the black had taken root. It was Shimmon's netbook, caught in the undergrowth where it had been thrown. Whether discarded by the killers or thrown by Shimmon, she had no idea. She bent to pick it up and saw the bullet hole. Battered and rain-damaged, the machine's secrets were probably lost forever. Nevertheless, her decision to retrieve it was more than mere sentimentality. She knew from experience that precious little was beyond the black arts of the digi-tecs.

While she was examining the netbook, the women became aware of a car coming up the lane. They heard it first, the murmur of an engine and the crunch of tyres on stone, then it came into view, a black 4x4 BMW with darkened windows. The women watched, curiosity turning to anxiety, as it pulled up behind their Golf. The front doors opened and two men emerged. They were dressed in tactical blue police uniform. The driver relaxed against the vehicle while the other came towards them. His back was to the sinking sun, his features in shadow. Beneath the peak of his blue cap he wore dark glasses. He was bulky with BDU pockets and belt pouches, but Ali could see that his handgun was safely holstered. The distinctive blue-and-yellow arm patches marked him out as a prowl officer. These men were apparatchiks rather than paramilitaries and, with that realization, Ali breathed more easily.

Then, as he came closer, she saw that he was holding a second gun against his thigh. Not his official issue Glock 17 but an old Czech CZ85. *A throwdown!* Her mind jumped to that curious conclusion by itself. She had watched enough TV cop shows to understand. *A throwdown is a kill gun!* The second man was now approaching, looping round to block their escape to their car. Her heart lurched off beat and her stomach tumbled loosely. Her hormones screamed *run!* but she had nowhere to go. Donylla had taken out her phone and was searching in vain for a signal. All Ali could do was slip the notebook into her bag and stand her ground with a cool that she didn't feel.

Donylla gave up on her phone. Some strange instinct caused her to step forward to protect Ali. The old woman knew better and scuttled off towards the house.

Without warning the man raised his gun and shot the old woman in the back. She sprawled headlong without breaking stride. Ali heard a scream, didn't know if it had come from her or Donylla. The old woman's right hand scrabbled at something unseen on the ground, and then she was still.

Casually, as if he was fetching the Sunday paper, the man strolled over to check the old woman. He prodded her with his boot and was met with dead, floppy weight. Satisfied with his handiwork, he turned to Ali.

Now the light caught him, picking out olive features that were as sharp as a blade. It was the guy who had baited her at the Decani. He smiled a smile of recognition, but there was a blankness about him that stopped Ali's heart.

'Don't you English ever learn?'

Donylla stepped in to confront him with an explosion of finger-jabbing fury. He listened to her impassively for a few seconds then he threw a vicious right hook that glanced off the side of her head. A look of surprise etched on her face, the interpreter crumpled backwards onto the grass.

Decani stared at Ali and she turned to ice. There was no escape. The pimp was police, the police were gangsters. His breath seemed to reach out and touch her cheek, like a dirty finger. He removed his shades and a savage flame flickered in his rheumy eyes. It illuminated brutal rape and murder, and fresh blood melting through white snow.

Ali turned to run. Too late. His hand snaked out and grabbed her arm. She tried to wrench herself from his grasp, failed, then lashed out with her free fist and caught him across the ear.

He cursed and slammed a hammer blow into her jaw. Her world pulsed scarlet and faded quickly into nothing.

Chapter 11

THE GIRL EMERGED from the house in Copenhagen Street and the Watcher's cold eyes darkened with cruel anticipation. He knew, even without checking the photograph on his phone, that he had located his target.

The girl known as Sarah York was in his cross hairs.

Cell phone to her ear, Sarah York was so preoccupied with her conversation that she didn't notice his loitering presence. She set off towards Caledonian Road and he fell in behind her, keeping a discreet distance as she slalomed through the quiet streets of Pentonville. At Caledonian Road, she turned towards Kings Cross Station, still glued to her phone and apparently oblivious to the roar of traffic. He shadowed her past the Cross and into the station, holding himself anonymous among the City boys and tourists as she jostled her way underground to the Circle line.

He waited for the rumble of an approaching train then edged up behind her. He half-expected her to spin around and scream *Murderer!* but she didn't even sense his presence. That puzzled him. Where was her survival instinct? How could a girl on the run be so careless and unconcerned, so blissfully unaware of the dark shadow at her shoulder? He could have sent her tumbling beneath the wheels with a puff of breath. Right here, right now.

But he didn't. Death was his specialism but that wasn't the job. Not yet.

He followed her onto the train. Same carriage, different door. It was standing room only, but he had no difficulty in observing her from a discreet distance. She remained cocooned in her own world, paying not the slightest attention to whoever was around her. A slender five-six, she had a gentle, faraway beauty and a smile, when it came, that lit you up inside. She was as soft a target as he could have hoped for.

Not so long ago, it would have been an improbable ask to find a young woman in the choking anonymity that was London. Certainly not one like Sarah, who was using a throw-away cell phone and carried no plastic in her own name. But SO15 (the Counter Terrorism Command, formed by the merger of the old Anti-Terrorist Branch (SO13) and Special Branch) had recently acquired Smartrecon, the most modern computer-driven facial recognition system available. It used 3D imaging and HD epidermal mapping to identify faces from digital stills or video images. Feed in the capital's all-seeing CCTV and there was no hiding place for an innocent abroad.

SO15 had located her through its routine monitoring of Green activists. She had visited the Pentonville office of the Scorched Earth Information Exchange, and Smartrecon had picked her out. A clandestine follow-up visit - euphemism for a late night B&E - had established that Scorched Earth didn't have her new address or contact details. But a few hours of watching the office had resulted in this pick up.

At Baker Street, Sarah switched trains, disembarking minutes later at Queens Park. The Watcher allowed her to ease in front of him, waiting until the train had rattled off towards Harrow before following her to the exit. The drab skies threatened rain and Sarah toyed with the hood of her cagoule before turning south into West Kilburn. Minutes later, she was letting herself into the ground floor flat of an elegant little red-brick terrace.

Her lounge fronted onto the street and the Watcher could see immediately that she didn't live alone. There was another girl. Early twenties. Dark long hair. Student garb. From their body language, he judged them to be flatmates rather than intimates.

The presence of the other girl was a complication that he hadn't foreseen but it wasn't a problem. He would come back when Sarah was alone.

He took out his cell phone, the one with scrambling features, and selected a speed dial. His call was answered after four rings.

He said, 'I have the girl.'

Chapter 12

ALI DIDN'T ACTUALLY lose consciousness, though she was adrift in a fog of white noise that amounted to the same thing. Time went on without her until, after what seemed like days but could only have been minutes, the hurt began to leak in. It came as a throbbing pain in her jaw that quickly grew in intensity and spread like a virus to all parts of her body. Her throat was dry and the inside of her check felt like a bloody mess. Groggily, she made to touch her face but she couldn't move her arms. At first, she thought that it was a kind of waking sleep paralysis, but the more she tried to move, the more constricted she became, and she bucked and wriggled like a rat snagged by a boa. A few seconds of that and she was exhausted. A few more seconds and she realized that she was trussed to an upright chair. For some reason, she found that comforting, and her fear gave way to an unreal sense of complacency. She didn't want to move and, now that she couldn't, she didn't have to. If she kept still, the pain was bearable.

Outside, the low sun was blazing through strips of cloud to turn the world crimson. The light seared her eyes and she shifted her gaze inside to where it was dusky soft and soothing. It was then that she noticed the shadowy bundle on the floor.

Someone was lying there!

Quickly, she averted her eyes. She couldn't remember what had happened, or what she was doing here, but the bundle evoked grainy memories of death. She closed her eyes. She didn't want to look, she was determined not to look, but she couldn't help herself. Her eyes opened and she had to steal a glance. It was a woman, trussed and silenced with duct tape. She looked extremely young and vulnerable but she was alive. Their eyes met and the woman tried to smile.

Donylla!

All at once, Ali had total recall. The man from the Decani had shot the old woman, felled Donylla then turned on her. She had tried to escape and he had punched her. Just like that. No holding back because she was a woman. No respect for the fair sex. Just a right hook thrown in anger, disconnecting her nervous system so that she had collapsed like a drunk. That's why the pain was arcing through her brain. That's why the inside of her cheek was leaking blood with its nauseating taste of copper. That's why she could see the old woman outside, crumpled on the lawn where she had fallen, a rust red patch drying between her shoulders.

'So, English, you are awake.'

Decani appeared from behind her and stood over her, amusement, curiosity and anticipation pasted over his blank smile. The CZ85 that had killed the old lady was stuck in his belt.

Ali tried to wriggle free but there was no fighting this. Her bonds were too tight, the pain of movement too great, the memory of Decani murdering the old woman too vivid. She should have been terrified, she knew that. Yet she felt quite dispassionate. It was as if she was inside her dream looking out.

'You won't get away with this,' she heard herself say, her voice a hoarse, pompous whisper that barely rose above her churning fear. 'I am a British citizen. Release us now and no more will be said.'

'No more will be said,' he echoed, clearly amused. There was dead meat on his breath and an unfamiliar deodorant that seemed to enhance the wretched stench of urine and faeces that must have been her own. 'But I want you to talk, English. I want you to tell me what you are doing here.'

'That's easy,' she said, her voice gaining in strength as she spoke. 'I'm looking for investment properties. If I'm looking in the wrong place, then I apologise. But why is that a police matter?'

'A police matter?' he echoed with a leery smile that told her there was no appealing to his uniform. He held up her journalist credentials. 'Why would a reporter be looking for investment properties?'

'Reporters make investments. Why not? We all have to look to the future.'

He leaned forward and cupped her face in his hand. She couldn't believe how painful such an unremarkable act had become.

He asked, 'Do you think I am stupid?'

She felt the sickening beat of his breath on her face and she wrenched away. He glanced beyond her and someone seized her head from behind. It was the driver of the BMW. She hadn't realised that he was there and his action brought an involuntary little scream. Decani gripped her face again, inducing a hot pain that stabbed through her jaw. Then he let go and ripped open her blouse and bra.

A surge of revulsion and fear and rage ran through her. She wondered fleetingly if she had already been raped but knew that she hadn't.

'Don't touch me, you fucking animal! Touch me and I'll kill you.'

The driver struck her on the side of the head, not too hard, but enough to cause her to gasp. She didn't cry out, wouldn't give him the pleasure, though she could do nothing about the tears that rolled over her cheeks.

'You are out of your mind to come here,' Decani said. 'Do you have any idea who you are dealing with?'

'Do you?'

Her defiance brought a smile. He stared dispassionately at her breasts, a farmer appraising the livestock. This was beyond her darkest imaginings. She had been threatened before, many times, but her run-ins had never actually become physical. She tried to persuade herself that she was beyond his reach, that he might be able to touch her but would never be able to *touch* her. Then he reached out to prod and squeeze her breasts and the fantasy dissolved. She bucked and squirmed, her face taut with desperation as she struggled to escape, but she was gripped too tight. She yelled and screamed but it only encouraged him. She tried to spit into his face but her mouth was parchment.

Then she did the bravest thing that she had ever done. She stopped fighting, tried to blank out his touch and conserved her energy for the opportunity that she sensed would come,

As if confounded by her submission, Decani stepped away. He took a cigarette from his pocket and lit it, alternatively sucking on it then blowing the embers, intent on creating a tool to cut through steel.

'I have been trying to give them up,' he informed her conversationally. 'I know they will kill me. I know what the doctors say. But I have enemies more dangerous than this.'

Ali eyed the glowing cigarette warily. 'I'm not your enemy.'

'So, you are my friend?'

Ali had nothing to say to that. She waited for his question but it didn't come. Instead, without preamble, he touched the glowing cigarette to her body, just below her left breast. There was a gentle sizzling sound, and a smell, not altogether unpleasant, as though someone had dropped the pork into the barbecue. A brief, painless instant, then an unfocused agony racked her body. Her cry echoed through the house and beyond. Decani's impassive features didn't budge, but the light behind them flickered a little.

'Why have you come here, English? Why are you interested in Boletini, a dead man?'

She tried to move but her head was clamped. 'Please!' she whispered. 'Please! No more!'

He waited, a moment of silence. 'Who sent you to spy on us? Who have you come to see? I want names. You understand?'

'I understand but I don't know.' Her voice was a whimper. 'I don't know a Boletini. I'm trying to find my colleague, Steven Shimmon. That's all. I'm not here to spy.'

He sighed, as though this was hurting him more than her, fanned the glowing cigarette and re-applied it, this time below her other breast. Her every nerve end fired up, as though she had been rolled in hot coals. She uttered a heart-stopping howl and writhed helplessly against her restraints.

'If you die here today,' he said reasonably, 'who will know? You should be at home with your husband and your children. Why are you doing this to yourself?'

At last, the reality of her situation penetrated her defences. He was going to kill her! She was going to die in this cold and lonely place, in a land that she had never even wanted to visit.

Be calm! she told herself. *Keep him talking. Stay alive.*

But she didn't know how to stall him. She was overcome with a curious numbness. Her mind had blanked the pain but it had also dulled her thought. She started to shiver uncontrollably. Dissociation loomed, as lethal as hypothermia. Faced with her silence, Decani prepared to brand her again.

'No, no, no! Wait!'

He waited.

'Please!' she whispered between sobs. 'No more! Please! I'll tell you everything!'

And she did, the words tumbling out like tokens from a slot machine. She told him all she knew and all she surmised as one and the same thing. How the death of Shimmon had caused her editor to send her in his footsteps. How Irvine claimed to know nothing.

How Shimmon was investigating the involvement of the SAS and possibly the British government in the death of Lucca. How everyone, from the FCO to the local police and residents, was trying to keep her away from the story.

By now the cigarette was little more than a stub. Decani made to light another and Ali closed her eyes in surrender.

'Open your eyes!' he instructed her.

She did as she was told and immediately wished she hadn't. A third man had appeared in the hall doorway. Another of their kind. More Kosovan pain. She blinked hard, twice, and he was still there, a Sig Sauer P226 pistol in his hand. She groaned. Was there no end to the nightmare?

Decani picked up on her bewildered gaze and turned towards the door. His face twisted in alarm and he reached first for his holstered Glock then for the CZ85 in his belt.

The sound of the Sig was deafening in that room. With a strangled gasp, Ali's tormentor stumbled and fell against the wall. His eyes popped open and he seemed to be struggling for breath. A pink mist hovered in the air where he had stood. Blood splattered the wall and ran down his face. There was the briefest delay, then he slipped to the floor.

The police driver glanced from his fallen partner to the man in the doorway and, in blind panic, turned despairingly for the French window. Another man appeared there to block his escape, his Beretta 92G aimed at the driver, centre mass. The latter reeled away in panic, fumbled unsuccessfully to draw his gun, then dropped to his knees. It was as though someone had cut his invisible strings. Hands together in supplication, he gazed up with the astonished eyes of an animal under the butcher's knife. He spoke rapidly. His words were unintelligible, but his pleading tone said it all.

'You can have mercy,' the newcomer told him. The words were English, the accent Estuarine. 'The same mercy you showed Kenny Moorhouse.'

The two shots were so close together they could have been one. The driver slumped to the floor and lay still.

Decani groaned and moved. The newcomer fired a third time and Decani's chest deflated like a balloon and his lips parted into the stillness of death. The newcomer checked both men. Satisfied that their threat was neutralised, his eyes flickered over the two women then came to rest on his associate.

'Avni. Make sure they're alone.'

Avni nodded and slipped out through the French windows.

The Englishman took out a small switchblade and cut Ali free. She came unsteadily to her feet and he held her arm for a moment. She gave him a nod, and a forced smile, and he let her go.

'I'm Chris Keaton.' His voice was gentle, reassuring. 'You're safe now. You're fine.'

Fine! Her head was heavy and bloated, and she ached all over. But her fear and pain had been neutralised. Maybe he was right. Maybe she was safe. If detached was safe. If being a terrified spectator to her own life was safe.

'Who are you?' she asked lamely. 'What are you doing here?'

He smiled. 'I'm your airport taxi.'

She tried for a smile in return, but shock now numbed her relief. She realised that her breasts were naked and tried to cover herself. She needn't have worried. Keaton had already turned to Donylla. Ali pulled her bra into place. It was then that she saw her burns. Surprised, she touched one, as if to confirm that it was real, and the pain returned, gathering intensity as it ran through her chest and up her spine. She gasped, then began to sob, silently, tears and mucous streaming down her face as she struggled to close her blouse.

Keaton freed Donylla then inspected the abrasions on her face. She waved him away.

'I am not hurt.'

A curt little nod and Keaton returned to Ali. He prised apart the fingers that held her blouse together and inspected her burns. Donylla came to stand beside them, ready to intervene.

'That's got to hurt,' he said. It was the voice of a man unimpressed by pain, his own or anybody else's, but his touch was gentle and sympathetic.

'I've known worse,' she grunted.

The ghost of an appreciative smile crossed his face. 'Sure you have.'

He traced his fingers over the centre of the bruise spreading out from her jaw. She flinched, somehow stemmed the tears.

'These boys don't hold back.' He shook his head. 'I don't think there's a break but you'll need an x-ray. Hold on, I'll be back.'

He disappeared through the French window.

Ali was trembling with fear, but there was triumph in there, too. She caught Donylla's eye and a flash of understanding passed between them. Donylla took Ali's hands in her own. There was no sense of recrimination towards the journalist whose stubbornness had brought them here, just a sweet charge of pathos between two people who had suffered at the hands of brutal men. Together, they stared down at the bodies of their tormenters.

'Death is too merciful,' Donylla said, her voice cold and vicious. 'They should not be free of pain.'

Ali nodded. She, too, wished that the men had suffered, died in lingering and excruciating agony, but she was unable to put her feelings into words. This intensity of hatred was beyond her experience.

Keaton returned. He was carrying a medical pack and a small rucksack. His eyes followed their gaze to the men on the floor.

'Even God regrets making these people,' he observed, 'so what the fuck are you doing here?'

'Tracking a story.' Ali gave him a penetrating stare. 'And what about you? Did Irvine send you?'

'Who's Irvine?'

'My boss.'

He stared blankly and she knew that he wasn't there for her.

'So why are you here?' she demanded.

More blankness. She stared at him, desperate for understanding. Finally, he relented, nodded at the men on the floor. 'I'm here for them.'

'But why now? Why this very moment?'

'Do you only speak in the interrogative?' he smiled. He read her face, which was wired to the edge, and stopped with the humour. 'It's just karma. I've extracted some street justice. Are you comfortable with that?'

She took her eyes off his and tried to imagine what would have happened if he hadn't arrived. She gave him a single nod.

'I'm glad that's settled.' He opened the medical bag. 'Let's get you sorted.'

Ali continued with the stare. 'So who are you?'

'A friend.' His voice was firm; this was his final word. 'Now, keep still.'

With practised ease, he covered Ali's burns with Burnshield dressings. For the pain, he sprayed her jaw with a topical analgesic then gave her two Kapake tablets. While he worked, Ali appraised him with frank curiosity. Late-thirties, he was five-ten, lithe and wiry, with brown hair, weathered skin and bright green eyes set in a wide, handsome face. There was something about him she couldn't fathom, an innate contradiction. He had been cold and ruthless in dealing with the Kosovans, he had taken control of the situation with natural ease, yet his treatment of her was so gentle.

'You kill and heal.' She gave him a grimace that was meant to be a smile. 'I love a man who can multi-task.'

He chuckled lightly, then disappeared into the depths of the house, returning moments later with a pair of denims. Fake Versace. He handed them to Ali. They were several sizes too large.

'Better clean up a little,' he told her. 'Change into these. Three minutes and we're out of here.'

'Three minutes!' The thought of lingering in this place a moment longer and Ali cracked. 'We have to go now!' she shrieked. 'We can't stay here!'

'We have to sterilise the place. Police up shell casings . . .'

'No.' Wild eyed, chest heaving, she grabbed him by the jacket. 'We have to *get to* the police!'

'These guys were the police.' He took her by her wrists, using just enough strength to hold her still. 'We can't trust the local cops. They'll give you up.'

Ali struggled hysterically. 'We have to get away from here! It's not safe! We have to go!'

Without warning, she vomited. She hadn't felt it coming. There was no time to lean forward or turn her head. She just opened her mouth and out it came. Keaton's face was spattered, his jacket streaked, but he didn't flinch. He held on to her as she bent over and was sick on the floor, then he helped her upright again. Still holding her wrists, he looked into her despairing eyes and clamped them with his own.

'You're safe. Nothing bad can happen to you as long as you do as I say. Do you understand?' He waited for her nod. 'Just do as I say. Trust me. Do you trust me?' Another nod. 'You'll be fine.' She nodded again, but he continued to hold her.

Eventually, she said. 'I'm fine.'

Still Keaton didn't release her, not until he saw the change in her eyes, the giving way of fear, the knowledge of safety. Then he reached into his medi-pack and produced a small blue pill and a water bottle.

'Here, take this.'

She grasped the pill. 'To take me out of the matrix, right?'

'Something like that,' he grinned.

Ali nodded. Then she did something she had never done, not even as a child: she took her medication without protest or question.

Chapter 13

THE NEXT TWENTY minutes flew by in a daze. Ali and Donylla did their best to cleanse themselves and purge the odium of their encounter with Kosovo's finest. Keaton made a couple of calls with his satellite phone then, with Avni, heaved the bodies of Decani and his driver into the BMW and dumped the car in a ravine. The two men policed up bullet casings and other evidence, carried the old woman indoors, staged her asleep in a chair, then set a makeshift incendiary device to torch the house.

Darkness was on them by the time Keaton led the women to his SUV, a Cross Lander 244. He waited for Avni to get behind the wheel of Donylla's Golf, then negotiated the dirt road down to Route 25 and turned south towards Prishtina. Ali stared into the wing mirror and watched the Golf's headlights tuck in behind them.

'Where are you taking us?' she demanded, close to panic. 'The Embassy is north!'

'Prishtina's closer,' Keaton told her. 'We'll collect your bags and be in London before they know it.'

'I don't have a valid plane ticket!'

'We're booked on the next flight out of PIA,'

'How does that work?' Ali's lips were parted on her teeth, her fingers curling into a fist and uncurling. 'We bump some hairy businessman off the plane? *Sure, I'd be happy for this bitch to take my seat. Anything for the fifth estate.*'

'We have tickets.'

Ali recalled Keaton's phone calls. 'The airport won't be safe. It's the first place they'll look.'

'The alternatives are not so attractive.' He was smiling in the gloom. 'We could try the Embassy but we'd never get past the border crossing. There are smugglers' routes through the mountains but, even if we made it, the Bulgarians would send us straight back. We could hole up here for six months, until they've forgotten about us, but you'd die of boredom. The only other way is to punch a hole in the dimension but there's no telling where that would take us.' He sensed her seething anger, changed tack. 'No one's looking for us, Ali. There's no reason why they should be. There's nothing to connect us to the house. The only downside is that we have to wait until we're on home soil before we can get a doctor to look at your injuries.'

She had nothing to say to that. She just stared ahead through the windscreen. There were no other vehicles on the road, just a ground mist that formed and reformed itself into random shapes in their headlights. Above them, constellations glowed brightly, as if Edison had yet to invent light pollution. The air tasted sickly sweet, pine laced with diesel, and she could smell the faint aroma of vomit and other human waste. Keaton had removed his jacket so it had to be coming from her. She cringed with embarrassment.

'I can't get on a plane stinking like this. I need a shower.'

He nodded agreement in the dark. 'A quick hosedown, that's all. Use plenty of deodorant. You don't want to miss this flight.'

'What about Shimmon?'

'The Consulate will sort it. Your friend won't mind waiting for another day. Not if it sees you safe.'

Ali fell silent. She knew that she had to take stock, put a layer of rationale on the day's horror. But, lulled by the hypnotic rattle and hum of the Cross Lander, she couldn't process her thoughts. A feeling of heaviness and relaxation was beginning to settle on her. She no longer felt so cold, or hurt, or filthy. Her mouth was still clotted with blood but her nerves were healing. That little blue pill, she guessed. It wasn't so much that the pain and fear had been eradicated, more that they didn't seem to matter.

Soon after passing through Tregu, the two cars rolled to a halt on a remote stretch of tarmac. Avni drove Donylla's VW off-road into the forest, removed the plates and torched it. Ali watched, entranced, as the flames leaped up to perform a manic dance with the Transylvanian shadows, a dance that she could still see on the back of her eyelids long after Avni had joined them in the 4x4.

'Sorry about your car,' Keaton told Donylla as they drove on. 'But you never know who's clocked it. Avni will sort you another vehicle.'

'It was just a car,' Donylla said, her voice matter-of-fact dull. 'There are many cars.'

At the hotel, Ali slipped up to her room, showered, dressed and packed. She grabbed Shimmon's bag with her own and hurried down to reception. Miro was not there and a young woman checked her out. Ali fixed a tired, self-effacing smile onto her face and explained that her boss had called her back to London. *Seems they can't do without me.*

A tense twenty-five minutes later, they were at the airport. Keaton slipped his gun to Avni, exchanged a hug and muttered word, collected his rucksack from the boot and hefted Ali's bags.

'I'll collect the tickets,' he told her. 'I'll see you inside.'

Ali turned to Donylla and the two women embraced tightly.

'Goodbye, Ali,' Donylla said. 'I will be thinking of you.'

'You should come to London with us,' Ali entreated her. 'Come and see the world.'

'I will go to my family in Djakovica'

'You won't be safe here.'

'I am safe. You are the one who looks for danger.' Donylla paused. 'These people are evil. In your country, I know, it is not politically correct to believe in such a thing. You pretend there are no evil people, only bad acts made by good people. You think such people can be cured. This belief permits evil men to thrive. Evil cannot be controlled. It must be destroyed.'

'I'll be okay.'

'I hope so. And please, Ali, don't judge us all by the men who did this to you. My people are good people. We want nothing to do with the madness. We want only to live and work and love our family.'

'I know.'

Avni touched Ali's shoulder. 'You must go.'

Ali squeezed Donylla for the last time. She shook Avni's hand then turned abruptly and went directly into the terminal. She didn't look back, couldn't look back.

Keaton was waiting inside. They checked in, made their way airside and found a seat in the lounge. She took out her phone to call Irvine only to be denied by the battery warning bleeps. She eyed the bank of public phones, decided against it. When it came down to it, she didn't know what to say to him.

While they waited for their flight, she couldn't get Donylla's words out of her mind: *You pretend there are no evil people, only evil acts. This permits evil men to thrive.* There was no arguing with that. She scrutinised every face that entered the terminal as though it belonged to Satan himself. No assassin came to kill her, no policeman to arrest her, but her fear, adrenaline and pain mixed into a thickening fog of paranoia that was still with her as the runway receded beneath them.

She said, 'We should have made Donylla come with us.'

Keaton shrugged. 'She's safer here than in the UK.'

His words brought a real psychic wobble 'Is that supposed to be reassuring?'

BY THE TIME they reached Gatwick, Ali was too wasted to drive. Keaton guided her through customs and baggage then took the keys to her Renault. She didn't register the journey - north on the M23, clockwise on the M25 then east on the M4 - until they had left the motorway at Hounslow and pulled up on the forecourt of a private clinic on the edge of the Heath.

Ali blinked about her. 'What are we doing here?'

'You'd have difficulty explaining those cigarette burns in A&E.'

'I've got nothing to hide.'

'Maybe not, but you want to keep a tight control on information, trust me.'

She stared at him, then nodded. She didn't quite trust him – couldn't bring herself to trust anyone - but he had brought her this far. She went along.

The doctor was mid-thirties though, with his cropped hair, slim body and boyish looks, and his insistence on being called Marcus, he seemed much younger. Keaton settled into the waiting room, eyes closed, while Marcus took Ali into a consultation room. It was sparkling clean and, scattered with machines for diathermy, anaesthesia, resuscitation and ventilation, equipped for all eventualities from man flu to emergency surgery.

Marcus had her sit on a half-way couch.

'Burns first,' he said. 'I expect that jaw hurts like hell but it'll wait.'

She removed her blouse gingerly and gritted her teeth in anticipation as he eased off the Burnshield dressing. Surprisingly, it didn't hurt. Small yellowish blisters had already formed over the wounds. He inspected them carefully.

'Perfect. They look nice and sterile. I'll leave them intact.'

He covered the incipient blisters with a Jelonet gauze dressing, then applied gauze, cotton wool, crepe bandage and tape. He kept up a neutral, stream-of-consciousness patter as he moved on to x-ray her jaw. The image revealed no break.

'The bruise will spoil your good looks for a day or two,' he grinned, 'but it'll fade.'

He gave her some spare dressings, antibiotics to fight infection and a box of Kapakes for the pain.

'Don't take too many painkillers. They'll knock you out. If the burns haven't healed in two weeks come back and we'll see about a burns surgeon. But I'm confident they'll be okay. Keaton did a good job.'

She nodded. It was only when they were back in the waiting room that she realised that Marcus had taken no personal details or history. That kind of medical treatment didn't come cheap.

Keaton opened his eyes and smiled. She fixed him with an unfriendly, quizzical gaze, asked, 'Who's picking up the tab?'

'Tab? Oh, don't worry about that.'

She continued with the hard stare but he was no more forthcoming. She didn't have the energy to pursue it, not now. Instead, she muttered:

'My Dad will never forgive me.'

'Forgive you what?'

'He's a GP. And very catholic. He thinks private medicine is the work of fallen angels. *Greedy doctors will be the death of the Health Service. Mark my words, Ali. There's only so much meat on the Service and they won't be happy until it's all on their plate.* It's his mantra.'

'Mantra's are just comfort blankets,' Keaton said matter-of-factly. 'Your Dad would want you safe and well.'

She tried to come back at him but, once again, her fatigue and his simple logic had disarmed her.

THEY REACHED COLINDALE in the small hours. Keaton put her car in her garage, located in the service road behind the shops, and they walked the short distance to her flat. After all that had happened during the past few hours, she should have been falling apart. But her adrenaline was on slow, blue tab burn and the Kapakes that masked the pain were cocooning her brain. As they entered the flat, she had the sensation of floating. She filled the kettle for coffee and put her phone on charge, but all she wanted was to sleep.

'I'm sorry,' she said, her voice scratchy and robotic, 'we have to talk but I need my bed. Can we leave it until the morning?'

'Morning is good.'

'Help yourself to a drink and whatever you want to eat. And take the spare room. It's too late to be kicking you out.'

She tried to make the offer routine and impassive, but Keaton sensed the need in there. She didn't want to be left alone, not tonight.

'Thank you,' he said. 'At this time of night, I'd have to jack a car to get home.'

Chapter 14

SARAH YORK WAS eating breakfast on the sofa when the call came. Muesli, coffee and a recycled game show. She reached for her phone. Number withheld. A moment's hesitation then she took the call.

'They've found you.' The message was boiled down, the voice that of her guardian angel. 'Be gone in ten. Understood?'

'I understand.'

'Queens Park. I'll call you in twenty.'

Pre-programmed, she abandoned her breakfast, grabbed her toiletries from the bathroom, and hurried to her bedroom. There was not much to pack. She had brought few belongings with her and she hurriedly stuffed them into her backpack. Textbooks and other impersonal possessions she would leave behind. They contained nothing of her. She knew that. Wasn't she ever vigilant?

She didn't understand how they could have found her so quickly. It shouldn't have been possible. Was there no escaping?

Her heart began palpitating, slowly at first but then it was hammering so hard that she had to sit on the bed. In the past, she had always been so prepared for moments like this, so calm, so controlled, but now the absurdity of her situation threatened to overwhelm her. She was running in fear for her life from people who were supposed to love her! How could this be right?

Right or wrong, it had always been thus. Flight, for Sarah, was a lifetime's routine. As a little girl, she had fled with her father to the West, two survivors of the Yugoslav wars and its ethnic cleansing. They had pulled up the genetic roots of centuries to live in France, South Africa then England. Thereafter, as her father had re-built his fortune, they had commuted between a range of luxury homes: England, Switzerland, Bermuda and New York State. A few months here, a few months there, using air travel as most people used a car. It was a singular way of life but she had always accepted it as *her* way of life. Now, like a seed that had been blown hither and thither in the wilderness, she just wanted to drop out of the wind and germinate.

Calmer now, she scanned the flat for anything she might have forgotten. There was nothing. Once again, she was leaving fingerprints but no footprint. That brought a pause. She considered writing a goodbye note to her flatmate, Amy, decided it was safer for all concerned if she simply disappeared. Her rent was paid. She owed no allegiance and no explanation.

She opened the front door cautiously, her eyes flickering up and down the street. Seeing no threat, she stepped outside, hunched down into the hood of her fleece jacket and turned north towards Queens Park station. The platform was almost empty at that time of day and she could see no obvious tail. She slipped into the shadows, from where she had eyes on the stairs. Precisely on time, her phone rang. Keeping a wary eye for danger, she listened carefully to the cryptic instructions.

She caught the first train to Oxford Circus then joined the throng on Oxford Street, dodging in and out of shops as she made her way to Tottenham Court Road. She descended once again into the cavernous depths of the Tube and took the first westbound Central train. At Holborn, she crossed over to the eastbound line and caught the next train to Bond Street. She waited on the platform, boarded the second train to come along and got off at Baker Street. From there, she caught a Jubilee train heading north, disembarking two stops later at Swiss Cottage. She waited on the platform until it was empty then walked up to the exit to catch out any stalker. Finally, as certain as she could be that she wasn't being followed, she caught the next train north.

At Canons Park, she left the station and walked swiftly along Donnefield Avenue into the park. She skirted the children's playground then climbed the steps of the pedestrian bridge that crossed over the railway. From the top, she had a panoramic view of the route she had taken from the station. There was a solitary mother and child in the playground and a small dogwalkers' convention on the path. Satisfied at last that no-one was following her, she carried on into Cheyneys Avenue.

As promised, a car was waiting, a sporty little Peugeot. The driver was late twenties and wore a dark suit. She was used to men hitting on her so she had mixed feelings when he avoided her eye as if she might turn him to stone.

'The SatNav is pre-programmed,' he informed her curtly. 'Keys are in the ignition and there's a new passport and paperwork in the glove compartment. Good luck.'

Good luck. Meaningless tick. Without another word, he walked off towards the station. She watched him go, then dropped her bag onto the passenger seat. The digital voice of the SatNav guided her north to the M1, anti-clockwise on the M25 and then south on the M3 to Southampton.

She spent a lonely night at the Holiday Inn at Southampton Airport then caught the early flight to Cork. From there, she took the three hour bus trip to Shannon Airport. She sailed through check-in, security and boarding, and, seven hours of in-flight movies later, she was approaching New York.

At JFK her heart hammered loudly against her chest, her face burned and her eyes wandered restlessly. She was convinced that her new documentation would fail scrutiny, or that her nervous tells would betray her. She needn't have worried. An attractive Caucasian girl doesn't register on any passenger profiling index.

Her guardian angel had arranged for her to be met but no one waved, or came forward to greet her. It took a couple of minutes before she realised that the woman holding the card for *Rachel Carson* was actually waiting for her.

Sarah York had ceased to exist.

Chapter 15

ALI WAS UP early, the pain of her injuries burning through the neural gate to overcome her exhaustion. She popped a couple of Kapakes, pulled on a dressing gown and went downstairs in search of coffee. Almost immediately, Keaton appeared at her side.

He asked, 'How are you feeling?'

'I'm good.'

He nodded, but his shrewd gaze made it clear that he didn't believe her. For a man who must have seen and done terrible things, his eyes were remarkably gentle. They saw right through to her trauma and soothed it. The sensation was like a laying on of hands and Ali shrank from the intimacy, holding her gown closed like a self-conscious teenager.

Keaton sensed her discomfort and turned away to inspect the contents of the fridge. It was all but empty. The cupboards likewise.

'Get dressed,' he said. 'I'll buy you breakfast.'

'Coffee's all I need,' she said. 'Black. One sugar.'

'You need to boost your energy levels.' He cleared his throat, as though about to lecture her on the importance of good nutrition. Instead, he contented himself with a nod. 'Black. One sugar.'

She left him to it and went through to the lounge where she retrieved her phone from its charger and watched as an assortment of comms popped in. Missed calls, messages, emails, notifications. Too wired to read them, she deleted every one and took out Shimmon's netbook. She studied it carefully, flipping and rotating it like it would magically regenerate. The obvious course would be to take the netbook and thumb drive to the Echo's techs but she didn't quite trust them. Sure, they had the knowhow to retrieve the data but they also had an unwelcome tendency to take their stated mission - *to grease the information flow* – to the extreme of selling it on. She couldn't have them sharing this material with the world. That left Paul Stewart, long-time friend and computer geek with a difference.

She scrolled his number.

After half-a-dozen rings, he picked up. 'This had better be important!' he snapped.

His petulance brought a sudden awareness of how early it was. A night bird, Stewart hated to be disturbed before midday. Quickly, she switched to her business voice and came to the point before she lost him. 'I need to retrieve the data from a damaged netbook and memory stick. It's urgent, Paul, or I wouldn't bother you.'

'I'll be in the office this afternoon. Probably sooner now you've woken me.'

'I'll see you there', she said, but she was talking to a dead tone.

Keaton came in with two mugs of coffee. She took hers and they drank in silence, distracted by their own thoughts.

Eventually, she said, 'So, who do we report this to?'

'What do you mean?'

'Our little brush with the dark side. Who do we go to? The Met? The National Crime Agency? The Foreign Office?'

He put down his coffee and turned to look into her eyes. 'The first thing the authorities will do is contact the Kosovan police.'

'Excellent. The Kosovars will have to explain what they're doing to catch Steven's murderers.'

'No. They will interrogate you about the deaths of two of their own.'

'Then the world will know all about those bastards.'

His face flickered with alarm. 'You can't write about Prishtina, Ali! You do know that. Tell me you know that.'

'Three people died. We can't just ignore it.'

He pursed his lip and shook his head. 'I killed two of them.'

'It was self defence!'

'Prove it.'

'Okay.' She allowed condescension to creep into her voice. 'If you're worried, we lawyer up. The Echo will provide. Any half-assed brief can finesse a little problem like that.'

'We killed two cops, hid their bodies and fled the country. Finesse that!'

Ali paused. He had all the answers. 'If we don't front up, what happens when they do find the bodies?'

'They'll take some finding. At which time the cops will put it down to a little blood on blood. As will the local mafia. With any luck, they'll avenge themselves into extinction.'

'And when the police come calling?'

'They won't. Why would they? We don't connect. You flew into the country, identified the body of a friend and flew out. As for me - no-one even knows I was there. We're in the clear, Ali, unless you give us up. If you do that, the Kosovan police will inform the mafia and we'll spend what's left of our lives looking over our shoulders for the psycho avengers.'

'You're a real harbinger of doom,' she complained. 'You've spent too long playing at soldiers,'

'Long enough to know this,' he told her with exaggerated care. 'Broadcast where you've been and what you've seen, and they will come after you. You won't see them coming. No one will know what happened to you. There'll be no body, no witnesses, no trace. But you won't be any less dead for that.' He stopped briefly to gauge her reaction. 'You think I'm making this up? These people live for the simple pleasures in life, like torture, slaughter and rape. And, the news of the day, Ali, is this: the Kosovars are already here!' He might have added *duh!* 'It doesn't matter how good you are at your job, you can't take a notebook to a gunfight and expect to live.'

Ali felt as though she was trapped in a revolving door. If Keaton was correct, she couldn't report events in Kosovo. Yet she couldn't not report them. She knew that he was close to losing patience with her but she wasn't about to concede.

'We have to talk to someone.'

'You need to talk? Go see a priest.'

'People should know the truth about Steven.'

'Why? It won't make him any less dead. People die all the time, Ali. The world keeps turning. By all means remember your friends but don't fool yourself that anyone else cares. . . . The important thing is that justice has been done.'

'That's not justice, it's revenge.'

'Oh, it's justice, Ali, believe me. Natural justice, Kosovan style. It's the only justice you'll get here.' He paused, softened his tone. 'It's over. You're back in your own world. Forget it happened. Put it down to a nightmare, something bad you watched on TV.'

'Something bad I watched on TV!' She glared at him. She felt patronised and that brought her a new focus. 'What were you doing at that house?'

'I'm not sure I understand.'

'Don't play dumb, Chris, it doesn't suit you.' He offered her the hint of a smile and Ali reacted with anger. 'You're some kind of mercenary, right! Who paid you to be there? Irvine? Echo Newspapers?'

'No one paid me.'

'Stop lying to me!'

'Okay,' he shrugged. 'Stop asking me questions.'

She fenced eyes with him, trying to penetrate that shield of his. *Who the hell are you?* The question had crossed her mind last night, but briefly. Now it was back, and this time it wasn't going away. What little she knew about him she had gleaned from close-hand observation. He was some kind of security operative who moved undetected in a foreign country, was an accomplished medic, could magically conjure up plane tickets and had access to a private hospital that treated strangers anonymously. He was also capable of killing a man without a flicker of remorse.

That upped the ante. Made him a stone killer. Yet, she didn't see him as a threat. Not to her. He was a scary man, certainly, but for some reason he didn't scare her. It made no sense, of course. Nothing made sense. She couldn't think it through! The Kapakes were warping her judgment, leaving her in a haze of frazzled ambivalence. She retreated to her comfort zone and slipped into journo mode.

'So you arriving when you did was a coincidence. Nothing to do with me.' Her lip curled. 'I'd have to be a vegetable on life support to believe that.'

There followed a lengthy silence during which he fielded her stare with maddening calm.

'Moorhouse!' Her mind flipped back to that Kosovan lounge. 'You said you were there for him! He was Shimmon's bodyguard. That's why you were there. To avenge Moorhouse!'

For a moment, she thought that Keaton would maintain his silence, then he stared off, speaking quietly, self-consciously.

'He was brave and loyal. A real friend. He never let you down, never flinched from a fight. *He ate his pain and swallowed his blood.*' Keaton paused, seemingly embarrassed to have uttered the barrack-room cliché. 'It's important, if you live that way, to know that your mates will avenge your killing.'

'Violence and vengeance!' That lip curl again, 'It's all just a pissing contest for men like you.'

'Men like me?'

'Yes. You're a security consultant, right? A mercenary?'

'I'm not part of your story.'

'Moorhouse was an old mate,' she continued. 'He was also a Paratrooper and served in Kosovo. That was in his CV. He was probably SAS. You served with him, didn't you?' Keaton's acknowledgement was almost invisible - a momentary shudder behind his eyes quickly covered by an awkward smile. 'If you didn't serve with him, I'm a Trappist. Tell me I'm not right.'

He shrugged. 'The past is a grey area.'

'For people like you. What was it like? Kosovo?'

'You've been there. It's cold in winter, hot in summer.'

It was her turn to smile. She was still smiling when she threw her curve ball. 'What do you know about Operation Mammon.'

Another flicker ran through his eyes but she still couldn't read him. 'That's a new one on me.'

She smiled again, despite herself. 'You're a tricky bastard.' They stared at each other, each uncertain of the other's mood. 'I guess, now that you've avenged your friend, you've finished with this.'

His eyes sought hers and took a firm grip. 'So have you, Ali. If you keep snooping around in this mess, if you discuss it with anyone, or write it up, or mention it on the phone, then someone will hear about it. You people are not the only ones who monitor phones and computers. Someone will come calling.'

'I don't hack! . . .' Something in his tone caused her to take a mental step backwards. 'What are you talking about? Who would come calling?'

He shrugged. Concern touched his eyes. 'You're opening a door to a world of pain you couldn't even dream about.'

'People should know the truth!'

'People will never know this truth.' He took a breath that was pure exasperation. 'Do what you must, Ali. Just leave me out of it.'

Ali shook her head at him. The journalist in her understood that he had told her nothing and would continue to tell her nothing. She couldn't contain her frustration. But neither could she ignore the fact that he had saved her life. She realized a little guiltily that she hadn't even thanked him for that. If it hadn't been for his intervention, it would be her lying in that Kosovan gully.

'Thanks for your concern, Chris, but I'm not some helpless bimbo.'

He shook his head sadly. 'It's a pity you're not. You might grasp what you really need.'

'What I really need!' Her voice grew thick with anger. 'A good seeing to, right! And you're just the macho fuck to do it.'

He coloured up, genuinely shocked to be so misinterpreted, and she saw a level of injury in his eyes that she could not have anticipated.

'Take a sabbatical, Ali,' he told her, his voice dry and scratchy. 'Step back from this one. You're in over your head.' He stared at her with frightening intensity. 'This is not worth your life. It can't be. There are plenty of other things to care about, a hundred lifetimes of causes.'

She could see his point, though she wouldn't concede it. *Move on to survive,* he was urging her. *Leave this story behind and find another.* But she knew that she wouldn't. She had too great a capacity for denial. She had been complicit in the killing of two men and that made her an accessory after the fact. She had also witnessed an old woman shot dead and had herself been subjected to physical and sexual assault. By rights, the fear and loathing should have kicked back in. By now, she should be suffering emotional overload. PTSD. Yet she felt nothing. No shame, no guilt, no fear, no anger. The terror and rage of Kosovo had gone. She had no flashbacks. Her wounds had recovered to a background throb. Even the brutish hatred for her attackers had left her. Events in the Balkans badlands seemed to have tripped a switch inside her, fusing her circuitry and shutting down her emotions. She heard the sound of Keaton's words but not the meaning. Nothing bad could ever happen to her. Nothing ever did.

'Steven was a good man,' she said. 'This may be a shit world, but good things do happen and Steven was one of those who made them happen. Someone killed him and I want to know why.'

He came to his feet and they stared at each other. The tension in the room was almost sexual in its intensity. She felt two conflicting, irreconcilable emotions. On the one hand, she was anxious for him to go, to go and take his protective bloody instincts with him. On the other, she felt curiously anxious that he was about to walk out of her life.

At length, his eyes disconnected from hers. 'Please keep me out of your story.'

'Don't worry,' she said. 'You don't even rate a mention.'

He nodded, took a business card from his wallet and placed it on the table. 'I won't be far away. Call me when you need me.' He said *when*, she noted, not *if*. 'Any time, any place.'

He picked up his rucksack and turned to go.
'Chris!'
He looked back at her from the door, his face unreadable.
'Thank you,' she said. 'Thank you for my life.'
He reached out a hand, as though he was going to stroke her cheek, but she was too far away and he let it drop.
'Guard it well, Ali. It's too precious a thing to throw away on nothing.'
Then he was gone and she was sorry. She hadn't felt this hollow and vulnerable since her mother had died.

Chapter 16

SANDFORD WATCHED AMY Harris leave her flat, adjust her backpack and walk off towards Queens Park. Six and a half minutes later, his phone vibrated and the voice told him that Amy was on a tube train heading into the City.

Sarah York was home alone.

He eased himself from the car, strolled with casual purpose along the street and stopped at her front door. His task was simple. Stun the girl and acquire the data stick, then walk her the few steps from the house to the SUV. He took the Halothane spray from his pocket and tapped on the door. No-one came. He rapped harder. Still no answer.

No hesitation, no glance about him to attract suspicion, just a moment's work with a rake and pick and he was in. He closed the door behind him, and then stood still, listening. There was no sound of life. Just the hum of a fridge and the aroma of cheap perfume and old curry. He wore no deodorant himself. His aim was to come and go undetected. His synthetic clothes, hat and gloves would leave no trace and he moved soundlessly. It wasn't for nothing that his colleagues in the old Five had dubbed him the Ghost.

The lounge was clean but untidy, littered with papers, books, CDs and coffee mugs. Furniture was a sofa and armchairs, and there was a standard data rack of hi-fi, TV, satellite box and Blu-ray player. An airer loaded with washing stood in a corner of the room.

He moved into the narrow hallway. Before him was the kitchenette. To the left was a small bedroom with a card stuck to the door. *Amy's room*. Next to the bedroom was the bathroom. It was messy. Dirty underwear and t-shirts on the floor, and a pink towelling bathrobe discarded by someone late for college. The two rooms had been carved from one. To his right was another bedroom. There was no nametag here but it had to be Sarah's. Halothane at the ready, he pushed open the door.

The room was empty. He wasn't often surprised but this brought him up short. The room wasn't just unslept in. It had been cleared out. No personal belongings. Bare shelves and empty cupboards. Sarah York had left and had no intention of returning.

'Bitch!'

In a controlled fury, he searched the room. It was barren. The bin contained an empty crisp packet and a plastic water bottle, but no discarded scrap of paper with a forwarding address, no name, or phone number, or email. She had left nothing for him.

He didn't like the unpredictable. He preferred control, precision and order. This was his own fault. He had found her, hesitated and lost her. Someone must have tipped her off but he should have expected that. He cursed his own complacency though he didn't dwell on it. There was no point in looking for excuses where none would be accepted.

He returned to the lounge. There was plenty to sift through but he quickly realised that it was the roommate's mess. He moved on to Amy's room. A clutter of stuffed animals, dirty clothes and books, with a bed, a desk, another TV and CD player. Amy, he learned, was studying IT and Business but there was nothing to connect her to Sarah, nothing to indicate where Sarah might have gone. The kitchen revealed no clue, the bathroom just circles in the dust where toiletries had once stood. There was no evidence to indicate that Sarah York had ever lived here.

He took out his phone and selected Seymour's number. There was a brief pause, a few hollow clicks, then the phone was picked up.

Sandford said, 'She's gone.'

LATER THAT DAY, Miles Martin found himself sitting on a cold, hard concrete floor. He was blindfolded and gagged, and his hands were plasticuffed to something immovable behind him. He had tried to pull his arms free but had only succeeded in cutting his wrists. There was no escaping the cuffs and that meant there was no escape. Worst of all, he felt nauseous. He was terrified of vomiting into his gag. Suffocating on his own puke was no way to die. The more he thought about it, the more likely it seemed.

He had no idea where he was. The air was cool and musty. Every now and then he sensed a distant rumble as if a lorry or bus had passed by. He could hear men in the background, their voices muffled by a closed door. The same men, he presumed, who had come for him that afternoon. He had been on the street when the hoodie had approached him. Just another guy on the fringes of his consciousness. Too late, he had seen the gun. Before it had registered, a second man had taken him by the arm and guided him into an SUV with darkened windows.

And now he was here.

The voices stopped, the door opened and he sensed people moving towards him. They were going to kill him, he was convinced of that, though he didn't know why. He wondered if it would be quick: a bullet to the head; a knife in his chest. Or slow and horrific: a blade slashing at his throat; a slow drowning – his worst nightmare. Despair and helplessness overwhelmed him. His chest heaved, he had to fight for breath, his tears streamed. He wrestled against his restraints and pushed himself backwards in a vain attempt to make himself small.

Someone tore the tape from his mouth, the pain sharp but short-lived. They left his eyes covered but at least he could breathe freely.

Silence.

'Who are you?' he asked, his voice little more than a whisper. 'What do you want with me?'

No one replied.

'Who are you?' he begged. 'What do you want?'

A voice at last. 'How good are you with pain?'

'What do you mean?' Sweat was running freely over him. 'What do you want?'

'I'm wondering what kind of incentive you would need to tell the truth.'

'I've got no reason to lie.' His words trembled. 'What have I got to lie about?'

'All terrorists lie.'

'I'm not a terrorist.' He felt a sudden surge of hope. He saw it now: they were some kind of anti-terrorist police. They had simply taken him by mistake. With that realisation, his words flowed with relief. 'I'm no terrorist. You've got the wrong man. It's not me you want. Please. It's easy to check. You have the wrong man.'

'Miles Martin,' the voice intoned. 'Born in Guildford, twenty two years ago on May 26th. Your father is a solicitor, your mother a teacher. You attended the Royal Grammar School then LSE, graduating last summer. You joined Amnesty International and the Greens during your first term at the LSE. Eighteen months ago, you co-formed the Scorched Earth Information Exchange with Alice Newman and Ben Claxton.'

'We're not terrorists.' His breathing was calmer now, now that he understood the nature of their error, now that he could explain. 'We're a campaigning and pressure group. We educate people on the dangers of global warming. We're about non-violence, sustainability, social justice, ecological wisdom.'

'I know people like you,' the disembodied voice told him. 'Retros. Watermelons - green on the outside, red in the middle. In another age you'd have been a Marxist or a religious fundamentalist. If you were a raghead or a Packi, you'd be slaughtering innocents in the name of your god. You have a beef with society because you can't hack it. You share the same mantra: *I have to kill you to save you.* Emphasis on the killing. With people like you, it's in your genes.'

'No, no!' he cried. 'You've got it wrong. We're not terrorists. We're sworn against all violence. What would be the point? We want to save people, not harm them.'

'We have your computer. We're finding enough incriminating material to put you away for three lifetimes. Your files. The sites you've been browsing. Your emails. Your links with other terror groups.'

'There's nothing like that!'

'You can't hide it from us. We will find it.'

'There's nothing!' He paused as another reality struck home. 'You mean you'll plant it! . . . You can't do that. Why would you do that?' Silence. 'You can't get away with that. There are laws.' Another silence. 'We're not terrorists. We're nothing. A talking shop. We don't do anything. No one listens to us, or follows us. Just look at our social media. We're totally transparent about what we do. We even have a web site!'

'I know, Miles. I've seen it.' Pause. Martin could hear the contemptuous smile in the man's voice. 'In fact, we know all about you and your schoolboy politics.'

Pause.

'Then you know we're harmless.' Another silence. 'What do you want?'

'Sarah York.'

'Sarah?'

'Where is she?'

'She has a place in West Kilburn. That's no secret. You could have found that out by asking.'

'She's gone. We want to know where.'

'Gone? She'll be at uni.' A pause. 'You mean *gone!* I don't understand. I didn't know. I don't know where she is. How could I? She doesn't confide in me.' Pause. 'Why Sarah? What has she done?' Another pause. 'You mean she is a terrorist! How could we know?' Another moment of stunned silence. 'I dunno where she is. Maybe one of the others will know.'

'We're talking to your friends, Miles. Why not get onside. Do yourself a favour. Be the first to tell us.'

'She keeps her private self just that, private. I don't know where she comes from and I've no idea where she might have gone.' Another pause. 'You can't do this. There are laws!'

'There are no laws for terrorists, Miles. No human rights for the anti-human. Talk to me here or we'll fly you straight to hell.'

Chapter 17

THE WORKADAY EXCITEMENT and energy of the newsroom gave Ali an unexpected buzz. She smiled her way to her pod, deposited her bags, then carried on to Irvine's office, She knocked once and, without waiting for a reply, opened the door. Irvine was hunched over his keyboard, eyes asquint, brow furrowed. He glanced up as she came in and gave her a languid smile. Then he saw her bruised face and snapped to as if she had kicked him.

'That must hurt.'

She tried for a wry smile that turned into a scowl. 'I won't be turning the other cheek for a while.'

He came around his desk to examine her. His fingers hovered just short of contact. 'Jesus, kiddo! What happened?'

'I found out that Steven's murder was no mugging. . . .'

'What!'

' . . . Someone didn't want me to know and they made their feelings plain.'

'And they did this! Buggar me!' There was a moment of silence during which the temperature in that room seemed to plummet. 'What happened over there?'

With a surprisingly clear head, Ali recounted the events in Prishtina. She explained what she had been told about Shimmon's murder, then related in detail her own experiences, including her visit to the Decani, her trip to Pozderka, and her hasty return to London. As she spoke, Irvine accompanied her, beating out *fuck . . . fuck* every fourth bar. For some reason that she didn't quite understand, she redacted the events at the killing house and the role of Keaton.

'Jesus Ali!' he said at last. 'Why didn't you call me? I would have got someone to you.'

'We would have passed in mid-air.'

'What are the police doing about it?' He read her expression. 'You didn't inform them, did you?'

'Like I said, the Kosovan police covered up Steven's death. It would have been counter-productive.'

'Counter-productive!' He paused, just long enough to regain his equilibrium. 'I should never have sent you. A mugging, they said, and I believed them. The bastards.'

'Steven was murdered and his flat turned over! It was always more than a mugging! . . .'

'I didn't *know*, Ali,' he insisted. 'If I had, I would never have got you into it.'

She nodded. 'If I thought otherwise, we'd be having a different kind of conversation.' She stared at him, frankly quizzical. 'Did you hire me a minder?'

'I should have done,' he said apologetically, 'but no. It never occurred to me.'

'I ran into this guy, Chris Keaton. I checked him out. He's an employee of Corbin Defence Services. Same as Moorhouse, the guy who was minding Steven. The name doesn't ring a bell?'

'I think I would have remembered.' He sighed heavily, scratched his neck. 'What's going on, Ali. I know you. You're holding something back.'

'Why would I do that?'

'Because you're you.' He glanced out of the window and back again, no more than a breath. 'Look, no story is worth this grief, kiddo. I'm killing it, as of now.'

'No!' She took a half-step forward, her eyes blazing. 'You can't do that! The local police have as good as closed Steven's case! The killers are getting away with it! Steven deserves justice, John! It's up to us to close the loop! We have to keep going!'

'Up to us?' he echoed sceptically. 'Listen to yourself, Ali. How do you keep coming up with this stuff? *Up to us!* It's like you've got some thinking disorder. You hardly knew the guy!'

'But you knew him. He was working for you. He was your friend! He was killed because of the job he was doing for you!' She hesitated. 'If you had seen him lying in that morgue you would want to stand up for him, John, I know you would.'

'Don't give in to your emotions, Ali. I need you to be professional in this.'

'Do I sound emotional?' A reflective pause. 'Okay, so I'm bloody mad. But, take Steven out of the equation and this is still our kind of story. *My* kind of story.'

He shook his head. 'I can't afford to put my best investigator on a story that could run for weeks and come up with nothing.'

'Every story carries that risk.' Silence. The heat of anger drained from her cheeks, slowly. 'You pay me to expose the sharks who abuse power for their own ends. People with the clout to cover their tracks. And I'm good at it. You sent me to Kosovo blind, chasing some story about our government colluding with Kosovan organised crime, and in just two days I've come up with Operation Mammon, Lord Figgis and the Kosovan mafia. This is no dead end.'

He read the mutiny in her face and smiled, affability encased in steel; it was an irritating gesture, disingenuous. 'Think about it, kiddo. A hot investigation can be difficult enough - a maze of dead ends and obstructions, countless hours of wasted time and effort. But this! This is as cold as a marble headstone. How do you propose to find his killers when you can't even go back to Kosovo?'

'I'll succeed because I want to,' she responded evenly. 'I'll unravel what I can from the London end and force the FCO to get their finger out. Nothing succeeds with this government like a tabloid campaign.'

He folded his arms, a sign of his own intransigence. 'I'll tell you what I'm going to do. I'm going to arrange a meet with the lawyers and devise a strategy for progressing this with the authorities.'

'No.' She stared at him, grim and intense. Suddenly, Keaton's words made sense. The last thing she wanted was any kind of investigation. It might uncover what had really happened in that hillside house. 'You assigned me, remember. You got me into this and now I have a real story. If you don't want it, I'll take it elsewhere.'

'Take it elsewhere!' He was genuinely shocked; she actually meant it! 'Jesus, Ali! What the fuck happened to friendship and loyalty?'

She caught the jibe and threw it back. 'Ask Stephen Shimmon.'

'Listen to yourself!' His face was flushed with anger but his eyes were pools of sadness. He knew that, if he called her bluff, she would simply shrug her shoulders and be gone. He didn't want that. Not just because she brought in the stories, or because he had profound respect for her skill and integrity. He was genuinely fond of her. He cleared his throat. 'Let's say you're right, and Steven was killed for something he found out. It's not like the old days. There is no respect any more. Did you know that the number of journalists murdered on the job doubled last year. Many, too many, were women, like you, so obsessed by their investigations they lost their heads then they lost their lives. Am I supposed to stand by and watch you put yourself in harm's way over the same story that got Stephen killed, a story we can't even bring in?'

That almost pulled the rug. She felt strangely affected by his concern. Not so long ago, she would have snapped his head off for having the nerve to suggest that she wasn't up to looking after herself. Now she was touched, and that pained her. It was as if moral decay had eaten through the enamel of her psyche and reached the soft core.

'I will bring it in, John. Nothing and no-one will stop me.'

He sighed, exasperated. 'If the story's so important to you, let me give you a couple of guys to help with the legwork.'

'A couple of guys!' she snapped. 'You want me chained to a desk like some helpless bimbo! Since when has being gynec been a disability?'

'Gynec? You'd win a pissing contest with any man I know.' Irvine eyed her like she was a guileless idiot. 'Macho posturing is a futile and dangerous liability in our line of work. You know that as well as I. Anybody else who'd been through what you've experienced would be in therapy for a year! '

She said nothing to that, just stared at him.

He stared back. 'You know how much we value you, Ali - how much *I* value you. You're the best hack I know. Don't walk out of this room thinking my opinion is otherwise. But you have this psychic flaw: you can't control what's inside you. Stephen was the same. He had to do everything in a contrary and unpredictable fashion. And look where it got him.'

She carried on with the stare.

'You know your trouble?' he said. 'You think if you turn your back on the world, just for a moment, chaos will overwhelm us.'

Her tight-lipped gaze was unrelenting.

'This is not something you should handle on your own.'

'If I wasn't a woman,' she said, 'would you be saying this?'

'If you weren't a head-case,' he responded, 'would you be listening to me?'

She allowed herself to smile at that. 'We'll never know.'

'Okay.' He didn't smile. 'Go ahead. I can't stop you anyway.'

She felt no sense of victory. Very detached, she said, 'Thank you.'

'Look into the London end, but no more. And you report to me every day.'

'I'm good with that.'
'And touch base with the lawyers.'
'Of course.'

They both knew that she was just saying that to placate him, both knew that the other knew.

He changed tack. 'I'm arranging a memorial service for Steven, something Humanist. After a lifetime of investigating the dark side, he had turned his back on religion. As for the wake? . . . The man hated a fuss. Remember his leaving do? A quiet hour in a bar. He would want us to raise a glass or two, that's all.'

'Sounds about right.' She averted her eyes lest she well up. 'He used to tell me: get mad about what you can't change and maybe you'll get to achieve something.'

Unexpectedly, he reached out and gave her arm an affectionate squeeze. She stood still for a moment, conscious of things unsaid, then turned to leave. As she reached the door, he called her name.

She turned. 'Yes?'

'You should think about going to the police with what you know.'

'They'd have me committed.'

His gaze played about her, touched with melancholy. 'Then count yourself lucky that you own your own soul.'

'What?'

'Get the fuck out of here.'

ALI COLLECTED A coffee and went to her cubicle. On the way, she exchanged greetings with colleagues but avoided eye contact. She didn't want to explain her bruises. She ducked quickly from sight, like a soldier dropping into a foxhole.

The Kapakes were wearing off so she popped a couple more then sipped slowly at her scalding drink as she glanced through her messages. There were plenty of them but nothing to grab her attention. She Googled Keaton and Jones of the Foreign Office, hit nothing relevant. There were no results for Operation Mannon involving British Special Forces in Kosovo. She tried every combination of key words she could think of. Nothing. She found a list of former SAS personnel but it was only names already in the public domain.

For the next hour she worked the phone, running through contacts in government, the military, police and academia. All denied knowledge of Mammon. She considered calling Keaton, couldn't make up her mind and left it. She would have to call him for news of Donylla but, for some reason she couldn't explain, she wanted to maintain distance between herself and her Good Samaritan.

Instead, she called Jim Marriot. Marriot was an ex-SAS soldier who had contacted her three years previously to discuss the growing attrition rate of special forces personnel. Like many of his colleagues, he had quit because of their increasing use for political purposes. He objected to being tasked for illegal ops that crossed the boundaries of morality, legality and accountability. As it happened, Marriot had decided, at the last minute, that their conversations were too sensitive for publication. Nevertheless, they had remained on good terms, not least because she had never betrayed his trust.

After exchanging pleasantries, Ali asked him about Operation Mammon.

His immediate reaction was surprise. 'Where did you hear about that?'

'So it existed?'

He hesitated as he realised what he had just confirmed. 'I've not come across it,' he told her guardedly. 'The only Kosovo special op I recall was a patrol rescuing an aid worker from southern Albania. I can't recall the name. The team located him, went in with a Land Rover, then drove straight into a Chinook and lifted out of there. The operation went off without a hitch.'

Ali realised that he was quoting an op that had received wide media exposure. He was covering himself. She recalled Marriot's earlier conviction that he was being monitored by the security services.

'That's not the one,' she said. 'Mammon was an assassination.'

He grunted. 'Wet ops are a myth, Ali. Regimental secrecy is so tight it's given rise to all kinds of madcap rumours.'

'So it didn't exist.'

'No,' he said gruffly. 'You would be wasting your time thinking otherwise. You shouldn't be pestering people like this. Fucking journalists.'

The phone went dead. Ali was deflated to receive such a firm rebuff. In their previous dealings, Marriot had regaled her with numerous tales of wet ops, so why would he deny them now? And why admonish her? *You shouldn't be pestering people about this.*

Was he warning her off?

Her thoughts turned to another snub. Connolly, the guy she had rung from Kosovo, had told her, *I won't talk on the phone*. Did that mean he would talk face-to-face?

She went back on line and learned that Connolly was an economics lecturer at Dublin University, a specialist in international banking and money laundering. Curious, she followed links to his more recent work, an article on the London banking system, *The tip of the Iceberg*. The links were broken. Even the cached pages had gone. There had to be something out there. Her fingers returned to the keyboard but her mind refused to follow.

She stretched back in her seat. Her neck and back muscles were starting to cramp and her eyes were red and sore from the screen burn. She had had enough computer search for one day.

She knew, intuitively, that Shimmon's Balkan stories were a dead end. Just one of the many loose ends she had tugged on. A mind map would help her make sense of it all but how was she to connect all those floating synapses? Another time, she might have brainstormed Irvine, but she sensed that he would interpret any such request as a cry for help – in other words as an admission of failure - and pull the plug.

Instead, she took the lift down to the Morgue, where she sought out Danny Fitch, one of the paper's archivists/researchers. Fitch had been with the Echo since the epoch of typesetting and, now semi-retired, he was no longer the quickest kid on the block. She could have requisitioned one of the paper's 'leading edge' researchers - intelligent, ambitious and remorseless, each had been selected from an applicant pool of hundreds - but, for her, Fitch was still the best in the business. He combined the most extensive network of contacts and knowledge bases outside the internet with a bull terrier approach to investigation that matched her own. He was also the most reliable and trustworthy of men: his secrets weren't for sale to anyone, in-house or out.

'Hi Fitchy,' she greeted him breezily. 'You busy?'

He stared at her. 'Who gave you the black jaw?'

'Nobody gave it me. I had to fight for it.'

He kept up with the stare. 'So who did you fight?'

Under his scrutiny, her cheeks were suddenly wet from tears. He rose from his desk and gave her a much-needed hug. He stepped back and regarded her with concern.

'You look as if you could do with a rest. When was the last time you took a vacation?'

'What I need, Fitchy,' she told him bluntly, 'is some information, and I need your help to get it.'

He grinned. 'You're a hard lady.'

He led her into a back room. His room. It was a cheerful, well-light place, decorated with an array of football memorabilia and boasting a computer terminal and a large table covered with old papers. He bade her sit at the table then trundled another chair across the room to join her. He was dressed in brown slacks and checked cream shirt, and his dark eyes twinkled beneath his cropped grey hair.

'I need to ID these two guys.' She displayed the images of Keaton and Jones on her phone. 'The first guy is one of those private security types, ex-British army, probably special forces. Calls himself Chris Keaton. The other one goes by the name of Jones. He claimed to be working out of the British Embassy in Belgrade. Both names are probably bullshit. I need anything useful you can find on them. History, addresses, aliases, known contacts, the works.'

He took her phone and began downloading the pictures. 'I assume it's a matter of life and death.'

'As is this,' she said without irony. She showed him the SAS report. 'How can I find the source?'

He read it in silence then raised his eyebrows at her. 'Where did you get it?'

'Steven Shimmon.'

'Is it genuine?'

'I don't know. There's nothing in the public domain.'

'Okay. I'll try my usual contacts but it sounds like the kind of enquiry where the people in the know have quit, or retired, or they don't remember, or the files have been misplaced, that sort of thing.'

'We have the initials of the soldiers who took part. Surely we can pinpoint them.'

He nodded slowly. 'If they're genuine, it should be possible to ID them. I have some ideas but I would need to be sure before I tell you.'

'Just tell me where to look.'

'Pandora's box, if you can find it.' He saw her scowl and smiled in apology. 'The APC [*Army Personnel Centre in Glasgow*] will have your information, but it would be difficult without names. If you had their parent regiment, initials might do it since you can pinpoint the date. But you've still got the numbers problem – the SAS alone would have had more than 500 men in 1999. I'll try my contact at Credenhill [*the SAS HQ*]. But even if I could get you a list, it would still be a question of working through it. I seriously doubt that anyone would talk to you, let alone admit to being there. And, the moment you start asking, you'd be rumbled and shut down.'

'What about operational files?'

'You'd have to steal them or buy them. You might find someone with a grudge, someone who wants to embarrass the brass or the government, but I doubt it. You could try advertising for someone to come forward.'

'You're joking.'

He smiled: *of course I am.* 'There's always Malci Macleod. He still plants stories on gullible and corrupt journalists for IOPS [*the Information Operations Planning System within MI6*]. He also gives kosher intel to his friends. Steven was his soul mate.'

'I've called him. He says he'll get back to me sometime never.'

'Keep at him,' Fitch advised her. 'He'll break. Get eye-on-eye and just stare at him without speaking. The silence will do for him. He'll *have* to talk. Now, tell me about that face of yours.'

She grinned. 'You should see the other guy.'

ALI RETURNED TO the fourth floor and picked her way through the work stations to Trevor Turow, the Echo's financial correspondent. Short and overweight, he was a slightly stooped man with a sparse head of greying hair coloured ash with a tint of orange. Coffee in one hand, biro in the other, he was busy with the Echo crossword. He sensed her approach, half-swivelled in his chair and greeted her with a show of brilliant white teeth.

She asked, 'What can you tell me about a guy called Brett Connolly?'

'Jesus Christ, Ali,' he complained, 'I'm up to my arse in work. What the hell do you want to know about him for?'

'I'm writing a piece about morbidly-obese financial journalists who sell column inches to crooked traders for perverted sex!'

He stared at her blackened jaw and gave her a wicked grin. 'Word of advice. If you're taking up boxing, learn the defence moves first.'

'It's kick boxing, Trev. My specialist move is the gonads if you'd like to try me.' She stared into his amused eyes. 'Connolly.'

'What's your interest?'

'Just background. He might have a bearing on a story.'

He gazed at her in silence, waiting for an explanation that she wasn't prepared to give.

'I need a favour,' she said at last. 'Show some love, just this once.'

'You want love, come and sit on my lap.'

She sighed, in no mood for his banter. 'Humour me, Trev.'

'Bite me,' he grunted, feigning hurt. He took a theatrical moment to reflect. 'If it's the same Brett Connolly, he wrote an article claiming that London is *the* money laundering centre for organised crime, major corporations and governments. It got him into a heap of bother.'

'Is there any truth in it?'

'Truth?' He gave her a cynical, lopsided grin. 'No poet ever interpreted life as freely as we hacks interpret truth.' He paused. 'It is said that Connolly based his article on First Garanty Bank. Garanty is an old established merchant bank, maybe two hundred years old. It was founded, owned and run by the Laughton family. In 2005, it was taken over by Leke Corporation, a major multi-national company which had no banking tradition but apparently wanted their own bank. It was a very secretive takeover, taking Garanty from private ownership to what amounted to very private ownership. Part of the deal was that Laughton be kept on as chairman, but within three months he was ousted from the Board. Rumour has it, the takeover was preceded by a financial attack on the bank itself that forced Laughton to sell. The same rumours claim that this attack was investigated by the financial authorities and that Garanty has since been investigated for money laundering. Both investigations came to nothing. It could have been a big story but it went the way of most rumours.'

'You mean there was nothing to it?'

'According to unpublishable gossip, the very threat of investigation had the great and the good running for cover. That got us slavering, us lowly financial hacks. We were interested in uncovering links with the political establishment. Our spin was to be corrupt politicos. You know, *yet another politician in it for personal gain*.'

'Any names?'

'Nothing we could whisper outside these walls. Terminal law suits are a fearful way to go.'

Ali thought back to the notes scribbled on Shimon's documents. 'Did the name Figgis feature in this gossip?'

'Lord Harry?' In a melodramatic gesture, Turow looked about them for eavesdroppers. 'His name was very prominent. The Man in the Street [*in-house nickname for Irvine*] was convinced that he had something big to hide. You know what Irvine's like: *Figgis is panicking because he's worried where real scrutiny would lead. Someone's going to get him because that's what happens when a villain with a high profile tries to dupe the British media. And that someone had better be us.* No one got him, of course. Is that what this is about? Have you cracked the code?'

'I wish.' She gave him a little smile of regret. 'What dirt do you have on him?'

He groaned in protest. 'You expect me to know this shit off the top of my head?'

'No. I was thinking maybe you could stroke those little crystal balls of yours.'

An amused smile tugged at his lips. 'His Lordship is old money, and that's as dirty as it gets.' He shrugged. 'It's difficult to get good craic on the man. And plenty have tried, believe you me.'

'Perhaps they didn't try hard enough.'

He frowned, letting her know that she had overstepped some invisible mark. 'And you're about to show us how, right?'

'I don't do finance,' she told him unapologetically. 'Everything I know about the banking world would fit on a baked bean.'

He thought for a moment, sucking on his tongue as he did so. 'I could dig out my research. Later today. When I'm not so busy.'

'Thank you.' She paused, her eyes lingering on his crossword. 'So there's a link between Figgis and money laundering?'

'I didn't say that.'

'Are you saying there isn't?'

'I'm saying: Don't get caught with those words in your mouth!'

Chapter 18

PAUL STEWART WORKED out of Nile House, a 1930s art deco office block lost in the back streets of Southwark. The building was dated and neglected, its fascia spider-crazed, grimy and pitted. No-one knew how it had managed to survive into the steel and glass world of the twenty-first century, Maybe, as the story ran, some speculator really had bought the place then died, the paperwork lost forever. A big loss for someone but an opportunity for others. Its five-storey maze of corridors and rooms had been converted into small spaces for fledgling businesses. Most were stillborn, or enjoyed ephemeral lives before slipping, unnoticed, into extinction. A few were strong enough to thrive, and they soon moved on to bigger pastures. Only one both survived and stayed, and that was the IT consultancy run by Stewart.

The lifts were out again, and Ali took the staircase to the second floor. A confusion of Photoshopped ads and direction indicators vied with each other for her attention, while, from behind closed doors, came the unintelligible clatter of busy offices and workshops. On the door of a corner office was a tiny card: STEW'S COMPUTER SERVICES. The reception area was unoccupied, so she pushed open the glass door to the inner sanctum and entered Geek Heaven.

It was a large room, converted from a corridor and four times longer than it was wide. The floor groaned under the weight of IT equipment - PCs, Macs, servers, laptops, scanners, printers, routers, drives, wires draped everywhere and electrical outlets jammed to capacity - but the room itself was backspaced into the typewriter age. Stuffy and stale, it was all marbled paint and mahogany veneer. Testament to a man indifferent to workplace aesthetics.

In the middle of it all crouched Stewart himself. His back was to the door and he was so engrossed in his work that he didn't even notice her come in. She smiled fondly. Same old Paul. Dark, boyish looks, lively promiscuous smile, crazy enthusiasm and companionable manner, but a geek to the core. Even his personality was perfect for his most effective form of hacking, social engineering.

He had been writing commercial games and software since the age of twelve, yet he had never been interested in exploiting his financial potential. No Bill Gates route to nirvana for him, he was content with life at the coal face. He made money by occasionally selling software or undertaking contract programming but his main earner was security. A white hat hacker, he had ridden the new wave of public-key encryption and he now hacked into clients' systems and wrote algorithms to block the crackers.

She cleared her throat. 'I've always considered these premises a tad pretentious.'

He looked around, grinned. 'Beats working from home.' He jumped up and kissed her lightly. 'You alright? You look like you've just parachuted from a dog's arse.'

She shrugged off his concern. 'Got hammered last night.'

'In more ways than one.' He inspected her jaw, knew that it was more than a hangover. 'What happened?'

'Accident.'

'Right. As in, *She fell down the stairs, guv.*' He shook his head. 'You good?'

'I'm good.'

'Okay,' he grinned, quick to take a hint. 'None of my business. Give me your tech and make us some coffee.'

He took the netbook from her and ran a finger over its ultra-slim body. 'Hot little machine. Amazing as a word-processor but I'd never use it online. These netbooks are a hacker's dream.'

'Hot little machine! You are such a pervert.'

'Someone's punched a hole in it. Who'd do a thing like that?'

'The owner was murdered. That's a bullet hole.'

'Yeah, right.' He saw her expression. 'You're serious! Is that how you got the face?'

She shrugged. 'It's not something I can talk about.'

'Just as well. I wouldn't sleep nights.'

'You can retrieve files from the netbook, I take it.'

'A trained monkey could do it.' A pained expression crossed his face. 'Oh shit! I walked into that one. Okay. I've got a forensic retrieval program similar to those used by law enforcement, only mine's better.'

'There's something else.' She handed him Shimmon's USB drive.

He took the stick from her, inserted it into a computer and tapped a few keys. The screen changed colour and asked for a password. 'I'll run my password override. It could take a while. Might never happen. Depends how clued up he was.'

'He was OCD about security but he was no geek.'

He nodded. 'Simple phishing scam should do it. But if he used an AES key *[Advanced Encryption Standard]* it might never happen. It's supposed to take a billion billion years to crack a 128-bit key using a brute force attack. You're not known for your patience.'

'I'm patient. Tomorrow will do.'

He threw her a smile. 'Good to see you by the way. How come you only drop by when you need something?'

'Come on, Paul, who in their right mind would come here voluntarily? It smells like an elephant house. There must be a cleaning contractor in the building. At least someone who could show you how to open a window.'

'Cleaners pull plugs and splash water.' He gave her a wan smile. 'Fresh air means dust and other nasties.'

She frowned. 'Aren't you worried that your neighbours will call in environmental health?'

'Okay,' he grinned. 'I'll promise you this. Whatever you pay me, I'll spend on a cleaner.'

'You don't need a cleaner,' she came back, quick as a flash. 'They pull plugs and splash water.'

'Pay me enough and I'll employ a careful one.'

She smiled sweetly. 'You're so much more to me than a deductible expense.'

He laughed, picked up the netbook. 'Where's that coffee?'

While he set about assessing the damage, Ali dumped her bag on the table and switched on the kettle. She found some clean mugs and spooned coffee into them, then fell to staring at her reflection in the glass fronted cupboard.

The eyes that stared back at her were sad and dark ringed, and the faint webbing of lines at the corners had suddenly become deep enough to cast shadows. All in all, she looked a mess. The bruises on her jaw had peaked, creating an unwanted symmetry with the tiny bony lump on the bridge of her nose and the thin, white scar that followed her other jawline. Lump and scar were the results of a childhood accident on the ice rink. Mementoes of times when she had been happy without reservation.

She could still recall events from those days, but they were inert and stale, like someone else's memories. The walk up the Cwrch Valley to picnic among the rocks by the stream, her father slipping in the water and losing his glasses, her mother leaning on a boulder, hysterical with laughter. She tried to conjure images to go with the memories, couldn't penetrate her own reflection.

Stewart called out, 'What are you doing?'

'Taking a good look at myself.'

He came next to her, put his arm around her shoulder and stared at her face in the glass. 'Mind if I join you?'

'Look *through* the mirror,' she told him bleakly. 'That way you see the real me.'

'Cool. Very Lewis Carroll.' He caught her eye. 'What's wrong? You got man trouble again?'

'What do you mean, again?'

'You always choose the wrong guy,' he reminded her solemnly. 'When are you going to face up to the fact that the right man is here, ready, willing and able.'

She smiled at him, affection clouded by contrition. Her hot pursuit of career had all but destroyed her social life. Men peeled from her like dead skin, tired of being stood up, or just plain unwilling to get involved with someone so committed to rooting around in society's detritus. She was well aware that her immersion in work was denying her own emotional and physical needs, but there was no one else to blame for that but herself.

'I won't hook up just for the company,' she said, her voice imbued with a touch of defiance that she found embarrassing. 'Anyway, I'm not sure I'm capable of that kind of commitment, that kind of love.'

He laughed. 'Did I just ask you to marry me? I don't mean to shatter your ego, darlin', but I'm not the one scratching for favours here.'

She gave him a weak smile. 'Then what are you after?'

He indicated the empty cups on the table. 'Coffee.'

She turned to him, sharp with anticipation. 'You finished?'

'I'm a genius not a miracle worker. You've caught me in the middle of a big job, Ali, a major contract. If I miss the deadline, I lose what amounts to a considerable hit for little ole me. I'll get to your bits overnight, let's say mid-morning to be realistic.'

'You're a real friend, Paul. The best.' She planted a kiss on his cheek. 'And you still like booze! Everyone else I know is into Class A drugs!'

He touched his face, Mills & Boon parody. 'That makes it all worthwhile.'

She smiled. 'Is there a way to get into his emails? You know, without his computer?'

'Sure. If you have his address.'

'I've got that. But I don't have a password.'

'No worries. I just need a few personal details. He's got a bio on the web, right? Facebook?'

She nodded. 'It's pretty basic. Can you hack into his ISP? I need to trace his informants.'

'Consider it done. And he's probably backed up in the Cloud. That'll be there forever, gathering cyber dust until his subscription runs out. I'll get to it.'

Chapter 19

BY THE TIME Ali arrived home, it was mid-evening. Tired and sore, she popped some Kapakes, kicked off her shoes and curled up on the settee with a glass of wine. A few sips then she called her father. He wasn't in so she left a message: *'Hi Dad. Catch you tomorrow. Love you.'* She stabbed the remote and the TV blinked to life. It was pre-tuned to the BBC News channel. She tried to focus but the world was too heavy. Her eyes closed and the remote dropped to the floor. She hadn't intended to sleep, but sleep she did.

THE BUZZING OF her mobile phone woke her. It felt like morning but it was five past ten in the evening. She was hungry and thirsty and not a little confused..

'Oh dear,' Stewart said, enjoying the irony. 'Have I woken you?'

'Of course not.'

He chuckled. 'I've dipped in and out of your stuff.'

She came awake. 'And?'

'I can retrieve the stick but it'll take time to decrypt. Your friend was no fool. As for the netbook, it's not as bad as I thought. The hard drive is intact and in fair condition, considering how you found it. That's the upside. As for the down: I don't know what you were expecting but there's not much on it.'

'There wouldn't be. He used the netbook as a notebook - literally. He transferred his notes to his laptop and deleted them from the netbook.'

'That explains it. The netbook is new but I can retrieve any deletes that are on there. There's a few jpegs but they're corrupted. I'm trying to recover them but don't hold your breath. There's a folder, too, and some emails. Your friend kept a clean board. He deleted his mail, both incoming and outgoing. All I've found are his unopened mails, the ones that came in this week. If you want old mail, I'll need a bit more time. I've sent all I have so far.'

'What would I do without you?' While she talked, she booted her MacBook. 'I owe you big time. What's it to be? Lunch? Dinner? Concert tickets? All three?'

'You can take me to *Kings of Leon* at the O2.'

That made her smile. Stewart knew how much she hated the group. 'Deal. On condition that you have my information by tomorrow.'

'I'm flying to Edinburgh tomorrow and I should be back the day after. I'll see you then. If I get anything in the meantime, I'll let you know.'

When he was gone, she turned to her computer. Professional habit, she held her eager anticipation under as two emails dropped in. Each contained a zipped folder.

She opened the folder labelled: <docs>. It unzipped into three sub-folders. The first was entitled, <griffin> and contained a single file of notes derived from a source *T*, who appeared to be a police officer.

According to *T*, the name Griffin had first appeared when the police had smashed a drug smuggling ring. Seven people had been arrested, one of whom, Jeff Glenny, had begun talking a witness protection deal while the cuffs were still cold on his wrists. He had told the interviewing officers about a man known as Griffin who controlled a dark empire of multinational businesses and criminal enterprises via a labyrinth of dummy companies and crooked banks. This empire was protected by politicians, lawyers and a private army.

Glenny had no concrete proof to back up his story and the police had dismissed him as a fantasist, a criminal weaving a web because he was terrified of gaol, A justified terror, as it turned out. Within three days of being remanded to Belmarsh, Glenny was murdered in his cell. The killer, who was never caught, was assumed to have been a member of a rival gang. *T* believed that Glenny had been silenced by his nemesis, Griffin.

The name Griffin had turned up in two other cases related to organised crime, involving drugs, weapons and prostitution. Griffin had even appeared on the agenda of a meeting between the Met, the National Crime Agency and some other, unnamed, agency, possibly one of the security services. This meeting had concluded that there was no evidence that Griffin existed. They had no ID, no location, no associates and no crimes. Sources had variously indicated that he was East European, a Serb perhaps, or a Russian, maybe even a Bulgarian, but none offered evidence. A file had been opened but it contained hearsay, speculation and nothing else, and Griffin had been dismissed as a street myth. *T*, however, remained convinced that he was real.

The second sub-folder contained two files, a scan of the Agence France Press article on Figgis that Ali had found in Prishtina and a Word document tagged <figgis>. The latter started with a thumb sketch of the man. Nothing new there. But Shimmon went on to discuss his Lordship's role in nineties Kosovo. Shimmon believed that Figgis' contacts with freedom fighters had been more than diplomatic, that he had been the conduit for the flow of arms, intel and aid from the UK to Kosovan Serbs. He speculated that Figgis had also gone into business on his own behalf, and that the conduit had become two-way. Considering that the Kosovans dealt in sex slaves, arms and drugs, that accusation carried some pretty serious implications.

Shimmon concluded with speculation that Figgis had been involved in money-laundering via First Garanty Bank. According to Shimmon's sources, the Kosovan mafia had been involved. So, too, had the nebulous Griffin. Those same sources claimed that the investigation into this laundering had been shut down on national security grounds.

Ali opened the third sub-folder and found a scan of the Operation Mammon report together with a file named <lucca>. The Lucca file outlined the life and death of the most notorious of the Kosovan war criminals and reiterated the Figgis relationship. The crucial point came at the end. Shimmon believed that Lucca's assassination had been approved by UK Plc, facilitated by UK intelligence agencies, and observed by the SAS. He also believed that Figgis had acted as broker and set-up guy for the murder. Once again, there were esoteric references but nothing Ali could consider proof.

Stewart's other folder, labelled <mails>, contained a batch of nine emails. Two messages caught her eye. The first concerned Griffin.

According to V, Griffin is in Switzerland.

The mail was from BIGT. She had no idea who V might be, or why it mattered where Griffin was. BIGT could have been *T*. Again, she had no way of knowing.

The second mail was a note from a London-based literary agent, David Bulman.

I've just had a visit from your security service friends seeking a preview of your book. I told them they could pre-order through Amazon but they're not prepared to wait. Please call me as a matter of urgency.

Shimmon had been writing a book!

That surprised her. The news triggered a cascade of questions. Was this book about his Lucca investigation? How far had he got with it? Did Irvine know? Was there a manuscript she could read? Why were MI5 interested? Did the existence of the book explain why his flat had been turned over? Had it been MI5 trying to steal the script?

Question leading to question leading to question. Each question without answer. She felt like a dog chasing its tail. She had been keyed up waiting for Shimmon's information and now that she had it she was desperately disappointed. The netbook had assumed real significance just because its content had been a mystery, but so far it had revealed toilet jottings and nothing more. Here and there, Shimmon had inserted reference numbers that alluded to information held elsewhere, presumably on his laptop. But the laptop had gone. She had no way of knowing what that information was and there was nothing in his notes that represented proof of anything.

Not for the first time in this investigation, Ali felt a sense of dislocation. She was no longer a reporter but a pawn in some after-life game of connect-the-dots devised by Shimmon. The dots being Figgis, First Garanty, Griffin and Lucca. She tried to get her head around it but she kept getting into arguments with herself in which crucial pieces of information were missing and she always ended up back where she had started. She had no doubt that the names actually did connect. Shimmon had been no hysterical conspiracy theorist. She would always trust him over a story. But she could do nothing with information that was pure speculation. She had to find his sources, in particular the one referred to as *T*.

But that could wait until the morning.

JUST AFTER THREE, Ali was woken again by the relentless ringing of her phone. It had to be Stewart-the-Nocturne with more data. Wondering whether to curse or thank him, she took the call.

'How did you like Prishtina, Ali?' It was a voice she didn't recognise. It sounded male and oddly robotic. 'Why go all that way just to eyeball a corpse. The dead look pretty much the same everywhere, don't you think?'

'What? . . .' Ali was momentarily confused. 'Who is this?'

Her caller laughed a mechanical laugh, like a faulty replicant. 'That was a melodramatic touch, touring

Shimmon's flat like it was some theme park for nosy hacks.'

'Who the hell is this?'

'You should ask yourself, Ali: what happens to a journalist who gets sucked into her own story?'

She realised that she was listening to a digitally-filtered voice, one that was actually threatening her. The knowledge snapped her into a sudden fury. Somehow, she kept it in check, resisting the impulse to hurl a mouthful of venom. Or to cut the call. Why give him what he wanted? Instead, she muted her phone to conceal her nervy breathing.

'We are your worst nightmare,' the voice hissed. 'We are everywhere. We see everything, know everything. This is your last warning. Stay away.'

'Fuck you!' she breathed.

There was a moment of silence. He seemed to be waiting for her reaction but she wouldn't give him the pleasure. Outside, there was the sound of a bottle smashing onto the pavement, followed by raucous laughter. At least someone was having fun!

'You seem like a nice girl, Ali,' the voice said at last. 'Don't make us come for you.'

Chapter 20

'I hear we're picking up chatter.' Burns' soft voice filled the Gower Street Cage. His sallow face was drawn into the hint of a smile, unnatural yet menacing and immutable, like a childhood scar. 'Mammon, Figgis and Griffin. You assured me that the risk died with Shimmon. Yet here we are again. For all your vaunted spycraft you have somehow contrived to be deaf, dumb and blind. You want to explain that to me?'

'It's Feysor,' Sandford said, sounding confident and in control of events. 'She's trying to track Shimmon but all she has are bits of data that she can't interpret. She can run with that forever and never hurt us. Shimmon's story died with him. Feysor is groping in the dark.'

'That woman doesn't go in for groping.' Burns' smile lacked humour and warmth, and its persistence gave him a sinister edge. 'I need to know what she knows and who she is talking to. Can you tell me that? No, I can see you can't.'

There was a moment of awkward silence. The small, spartan room, normally as crisp as a cooler, was hot with tension. The internal recorders were off and the cherry wood and black leather surface of the table was clear. Not even a bottle of water. This meet, like many at Alpha, had no agenda and required no record.

'She's not a problem,' Sandford said. 'We've bugged her flat and we're intercepting her comms. She's got Shimmon's Netbook and a flash drive but she can't access them. We're running interference on the tech who's trying to decrypt them. If it comes to it, she's breakable. They've all got their weak spot.'

'A gorilla grunting into a phone won't neutralise that bitch,' Burns said. 'What she went through in Kosovo would scare off most men, let alone a woman, yet she is still with us. The harder we shake someone like Feysor, the harder she clings on.' He paused, looked from one to the other. 'Worst case scenario?'

Seymour hesitated, 'She puts some flesh on the rumours and the problem goes viral.'

'Take her out of the game,' Sandford suggested. 'Plant some coke in her flat. Toss in ten grand in dirty notes, tip the Met and Feysor is history.'

Burns dismissed the idea. 'No-one would believe it. You would plant more questions than answers, just as you did at Shimmon's flat.'

Sandford's face turned to stone. 'What do you mean?'

'The job needed a ghost sweep and you blundered about like a poltergeist.' Burns stared at Sandford with cold contempt. 'If you had left the bulk of Shimmon's files in place, cleaned the incriminating information and planted disinformation, there would have been nothing to arouse suspicion. But you were lazy. You took it all and tipped Feysor that something's up. Planting drugs would have the same effect.'

'The Met have dismissed the break-in as the trashing of a dead man's apartment,' Sandford responded icily. 'A loose end.'

'The police are not the issue here,' Burns responded. 'Feysor is altogether more intelligent and diligent than our friends in blue. If she tugs on this loose end, something will unravel. If you continue to hush everything up, the silence itself starts to talk and the conspiracy theories multiply out of control until you can't stop them. You have managed to achieve the last thing we wanted: you have wetted Feysor's appetite.'

'We have her under control,'

'We do?' Burns gave a contemptuous shake of his head. 'Then why is she still active in our business. And what have you done about Analytic's mole? He has an agenda, like all insiders. He wants to get his information out there while preserving his own skin. We know he was feeding Shimmon. What happens if he decides to help Feysor?'

'That's what we want him to do,' Sandford informed him smugly. 'The moment he contacts Feysor we have him.'

'By the very act of contacting her,' Burns responded, 'he will confirm to Feysor that she has a story. This woman is not going away. We might silence her newspaper but we can't stop her screaming in cyberspace.'

'In cyberspace,' Sandford said, 'no one can hear you scream.'

Sandford's attempt at humour induced a condescending silence.

Undaunted, Sandford said, 'When a man becomes a problem, you need only eliminate the man to eliminate the problem. Or, in this case, the woman.'

'Stalin,' Burns grunted, unimpressed. 'Now you're quoting Uncle Joe! We can't afford to put her in the ground. Not yet. A second journalist working for the same paper on the same story dies and the media will be swarming over us like the flies on her corpse.' Pause. 'Right now, she represents a greater threat than Analytics. All the algorithms in the world can't discover what legwork and small talk can uncover. We need to find her contacts and roll them up. For the time being, we have to leave her out there. Listen and watch. It's the age of fake news and alternative facts, isn't it? Let's discredit her story even before she publishes. We have to get her off the story in such a way that no-one steps in to fill the void. There must be no story.'

Burns stared from one to the other. A question mark formed on his face, then dissolved into an expression that the other men couldn't read.

He asked, 'What progress with the York girl?'

'She has gone off the grid.' Sandford told him. 'She seems to have dumped her cell phone and abandoned her social networking sites. She hasn't shown up on airport or port lists. We're looking at her history, interrogating her old comms and search history for places she's familiar with, places she's researched, places she might go to. We're also identifying and questioning the people in her life, significant, non-significant, her most trusted people. We're monitoring communications between them, putting their vehicles through ANPR. We've got it all covered. It won't be long, now.'

Burns grunted in frustration, 'So, this innocent child has managed to steal Griffin's crown jewels and vanish into the ether?'

'If she is Griffin's family,' Seymour said, 'why would she go on the run? How do we know this Jackson hasn't snatched her. She would be worth quite a ransom.'

Sandford shook his head. 'The girl packed her own gear and left of her own accord. She was a month into her semester at Imperial College and she just cleared out her flat and left. It surprised a lot of people at Imperial. She was a top student, well-liked by everyone. No one - that's staff and friends alike – none of them knows why she went, or where.'

'Shimmon is killed and she runs,' Burns said. 'Is she Shimmon's source?'

'We can't discount the possibility.'

'Griffin blames us,' Burns said. 'The girl was tipped off within hours of you finding her. The only people who knew about that were your people. The leak must have come from your side.'

'Not a chance.' Sandford saw that Burns was ready to challenge him, so he continued quickly. 'I notified Griffin's people the moment we found her. One of them tipped her off.'

'Griffin will not accept that,' Burns told him. 'The girl must have noticed your man watching her.'

'Our people are the best in the business,' Seymour informed him trenchantly. 'No-one would see them. And not one of them has a motive to warn her off. The leak has to come from his side.'

'You had better be right in this.' Burns looked from one to the other, his doubt plain to see. 'This York girl is a real danger. If anyone starts burrowing about in her past and listening to what she has to say, there's no knowing what might come out. We have to bury her so deep that she'll never come back to haunt us.'

'We found her once,' Sandford said confidently, 'we'll find her again. She lacks the skills for evasion.'

'It won't take skill to broadcast what she knows, just a smart phone. Finding her is our top priority. We need that data drive.'

With calculated nonchalance, Seymour stretched back in his chair, 'So what do we do?'

'For now,' Burns said, 'we finesse the situation. Raise the search status on the girl and put Feysor in a straitjacket. Make absolutely certain it doesn't turn from bad to worse.'

Chapter 21

ALI WOKE EARLY after an untroubled sleep, the events of the night all but forgotten. She was no stranger to abusive calls. They weren't pleasant, were occasionally frightening and were invariably maddening, but they couldn't hurt her. She took them as confirmation that she was on the right track. She grabbed a coffee and went into the lounge where she opened her Macbook and reviewed Stewart's data. But, however she approached it, whatever system or strategy she employed, she could not connect the cryptic references to T, V and BigT to Griffin, or Figgis, or First Garanty, or Lucca. There just wasn't enough data.

Not that she was convinced that they did connect. There was no telling with Shimmon. Secretive and obsessive, he would take the simplest investigation and entwine it within layer upon layer of secrecy, endowing it with some whimsical mystery whilst making it all but impossible to follow. The story might be huge, it might be nothing. Either way, he would have preferred it lost rather than go to a rival. But Ali was no rival. He had been fond of her, in a withdrawn kind of way. In fact, he had probably been as close to

Ali as he would ever get with anyone. He might even have thought of her as a friend. Which was a pretty flimsy basis for the sense of obligation that she felt. But it was real, for all that.

There was another person he might have considered a friend. Malci Macleod. If anyone knew Shimmon's sources, it would be Macleod, with his network of security service contacts. She had already left him several voicemails but he hadn't got back to her. She called him again. This time, to her surprise, he picked up and offered to meet her for lunch.

That gave her time to chase down the book Shimmon was supposedly writing. It might have turned out to be a cookery book, or a children's novel, but she had to find it if only to eliminate it.

She got Irvine on his cell.

'Did you know that Steven was writing a book?'

'No.' Irvine sounded intrigued. 'He was always talking about it but it never got off the ground as far as I know. What was it about?'

'I was hoping you could tell me.'

'Sorry kiddo. Looks like we're both out of the loop.'

Before he could expand the conversation, she killed the call. According to her information, Shimmon's literary agent was David Bulman. She brought up his website from which she learned that he worked out of his Hampstead home which doubled as his office. She punched in his number, intending to make an appointment, but his secretary put her straight through. She introduced herself and asked if he was looking after Shimmon's book.

He hesitated momentarily. 'How do you know about that?'

'I've been asked to finish it.'

'I hadn't heard that.' His voice sharpened with curiosity and anticipation. 'Who asked you?'

'I'm an old friend. A journalist. I spoke with his family in New Zealand.'

A pause. 'In principle, it's a sound idea. It would facilitate the recovery of a great deal of work, not to mention the costs incurred. There would be various things to discuss, of course, not least the continuity of content, structure and style.'

'Of course. To be frank, I'm not even sure that I want to do it. I'm not averse, in principle, to taking it on, but I'm in the dark. I would need to see his synopsis, and whatever chapters he had written before deciding.'

'I can't help you there, I'm afraid.' He paused. 'Two days ago we had a visit from two men who claimed to be police officers.'

'Claimed?'

'I think they were from the Security Service. They had a warrant to take away everything pertaining to Steven's book. We would have complied, of course, but we couldn't do that since Steven kept the book to himself. He wouldn't leave anything with me. I had to read the draft chapters in his presence then give them back.'

'Isn't that unusual?'

'Steven was an unusual man. But he was an old friend and I was used to his ways. He kept everything close to his chest.'

It was the answer Ali should have expected. It brought a wry, affectionate smile. 'You've read his drafts. Perhaps you could give me a verbal synopsis to be going on with.'

He hesitated long enough for his tone to turn wary. 'I have a meeting scheduled within the next few minutes. Give me your number and I will check my diary and get back to you.'

ALI LEAPED OUT of the taxi by Stanford's, the Long Acre map shop reckoned by many to be the largest on earth. This was jump off point for the world's great couch explorers. She was travelling no further than Covent Garden but already she was running fifteen minutes late. Worried that Macleod wouldn't wait, she hurried into Hanover Place and jinked her way through the tourists and lawyers to the *Café Des Amis*.

There was a thin but penetrating drizzle, and the street tables were unoccupied, their chairs tilted forlornly and umbrellas furled. With the action driven indoors, the Brasserie was heaving with the early lunch crowd, and it took her a while to thread her way down to the basement wine bar. There, among the French wines, chalked menus and Gallic cheeseboards, she found Macleod. The retired journalist looked as sharp as ever, despite his quivering jowls, bursting waistline and smoker's cough, and he wore his careless suit and fifties hairstyle like an eccentric country squire.

He greeted her with a smile. 'What are you drinking?'

'I'm good, thanks,' she said, settling down next to him. The swelling had gone out of her jaw and her mouth no longer bled when she ate, but she was still on a self-imposed minimum-by-mouth diet. 'I need my thinking head.'

'Ah,' he said with feigned anti-climax. 'I see I'm to be denied foreplay.' Good humour deepened the lines of his milky face. It amused him to intrigue in the heart of London's theatrical quarter, where barristers, actors and the ghosts of journalists conspired with time to frighten off the truth. 'So, get to it girl: what am I doing here?'

She hesitated, drew her chair closer to his. She didn't want to conduct this conversation at a shout. 'I'm trying to figure out Steven's story, the one he was working on when he died.'

Macleod's eyes narrowed. 'I was sorry to hear about Steven,' he said softly. 'He was a good man. And you're taking up his baton? Is that wise?'

'Probably not. That's why I need your help.'

'My help?' He raised his eyebrows, the picture of guilelessness. 'You do know that I'm out of the game?'

'Of course you are.' She gave him a dry smile. 'You never talked to Steven about Figgis, or Kosovo, or Mergim Lucca or Operation Mammon.'

'Why would I do that?'

'Because you're depraved. You revel in that shit.' She paused, changed her tone. 'Steven has been killed and his research destroyed. I need to know what you told him.'

'*Need* to know?' He smiled. 'What makes you think he would have shared with me?'

'Like I said, this is your kind of shit. You're the obvious source, Malci, so please don't play me.'

Macleod put his head to one side and his face took on a pained, contemplative look. 'I just don't want you wasting your time. Steven was a genius at what he did. The best there was. But he had a fatal flaw, Ali. He thought he could change the world. Make it a better place. That was never going to happen. Poor Steven, he became a specialist in writing the wrong story.'

'You mean he was guilty of honest journalism.'

Macleod smiled amiably. 'You're a hack. You know how it works. You collect a bundle of facts and frame them into your story. Someone else takes those same facts and juggles them into another story. The facts are the same, the stories are different. It makes no sense but only fiction has to make sense. In our world, whoever tells the most interesting story is the one with the truth.'

'Steven was murdered,' she said pointedly. 'How's that for *most interesting*?'

Macleod retreated behind a veil of distance, as if trying to escape her presence. His face became empty, his brown eyes remote with thoughts he couldn't resolve. Waiting for a response, Ali could feel her impatience welling up, but she sensed his unexpected angst and uncertainty so she waited in silence. When, eventually, he spoke, it was with a steady, held-under tone, devoid of the affectation that she had come to think of as natural.

'You can't understand Stephen's life – his journey, if you like – without understanding how deeply the Yugoslav conflict affected him. He covered the war at a time when ethnic cleansing was at its worst and he saw things that come close to breaking him. The one factor that helped him through was knowing that we were the good guys. The allies were there to save lives and help people.' He paused, the theatricality for once unintended. 'Years later, he stumbled upon the fact that we weren't the good guys at all. It was all a lie.'

He broke off to sip absently at his wine. Ali said nothing, just waited to see where he was taking this. At length, she realized that he had made his point.

She asked, 'What do you mean: all a lie?'

Macleod was quiet for a long moment. Then he nodded, just slightly, and moved in a little closer. 'I suppose you have to start with the realpolitiks of the Yugoslav break-up. Different governments within NATO were pursuing very different agendas. At the time, HMG was convinced that the real threat to our interests in post-cold-war Europe came from the U.S. and Germany. The French thought the same. We - the French and the Brits - regarded the Serbs as allies against Washington and Bonn. As a result, we opposed intervention in Yugoslavia, sabotaged the peace effort by promising to with-hold recognition for the break-away states and backed a negotiated solution. All on the QT, of course. The effect of this policy was to give the Serbs a free hand on the battlefield.'

'That doesn't gel,' she said. 'NATO kept the Serbs in check. We contributed peacekeepers both during and after the conflict.'

Macleod waved a dismissive finger. 'I fear you underestimate the Machiavellian skills of our political masters. Let me illustrate. Undercover SAS teams were assigned to the UN as forward air controllers. Their job was to locate Serb artillery positions firing upon safe havens and call in NATO airstrikes to destroy them. But British Command ordered the SAS not to identify the targets, so the NATO planes flew missions without engaging the Serb guns. It was a highly secret instruction and it left the Muslims at the mercy of attackers who knew no mercy. As you know, they were slaughtered.'

'That,' Ali pointed out sceptically, 'would make our Government an accomplice to ethnic cleansing.'

'Hence the ultra-secrecy. If the truth got out, it would upset too many people - the great British public, our NATO allies and the whole of the Muslim world.'

'I can't believe the Americans didn't know.'

'Of course they knew, but quid pro quo, we had too much dirt on them.'

'What kind of dirt?'

'They learned about the FAC [*Forward Air* Control] scandal because they were listening to our comms. They can't admit to that so, officially at least, they don't know. We also know that they used military consultants to retrain the Croatian army, and that they dropped weapons and military equipment to the Bosnian army - all in breach of the arms embargo. And the clincher? We loaned them people, from time to time. The Increment as it was then known [*now E-Squadron*]. A cadre of special forces that worked for SIS and did favours for the Yanks. We can't afford to let that get out.'

'What kind of favours?'

'Covert intervention. So-called wet ops.'

'You mean assassination?' Macleod's lack of denial was enough for Ali. 'Did that include Operation Mammon?'

'Mammon was a wet op. The SAS assassinated Lucca to cover up government involvement with the Kosovan mafia.'

'So the SAS weren't just observers!'

A nod, barely perceptible. 'After Lucca's death, there were complaints from locals who claimed to have witnessed what happened. That led to an internal enquiry, held under wraps, of course. It never took evidence from key witnesses. The testimony of locals was dismissed as tainted and the enquiry concluded that there had been no British involvement. Nothing else came out. Not a single word of evidence.'

'Could a routine patrol have run into Lucca and killed him in a firefight?'

'They don't send out patrols to blunder around hundreds of square miles of mountain and hope for a random encounter. That's no kind of mission planning.'

'Who hushed it up?'

'The security services. Mammon was part of the Balkans Shadow Protection Programme run by SIS *[Secret Intelligence Service, or MI6]*. Basically, ethnic killers were put into the programme in exchange for information on higher profile killers. In other words, giving up information on the *Most Wanted* absolved lesser-known mass murderers of their crimes. They were given a new identity and spirited away to God knows where. London or New York would be my guess. Lucca should not have been on the programme. He was a key player.'

She stared at him in open disbelief. 'A twenty year old secret on that scale and nothing leaked out. That's impossible and you know it. Sooner or later, someone is born again, or exacts revenge for some imagined slight. They go running to the Guardian or Wikileaks or just hang it out there in cyberspace. There's always someone too weak to handle their conscience.'

'That's the point!' he told her, passion unexpectedly lighting his face. 'There's been nothing to corroborate the notion of a cover up, nothing to cast doubt on it. There hasn't been a whisper. A wall of silence is one thing, Ali, but I've never come across a wall that didn't crack over this length of time.'

'Perhaps there's no word because it didn't happen.'

Macleod twitched his head and settled back in his chair. 'If it was just a detail of history, it wouldn't matter. But this is about the future, not the past. To admit our involvement in those ops would be a geopolitical disaster. If it got out, not even our closest allies would want to work with us.' Macleod abruptly changed mood again, leaned across the table, his attitude serious and confidential. 'What our masters now want, Ali, is for this whole affair to be cleaned up.'

'Cleaned up how?' A shock ran through her like an ice taser. 'Oh My God! Are you saying that the government had a hand in Steven's murder?'

'I wish I could discount it. Truth is, I don't know.' He paused. 'Modern security services have to be beyond reproach. The watchword is accountability. There must be no more shady dealings, no more covering up the activities of their own.' He paused, this time for deliberate effect. 'But there are still things to clean up. With all these accusations of extraordinary rendition, torture and Deep State, the Security Services are running scared. The last thing they need is the resurrection of past embarrassments. So now we have clandestine units operating within but independent of the security services. The real irony of the new transparency is that parts of the security world have become murkier than ever.'

Ali fell silent. Her own government supporting organised crime and kill squads! It was worse than she had imagined. Could such evil really be lurking in the fibre of her nation?

She took a deep breath and exhaled. 'What about Figgis? What was his role?'

'He was in the Balkans as a diplomat and administrator. His key role was to get intimate with the Serbs, to make them feel loved and indispensable. He was under instruction to liaise with the paramilitary and mafia gangs. Not surprising in itself. We maintained unofficial channels with all kinds in those days. Probably still do. But he also orchestrated the black side of things. I believe he ran liaison on ops like Mammon. He also ran weapons through the mafia into the paramilitaries. It seems probable that he facilitated trade the other way.'

'Trade? What kind of trade? These people deal in drugs, people, arms and God knows what else!'

'You lie with the devil! . . .'

Another silence, dismayed, thoughtful.

She said, 'How big a deal is this?'

'For you? As big as it can be. Because right now only a handful of people know. Few enough to silence. If a million people knew, or a thousand, or even a hundred, there's not a lot anyone could do about it.'

'Are you trying to scare me?'

'Of course I'm trying to scare you.' He glanced about them. 'Steven was always fascinated by the idea of a corrupt feral elite, a crossover of state and corporate interests that has the power to manipulate political and economic processes. He was convinced that he had stumbled across some Deep State nightmare. He got so carried away with himself he was blinded by the obvious. He was bringing undue attention to some organised crime bosses and they murdered him. You want my advice, Ali. Move on. Leave it be.'

'So this isn't about Mammon.'

He shrugged like he had said enough.

She thought for a moment. 'Were you his source on this?'

'He was mine.' He stared at her, defying her to contradict him. Then he leant in close again, this time his voice was barely audible. 'His initial source was a computer hacker, someone who hacked Figgis' computer, found the Kosovo link and sent the information to Steven. Steven told me this was done anonymously. He claimed he never knew the source. He asked for my help and I introduced him to a source of mine. I don't know how useful this source proved. I never asked. Some time after Steven started his investigation, another source emerged, again anonymous. This source was a genuine Deep Throat.'

'What's the name of this source? The one you gave Steven.'

He shook his head.

'What about this Deep Throat?'

Another head shake.

She said, 'Steven listed some of his sources - T, V, BigT. Could be shorthand, could be code. Can you identify them? Could one of them be this Deep Throat?'

'You are not listening, Ali. Stephen trusted my contact and he is dead. Would you trust that same contact enough to approach him? Yes, I can see you would.' He sighed. 'I thought you would have learned by now. You can trust no one. The best I can suggest is that you take care and follow your instincts.'

'I am following my instincts,' she told him. 'That's why I'm so disconnected.' She considered pressing him, decided it would be pointless. 'So what can you tell me?'

Macleod locked his gaze on hers. 'Use a wider lens, Ali. How do you think a man like Figgis can survive governments of all hues – Tory, Labour, coalition? Forget Shimmon's story. Not even you can bring it in. Now, can we change the subject here? I've already said more than I should.'

Ali nodded dubiously. Macleod's careful calculatedness went beyond his intelligence role to his very nature. Ever the confectioner, he would be feeding Ali precisely-measured quantities. Not even the murder of his old friend would affect his approach.

'What do you know about his book?'

'Steven?' Macleod's surprise seemed real enough. 'What book?'

'How about David Bulman? His Literary Agent?'

'I have met the man. I had no idea he was representing Steven.'

'Come on, Malci,' she entreated him. 'I need help here. Friend to friend. For Stephen.'

'Friend to friend, I can't help you.' His gaze faltered and his lips pursed into silence. 'You may have stumbled into a genuine *conspiracy*, but that doesn't mean that everybody involved has the same agenda. The only thing they have in common is wanting the same people dead.'

'Help me, Malci,' she pleaded. 'Give me something I can use.'

Avoiding eye contact, Macleod picked dispassionately at the remnants of Normandy Sausage that lay on his plate. 'There are two types of journalist, Ali. Those who dig for the truth and those who bury it. Steven believed in exposing the truth – the truth, the whole truth and nothing but the truth. He pursued it beyond all distraction. As, indeed, do you. Me? I'm the burying kind. I believe in personal survival and my own disillusionment with the world. So do *me* one favour, if you please. Keep this little conversation to yourself.'

'Keep what to myself?' she grumbled. 'You haven't told me anything.'

'That's because I don't trust journalists,' he explained gravely. 'Never have.'

She leaned in and pecked him on the cheek. 'Be careful what you get up to, you old dog. And go easy on the women. Don't be giving yourself a heart attack!'

He smiled, 'Would you deny an old man the last of his vices?'

She laughed. 'Since when have booze, cigars, hi-fat-sugar diet and lack of exercise counted as virtues?'

He started to chuckle, but all of a sudden his eyes darkened, his smile vanished and he gestured for her to bend closer again. 'It was Steven's obsessive secrecy that killed him. His insistence on putting his story together before bringing anyone else into the loop. He didn't trust anyone. He wouldn't share. He thought hubris was a virtue. He was like a drunk searching for lost keys under a lamp-post because that's the only light source. Everyone could see him. He couldn't see them. He made it too easy for his enemies to kill his story. They just had to kill him.' He shook his head morosely. 'Sharing is the only way to protect yourself, Ali. Don't repeat his mistake. Poor Steven. He never understood that this has nothing to do with truth, it's about power and those who yield it.'

The air between them had become charged and Ali sensed that Macleod wasn't talking about spooks on the rampage. 'What kind of power?'

He offered her a shamefaced little shrug. 'The Y half of me wishes I knew, the X is glad I don't.'

Chapter 22

DAYLIGHT HAD GONE and night lights shuffled shadows as Ali entered the Washington Bar, a peppy, catholic pub at the heart of Belsize Park. City pin stripes mixed freely with builders' denim, Green Day punks with Glastonbury vets. The huge wooden bar and polished rustic floorboards were pure spit and sawdust boozer, while art deco lighting illuminated designer leather sofas and wooden tables and chairs.

Most of the tables were occupied. A handful of punters turned their heads and Ali exchanged nods of recognition. She spotted Kate and Prisha lost in animated conversation in the far corner of the room. It was the first Wednesday of the month, habitually girls' night out for Ali and her friends. Tonight, just the three of them could make it. Ali had been tight with Kate Turner since their days as law students at Birmingham University, sharing intimate thoughts, joy and pain for fourteen years. Both had been first class graduates but neither had chosen the law as a career. Ali had gone into journalism while Kate had entered the Met on the graduate fast track scheme. Now in their early thirties, Ali was a senior investigative reporter for the Sunday Echo, her friend a DI in Homicide and Major Crimes. Kate was short for a police officer and, clear-eyed and rose-cheeked, she carried the vulnerability of an innocence not yet stretched tight and hard. It was an image that had fooled many an offender and rather too many of her colleagues. Prisha Nell was four years younger, an IT graduate who worked for the Met's computer branch. She was about the same height as Kate, smaller boned, with golden brown complexion, brown eyes and black hair.

Each greeted Ali with a kiss. They had a TVR waiting for her, the glass brimful. Ali sat down, took a careful sip to avoid spillage then pulled a deeper draught. Satisfied, she glanced at the others.

'Why are you looking at me like that?'

'Our weekend in Florence,' Kate said. 'We want you to come.'

Ali blinked in surprise. 'Well, thanks for the thought, but I have to pass. I'm in Dublin tomorrow, goodness knows where the day after that. I barely made it here tonight.' She paused, glanced from one to the other. 'Anyway, I couldn't do that to you. It's your anniversary. Be like taking your mother on your honeymoon.'

Kate grinned. 'We'd like you along, that's all. It'd be fun.'

'A weekend with an old married couple?' Ali mused. 'Now there's a definition of fun.'

'Come on, Ali,' Prisha said; she was too busy browsing her iPhone to look up. 'You need it more than we do. Think of all those horny Italian men.'

Ali shook her head. 'I've been to Italy. I came home black and blue from all the pinching and groping. You want to know my lasting image of that country? Not the Capitoline museums, or the Sistine Chapel or St. Mark's Square. It's some guy openly masturbating on the beach at Rimini! Fucking pervert. It almost ruined my adolescence. I've never been able to look an Italian in the face since.'

'Such a delicate child,' Kate sympathised. 'No wonder you've morphed into this celibate figure of fun.'

Ali smiled wryly. 'I'm not dead yet. Though I'm pretty sure my cherry's growing back.'

They all laughed.

Without looking up from her screen, Prisha said, 'There's no mention of Dublin on your social media.'

'I've been too busy to update it. Oh My God, Prisha! You're checking up on me!'

Prisha responded with an unreadable smile. 'You do know there are apps that will post all your social media accounts at once.'

'Uh-oh,' Kate groaned. 'The nomophobe's going all OCD on us.'

'What's this?' Prisha's smile vanished and she scrolled and swiped with sudden intensity. 'Sorry to tell you, Ali. You've been doxxed!'

'What?'

'You haven't put your phone number on-line, or your address, or your current location?'

'Of course not.' Ali shifted closer to see the phone and a dark cloud passed over her face. 'Oh, no! Not again!'

'It's all out there,' Prisha said, an edge of distress sharpening her tone. 'All your personal information. And there are links to what look like! . . .' She paused, dismayed, and her voice dropped a notch. 'I missed this. These Twitter posts are fake. They must be. Oh My God! You'd never do that, would you?'

She passed her phone to Ali who read tweets on her own Twitter account boasting of her sexual adventures. There was a video clip depicting Ali entangled in painful-looking contortionist sex.

'This isn't me!' she muttered incredulously. 'So how? . . .'

'Someone hacked your account.' Prisha explained the obvious. 'The pictures are Deepfakes. Some perv used AI software to generate a version of your face that closely matches the woman in the video. And there you are!'

Kate crowded in to watch as Ali viewed the video again. 'Are you sure it isn't you?' she grinned. 'That mark on your bum! . . ."

'If it is,' Ali said slowly, as if trying to recall, 'I can't remember it.'

'It's a fake,' Prisha explained firmly, not tuned to their banter. 'I can see it's been tampered with even without looking at the raw files.'

Ali grinned, suddenly, expansively. She passed the phone back to Prisha. She felt surprisingly calm. 'How do they do that?'

'Deepfakes?' Prisha asked.

'No. Have sex like that without losing a limb.'

'Doesn't it trouble you?' Prisha asked. 'Being targeted like that?'

'I'm always being trolled. Fake stories and genuine abuse. Though I've never been deepfaked before. That's one for the CV.'

Kate said, 'You didn't tell us.'

'The Echo techs sorted it.' Ali shrugged. 'It goes with the job. I don't take it personally. If anything, it's confirmation that my story is good. The real hassle is changing phone numbers and emails. I hate that.' She reached for Prisha's phone and watched the video again. 'I didn't know I could do that? I could set myself up as a sex guru.'

'Leave the video up,' Kate advised her. 'With a promo like that the guys'll come flocking.'

'Might do,' Ali responded cheerfully. 'The only guys I meet now are grubby womanizers. Or sad bastards hooked on golf, wine and cars. Sex with them is like a visit to the dentist: lay back and relax, and you won't feel a thing. A queue of perverts at the door is just what I need!'

Prisha chuckled, 'You'll regret saying that when you're a sad old sex beggar.'

For a long moment, nobody spoke. Prisha took a sip of beer. At the same time, she forced herself to swallow her misgivings about Ali's attitude. For Prisha, online attacks were as remorseless and undefendable as an advance of the living dead. They weren't real but there was no fending them off. But if Ali was genuinely unperturbed, what could she do?

Kate said, 'Maybe it's time you lowered your sights, Ali. Why hang on for Mr Perfect when there are so many sex Gods in the world.'

Ali laughed. 'What would you know about Sex Gods?'

'Just admiring the opposite sex. It's what we girls do.'

'Not you. You're a batty girl. You don't have an opposite sex.'

'Maybe,' Kate said, a coy eye on the bar. 'But I can still attract them.'

Ali followed her gaze and focused on a familiar face, Tom Chambers. Once of The Correspondent, he was now some kind of spin doctor with Whitehall connections. Slight and unmuscled, he had pale blue eyes and the kind of translucent skin that struggled in sunlight. He was wearing his trademark Hugo Boss suit over a grey t-shirt, and his hair was newly cropped. In all the time that she had known him, she had found him to be affable, kind and charming, yet she had never trusted him. She had seen in action the sharpness and ruthlessness that belied his little boy lost look, qualities which, together with his *black* contacts, had shaped his career. He was standing alone at the end of the bar. He saw her glance over and he raised his glass in greeting. From the expression on his face, his presence here was no chance occurrence.

Ali grimaced. 'A night with him would bring out your feminine side alright.'

'You know him?'

'I know him.'

'Don't tell me. He's another of your evil creed.'

Ali grunted. 'You don't need a degree in faecal parasitology to work that out. Be back in a minute.'

She eased herself from her chair.

'I'll put a temporary block on your sites.' Prisha offered. 'Are you still using the same password?'

Ali nodded.

'That figures. Won't you guys ever learn! Even toddlers know you have to change your passwords every week!'

Ali grinned at her friend, handed over her phone then went over to the bar. Chambers smiled as she approached and her heart went cold.

He said, 'This is a coincidence.'

'Coincidence. Right. You just happened to turn up in a pub the other side of town from where you live and here I am. You're dogging me.'

'Why would I do a thing like that?'

'Because it's the kind of sly, pervie thing you do.'

Without taking his eyes off her, he swallowed a mouthful of Lowenbrau. 'Beautiful and intelligent as you are, Ali, my taste runs to nine inches of solid meat.'

'Well, good luck with that.'

That smile again. 'If you don't mind me asking, what are you working on at the moment?'

'I do mind.'

That cut him short. He stared at her like he was disappointed, then reached into his bag and brought out an A4 envelope. He held on to it for a moment, like he was reluctant to part with it, then he passed it over to her.

'I think you might find this of interest.'

She took a peek inside and saw a thin wad of photocopied sheets. She eased them partway out of the envelope. The top papers were some kind of accounting sheets. She didn't bother reading them. Instead, she slid them back into the envelope and threw him a quizzical, suspicious look.

'What is this?'

'Your scoop on a rope.'

She snorted. 'You're asking me to do one of your hatchet jobs?'

'I wouldn't insult you. It's a real story.'

She stared at him and read an unlikely degree of truth in his eyes. 'Okay. I'll take the executive summary.'

'Pithy and to the point.' He smiled, took a slow, deliberate sip of his drink. 'Charlie Lawrence, high flying Home Office minister, tipped for the Cabinet in the next reshuffle. Church-goer, family man, hunky-dory and as clean-living as they come. I'm offering you proof that he violated banking and tax rules to set up a scheme to pay hush money. Just shy of half a million quid. He also lied to MI5 vetters.'

'Hush money?'

'To conceal sexual misconduct with an under-aged boy.'

'And you want this out there because? …'

'I would have thought that to be self-evident.'

'If you're so concerned about justice, why don't you just turn him over to the Met?'

'A story with these legs? A major scandal. Weeks of investigation. A succession of front page straps. It's the kind of story you give to a friend.'

'I'm not your friend. Oh, I get it. You don't have any friends.' She tapped the envelope against the bar. 'How do I know these are genuine?'

'Verify them. Then ask yourself who facilitated Charlie-boy's rise? Who knew about his past?' He smiled sweetly. 'Talk it over with Irvine.'

Her eyes climbed into his face. 'What do you get?'

'The satisfaction of knowing that my favourite investigative journalist is devoting all her time and energy to bringing this bastard to justice.'

'All my time and energy?' she repeated. 'In other words, drop everything else.' She paused, held his gaze. 'I know you're just the messenger boy. Tom. I have to ask: who sent you?'

'People who want to see an end to this man's activities. The same people who would like you to stop wasting your talent chasing non-stories into dead-ends.'

'Non-stories?'

'I know you, Ali. You dig and dig for you-don't-know-what until you unearth something it's better to leave buried. One day, you'll end up digging your own grave.'

Chambers had come to the point. He was here to bribe and intimidate her. After the phone call in the night and the attack on her social networking sites, she was getting the message loud and clear: someone wanted her off the story.

It was an odd paradox that, left to her own devices, Ali might soon have grown tired of chasing her own tail. By running interference, her unknown targets were confirming that there was a story whilst inevitably whetting her appetite for pursuing it.

Not that she was in much need of stimulation. She had just spent the early evening reading Shimmon's despatches from the Yugoslav war. Her old mentor had rendered colour, humanity and immediacy to random and senseless slaughter. Mortared marketplaces, play areas and water queues. Street snipers randomly killing civilians for fun. Systematic rape, murder and child abuse. Hamlet massacres, the bodies piled, bloodied and mutilated. He had drawn stark, ironic contrast between the unrestrained activity of the Balkan paramilitaries and the culpable inactivity of western politicos and peacekeepers. In none of the pieces had he hinted at British collusion in the ethnic cleansing horrors, but Ali knew that his knowledge of that betrayal had come much later.

Despite the exceptional quality and humanity of his journalism, Ali knew, intuitively, that Shimmon's Balkan despatches were no key to breaking his story, but they did explain why his commitment had been so emotional, blind and unbreakable. The war of Balkan fragmentation had passed her by. She had been too young, too caught up in her own life. Even with hindsight, she wasn't sure that she could fully grasp the horror of ordinary people indulging in such an orgy of sadism and murder. Or her government standing by and watching it happen. But Shimmon's belief in his story, and Chambers' confirmation that people were determined to bury the truth were enough to lock her in.

She placed the envelope on the bar. 'My friends are waiting. I'd ask you to join us but they've already got one vulture of the press to contend with.'

Without a backward glance, she returned to her table.

Kate looked at her with pity. 'Don't tell me you just blew off the chance of a date?'

'Tom Chambers!' Ali shook her head. 'You could call him a date. You could call Aleppo a prime holiday destination.'

Chapter 23

THE PILOT OF THE 737 hit the Dublin Airport runway like a man 0in a hurry, left wheel first, then the right, and he roared into the terminal as though his brakes had failed. By contrast, the driver of the taxi who took Ali into the city seemed unable to find top gear, reserving his speed for a line in anecdotes that made Dave Allen seem like a mute.

Brett Connolly lived in Marborough Street, in the zone of gracious Georgian streets and squares north of the Liffey. This once prosperous place carried the rotten air of a dying Tiger. Skips overflowed with rubble and old doors, flat conversions jumbled with grotesque adventures into modern architecture and partially demolished buildings propped up the partly-built.

Ali paid off the cab and approached Connolly's house. She had no idea how he would react to her visit, but she wasn't expecting an open-armed welcome. She hadn't called ahead, didn't want to give him the chance to blow her off. The university had told her that he was working from home that afternoon. She hoped that that wasn't a euphemism for shopping with his wife or visiting a mistress. She wasn't in the mood for door stepping.

She needn't have worried. Connolly himself answered the door. He was in his forties. With tartan trousers topped by a loose woollen sweater, and long fair hair streaked with silver, he looked more like an ageing hippie than a senior lecturer in Economics. An approachable ageing hippy. His untroubled, friendly face and instinctive smile suggested a man popular with his students.

He asked, 'Can I help you?'

'Brett Connolly?'

'I am.'

'I'm Ali Feysor. I called you a couple of days ago about . . .'

'First Garanty, yes, I recall.' A little frown of focus settled above his azure eyes. 'I also recall telling you that I couldn't talk about it.'

'On the phone,' she reminded him. 'You said you couldn't talk on the phone.'

He stared at her for a moment, as though trying to compute her meaning, then he laughed. 'And you took that as an invitation? I admire your line in logic, Ms Feysor, but I'm afraid you've come all this way for nothing.'

She smiled faintly, and her eyes hazed over as though gracefully accepting the rebuff. She said. 'You talked to a friend of mine, Steven Shimmon?'

He hesitated, a moment of courtesy and curiosity. 'What if I did?'

'Do you know that he's been murdered?'

Connolly was genuinely shocked. 'No. My God! When did this happen?'

'A week ago.' Ali found herself blinking away a tear. 'In Kosovo. He was killed to quash his story.'

'Kosovo.' He stared off, some inner conflict covering his face in misery. 'You'd better step inside, Ms Feysor.'

He stood aside to let her in then closed the door and led her directly into his study.

'Would you care for a drink? Tea? Coffee? Something stronger, perhaps?'

'Coffee would be fine, thank you.'

He left the room. Ali heard voices off, then he returned, sat at his desk and swivelled to face her.

'Please, take a seat.'

He waited while she selected a battered old leather recliner, then asked:

'What happened?'

'I'm trying to find out,' she said, her expression artless. 'Can you tell me about your dealings with Steven?'

His reluctance was undisguised. 'How did you get my name?'

'Steven himself. Anything you say would be strictly off the record.'

Another smile, this time amused. 'I like to kiss before I get fucked.'

She gave him mock offended. 'I don't put out on the first date.'

'And I'm to take you on trust?'

'I could write you a reference.'

He grinned. 'I'm sure you could.'

He eyed her thoughtfully for a moment, then he flipped through an old-fashioned rolodex on his desk. He picked up his phone and keyed a number. 'Jeff, a quick one. . . . Yes, I'm fine thanks. . . . And the family. . . . Look, I have a journalist with me, Ali Feysor from the Sunday Echo. Should I trust her? . . . Thanks. I'll catch you later.'

He replaced the handset and eyed her carefully. Ali wondered who the hell he had been talking to. The atmosphere in the room was charged and she was afraid of losing him if she pressed, so she waited for him to fill the void.

At length, he said, 'Jeff Powers. You know him?'

Powers was a journalist with BBC radio. 'Not intimately.'

'Nobody would want to know him *that* well. He just gave you a glowing reference.'

She nodded, for once uncertain what to say.

Connolly studied her for a moment, then plunged right in. 'Steven Shimmon was interested in an article of mine about money laundering. The article was a teaser for a book I was writing, an academic tome.' He paused, but couldn't stop himself talking. 'It touched a nerve somewhere. I was threatened with legal action and the end of my career. The article was pulled and the book project aborted.'

'Who carries that kind of power?'

'That's the weird thing. A gentleman came to see me in my room at the College. He said he was a lawyer but he didn't give his name. He issued his threat, very politely, of course. I was going to ignore him but then the university came down on me.'

'Did they say why?'

'Financial considerations. They were threatened with the withdrawal of substantial private funding if they let me continue. There was a carrot with the stick: close me down and the funds would be increased.

They did what I would have done in the same situation.'

There was a tap at the door. A young girl of about fourteen brought in a tray containing two cups of coffee, milk, sugar and some biscuits. She looked Ali over with frank interest, placed the tray on the desk and, with a final stare at the visitor, left.

'She wants to be a journalist,' Connolly explained with a fond smile. 'She doesn't mean to be rude.'

Ali tried to detect a hint of mockery, or irony, but there was none. She found herself liking the Irishman.

He asked, then added milk to her drink. To his own, he added milk and ladled sugar.

She said, 'What did you talk to Steven about?'

He opened his mouth as though to elaborate, then unexpectedly stalled. It was as if, having set the scene, actually going on to tell his tale was a step too far. But he was a compulsive story-teller and he had a good tale.

'He believed that Lord Figgis was using First Garanty Bank to launder Kosovan mob money. He wanted me to explain to him how it was being done.'

'Figgis and Kosovan mob money?' Ali sensed her mouth hanging open, quickly asked, 'Did I hear you right?'

'An unlikely combination, I'll grant you.'

'Why come to you?' she wondered. 'Plenty of people must know about money laundering.'

'But not about First Garanty.' He paused, then decided to elaborate. 'My article followed conversations I had with James Laughton, owner of the Bank until 2006. I didn't mention Laughton by name, nor the bank, and I was extremely cautious in what I wrote. The article was written in an academic, theoretical, way, positing how easy money laundering had become with modern asymmetric encryptions. There was real interest in the work, yet it has been very effectively censored. You won't even find it on the net.'

'I know,' she confirmed. 'I've looked. And you smell conspiracy?'

'Smell it. See it. Feel it.' He gave her a rueful smile. 'What do you know about money-laundering?'

'Not a lot.'

'Then I'll have to give you some context.' He paused, took a sip of coffee. 'Money-laundering is the interface between two economies, the legitimate economy – which is our world - and the illegitimate economy – which is the world of organised crime. Put simply, laundering processes the money from the illegal economy into the legal.'

Ali produced a recorder and held it up. 'I won't get this first time. Finance is not my strong point. Do you mind if I record?'

'I would prefer that you didn't.'

She nodded, replaced the machine in her bag. 'The interface between two economies?'

'Don't take that too literally,' he told her. 'The *Two Economies* is just a research tool, designed to help understand the process of money laundering. It doesn't mean that there are actually two separate worlds. Think of them as virtual worlds. The people who run organised crime live in both worlds. They survive by ruling their underworld but they thrive by acquiring influence and legitimacy in our world.'

She nodded carefully. 'And banks like First Garanty are part of this process?'

'Precisely.' He paused. 'In writing about the City, the media's usual focus is on casino banking and how it brought about economic meltdown. And, of course, on the obscene incomes of top bankers, with their taper tax relief, bonus culture and other special considerations. The moral outrage makes an easy story. But it's a red herring for the real scandal.'

'Money laundering.' Ali frowned, her belief suspended in incomprehension. 'I thought that was an off-shore business.'

'A not unreasonable thought. The City of London actually functions like an offshore island. It has a quasi-independence from the UK, controls dirty assets in tax havens around the globe and is officially classed as a Tax Haven by the IMF. A fact conveniently ignored, it seems, by everyone.' He paused for her to come in. When she didn't, he continued. 'The City holds four trillion dollars in offshore bank deposits alone. In these days of super computers, and public-key and other financial cryptography - tools that render electronic money and digital bearer certificates untraceable - it has become so much more convenient to manage the laundering process direct from London.'

She nodded slowly, as if taking it in. 'Tell me about First Garanty.'

'On the surface, it is a legitimate bank for banks, a financial clearing house. It facilitates money movements around the world. It manages the transfer of eurodollars. It handles transfers of stock titles and other financial instruments. Its public and audited face is quite legitimate.' A pause, perfectly timed for effect.

'It is also a huge international money laundering and tax evasion machine, used by major banks, shell companies, and organised crime all over the world.'

Another nod, even slower. 'Ok. Assume I buy into this. The thing I don't understand is how First Garanty manages to evade the regulators.'

'By solving the problem of transfer.'

She gave him an exaggerated Gallic gesture and eyebrow roll.

He grinned. 'Laundered money is safe enough in offshore banks and tax havens; it's easy to hide the points of arrival and departure. It's during transfer that it becomes vulnerable. Garanty overcame this vulnerability by adapting its long-established system of non-published accounts.'

'Non-published accounts!' she echoed, mocking his expectation of her knowledge. 'Of course!'

Another grin. A moment to redirect his thoughts and he continued with the economics lesson. 'Non-published accounts are used by banks and big corporations to make transfers they don't want listed on the open books. In theory, they are perfectly legal. When he ran Garanty, Laughton kept them under control, strictly legit. He personally authorized each non-published account, which would be known only to auditors and key members of the board.' Connolly paused to gulp down some coffee. 'However, once he relinquished control of the Bank, there was nothing to stop abuse of the system. The new man, Kevin Baker, activated dormant non-published accounts for *special* transactions. These accounts are opened in the morning, used for a transaction, then closed by the evening. They don't show on the accounts list so no investigator or auditor would ever know of their existence.'

'Why would Laughton permit that to happen? I thought Garanty was his family bank.'

'Ah! Small is no longer beautiful. It is merely vulnerable. Laughton lost control of Garanty in the mid-noughties. The bank came under a systematic and very hostile attack which it lacked the resources to withstand. Laughton was quickly brought to his knees. He was offered a straightforward choice: sell or go under and lose everything. Since the price offered was a premium, he took the money. He became a figurehead with no operational role. I believe he died recently, but you would have to confirm that for yourself.'

Ali ran a quick search of her memory banks. 'I don't recall this making the news.'

Connolly shrugged. 'Garanty was a private bank. No public assets. Since no-one - neither Laughton nor those behind the attack - wanted the bank to collapse, the attack was kept secret. The takeover itself only warranted a few lines in the financial pages. The price was fair and that was the end of it.'

Ali shook her head in disbelief. 'So this Baker saw Garanty's potential for money laundering and orchestrated this attack in order to take it over.'

'In a nutshell,' he agreed. 'Though it was a company called Leke that did the dirty deed. Leke is a holding company that specialises in mergers and acquisitions, leveraged buyouts, recapitalisation and partnerships on international investments. Its true ownership lies somewhere in a labyrinth of offshore companies. I've not been able to work it through. It's the enabling essence of the laundering operation. It was Leke that installed Baker as CEO. He's no banker, that's for sure. He brought in his own man, Cummins, to handle the banking side.'

Ali nodded. She didn't quite understand the details but the bigger picture was coming to her. 'And Baker is responsible for laundering money on behalf of the Kosovan mafia.'

'Yes.' Connolly offered her a teacher's smile, acknowledging her effort to understand but slightly patronising nonetheless. 'You have to bear in mind that First Garanty manages tens of thousands of non-published accounts for clients world-wide. We're talking institutionalized money laundering, tax evasion, capital flight and fraud on a massive scale. Not forgetting illegal commissions worth billions of dollars for arms, pharma and energy deals. The Kosovans are not their major clients by any measure, but they're in there somewhere.'

Ali frowned. She was almost a believer. She just needed to touch the relic. 'All this you learned from Laughton?'

'The man himself.'

'I am told that there were investigations into Garanty and that these were quashed.'

Connolly gave her a rueful smile. 'The authorities don't have a prayer of controlling this. Technologically, the private sector is just too far ahead.'

Ali kept her face non-committal. 'And you told this to Steven?'

A nod of regret. 'My advice was *Ignore Figgis, he's a bit player. Follow the money!* I'm a pompous ass sometimes.' He paused. 'I used to liken this business to spaghetti . . . pull on one piece and you unravel the whole plate. I got it wrong. The harder you pull the more tangled becomes the knot. If Steven went investigating on the basis of what I told him, I have to bear some measure of responsibility for his death.'

'No more than you're responsible for the weather. Steven would have got there whatever.'

He smiled. 'I detect the same cussedness in you.'

'I'll take that as a compliment.'

Connolly opened his mouth as though to contradict her then stopped himself. He began rubbing his arm and his focus shifted, like he was re-living the memory of some ancient hurt. Somewhere in the house, a door banged shut. A rumour of conversation reached them, bringing with it the smell of cooking.

Ali used the silence to circle Connolly's words. She had no interest in a financial investigation. The paperwork alone would murder her spirit. However, key aspects of Connolly's narrative were woven inextricably into the fabric of Shimmon's story. First Garanty, money laundering, Figgis, Kosovan organised crime - this represented a whole other web of intrigue. There was something about the sheer scale that intrigued her. Take Figgis. The man was no inbred dummy. An aristocrat with a lineage that went back centuries, he was one of the richest men in Britain and modern enough to be a Cabinet Minister in Labour government and Tory alike. If someone like him was a bit player! . . .

At length, Connolly broke their silence. 'Shimmon isn't the first journalist investigating this to have died. A year ago, a German journalist called Kurt Muller came to see me about that same article. A month later he was killed in a car crash. I thought nothing of it at the time. But now! . . . ' He smiled, a sad smile. 'Maybe I am being paranoid, but I don't think I should be talking to you. I could be putting you in harm's way.'

'If you were that dangerous,' she pointed out, 'they would have silenced you.'

'They have. Oh, you mean killed me!' His expression became introspective, saddened. 'Perhaps I'm too useful to them. The beacon that attracts inquisitive moths to their death.'

That gave her pause for thought. 'Did Steven tell you why he suspected Figgis of laundering mafia money?'

'No.'

She racked her brain for something else to ask, but it was already reeling under the information overload.

He said, 'You haven't touched your coffee.'

'You tell too good a story,' she said, picking up her cup.

'I'll get some fresh.'

She shook her head and downed the cold drink in one. 'Thank you but I've taken up enough of your time.'

They made their way out in contemplative silence.

On the doorstep, he asked, 'Can I get you a taxi?'

She hesitated. She needed a drink. And she was hungry. Temple Bar was just twenty minutes away at a brisk stroll.

'No, thanks,' she said. 'I'll walk.'

'Then tread carefully, Ms Feysor.'

'And you.'

Striding away, she switched on her phone. Amongst the chaff, there was a message from Stewart.

The eagle has landed. Mine @ 10.

He had returned early from Edinburgh. Getting to his apartment by ten was achievable but only if she bypassed the Temple. She would have to grab a snack at the airport. She texted confirmation to Stewart then called a cab.

Chapter 24

STEWART LIVED IN Camberwell in a one-time public housing condo sold off to speculators and refurbished as starter flats. He didn't reply to his intercom, so Ali called a neighbouring flat and was buzzed into the building. She walked the three flights of stairs and found his door ajar. She wasn't surprised. It usually was when he was expecting her.

The flat was an ergonomic collection of cubicles, one for sleeping, one for cooking and eating, one for toilet and shower and one for living. There were three internal doors, all open. The lights were on and Stewart's phone, keys and wallet lay on the coffee table. She could smell Indian food and she half-expected Stewart to emerge from the kitchen, Spanish cooking spoon in one hand, glass of Hock in the other, looking faintly ridiculous in his Chamart chef's hat and apron.

So far so normal. She took two steps inside then noticed the holdalls with their *Metropolitan Police* tag. Unzipped. Spilling forensic suits and equipment. That was enough to stall her even before she noticed that the room had been trashed. Shelves were swept clean, cupboards emptied, multi-media equipment trashed and Stewart's books, DVDs and relics scattered over the floor.

Ali froze. Something inside her withered and drifted away. She felt light headed and jelly-legged, realised that she was holding her breath and tried to fill her lungs. Instead, she swallowed air and it rested on her stomach like rotting fish.

Gradually, as if by osmosis, she became aware of a buzzing sound. The fridge in the kitchen. The traffic on the road. Then a new sound, voices, from the bathroom, held under, stripped of emotion. And the light, an eerie blue glow, again from the bathroom.

She needed to look into that room yet she didn't want to see. She felt the bile rising as she edged forward. She had to pass the other rooms. The kitchen, with its Indian takeaway, fresh bottle of wine and two glasses standing guard, one for him, one for her. The bedroom was empty. She knew that without looking.

The bathroom. A figure dollied into shot, clad in protective coveralls and boots. Then another - hard at work with camcorder and digital camera - and another, until there were three wraiths in that tiny space. Scene of Crime Officers, she reckoned, too engrossed in their UV, print and trace search to notice her.

Stewart was in the bath. Even from the doorway she could see that the water about his neck and shoulders was pink, and she didn't need the small but hideous wound in his throat to see that the expression on his face was not that of a man contentedly adrift in a warm bath.

She wanted to scream and run but she could only stand there, transfixed, held against her will by the pain and fear that were frozen into Stewart's passively drooping mouth and dead eyes. She found herself struggling against the sensation that she had become infected with death. With some difficulty, she extracted her gaze from the milky-caul membrane of his eyes, only to find herself focused on his genitals. Cruel fascination: they were withdrawn and miserable like a junkie on the nod.

Somebody moaned, a long horrible, low-pitched sound. She started, then realised that the sound was coming from her own throat.

'Not here!' A man's voice; one of the wraiths rushed towards her. 'You shouldn't be here, you can't be seeing this!' He manhandled her from the room. 'This is a crime scene for heaven's sake. Noddy suit, boots and gloves. We can't have you leaking all over the place.'

Under more usual circumstances, Ali the journo might have protested her right to be there. But the shock had gone and her emotions had kicked in. Sadness, grief, loss, anxiety, above all that sensation of her own dying. Her breathing was thin and shallow, and she clenched her hands to stop them trembling.

She managed to say, 'Sorry, I didn't think.'

'Wait here,' he said. 'And don't touch anything.'

He hastened out of the front door, pausing to slip off his gloves and booties. As he passed her, Ali instinctively stepped aside. Something crumpled beneath her foot. An empty Blu-ray case. *Chinatown*. Stewart's favourite film. He had made her watch it with him once, bombarding her with his enthusiasm: *the convoluted perfection of its plot and direction, the stunning performances of Nicholson and Dunaway, the magnificent cinematography.* She remembered yawning, grinning, responding, *Stunning.*

She realised that she was standing in the middle of Stewart's film collection and, for an instant, the awareness paralysed her. She was like someone who had strayed into a minefield and didn't know where to place her feet. This was Stewart's movie compilation, the one worldly possession that he truly cherished. It had taken him years to amass and catalogue and now it was scattered and trampled, cases opened and disks spilled as if they meant nothing.

As if Paul Stewart meant nothing!

Warm tears welled and a sudden white fury seized her, cauterising the unhappy emotions lurking beneath her surface. Someone was going to pay for this violation, and pay dear.

The SOCO returned with two uniformed officers and a man in a suit. The tech pulled on new coverall, boots and gloves and went back into the bathroom. The uniforms set about taping off the flat. That left the suit.

He took in the laptop bag slung over Ali's shoulders and searched the journalist's face. 'You're Ali Feysor,' he said as though that made her Bin Laden's clone. 'What the hell are you doing here? This is off limits to the press.' He frowned as he saw her emotional state and his indignation turned to bemusement. 'You're no scanner voyeur. What are you doing here?'

'I'm not. . . . ' Ali tried, but failed, to conceal her distress. 'Paul Stewart's my friend.'

He said nothing for a moment. Tall and bulky, with high forehead, chipped brown eyes and cropped black hair, he was an intimidating figure. He appraised her openly and she got the impression that he was wondering whether to eject her, arrest her or talk to her. But, when he spoke, his voice had lost its harsh edge. 'I'm sorry you had to see this. I'm Leon Nicholson. DI. Senior Investigating Officer.'

'How? . . . ' She coughed, an unconscious attempt to expurgate the dead air from her lungs. 'How long? When did it happen?'

He ignored her questions. 'Was he expecting you?'

She offered a wry smile. 'Me? Yes.'

He nodded, paused. 'Did he keep much of value here?'

'He didn't own anything of value. Except his movies – and they were only valuable to him. There were his computers, of course. He keeps those in his office. I'd guess they're valuable beyond their replacement cost. He has a laptop but nobody's going to do this for a laptop.'

'There's no laptop here. No computer equipment whatsoever.'

'He had a netbook and flash drive of mine.'

'There's no sign of them. Were they valuable?'

'Not really.'

She struggled to put her mind into gear. The killer must have taken them. He had killed Stewart and then taken everything to do with Shimmon's story. Or had he? Was she reading too much into this? Maybe her tech was still in Stewart's office. She glanced at his keys on the coffee table.

Nicholson was studying her carefully. 'What did he do for a living?'

'He was an IT consultant.' He waited and she elaborated. 'He was an expert in penetration testing, security consulting and custom software patches. Essentially, he hacked into his clients' computer systems then plugged the security gaps. It was all legit.'

Nicholson looked dubious. 'Could this be about industrial espionage?'

Ali shook her head emphatically. 'He was too straight. He's not some kid hacking for fun; he does it to order. He attacks his own clients' systems. He thought of himself as some kind of external systems administrator.'

'But he could have learned something he shouldn't?'

She shrugged. 'I'm the wrong person to ask. He never talked business with me.'

'Because you're a journalist?'

Ali's face flared with anger. 'Because he would never break a confidence!'

The detective acknowledged his error with a conciliatory smile. 'How about enemies? Wounded husbands? Gambling debts? Has he been threatened? Was he into drugs?'

'He was a good man with a good heart. Nicer than a cliché. Everyone loved him.'

The detective paused, as though mulling this over. 'Did he have any family?'

'Not a wife, or partner. But lots of family, yes. His parents live in Birmingham. Edgbaston. The address will be here somewhere.' Another pause. 'I know this place. Candid cameras in the lobby and lifts.'

He smiled carefully. 'We've got the security disks.'

Her head cleared a little more and she began to weigh him up, wondering if she could entrust her story to him. She was leaning towards trust when a

SOCO came out from the bathroom. He took off his protective clothing and she recognised the man she had spoken to earlier. He shot a curious glance in her direction then carried on out through the front door. But the spell was broken. She would have liked to have talked to Nicholson, test him out, put him on the right track. Off-the-record, of course. But it was too late now. Their conversation would be circumspect, polite and politic, a mix of bare facts, routine background, appeals, denials and stone-walling.

It would be a waste of time.

Suddenly, she didn't want to be here anymore. Didn't need to be. She couldn't help them. She didn't know who had killed Stewart, hadn't seen anything. True, she could suggest a possible motive, but she wasn't about to open up that can of worms to police investigation. If she told them what she knew, their size twelves would trample all over the story. Worse, some chancer would sell it to her rivals, in so doing alerting the killers to close it down.

Nicholson said, 'I'd be grateful if you didn't write about this without talking to me.'

'Paul was a friend.' She told him, as if that explained it all. In her eyes, it did.

He regarded her shrewdly. 'Is there something you want to tell me? Something that might help us find who killed him?'

She shook her head.

He said, 'We'll need your prints and DNA for elimination.'

'Now?'

'We'll call you.'

She turned to leave, then she paused, turned back and gave him her card. As he took it, she noticed a knife scar across his hand, pink against his black skin. She wondered briefly about the story attached to it. Then he was giving her his card in return.

He said, 'Call me if you think of anything.'

She nodded. Once again, she felt strangely drawn to tell him everything. She channeled the impulse into a barely perceptible shake of the head then she picked up Stewart's key bundle as if it were her own. With a final glance towards the bathroom, she turned and left.

SHE WAS EXHAUSTED. She wanted to go home. Raise a glass to lost friends. Crawl into bed. Crash into oblivion. But she couldn't overlook the possibility that Shimmon's netbook and all her information were in Stewart's office, just minutes' drive away. It was a long shot, of course. The killers were sure to have beaten her to it. But she couldn't bear the notion, however slim, that she might miss out.

Ali recalled nothing more until she opened the door to Stewart's office. The place was bomb-struck. Shattered computers littered the floor, their hard drives stripped out, and all of his external drives had been spirited away. She had expected nothing else but that didn't cushion the bitter disappointment. She didn't go in. No need to pick her way through the debris. She knew, even before she looked, that there would be no netbook and no flash drive.

Chapter 25

ALI REACHED HOME, dropped her bag on the sofa, flicked on the muted TV for company then filled the void with *Evanescence*, the *Fallen* CD. She couldn't focus. She felt as low as at any time since her mother's death. Stewart's dead eyes haunted her thoughts. His scent assailed her, a kind of stale, electronic mist that brought a cramping pain and unwanted pop-ups that she couldn't delete. She pictured him laughing at some story in a pub, managed to blink away that image only to conjure up his face wracked by the terror and pain of violent death. Gruesome image grabs that evoked even worse memories. The death of her mother. The call in the middle of the night. The fruitless drive from Birmingham to Winchester where she had been denied access to her mother's body, burnt beyond recognition in a high speed motorway crash. Days of limbo, of dreadful, gut-churning uncertainty: if she couldn't see her mother dead then she couldn't be dead. The horror of the second cremation, this time with full ceremonial. Literally ashes to ashes, though more David Bowie than Jesus Christ. After the funeral, she had turned her back on both.

Something sharp began poking into her mind and it penetrated her disconnection like an unwanted touch.

Stewart had been murdered and it was her doing! She had taken her problem to her friend, kissed him on the cheek and signed his death warrant. No longer could she take for granted the warm, musky strength of his friendship, the fact that he was always there when she needed him, the way he loved her but never tried to grope her, the intensity of his film-watching that precluded conversation, the way he would suddenly fess up to her: *I paid for a prostitute once. Just for the experience, you understand. It was my existential phase. It was so degrading. She sensed my abasement and it seemed to affect her. We fed off each other's humiliation until I could hardly get it up. I think we both ended up faking orgasms to avoid hurting each other's feelings.*

He had been a soul mate, a true friend, so full of laughter and joy that, even dead, he was more alive than she could ever be. He was the big cuddly bear of a brother she had never had and now he was gone.

She had thought that she had her emotions under control but shock, distress and guilt threatened to overwhelm her. Her stomach churned and her skin crawled, as though she was leaking some alien, acrid sweat. Then the tears came. She put her head in her hands and pulled a dark blanket over her pain, sobbing uncontrollably until at last the tears stopped and the pounding in her brain eased.

Making space for the questions.

If the killers had been after the netbook and drive, how had they known about them? How had they known that Stewart had them? Were they watching her? If they were the same people who had killed Steven, if they were so hell bent on killing people who had access to the information, how come she was still alive? Why had they killed Paul Stewart and not her?

Who the hell were *they*?

Macleod had convinced her that she was facing some kind of conspiracy but the who and the what eluded her. A nagging voice told her that she knew more than she understood, that she had the pieces but just wasn't making the fit. Shimmon would have put it together. The man had been a conviction journo, as straight as a motorway and just as dull, but his forensic mind had bounced her through many a block.

Hot tears threatened her eyes again but this time she fought them back. She knew that the violent death of a close friend should bring these feelings of sorrow, and anger, and outrage. She ought to have been glad of these emotions: they reaffirmed her humanity. But she wasn't giving herself over to grief. For Ali, there was a much better way to cope with her churning emotions: pour herself a vodka Red Bull and spew her feelings into her computer.

Her MacBook. Always there for her. The ultimate listener, the ultimate healer. She had no need for life's other comforts, no need for chocolates or teddy bears, pets or husband. Just touch the keys and the computer would extract the evil. Her fears, her worries, her anger, they would all leave her to re-appear magically as little black symbols on the screen in front of her. Her laptop was both her prison and her saviour. Her very own Green Mile.

Seething with unfocused anger, she began to write what she knew - and what she surmised - about the deaths of two men. She wrote of carefully planned and executed murders, of stolen computers and files. She wrote of shadowy forces in a shadow world, of powerful men, of money laundering that interfaced two worlds, of organised crime and Kosovan mafia, of police she couldn't trust, of the role of the British government and the assassination of Lucca.

But no story emerged. Her article, such as it was, came across as a stream of consciousness. Delirious. Paranoid. The hard truth sliced through her like an ice blade. If Irvine read it he would consign her to a mental health month. She couldn't even put it out there on her blog. All she could do was close her computer and keep it to herself.

She needed to talk to someone and, at this late hour, there was only her father. He answered after five rings. Upbeat as ever, he didn't comment on the time or the fact that she had promised to call him several days ago. He was just glad to talk to her and she was so relieved to hear his voice. He chatted blithely about his patients, his music, his plans to walk the Pilgrims Way with friends. What was she up to? Working! *You shouldn't work so hard, girl. Will you be coming to visit?* That was what he really wanted to know. She promised to visit soon.

Call over, her eyes filled up again and suddenly her conscience began gnawing like an aching tooth. This always happened after their phone conversations, though she didn't understand why. Ever since her mother had died, she had felt responsible for him. She kept in regular touch by phone and drove to Winchester to see him every month. Yet, he had coped very well with her mother's death. Much better than she had. For years, she had been overwhelmed by an image of his loneliness, convinced that he was putting on a brave front. But his contentment was genuine. Maybe because, as a GP he was used to death; maybe because, unlike her, he had retained his religious conviction; most likely because he was made that way. It had taken her a long time to realise that only one of them was scared and lonely, and it wasn't her father.

The gnawing in her stomach turned to hunger but she didn't much feel like eating. She went to the kitchen for some coffee and a bowl of cereals. Waiting for the kettle to boil, she mulled over the events that had brought her to this cold, grey desolation. From the moment Irvine had cheer-led her into going to Kosovo, she had been in too much of a hurry. She hadn't thought things through, considered consequences or analysed risk, and her carelessness had had terrible consequences. No miracle could undo what was done and there was no one she could turn to, no solace to be had. She had made her decisions and now she had to live with them.

It was never in doubt that she would carry on with her investigation. Stewart's murder had shaken her but, after her mother's accident all those years ago, death could never bring the same intensity of shock, helplessness and hurt. The long process of coming to terms with her mother's death had given her this coping mechanism. However bad her life experience, she could always boot her laptop or catch that plane. This was the part of her that some people mistook for a hack's callousness, others for consummate professionalism. None of them understood that she was just practising the dark art of denial. Practicing it until there was nothing inside, just this huge emptiness, as if she were anaesthetized.

More vodka would help, but she didn't trust herself to be alone with Mr Smirnoff. Not tonight.

It was time to get a grip.

Okay, she rebuked herself harshly. *You've had your meltdown and that's your fucking lot! Now lose the tears and nail the bastards!*

Chapter 26

RACHEL CARSON, THE girl who used to be known as Sarah York, sipped her coffee and contemplated her current home, an elegant row house just off Amsterdam Avenue in New York's Upper West Side. Light and airy, it had been completely renovated, with modern kitchen and bathrooms, air con and a full data rack supporting computer, cable, phone, internet and security. The improvements had been tastefully done, and the house retained much of the grace and beauty of the original, including fireplaces, chandeliers, cross-hatched doors and voice tubes. After hiding out in a succession of small apartments, culminating in the West Kilburn flat, it was a relief to have some of the space and luxury that she was used to.

The house belonged to Christian Aust, a New York banker currently on a year-long posting to Spain with his wife and four children. The Austs had put all their personal possessions into storage, but the place still reeked of happy families. It was an aura that made Rachel feel like an intruder and imposter.

It was clever of her Guardian Angel to have brought her here. Her people were on Long Island and the last place they would look for her was in their own back yard. There was a downside, of course. There was always a downside. She was living in the cultural hub of the Big Apple - fantastic bars, theatres and clubs, food aromas from around the world, pulsing noise and electric darkness. Yet, she feared to venture out lest she be recognised. Her world was restricted to the local supermarket and park; her gourmet highlight was a pizza-to-go from the Hot & Crusty Café; her most memorable mental snapshot the woman in furs disembarking from her limo, her dog handler in tow with four little shih tsus. Rachel had come to feel like a crazed anthropologist living with some remote, alien tribe. In limbo. Connected and isolated at the same time.

Though not quite alone.

Nadia Jackson, the young woman sent by her Guardian Angel to meet her at JFK, was sprawled on a sofa the other side of the fireplace. Coffee and brownies were on the table between them. It was early evening but the curtains were already closed. It made the room feel dark and claustrophobic, but Nadia had insisted, concerned that the large bay windows put them on display. Rachel had been surprised when Nadia had turned out to be her minder, even more surprised when she had moved in with her. Early thirties, short-haired, lithe and tough looking, Nadia had a built-in smile with a touch of rogue, but there was no mistaking the glint of steely determination in her black eyes.

Conversation was proving stiff and fragmented, and they had drifted into a silence that was threatening to become uncomfortable. Nadia brushed crumbs off her lap and smiled.

'So tell me about yourself. You got a boyfriend, or a husband?'

Rachel's face lifted in mock incredulity. 'No!'

'You like women?'

Rachel gave her an amused smile. 'Not in that way.'

'What about family?'

'My mother and siblings were murdered.'

'I'm sorry.'

'It was a long time ago.'

'And your father?'

Rachel shrugged, unable to get her head around a conversation that felt like an interrogation. She couldn't shift the sensation of being trapped and her mood was plummeting. She set her cup down and came to her feet.

'I'm tired,' she said. 'I'm for an early night.'

Nadia smiled, unfazed by the snub. 'Sleep well.'

Rachel had chosen the bedroom belonging to the Aust's youngest daughter. It wasn't the most comfortable of rooms, and it had been cleared of personal belongings, yet the little girl retained a real presence here that Rachel found irresistible. It wasn't the pink rugs and décor, or the faint fragrance of strawberries and soap, or the childish art that adorned the walls, or the posters of Elsa, Barbie and Tinkerbell. It was the feeling of being wanted and loved, of tucking herself away in a space that was intimate and secure.

Rachel's rucksack lay empty in the corner, a reminder to be constantly ready. Nowhere was for long. Her clothes filled only a fraction of the wardrobe space. On show, she had just the picture of her mother and siblings, together with her battered copy of *Little*

Women. A curious book for someone with such a hard and pragmatic background, yet she read it time and again to be transported into an exotic world of companionship, hope and loyalty. Rachel, as she now called herself, understood only too well that she was living proof of Alcott's belief that no amount of wealth can guarantee the happiness to be found in a close and loving family.

She picked up her family photo and stared hard at people she could barely remember. The photo itself was old and worn, from a different life. Her mother, sister and brother. All long dead. And, of course, Rachel herself. There was a hole in the picture where she had excised her father. He was the other survivor of the group but he was dead to her. Soon, she must make good her promise to scan the image, crop the gap and make her family whole again.

The picture reminded her that the madness would never stop. The search for Sarah York would be unrelenting. They would never forgive her or forget her and that was the really frightening thought. These people - her people! - were the ancient masters of vendetta. For them, everything was secondary to family honour and making money, and she had become a threat to both. Their code of retribution - the Hammurabi - was actually written down in a murderer's handbook called the *Canon of Leke*. Their violence was inbred, a function, not of abused childhood, or misfiring neurons, but of bad genes. Her people had taken a wrong turn in evolution. They had been programmed to kill each other until none were left alive. They were even prepared to kill their own blood to make a point. How could she live with that?

How indeed. By staying in the house. Subsisting on take-out food, bad TV and even worse internet. Forgetting love and intimacy. And remembering to be afraid. Always afraid.

Chapter 27

Standing unnoticed in the unlit service road, Sandford watched Ali arrive home, park her car in her garage then walk off towards Sheaveshill Road. Minutes later, he saw lights came on in her apartment, the kitchen first, followed by the living room then the flickering blue of the TV. Satisfied that she was not going out again, he settled into watching mode.

He didn't mind waiting. It was part of the game. Stalking losers. People whose heads had been turned by cash or sex or greener grass. Traitors, without loyalty, guts or self-respect. Feysor was different, of course. She was not for turning and that made her a genuine threat. Fiercely independent, she possessed the intellect to unravel Alpha's carefully tied knot and the stubborn courage to keep going until it was done. She was a worthy opponent. Yet, her strengths were also her vulnerability. Brave and headstrong, she was blind to her own limitations and to the ruthlessness of those she was investigating.

At length, the lights in her lounge went off. The upstairs windows of her apartment sparked into life and returned to darkness shortly afterwards. The journalist had gone to bed.

He had no curiosity concerning Feysor the woman. As a man, he took great pleasure from his relationships with women - the conversation, the warmth, the companionship, the sex – and it was a curious trait, to know so much about someone as attractive as Feysor yet be able to de-personalise her, to see her sexuality yet be oblivious to her sex. It was, he concluded with grim satisfaction, the mark of the true professional.

He set his internal alarm for 60 minutes and put himself into pause mode, a kind of semi-dormant state that permitted him to rest whilst maintaining a state of alert. Soon after two, he snapped into action and made his way to Ali's front door. No hesitant glance to betray him, he pulled on balaclava and latex gloves and set about picking the locks. It took three minutes.

He listened for another minute then switched on a hand-held scanner that resembled an iPod and pushed open the door. He went directly to the alarm box. A series of numbers shimmered across the scanner screen then began to settle, digit by digit. The scanner transmitted the code and the 'no alarm memory' message appeared.

He was in.

He closed the door behind him and waited a further minute to be sure that he had not disturbed anyone. Then he set to work. He didn't need a light. He didn't make any noise. He would leave no evidence or clue for the police to follow. In the lounge, he found her MacBook, notebooks and memory sticks. He scooped them into her laptop bag and put the bag by the front door.

Next, he ghosted up the stairs. First stop was the spare bedroom that Ali used as an office. There was a PC on the desk, together with some external data storage. She had compiled a wall display of pictures, articles, diagrams and networks. He noted with interest that she was connecting Mammon, Lucca, Figgis, Griffin, HMG and Garanty, but tentatively, as though she had no firm evidence. It was the work of moments to remove the hard disk from her PC. He took the display down and folded it into his own bag, then added her notebook and disks from the desk. He picked the lock on the filing cabinet. Nothing there. Just personal papers.

Mind cold and empty, he walked to the end of the hallway. Her bedroom door was closed. He put his ear to the door and listened for fully twenty seconds. Not a sound from within. Carefully, he pushed the door open. The journalist didn't stir. He could just make out her soft, rhythmic breathing. There was a yellowish light from the street and the air was slightly musky. Eyes glittering, he watched her sleep for a long moment, maybe ninety seconds, before he entered and crossed the room.

Now, as he stared down at Ali Feysor, his mind was neither cold nor empty.

Chapter 28

ALI AWOKE WITH a jolt, senses on full alert. Something had disturbed her but she couldn't make out what. A passing car, or a fox searching through the bins? She held her breath and listened but everything was quiet. She felt no sense of danger, just a vague feeling of dislocation. It must have been something in the air. A Will-o'-the-wisp darting across the room, leaving behind a faint square of light on the bed.

Awake now, she was thirsty. Her clock glowed 02.35. She made her way downstairs and gulped down a glass of water. It was only when she re-emerged from the kitchen that she noticed that the alarm was off. Her eyes switched automatically to the front door. It was unlocked. She must have gone to bed without locking up. She found that hard to believe but her recall was peppered with blanks. With a weary sigh, she locked the front door and set the alarm.

Something - that Will-o'-the-wisp again - prompted her to check over her apartment. Nothing too heavy. Just a cursory glance into each room. At first, everything seemed to be in place, not exactly neat, but Feysor tidy, just as it should be. But, when she reached her office, she saw at once that someone had been here. The wall had been stripped of its charts, photos and cutting. Her PC lay open, its hard drive removed. Gone, too, were her external hard drives and thumb drives.

That pushed her panic button. She rushed downstairs to the lounge and this time she noticed the empty spaces on the table where her Macbook, mini-drives and notebooks should have been.

Someone had been here!

They had been here!

They had come for her information, just as they had with Shimmon and with Stewart, and they had taken it all!

All at once, thought caught up with time. An intruder had just invaded her space, maybe the same guy who had murdered Shimmon and Stewart! And what had she done? Wandered dozily around her flat, guided only by some blind, cross-wired instinct. What if the intruder had still been here? What if he had come to harm her? Her heart began pounding in her chest as if it were trying to break free from some terror. With shaking hands, she re-checked the front-door locks and alarm. First thing in the morning, she would arrange new locks, an alarm system that worked and some very heavy door bolts.

She returned to the living room and perched numbly on the edge of the sofa. Her cell phone lay on the coffee table in front of her. Comfort blanket for the smart age, Instinctively, she reached for it but she didn't pick it up. She had left the phone on her bedside table so what was it doing here? Nothing good, she could be sure of that. Cautiously, she leaned forward and thumbed her way past the lock screen. It opened up to a photo. The shot had been taken just fifteen minutes ago but not by her. Steel bands clamped her chest, making it impossible to breathe. Someone had been in her bedroom! They had photographed her asleep in her own bed! They had done so using her own phone!

She scrambled to her feet, taking deep breaths to fight off the panic. Like a dog chasing its tail she moved to the window, then the door, then turned back into the room and grabbed her phone. She tapped out a triple nine then flashed on Keaton's warning: *if you call the cops the Kosovan mafia will come calling*. Keaton had been deadly serious. That didn't make him right, of course. But even if she did call the Met, what could she tell them? The truth was too incredible to relate, especially when she had no backup evidence. Moreover, calling the Met would put her on their system. Did she really want that when, as Keaton had been at pains to point out, it would flag her actions to her enemies? Was the risk of being killed worth a comforting word and crime number from a uniformed police officer?

No.

She killed the call.

Keaton would know what to do. But when she scrolled his number it wasn't there. Her Contacts had been deleted. As had her Gallery and all other data.

She sat, paralysed, staring at the phone like it was a live snake. For the first time in her existence she sensed that her life was in danger, and she realized, almost with a sense of surprise, that she wanted to be safe and protected. Keaton had promised to look out for her. The thought triggered a curious mix of emotions: relief, hope, warmth. And fear. It was that last, single, discordant emotion that took over. Keaton had entered her life along with these killers and there was no way of knowing if she could trust him.

She didn't want to think any more about violent men. All she wanted was to disconnect herself from the world. She put on the TV for company, pulled her knees to her chest and slipped unknowing into a black place.

AN HOUR LATER she snapped awake. Her heart was hammering, there was bile in her throat and her brain was struggling for reason. The vague image of a murderous figure was stuck at the back of her eyes. Her intruder. Stewart's killer? One and the same man?

Her sense of failure was overwhelming. She had lost everything, all those notes and pictures gathered at such cost, and in so doing she had let everybody down: Stewart, Shimmon, the old woman in Kosovo, Donylla, everyone.

A deep anger welled up, self-directed, ripping through her without mercy. Since taking on this assignment, she had experienced violation after violation until she had reached the stage where she no longer controlled her own life. In just twenty-four hours she had been warned off four times. Four times! She had been trolled, doxed, bribed and threatened. Maybe it was time to take notice. The self-assurance that had led her to believe that she could finish Shimmon's story was the stuff of vanity, her desire to see justice done no more than a self-destructive impulse.

She was lucky to be alive. She couldn't understand why, when they had killed Shimmon and Stewart, they had let her live?

Just be thankful they have!

But being a survivor didn't make her safe.

Irvine was right, just as Keaton had been: she was too weak to fight this particular battle. There was no-one to help her, no-one to turn to. Call in a friend and she would condemn them to death. Summon the police and she would condemn herself. There was only Keaton and she was too wired to trust her shining White Knight.

For an indeterminate time, she lay there, exhausted but unable to close her eyes for fear that her nemesis would burst in. And that's where she spent the rest of the night, slumped on the sofa, drifting in and out of a fitful sleep that she shared with a menacing stranger.

Chapter 29

Andrew Feysor pulled his Volvo XC40 onto his drive and almost ran into Ali's red Clio. Parked against the bay windows, its presence was unexpected but no surprise. His daughter rarely apprised him of her visits. He climbed out of his car, checked that the automatic gates were closing behind him and made his way into the house. Her battered holdall was on the floor, dumped by the Grandfather clock, and he shifted it onto the rug lest it scratch the parquet. There was no sign of her ever-present laptop and he guessed that she was outside working.

She was outside, sitting on a bench amongst the autumn pastels and perfumes of the cottage garden, but she wasn't working.

'Ali!' He couldn't conceal his delight.

She stood, stepped towards him and forced a smile. 'Hey Dad.'

They hugged then settled onto the bench. He could sense her subdued mood, but nothing could extinguish the grin of pleasure that had settled on his face. He was a third generation GP, with warm, hazel eyes, deep laughter lines and a relaxed, self-assured demeanor that commanded trust.

He asked, 'How long have you been here?'

'An hour. Two.'

'You forget your computer?'

She shook her head. 'Mum used to love it out here.' A little smile, rueful. 'I don't keep it as she would want.'

'She would understand. Gardening was her hobby, not yours.'

There was a moment of reflective silence.

He gave her a sidelong glance. 'Everything okay?'

'Sure. I'm tired is all.'

'Working too hard?'

'That's one way to describe it.'

For a while, they talked routinely, catching up with each other. Then she asked:

'Did you ever quit anything, Dad?'

'What kind of anything?'

She shrugged. 'Anything.'

'Anything.' He thought on that, his smile flickering on and off. 'I quit the school rugby team when I was sixteen.'

'Better things to do? Or were you running away?'

He arched his eyebrows at her intensity. 'All that mud-wrestling and chasing about. I loved it as a kid but as I got older I grew tired of dragging my knuckles. All that fake machismo.' He shrugged. 'It was too homo-erotic for my taste.'

'What did granddad say?'

'Dad? Nothing, really. When I told him that rugby was irrefutable proof that Neanderthals mated with Homo Sapiens he just gave me one of his famous inscrutable looks.' He chuckled affectionately. 'He thought he could communicate anything with those looks of his, but inscrutable is inscrutable! I could never tell what he was thinking.'

She smiled. 'What about your career? Do you ever have doubts?'

'Every time I lose a patient.'

'How do you cope with that?'

He thought for a moment, allowing the sounds of a late summer evening to come through: the rich musical phrases of the thrushes and warblers, the discordant racket of the collared doves, the distant hum of the M3, the laughter and electronic noise that floated from open windows.

'Why do you ask?'

She shrugged. 'I just wondered what you do when it slips beyond your control.'

'Work harder to do better next time.'

'That won't undo what's happened.'

'Of course not, but you have to accept that some things are simply beyond your control.' Another pause. 'When I lost my first patient, I was shattered. My father told me, *Death is a part of life, son. Sometimes you can put it off for a while but you can never prevent it. You can't do your job if you lay everything on yourself.*' Pause. 'You don't get used to it, you just get back on that horse for the benefit of the people who still need you.'

'Is that how you coped with Mum's dying?' She saw his frown, explained, 'I've been thinking about Mum a lot, lately. I don't know why.'

'That's different.'

'You never got back on that horse. You never married again.'

'I've never wanted to remarry. Never needed to.'

She sat back in her seat, somehow assuaged by his reassuring sentiment. It was at times like this, when she was in real need of succour, that she was glad that her father had never acted on his occasional talk of downsizing. Of course this house was too big for him. He didn't need five bedrooms, or a quarter of an acre lawn that rolled down to the tree-lined Itchen. But this place, with its rangy elevations, mellow Victorian bricks, clambering wisteria and soft grey tiles was more than a house. Much more. It was home. The heart of a lifetime. The ephemeral composition of disjointed memories.

She said, 'You're happy to spend the rest of your life alone?'

He shrugged. 'It's the past that eats you up, Ali. I'm content to let the future take care of itself.' He took her hand in his. 'You know, for a long time after your mother's death, it used to pain me to see you smile. It was such a sad smile. I was afraid that you had gone into a place inside yourself that people don't come out of. But then I realised that you had found your sanctuary within.'

She nodded. Her mother's death had certainly thrown her off course. In her final year at university, she had lived the life of an adrenaline junkie, binging on vodka, cheap wine, wild promiscuity and dangerous sports, seeking out ever greater thrills in what was closer to death wish than cry for help. It was only after she had returned home to the unquestioning love of her father that she had begun to heal. She had stopped drinking, stopped seeking out crazy liaisons, stopped subsisting on thrills. As her world had ceased to spin, and time had slowed enough for her body and mind to become whole again, she had come to accept her mother's passing. She had also come to chose life over death.

She shrugged. 'I guess I didn't have your strength to cope.'

'Strength has nothing to do with it.' He squeezed her hand, let it go. 'The death of a loved one hits us in different ways. It can take a while, then it hits you when you least expect it.'

She realized that he was talking about himself and she looked at him, silent, expectant.

'It was just after the funeral, the day you went back to Birmingham. I remember it was a beautiful morning. I was driving to work and I had to pull over. It was too much for me. My entire system shut down. Every breath became a physical effort. And everything felt so dreadfully pointless. I've never felt so totally alone.'

She knew all about that pain. She shuffled closer and put her arm through his, held him tight. 'You've never told me this before.'

'It passed.' He smiled at her, a wan gesture. 'That's human nature for you.'

'Sure.'

'I was lucky.' He shifted, put his arm about her and she snuggled close. 'You went through such a dark period.'

'I was such a bitch in my teens,' Ali confessed. 'I was horrified to think that her last memory of me was my dreadful behavior.'

'No, no. Of course it wasn't.' He paused. 'When you were a teenager, your mother used to liken you to an orchid. You know, one of those flowers that is hard to look after but is so beautiful when it blooms. . . . You had the strength to survive through the darkness. And now you're in bloom.'

'You think so? Then I wish mum was here to see it.'

'Oh she's seen it, sweetheart. She never saw anything else.'

For a while neither spoke.

Eventually, he asked, 'What's brought this on?'

She shifted uncomfortably. 'I'm not sure that I'm cut out for journalism.'

'If you're not, no-one is.' He realized that she was serious. 'I used to have doubts about it, too. I thought that your crusading journalism was a kind of apology for not going to Medical School. Then I saw how good you are.'

'Is that what you wanted? For me to follow the family tradition?'

'Good heavens, no! I wanted you to do what's right for you. Isn't that what you're doing?'

She thought a little. 'I grew up believing that our society had higher moral principles than any other, that hundreds of years of cultural development and law-making had raised us above the savagery of Srebrenica, and Islamic State, and Syria. Now I know better. The veneer of our civilization can crack at any moment, crumble away and expose the darkness underneath.'

'It holds most of us in check.'

'But not all. And what if I'm no better? What if I'm driven by the same darkness of the soul?'

'You're a story teller, Ali. And a story teller stands apart from the story.'

'Not always. What happens when the story teller becomes part of the story? When she becomes no better than an avenging angel with blood on her teeth?'

'Why then, she must have the moral imperative.' Pause. 'Would it make the world any better if no-one told the story?'

She shook her head. 'Of course not.'

'So you can't quit, can you.'

A little smile crossed her face. 'I guess not.'

He glanced at her, took a deep breath and sighed. 'Just remember who you are. Keep that special place inside you.'

She nodded.

He smiled. 'I could do with a drink.'

They stood and turned towards the house.

'I love you, Dad.'

'Me too. You staying for dinner?'

'Sure. As long as you're cooking.'

Chapter 30

SANDFORD ENTERED THE London offices of Leke Corporation and went directly to the elevator station. One lift had a key pad instead of a call button. He tapped in the day's six digit code and the door opened. There were no controls inside. He merely had to smile insolently at the camera and wait to be transported upwards.

The lift opened directly onto a top floor office that was large enough to accommodate the entire Alphaplus operation. A floor-to-ceiling bookcase covered one wall, an en-suite bedroom and bathroom led off through a second, and the lift, door and fully-stocked bar and kitchenette occupied a third. The fourth wall was a picture window with a stunning backdrop of the Thames spanned by the Tower Bridge. The room had three distinct areas. Centrepiece was a desk the size of a conference table, with four leather office chairs, one behind the desk and three in front. Over by the window was a suite of sofas and low tables. Near the book shelves was a standard data rack with computer and multi-media set-up.

Michael Ashe, CEO of Leke Corporation, was leaning against the front of his desk. Jackson, Sarah York's minder, was seated just in front of him. Behind

Jackson stood Upandar Vanavasam, Ashe's PA, Ashe was early sixties, maybe five-nine, with close-cropped greying hair, blue-grey eyes, handsome, jaundiced features and lean body. His voice was lightly accented, pitched somewhere between Eastern Europe and South Africa. His PA was a heavily-built weights man, more BG than secretary, darker than Ashe with a stronger accent that put him somewhere south of the Danube. Jackson was late twenties, a fair-haired Anglo, sedentary and slightly overweight. Blood and mucous trickled from his nose and he was looking nervously defiant. Ashe had obviously started without Sandford.

Ashe didn't acknowledge the MI5 man's arrival, except to say, 'You have the evidence?'

Sandford handed him an envelope: 'Courtesy of the National ANPR Data Centre.' [*ANPR was the automatic number plate recognition CCTV network that tracked car movements around the country, often in close to real time.*] Ashe took the envelope and extracted two photos. The first showed Jackson driving a BMW on the eastbound M4 with the girl Sarah in the passenger seat next to him. The second, taken just thirty minutes later, showed Jackson driving alone on the westbound Bayswater Road.

Ashe turned on Jackson and demanded, 'Where did you drop her?'

'Oxford Street. She said she was going shopping. I had no idea what she was planning to do.'

Ashe clenched up as if he intended hitting Jackson again but was distracted as Sandford passed over a second envelope. It contained CCTV images of Sarah on the London underground, in various stations and on trains.

'The date codes on all the images match the day of her disappearance,' Sandford explained. 'We have CCTV-batoned her from Queens Park to Canons Park in north-west London. It's a convoluted journey clearly designed to avoid surveillance. From Canons Park, she goes off the grid. It's a well-chosen location. She could have gone to ground locally, or travelled by car to the M1 or M25 then literally anywhere, or she could have made her way to another tube station or mainline station, or taken a bus. We're checking ANPR for a recognisable plate from a friend's car, or even a lucky glimpse of her face. So far, nothing.'

Ashe stared at Jackson, his expression inscrutable, even to an experienced people reader like Sandford.

'Where is she?'

Jackson spoke calmly; this was the truth. 'I have no idea.'

'You planned her escape.'

'Escape? From what?'

'You have a simple job. Look out for her. Make sure nothing happens to her. Keep her in sight. Yet you lost her! You let her get away!'

'I was never told she was a prisoner,' Jackson protested. 'How was I supposed to know she was planning to run away? You should have warned me. I can't be blamed for this.'

Ashe's fist snapped out and caught Jackson on the nose and left cheek. It was a hard shot and Jackson crumpled backwards in shock, silent, unwanted tears mingling with the blood now pouring from his nose.

'It's your job,' Ashe reminded him, his voice ominously soft. 'Watch out for her and watch over her. It's what I pay you for.'

Jackson fished some crumpled tissues from his pocket and struggled to stem the flow from his nose.

'I can't go everywhere she goes,' he objected, his voice nasal and quivering. 'You want me holding her hand when she takes a toilet break?'

Ashe fixed fathomless eyes on him and asked, 'Where has she gone?'

'If I knew that,' Jackson responded with a gallows smile, 'I would have done my job and gone with her.'

Ashe wasn't smiling. 'She must have planned her disappearance. You must have known. You must have helped.'

'I would have told you.' Jackson spread his hands. 'I wasn't her friend. She didn't confide in me. We never had heart-to-hearts. Some days she lost me, but she always came back, so I didn't worry.'

'She lost you before? And you never thought to report this?'

'She's not a kid,' Jackson said. 'I can't control everything she does.'

'You lost her and failed to tell me!' The pupils of Ashe's eyes expanded momentarily then contracted. It was a cold, reptilian response. 'What did she tell you about her plans?'

'Nothing. I would have told you.'

'What about her friends?'

'I don't think she has any.'

'What about a boyfriend?'

'I'm not aware of one.'

'Perhaps I am looking at him.'

'Me!' Astounded by the suggestion, Jackson couldn't quite suppress a cynical smile, despite the circumstances. 'She's way past my pay grade. I'm just part of the furniture.'

Ashe nodded, as if in agreement. 'Tell me, if you are so loyal, why did *you* run away? Why didn't you tell me that she had gone?'

'I didn't know she'd gone,' Jackson protested. 'She gave me a couple of days off. I was just hanging out when your people came for me.'

Ashe was coiled like a snake. Jackson had five inches and seventy pounds on him, but Ashe was the power, and when he took a step forward Jackson twisted away and fell to the floor. He stared up, his eyes wild with fear. Already, there was a purple bruise on his face and blood flowed freely from his nose.

'I don't know where she is,' he whispered. 'Please! That's the truth! I didn't help her. I swear.'

'You helped her run and now you're helping her hide!' Ashe regarded him thoughtfully. 'I gave my word to her father. I assured him that she wouldn't be a problem. I gave my word and you've broken it for me. You understand that? You broke my word and you know what that costs?'

Jackson was sweating now as a dread premonition overtook him. 'Please! I did nothing wrong!'

'You double-crossed me.' Ashe kicked him so hard in the ribs that all in the room heard the crack of bone. 'You made me into a liar, and you haven't got the balls to admit it. Tell me where she is or die, right here, in this room.'

Sandford looked ready to intervene but Vanavasam caught his eye and smiled. It was a gesture rimmed with menace and the Alpha man didn't move.

Jackson said nothing, just groaned with pain and tried to crawl away. Ashe kicked him again, grunting with the effort, and Jackson ended up on his side, curled into a ball. Ashe stood over him, breathing hard. 'Tell me where she is!'

'She's where you won't find her.' Jackson hissed, deep resentment rolling in and out of his fear. 'Sure I helped. She asked and I helped. She's worth a million of you. She told me her father was raping her, had been for years. I told her not to tell me where she was going so I couldn't tell you.'

The tension had reached breaking point. It was as though there were just two of them in the room, Ashe and Jackson.

Ashe leant down and spat into Jackson's face. 'Tradhtar!'

'You're the traitor,' Jackson whispered. 'She trusts you. You told her you're on her side and she believed you.'

With a howl of fury, Ashe lashed out with his feet, the blows unguided and wild, striking head, back, ribs, arms, legs whatever he found. Then he stamped repeatedly on Jackson's head and torso. Finally, he grabbed Jackson by the hair, pinned him down and began pounding at his face. Jackson's screams had already turned to groans and now there was only the sound of fist on face and Ashe's grunts.

Vanavasam tried to stop him. 'Not here,' he shouted. 'Not here.'

Ashe had completely lost it. Cursing incoherently, he started hammering Jackson's head against the floor. It took the combined strength of Vanavasam and Sandford to pull him off.

Jackson lay still, lifeless, his face a bloodied and unrecognizable mush. Ashe shook the others off and took a moment to regain his breath. He stared at Sandford, his eyes empty and bottomless.

'I want the girl back here, do you understand me? Safe and untouched. How long will it take to find her?'

'I don't know.'

'That is not what I want to hear.'

Sandford kept his voice calm and spread his hands in supplication. 'If she's living in London under her own name, using her credit card and driving a car with her own licence, I will find her today. If she has changed her name and gone trekking in the Himalayas, it will take longer.'

Ashe fixed him with his murderous eyes. 'You had better pray she is not in the Himalayas.'

The meaning was clear enough and it was more than sufficient to raise every hair on Sandford's neck. Sandford believed that Ashe was Griffin but there was no certainty. He wasn't in the know. He doubted that even those who did know could be sure of their knowledge. If it were his decision, the man would already be dead. Sandford had carried out many black deeds in his time, but he was satisfied that all had been in the cause of protecting his country. But Griffin's people were gangsters, pure and simple, and Sandford felt dirty just being in the same room. Sandford's masters wanted Griffin alive for now, so the Alpha man smiled reassuringly. It took the effort of every finely tuned muscle to keep the smile on his face but he managed it.

'We will find her,' he said. 'There is no doubt about that. Even if she has changed her name, she will have to access her bank accounts. That will leave a money trail a blind man can follow. And she will be caught on CCTV. That's as good as a highlights reel.'

Ashe didn't seem bolstered by the assurances. 'She has accounts even I don't know about.' He paused, changed tack. 'People are sniffing around. The journalist, Shimmon. And now Feysor. No-one must talk to the girl. We must do anything to prevent that happening.'

Sandford frowned. 'If the girl was going to use her information, it would be in the public domain by now. And you would still be safe. You no longer exist, remember? Courtesy of HMG, your identities have been erased from official databases, Whoever you were has ceased to exist. There is no official documentation to say who you are.'

Ashe looked unimpressed. 'This reporter, Feysor. Has she had any contact with the girl?'

'No.'

'What are you doing about her?'

'She is not a problem.'

'And if she becomes one?'

'We won't allow that to happen.'

Vanavasam said, 'I will take care of this reporter.'

'No.' Ashe kept his eye on Sandford. 'We must use outsiders.'

Sandford nodded. 'We can outsource this, insulate ourselves from the kill chain. I know people. Just let me know when you want this doing.'

'That sounds like the way forward,' Ashe said approvingly. 'It is progress. Only a fool stands against progress.'

Ashe looked at his bloody hands and clothes, seeing them as if for the first time. Without a word, he went through to his bathroom and closed the door behind him, leaving his heat and anger behind like a visible presence. After a moment the shower started running.

The others waited, studiously ignoring the dead body on the floor. Sandford allowed his eyes to drift to the Tower Bridge. Backlit by the silvery-golden shimmer of sun on Thames, Wolfe-Barry's stone-clad bastions were an awe-inspiring sight. But, the beauty was clouded by the knowledge that this was a view City predators would kill for. London had become like that, a city of solitary dying, empty and angry, its poor banished and hidden, its streets threatening and void, its inhabitants waiting for something terrible to happen, while nothing happened, and nothing continued to happen. If only they knew what was being done to preserve their playground.

'I'm not against progress,' Sandford said reasonably. He knew well enough that intelligence was a filthy business where people lied and died all the time. 'We all profit from progress.'

'Not all.' Vanavasam relaxed into his chair and crossed his legs. 'Always, when there is progress, there must be losers.'

Sandford's eyes drifted to Jackson on the floor. 'I prefer to be a winner.'

Vanavasam followed his gaze. '*Koke per koke*,' he said. '*A head for a head*. Blood vengeance is the best and most dangerous intoxicant God gave to humanity.' He looked up at Sandford. 'To win,' he told him diffidently, 'you must be more ruthless than your opponent. You must do what he will not do.'

Chapter 31

ALI WAS AWOKEN by the sound of a car crunching on the gravel drive. Her father was off to work. As a home-alone teen, she would have snuggled further under the duvet and gone back to sleep. But that self-possessed teen had long gone. This was still her room, beyond question: unchanged, light, cosy and surprisingly modern. But it was no longer her nest. The thought put her in mind of one of Shimmon's favorite quotes. *No man ever steps in the same river twice, for it's not the same river and he's not the same man.* There is no going back.

A blackbird started up on the wisteria outside her window, its song pure and optimistic. A call to arms. She showered and dressed and went downstairs. Her father had left a note on the kitchen table. *Didn't want to wake you. Wonderful to see you.* She took her cereals and coffee into the conservatory that overlooked the garden. She didn't go outside. The atmosphere was fresher this morning, and quieter, but she was impatient to get back to work.

When she had finished her food, she put her crocks into the dishwasher, scribbled a note to her father and locked down the house. She drove into Winchester and bought a cell phone to replace the one corrupted by her intruder of two nights ago. In Blues, she sipped a coffee while she entered some basic data into the phone then, satisfied that she was back on the grid, she joined the London-bound traffic on the M3.

As she drove, her mind began functioning again and it struck her that what she knew of Shimmon's story was still intact. The bastards might have stolen her digital data but they hadn't wiped her brain. It was all there. Balkan war lords; money laundering; suppression of information; violent death; Figgis, Lucca, Baker and Griffin; and the rest. And there was still hard data: Fitch had her pictures of Keaton and Jones. And, if she was really lucky, Stewart had put her on the cloud.

She allowed herself a self-satisfied smile. She felt like the prodigal daughter returning. She had come close to letting the story beat her, had been ready to draw a line under it and find something safe and simple. But the tired and fearful woman who had fled London was no longer tired and no longer fearful. Her whole being was refreshed with conviction. It was an old conviction but it was as alive and keen as when it had first gripped her all those years ago. A deep, unquenchable desire for justice. She was going to find out why her friends had died and why someone was threatening her. She was going to learn the truth, track down who was behind this madness and make them pay the price.

She hadn't yet configured her new phone for voice recognition, so she pulled into the car park at Heston Services and called MacLeod.

'Malci. I need a contact in the National Crime Agency. Preferably someone in or close to the

Financial Intelligence Unit. Someone in the know but not too close to the power. Someone I can trust.'

'My dear girl, you are asking too much. If I give up the name of an informant, my sources will all slip back into the darkness.'

'I know what I'm asking, Malci. I've never asked before and I never will again. I really am that desperate.' Silence. 'I need to know who killed the investigation into First Garanty.'

'The same people who killed Stephen and would think nothing of killing you. Or me, for that matter.'

Ali let the silence drag on.

'Okay,' he resumed, 'assuming that I agree to help, how do you propose to do it? This is a secretive world protected by an industry of censorship. The laws that protect information have nothing to do with national security or confidentiality, they are there to preserve personal power and private interests. And it's not just the written press. There are internet filters in place which secretly censor all kinds of websites. You can't break this open without getting your hands dirty.'

'Malci, you are the only source I can trust.'

Macleod said nothing for a moment. 'Okay. Give me a list of questions and I'll ask my man.'

'If you do that, you become involved. Come on, Malci. Have I ever shafted you? Have you ever known me shaft anyone? It won't come back to haunt you, you have my word.'

'Your word! Oh, that's all right then.' He mulled this over, clearly unhappy that she had asked. 'Okay. Brian Kaur. He works for some ultra-secretive unit investigating this very kind of thing. Give me an hour or two to warn him.'

She killed the call then searched a couple of phone numbers. First up was Baker's office. When she introduced herself and asked for an interview, she was told that Baker only talked to the financial press, and then very rarely. When she tried to engage the receptionist in conversation, she was politely cut off. Undaunted, she called the office of Lord Figgis. A PA informed her:

'His Lordship doesn't give interviews.'

'You mean he only talks to tame journalists.'

'Not at all,' the PA informed her pleasantly. 'He has me read your newspaper every week. He loves the food and gardening articles.'

Ali rang off with a smile. She couldn't help herself. It had been the cutest of put-downs.

ON REACHING ECHO House, Ali signed out a new MacBook Pro and took the best part of two hours filling in the paperwork, configuring the machine and setting up her apps and accounts. After, she took a coffee to her pod and called down to the morgue and Fitch.

'Good morning, Ali,' he said. 'So nice of you to call.'

Under different circumstances, his curious, retro manner might have brought a fond smile but Ali was feeling too driven for such niceties. 'Any luck with those IDs?'

There was a lengthy silence. She pictured him pushing back in his chair, with his grey skin, green cardigan and reading glasses perched on the end of his nose. He was not a man to be hustled.

'Your man Keaton is ex-SAS,' he said at last. 'His army service is restricted. I would have delved deeper but you did say you're more interested in the here and now.' He waited for her grunt of confirmation. 'He left the forces in 2010, since when he has worked in private security. He did some freelance contracting in Iraq before joining Corbin Defence Services - you might know it as CDS or Delta Securities. It's a UK-based private security company offering military and personal protection services – basically, it undertakes covert, illicit operations on behalf of governments and corporations. Keaton is listed as a risk and investigations specialist. I haven't had the time to find out what that means.'

'I can hazard a pretty good guess.'

'I hesitate to ask.' He paused. 'The man you know as Jones is, indeed, a Foreign Office employee. He's listed as a B3 Operational Officer. Perhaps he is what they say he is. Perhaps he's a spook. I've someone getting back to me on that.'

'What can you tell me about Baker and Laughton?'

'I need more time for an in-depth assessment.'

'The unauthorised biography will do fine.'

Once again, the line went silent, this time for so long that Ali was beginning to think that Fitch had fallen asleep.

At last, he said, 'Kevin Baker is a board director of First Garanty Bank but he is not a banker by trade. He calls himself a financier, entrepreneur and socialite. He started out in property, made a mint, got out before the collapse in the market and moved on to venture capitalism - the *Great White* end of the market.'

'How does he link to Figgis?'

'Apart from the bank? I don't know. He is new money to his Lordship's old but they both got it the same way. His lordships' ancestors cheated, stole and murdered for theirs. Baker cheated, stole and killed for his. Baker's killings were not literal, of course, just the destruction of livelihoods. People like Baker understand that there's no level playing field. You want a break, you break it yourself.'

'Are you aware of any link between Figgis and the Kosovan mafia?'

'Figgis attracts rumour by the gigabyte. Mostly financial and political in nature. Nothing sticks. He is the true Teflon man. But links with organised crime?' He paused. 'An army of hacks have been after him at one time or another, but I've heard nothing like that.'

'There must be something.'

'He is rumoured to have been involved in various arms trade scandals that the government covered up, but there's nothing you can print.'

'Maybe that was Steven's angle. He believed Figgis channelled arms to the Kosovan paramilitaries in the Yugoslav wars. Perhaps he's still at it.'

'Perhaps.'

'I called His Lordship's office for an interview. They gave me the brush-off.' She paused. 'I need a way in. What about his wife?'

'Hard as nails. She feeds journalists to her dogs.'

'I don't like dogs.'

'There's always the back door. He is opening some charity exhibition, this week. If you could lay your hands on a ticket. . . . .'

'Okay.' She said slowly, making a mental note to source credentials. 'Tell me about Laughton.'

'Not much to tell. Old school merchant banker. A patrician who insisted that everything was done the right way. First Garanty Bank was in his family for generations before he sold it. That finished him, selling up. He never got over the humiliation. Poor fellow suffered bouts of remorse and depression. He died in a sailing accident about four months ago.'

'Accident?'

'Actually, suicide by all accounts. The accidental death verdict was cobbled together to protect the family. You think different. What do you know?'

'Nothing.' She offered him an invisible shrug. 'Have you heard of Leke Corporation?'

'You want me to dig into them?'

'You're reading me again, Fitchie.'

'You're easy.'

'And you're such a star. I owe you one.'

'You always owe me,' he chuckled. 'Trouble is, you never pay up. It's why I don't date you.'

Laughing, Ali killed the call. She logged on to the Echo's website and discovered a snippet on the TV & Showbiz page. Lord Figgis was to open the charity 'Age of Innocence' Exhibition in London. It was a ticket-only affair, set for tomorrow. Gossip had it thick with celebs.

Ali wasted no time in seeking out Annie Leigh, the Echo's entertainments editor. After a brief chat, she came to the point.

'Irvine would like me to attend tomorrow's opening of the 'Age of Innocence' Exhibition.'

'You'll be lucky. Tickets are like gold dust.'

'But you can get me one.'

Leigh studied Ali suspiciously. 'Why would you be interested in a celebrity charity do?'

Ali gave her flip. 'I'm as generous as the next person.'

Leigh scowled. 'Who are you after? If people think I'm setting them up I'll lose all my contacts.'

'No one will ever know where the ticket came from.'

'The tickets are numbered.'

'I will be doing nothing that can come back on you.'

Leigh hesitated, then said, 'I'll see what I can do.'

'Thanks. I owe you one.'

Ali returned to her desk. There was a voicemail on her office phone, the voice male, the message cryptic:

D is safe with family

She replayed the message. She couldn't quite place the voice and there was no return number. But she was elated to learn that Donylla was safe.

She had to wait a few minutes for her heart to stop racing. Then she called Kaur, Macleod's NCA contact. She was left tapping her pen for several minutes while she was passed from office to office. When, finally, Kaur did answer, his voice was deep, friendly and tired. After introducing herself, she asked what he knew about Figgis and First Garanty.

His tone switched immediately to wary. 'Nothing I can tell you.'

'Has Malci Macleod spoken to you?'

'Who?'

Momentarily thrown, Ali asked, 'Can we meet?'

'What for?' he grunted. 'I don't talk to journalists and I'm faithful to my wife.'

The line went dead.

She sighed. *So much for Macleod and his contacts.* As she replaced the handset, she sensed someone at her shoulder. It was Irvine.

'I'd like a word, Ali.'

She followed him into his office. They sat down and he said, 'I've just been told that you intend to tackle Figgis at some charity do. Why don't you just ask me to call a press conference and ritually disembowel myself?'

It was obvious that Leigh had gone straight to Irvine. Ali put aside any thoughts she might have had of mentioning the break-in at her flat.

She shook her head. 'I never said I want to *tackle* anyone.'

'Why else would you want to go?'

'It's time I talked with the man. He won't grant a formal interview so I will approach him informally. There are things I have to put to him.' Irvine glared at her as if she was the most stupid person on earth and she reacted angrily. 'We're talking moral, political and financial corruption that goes right to the rotten heart of our establishment. A London bank that's an international money laundering machine for other banks, shell companies and criminals. A political and financial mafia acting without regard for legal niceties and relying on some perverted code of omerta. Steven believed that Figgis is the key to unravelling this and I agree with him.'

'Well, bully for you.' Irvine fell silent, staring contemplatively out of the window, then brought his gaze slowly back to his reporter. 'How prepared are you? How solid is your information.'

'Solid enough.'

He studied her like he was catching her in a lie. 'You don't have shit. You're just out to provoke a response.'

'I'm just out to do my job.'

They stared at each other, neither prepared to blink.

'Working with you,' he said at last, 'is like trying to get chewing gum out of your hair. What do you know about finance?'

'This isn't about finance,' she insisted softly, just a hint of suppressed anger at his attitude. 'It's about where the money comes from and where it goes. It's about the people who own the money. It's our kind of story, John, I promise you. An exposé of the corrupt heart of our society.'

He stared at her, saw she wasn't kidding. 'There you go again with your *'corrupt heart of society'* nonsense. You are not here to judge or preach. You're a journalist not a cliche. Your job is to stay on the outside, report what you see and leave the rest to the reader.' His voice relaxed into a kindness that Ali found infuriating. 'I'm informed that you're being trolled on the internet. Abuse and fake stories. The works.'

'They're trying to frame me as some kind of conspiracy nut. It's nothing new.'

'Yes, well, some people actually believe what they read.' Pause. 'I've got the techs on it. But you've become involved, kiddo. You've fallen into the rabbit hole and entered your own story.'

'I'm as detached as ever.'

'Nothing I say to you has any influence, does it.'

Silence.

Irvine sucked in his cheeks, his eyes studying a dead space between them. Ali's resolution was deep rooted and unwavering. He understood intuitively that she would never knowingly let him down. It was the unknowing that had him worried.

'When I came into this job,' he said, 'I wanted to see something new every day and write a story on it. I wanted to tell the truth but, when it came to the critical point, I could never decide which one. You, on the other hand, are too sure. Steven was always doing this, always putting my neck on the block for a promise and a prayer. When you get absorbed in something, you just plough on regardless. You don't know when you've reached your limit.' He paused, shifted his eyes to hers. 'Be gentle with his lordship. Keep me in the picture.'

'You'll be the second to know. That's after me and before God.'

ALI WENT TO the coffee machine for a drink and some gossip relief. It was while she was there that she fielded a call from Kaur.

'I checked you out. Let's meet.'

Chapter 32

WHEN CROWDED, THE Angel was life itself - with its pimps and pushers and lost tourists - so much so that in some circles they referred to this part of Islington as angry. It was untouched by gentrification and speculation, a dangerous place to be on a Friday night. But this was the tame end of the week, music respectfully low, conversation a gentle hum, only the jarring clink of glass bottles to disturb the peace. The heat was up high, too high, but Ali liked the way the extra warmth sharpened the aroma of beer and food.

Kaur was at the bar. He was medium height, slightly overweight, with thinning hair and an easy, infectious smile. Ali's return smile was schooled by manners. It didn't touch her soul.

She bought drinks and they moved to a quiet corner and sat down.

He leaned in immediately, determined to speak first, driven by the need to voice thoughts that had been troubling him. 'I'm not in the business of selling information to the press.'

'That's good,' she replied. 'If I thought you were bent, I wouldn't be here. There are people in the Met who can't be trusted. I talk to the wrong people and I'm toast.'

He studied her carefully. 'What makes you think I'm the right people?'

'I don't.'

'But you're here anyway.'

'Yep. Right or wrong, it's too late.' There was a pause in her eyes, like a fine bead of light. 'Macleod thinks you're okay.'

He regarded her sceptically. 'These people you don't trust, do you have names?'

'No. And that's the point.'

'So they could be people I work with.' He paused again, his face conflicted. 'What's this going to cost me?'

'Nothing.' She took a sip of lager, made her pitch. 'I'm after a fair exchange of information. You're a cop. You have to follow rules. I don't, which means I can insinuate myself into places you can't. Being a cop, of course, you have the power to go where I can't. It's the perfect symbiosis.' She saw that he was unconvinced. 'Gaol before betrayal. The old mantras are best, don't you think? I've never given up a source, Nothing you tell me will ever come back to haunt you.'

'Figgis and First Garanty?' he mused. 'It would have to be so far off the record even God wouldn't hear about it.'

'This is the age of the download,' she responded, just the hint of a smile. 'Records are so twentieth century.'

The detective retreated into his beer while the journalist watched and waited. To talk or not to talk. The conundrum slowly crumpled the smile from Kaur's face. At length, his dark eyes flared in her direction.

'Okay. We'll work it this way. You give me something. I'll give you something back. Like for like. Give me value, you get value. Give me junk . . .'

' . . . I get junk. Sounds like a deal.' She paused, collected her thoughts. 'First Garanty is a conduit for institutionalized money laundering, tax evasion, accounting manipulation, and fraud on a massive scale. Kevin Baker, a director of the bank, handles these transactions through the illegal use of non-published and dormant accounts. Organised crime is involved. Certainly the Kosovan and Albanian mafia, who operate through Lord Figgis.'

He regarded her suspiciously. 'Seems to me, you already have good sources.'

She took a mouthful of lager, her gaze fixed unflinching on Kaur's face. 'Are you confirming what I have?'

His smile returned. 'Can you prove any of it?'

'Can you?'

He gave her a silent, deadpan look. She decided to up the ante, told him about the murders of Shimmon and Stewart.

Now his eyes were slits. 'And you're investigating this?' He paused; the smile had returned and Ali realized that it was just a happy genetic quirk. 'Do you think that's such a good idea?'

Ali sensed another door closing. 'Do us both a favour - if you're not going to talk, if you're just here on a fishing expedition, tell me straight out. Don't claim you know nothing of what I'm talking about. It would make you look ordinary. It would make it look like you're covering up.'

He saw the glint in her eye, and the anger and injury it represented, and knew that his presumption of some kind of moral superiority was unfair.

'We have a long-standing investigation of First Garanty,' he told her carefully. 'And its leading players. Ostensibly, the case is open but in reality it's locked away in a vault.'

'Which leading players?'

'Figgis and Baker.' He shrugged. 'Unfortunately, we have no hard evidence. The bank audits clean. The players audit clean.'

'Maybe you should audit the auditors.'

He nodded slowly. 'Maybe.'

She stared at him, gauging his reaction as she told him, 'Steven Shimmon was investigating someone called Griffin.'

A slight tightening around the eyes betrayed his surprise and interest. 'What do you know about him?'

'The name comes up from time to time but I can't find the man to go with it.'

'We believe that Griffin is a code name for a major organised crime player, though it could be code for his organisation. We're not sure. What I do know is that when we started taking an interest in this Griffin we were warned off.'

'Who by?'

'Our friends at Thames House.' Contempt and bitterness laced his words. 'Apparently, we were impinging on matters of national security. Ours is a joint op with MI5 but that counts for nothing. There is intelligence that they refuse to share.'

'If they tell just anybody,' she said ironically, 'it wouldn't be a secret, would it?'

He gave her another smile, but she could see the contempt, the cynicism, the anger behind it. 'For years now, we've been aware of large sums of money being channelled into enterprises across the globe. The sources of this money are unknown, the destinations both legit and otherwise. Our Financial Intelligence Unit has picked up enough broken threads to suggest at least one serious player. We think that someone is Griffin.'

'So Griffin is real.'

'If he is, Griffin is not his real name.'

'But he is real.'

Kaur shrugged 'It's hard to live off the grid. A trail of records follows us from birth. Of course, it's possible to create a new identity, but you can't exist without being on some database or other - Inland Revenue, Social Security, NHS, PNC, DVL, bank. These databases talk to each other all the time. We can find out everything about everyone - medical, financial, criminal, internet, telecoms. I can find out what you buy at the supermarket, so how come we can find nothing on this Griffin?'

Ali didn't know what to think. She decided that it didn't matter for the moment. Focus on what you know. 'What about Figgis and the Kosovan mob?'

'We had files connecting Figgis with the Kosovans since the mid-nineties. MI5 took the lot.'

'But you remember what was in them, right? Did Mergim Lucca rate a mention?'

'Lucca was something else.' Kaur said it with a kind of grudging admiration that made her uncomfortable. 'Kosovo has been under the heel of criminals since antiquity, but it was always local, clannish, inward-looking. Forget the Sopranos and Armani suits, think Gomorrah and survival of the fittest. These were small gangs of illiterate losers. Their bosses kept control through brute force and treachery.' He took a long drink of lager. 'After the collapse of the Soviet Union, and the subsequent break-up of Yugoslavia, the Kosovan mafia became a problem to the rest of us, and that was all down to Lucca. Lucca thrived by the sword then died by the sword. By the time of his death, he had built an international crime empire that made Don Corleoni look like a corner boy. The Kosovans now have links with the Albanian mafia who control much of our drugs trade. *The Evil Empire is dead, long live The Evil Empire!*' Kaur looked defeated. 'We believe Griffin to be Lucca's spiritual heir. His name – whatever it is - has been polished clean by success, the move into legitimacy and the passage of time. His blood has turned from red to blue. He no longer gets his hands dirty. If someone crosses him, he uses lawyers, PR agencies and private security companies to clean up for him.'

'And Figgis?'

'He's what we call a clean associate. He won't set up a deal or muscle into a business, but he invests for guys like Griffin. He's a pillar of the establishment. Protected. Closely protected. We've been trying to get him for years, without success. He audits clean.'

'You really must get yourself new auditors.' She paused for thought then asked, 'Does this involve the illegal arms trade?'

'It's part of it.' That caution again. 'Why do you ask?'

'Shimmon thought Lucca was killed to cover up links with HMG, probably concerning illegal arms deals.'

Worry registered heavily on Kaur's face. 'The arms business is very ethical these days. You can't just hawk weapons to dictators and guerrillas off the back of a lorry. But the arms trade is a complex and murky affair. You have the above board trade, which ostensibly is both legally and morally okay, and the below board trade, which is both illegal and immoral. In between are the grey areas, which are legally and morally questionable. We believe that Figgis and his associates are involved in all three areas. Therein lies the problem. Investigate the illegal trade and you end up investigating the legal and then you get shut down.'

'How does that happen?'

'The Government is an active player in the legal side, via the Defence Export Services. The DES is part of the MoD and is a marketing tool for the British Arms industry. The biggest customers are Saudi Arabia, the US, Malaysia, Pakistan, India and Afghanistan. Our investigations have shown that Figgis has acted as an agent to pay the bribes that grease many of these sales.'

'Using First Garanty?'

He nodded. 'We actually have the proof of that but no mandate to use it. Our investigation has been stopped in the national interest.'

Ali said, 'Are you prepared to give me any evidence?'

His cell phone trilled and he reached into his pocket.

'This is a seriously dodgy area, Ali. Last year, a French arms inspector uncovered illegal arms sales to Iran and Iraq. High-level politicians were receiving millions in kickbacks. The guy was murdered. execution style, and his evidence was *lost*.'

She let out a deep breath. 'So what's your answer?'

' . . . His murder was a clear message to others like him, people like you and me: back off. Excuse me.'

He took his call. As he listened, his features tautened and his eyes began darting about them. He spoke tersely. When he rang off, he looked concerned.

'I'm afraid we'll have to continue this conversation another time. I'll call you.'

Without another word, he pushed his chair back, rose abruptly to his feet and walked out of the pub.

Ali watched him go with sinking heart. There was so much she hadn't asked about. Shimmon's police contacts. Leke Corporation. The list would have kept them there until closing time. Kaur's sudden departure could have been official, an urgent shout perhaps, or a family crisis, but she didn't think so. Someone had got to him, which meant that he was blown. Either Kaur was being watched or she was. Either way, this particular source had gone for good.

Chapter 33

NADIA SHUCKED HER fleece jacket and hung it over the back of her chair, revealing a cool-grey, sleeveless T-shirt designed to show off her sculpted body. Rachel took in the lean and powerful arms and shoulders, and the admiring glances they attracted from around the bar, and a glint of devilment entered her eyes.

'Since I'm stuck with you,' she said, 'I think I'll adopt you as my personal trainer. Getting ripped might help attract the guys.'

Nadia shook her head. 'You'll just frighten off the good guys.'

Rachel looked around them. 'They don't look frightened to me.'

'Don't let that fool you. Who, in their right mind, wants a gym bitch? Dehydrated, curveless, breastless, front-loaded with carbs, not a hint of sensuality. Why would a cute girl do that to herself just to get a man?'

'It suits you well enough.'

'It happens to be my thing: fitness, martial arts, travelling and beating up on perverts.'

'Beating up on perverts?' Rachel giggled. She was powerless to stop herself. She couldn't recall being so carefree and it wasn't just the alcohol. Truth be told, she had never had a close girl friend. She had always considered herself to be an independent spirit who enjoyed her freedom and cringed in the face of intimacy. When she had first learned that Nadia was to stay with her, she had been dismayed. But spending time with her minder had exposed her self-image as delusional. She was no free spirit, singular, content to roam the world alone. She was a prisoner. Protected. Watched. Leashed. And lonely. The more she let Nadia in, the more she understood that she hadn't been doing so well in solitude.

According to her Guardian Angel, her father's people had no idea that she was in New York. On hearing that, Nadia judged it safe to explore their neighbourhood. Hannigans was their nearest bar, a five minute walk away. Until recently, it had been Fenians, an emerald green gin palace, all rebel songs, nightly fist fights and weekly collections for the killers back home. Now it was an Irish theme pub: plastic shillelaghs, Victor McClaglen look-a-likes and the Corrs on the juke box. Danny Boy had left the stage and trendy young couples had taken the place of cloth-capped old men.

'I've spent my life being a sheltered little girlie girl,' Rachel explained, 'and I've never met the right guy. Beefing up might change my luck.'

'The right guy?' Nadia turned her head to one side and made gagging noises. 'This is the twenty-first century, kid. People don't *fall in love,* they have sex. I mean, get real. You're in New York, a city renowned for fabulous orgasms. Believing in love is about as plausible as believing in UFOs, or Jesus Christ.'

'I believe in Jesus.'

'Then you're beyond all hope.' Nadia shrugged. 'I guess I was as green as you at some time in my life. Although . . . maybe not. You've seen the way the world works, Rachel. How can you be that innocent?'

'I've seen the world alright,' Rachel said mordantly. 'Motels, rented houses, holiday villas. But only from the inside. Like a perpetual tourist who never leaves the bus. We've got estates all over the world but we just rotate from place to place. None of these places is *home*.' She stopped to take a drink, changed her mind. 'As I grew older, I realised we were actually on the run. Nobody would tell me why, or what from. I had to learn that for myself by snooping around my father's office.' She offered Nadia a bitter smile. 'Now I'm on the run for real.'

Another pause. This time, Rachel took that drink. Nadia, precluded by training and inclination from intruding into another's private thoughts, waited patiently for her to continue.

Eyes hooded, Rachel said, 'I swore to myself that when I was old enough I would have my own home and stay there until I die. I'd have my own friends, my own pets, my own family, and I'd keep them safe.'

She stopped as something inside tightened, her eyes misted and her heart went everywhere. *How do you keep a family safe?* She had trusted her father to do it and he had murdered his own wife and children.

That, she reminded herself, was the reason she never formed attachments.

They only betray you, those nearest to you.

But, though she knew the truth of it, she couldn't say it.

Nadia watched her struggling and stepped in. 'You know, I think you're right about the personal training gig. You're tougher than you look. A hard body would fit well on you. You can start working out with me in the morning.'

'*With* you! I'd be dead in five minutes.'

'I'll start off slow.'

'You'd have to start backwards.'

Chapter 34

WILLESDEN GREEN POLICE station resembled a faded Victorian elementary school, so unassuming that only those in the know could find it first time. Long redundant, it was undergoing death by slow closure. Hence its peeling paint, dirty floors, desperate graffiti and, most telling of all, skeleton staff.

Ali had been invited here by a man calling himself DI Coates for an informal chat about her meet with Kaur. The invitation had come by phone, just twelve hours after Kaur had so abruptly exited the Angel. On another day, she might have exercised sounder judgement and shied away. But, this time, she had gladly accepted. How else would she get a chance to probe these people? Anticipating a freer conversation without a nagging legal presence, she had even kept the Echo and its lawyers in the dark,

The custody suite was small, cold and under-occupied. Two detectives were waiting for her, an older guy, dark and balding, with the body of a rugby forward going to seed, and a younger guy, slighter and with a full head of ash blond hair, Outsiders, she guessed, too full of self-importance to have called this inconsequential place home. Which meant they were here for the same reason as her: to stay off the record.

The older man shook her hand. 'DI Coates. This is DS Pearson. Thank you for coming in.'

'Thank you for inviting me.'

Coates blinked at her unexpected reply. 'I'm afraid you will have to leave your bag and phone at the counter. Edicts from the bureaucrats cannot be ignored.'

Ali took in his irony and thought about contesting the regulations, then questioning Coates' interpretation, but decided that protest would be futile. She carefully checked her bag and its contents and exchanged them for a receipt which she stuffed into her pocket.

Coates led the way to an interview suite, four rooms that opened onto a common area furnished with grubby and stained sofas. Coates looked into each room, rejected the first three and accepted the fourth with a look of grim resignation. It was depressingly dull but its blue walls and tiled floor were reasonably clean. The table and shelves were dark walnut and the Captain chairs had leather seats and backs with wheels that still turned. A grey, amorphous light came from overhead strips that were choked with cobwebs and dust, and from a window, the bottom half of which had been painted over. Through the window bars, she could see the light of the sun reflecting off an adjacent office block.

Ali looked about them. 'Wow! I've been into some time warps, but this! . . . When does Sherlock Holmes appear?'

Coates shrugged. 'As you can see, the building is undergoing closure. We could have chosen a more pleasant venue but this gives us the best guarantee of privacy. Please, take a seat.'

Coates and Ali sat on opposite sides of the table while Pearson stood by the door, as if he expected her to make a break for freedom. There was a moment of silence as they appraised each other. They could hear voices in the suite outside, amplified by emotion and poor acoustics, the drone of the elevator rising and falling, and traffic outside on the A407.

Coates gave her a friendly smile. 'I'd offer you coffee but you might say yes. I hear the machine's not working.'

'No doubt your new offices will have coffee on tap, bowling alleys, hammocks and inter-floor slides.'

Coates allowed himself the ghost of a smile. 'Only the IT suite.'

The two men watched her silently. Ali knew all about interviewing techniques, knew that they were waiting her out, so she wasted no time before speaking. 'Okay. What am I doing here?'

'We have some questions.'

'That much I guessed.'

'I believe you met with DS Brian Kaur last night. As you are probably aware, DS Kaur is attached to a special unit working on matters of national security.' He waited for Ali to reply but she kept her counsel. 'What you probably don't know is that DS Kaur is under investigation for various security breaches. You, I hasten to add, are not a part of the investigation. Not yet. However, we would like you to tell us what was said at your meeting.'

She tapped the empty desk. 'No recorder. Has your colleague got an audiographic memory? Is that why he's gone into a mute state by the door?'

'I thought it would be better to keep this chat informal and off the record.'

'Better for whom? The recording is there to give me protection.'

'Do you need protection? If you are worried about self-incrimination, we can always send for your brief.'

She shrugged away the suggestion. 'You're not Met,' she said. 'So who are you?'

'SO15 at your service.'

'SO15? Counter Terrorist Command?' She gave him a curious look. 'There are terrorists out there planning real attacks, people with knives, bombs and cars, and you want to talk to me! If there's a law against having a drink with one of your buddies, I haven't heard about it.'

Coates stared back. 'Why did you meet with DS Kaur?'

'To share a drink and a chat. Why else do people go to the pub?'

'What did you talk about?'

'That would make you blush.'

'I asked you a serious question.'

'In that case, I gave you a serious answer.'

He shrugged, as though unfazed by her attitude. 'I would like to establish a basis of trust so I am going to be as forthcoming as I can. But first, I must have your assurance that what is said here will stay between us.'

'Between you, me and the reading public. You have my word on it.'

Coates rolled his eyes as if he was dealing with an antsy teen. 'We know that you've been contacted by individuals who are feeding you fantasies with lies. These people are a danger to the security of the state. We would like your cooperation in bringing them to justice.'

'If you mean people like Harry Figgis, I would be delighted to help.'

He put on a hurt expression, as though she was deriding him. 'You're not the first journalist to go after his Lordship. He is off limits to you or anyone else. Lord Figgis is ours. Poke into his affairs and we will hit you with a PII Certificate.'

'A Public Interest Immunity Certificate?' She didn't conceal her surprise. 'You're protecting Lord Figgis?'

'He has business and political contacts in the Arab world that are of paramount importance to the security of this country.' Coates kept his face neutral, but his eyes were liquid nitrogen set behind a thin film of ice. 'By attacking him, you threaten the integrity of those contacts and undermine the interests of the state.'

'If Figgis and his kind are clean, there is no way I can hurt them. But if they're mired in their own filth! . . !'

The cold film seemed to be spreading over his face. 'Mud sticks if thrown. You could do real damage to London's financial institutions. Bring them down and you bring down the whole country.'

'Oh My God!' Ali almost giggled at the thought. 'You think little ole me is going to bring down the country?'

His face darkened, allowing Ali an unwelcome glimpse of crumpled fatigue. 'You've been asking about something called Operation Mammon. It has been established that there was no such thing.'

She shrugged. 'So why are you tapping my phone and intercepting my emails? I do hope you have a warrant, by the way.'

He ignored her words, neither confirming nor denying her accusation. 'The MoD conducted an exhaustive investigation of Lucca's death and found absolutely no evidence of British involvement.'

'The MoD investigated themselves and pronounced themselves clean. That's reassuring. According to my sources, the investigation was snagged.'

Coates sighed. 'The investigation lasted a total of three months and involved a team of senior investigative officers from the military police. Their findings were scrutinised by a Board of senior officers and MoD and FCO personnel. Hardly perfunctory, Ali. Not a single allegation, or document, held up to scrutiny. The investigators talked to dozens of servicemen and locals in the search for witnesses. There was no truth in any of the allegations of British involvement.'

'So why the cover up?'

'There is no cover up.'

'Let me put it another way: who would hope to gain by setting up Steven Shimmon?'

'Shimmon had a reputation for unimpeachable integrity. If he were to write a story about NATO countries working secretly against each other, it would carry genuine credibility. It would create a rift in the alliance. At bottom, this is all about geopolitics. The

Russians are hell-bent on breaking up NATO and the EU.'

She pulled a dead mask over her concern and said, 'The Russians set Stephen up? I don't think so. He was too experienced to fall for that kind of bullshit. He had real contacts. He checked and rechecked his sources ad nauseum.'

'Nevertheless, he was set up.' Coates waited for her reaction. When none came, he ploughed on. 'A source told him that Figgis was dealing with the Balkan mafia, channelling money on behalf of HMG for weapons deals and working against the interests of our NATO allies. The source seemed genuine enough. He even had documentation to back up his story. But the documents were skilful forgeries. This source wrapped enough truth inside the lie to make it believable. He even put Shimmon in touch with other sources who confirmed the story.'

Ali had an empty feeling, like she was consuming sugared confections. 'So who killed my friends?'

'Shimmon was mugged in Kosovo. I'm told they have made an arrest in that case. As for your friend, Stewart? The police have concluded it was a robbery gone wrong.'

'We both know that's bollocks.'

He opened his hands and shrugged: he didn't care whether she believed him or not. 'You are like a child throwing stones into a pool, causing ripples for the hell of it. But you are compromising a lengthy and complex investigation that is vitally important to the security of this country. '

She paused, let her puzzlement show. 'How does my investigation compromise yours?'

Coates appraised her as though she was leading contender for the world's most stupid woman. 'You don't do investigations.'

She smiled. 'Then what are we doing here?'

'Tell me about Kaur.'

'I really have nothing to tell you.'

'If you prefer,' he snapped, 'we can take you to a secure nick and hold you until you grow a beard. Let's see how tough you are when you're carrying your shit in a bucket.'

'Very tough if it's my own shit,' she told him with an amused glint.

There was a conciliatory pause. Coates' eyes were tired and angry, his suit rumpled, like he'd been sitting in his car all night, but he was quickly back in control of himself. Pearson was watching her carefully with eyes that were relaxed and curious. Nothing about the body language of the two men was threatening.

Coates said, 'Let's try again.'

Ali had allowed herself to drift into provocative mood. 'If the reason I am here is because I'm doing a better job that you, then I'd be seriously embarrassed about that. Shouldn't you people be leading not following?'

Coates' voice grated with suppressed but genuine anger. 'Help us out. Stay away from this. Otherwise, you will sabotage a lot of hard work and help the bad guys.'

'I've never been into helping the bad guys. But someone killed my friends and I'm going to find out who was responsible. If it turns out to be the people you're protecting then don't stand in my way.'

'I'm telling you straight: rein yourself in.'

'Who are you protecting? It has to be someone more powerful than Figgis. I'm told he is a bit player.'

Coates' face hardened and she wondered if she had pushed too hard. She recalled the killer in Kosovo and began to sweat. She reacted to her fear in her usual way by pushing the boat further out.

'Is it Griffin?'

His face was unmoved but his eyes flickered with concern. 'What do you know about Griffin?'

She saw his interest, went coy. 'It's just a name I've come across.'

'In what context?'

She shrugged as if it was too trivial to remember. 'Is Griffin under investigation by the Security Service?'

'Not to my knowledge.'

'Is he a terrorist?'

Coates stared at her for a moment. 'The terrorism that worries us is down the line. Figgis is being targeted by people who seek to damage our economic and political influence in the Middle East. They want to turn the Muslim world against us, bringing Jihad and economic attack. The Americans and their friends the Saudis and Israelis are behind this. It is imperative that we insulate ourselves from this whole sordid affair. We need to get you on board before it's too late.'

She laughed, genuinely amused. 'You want me on board? You've cited as enemies the Middle East, NATO, the Russians, the EU, the Americans, Saudis, Israelis. The whole world is out to get us and you need *me* on board. Am I missing something here?'

'You have a reputation for missing nothing.'

She smiled and shook her head.

Coates studied her, his expression disappointed. 'I'm trying to play square with you, Ali, but if you're not smart enough to listen, there are other ways I can solve the problem.'

'Like you did with Shimmon?'

'That had nothing to do with us. But it could happen to anyone. Even you.'

A throbbing started in her head, quickly spread to her shoulders and arms. Ali had been leaned on all her working life and she sensed something deeper at play. They wanted her out of the way but she didn't know why. Unfortunately for them, shutting her out was the worst thing they could do - they were just inciting her to discover who and what they were protecting. And she would keep digging to find it. She swallowed her anger and spoke slowly.

'Do what you must. But, next time, make it official. Contact the paper and go through the Editor and lawyers.'

'That's your stance? Then we have nothing else to talk about.'

'Can I go?'

'Of course. What kind of people do you take us for?'

'What kind of people are you?'

Back at the counter, Ali handed over her receipt, collected her bag and glanced at Pearson.

'That went well,' she said.

Pearson ignored her. Ali noticed that her bag had been opened and her tech tampered with. That didn't surprise her. She held up her phone and Macbook.

'They're new,' she told them helpfully. 'All apps and no data.'

'You take care now,' Coates told her sourly. 'Don't get stopped for a traffic violation. You might find yourself doing gaol time in Pakistan, or Egypt.'

AS PEARSON LED her out of the building, a balding, fair-haired man in a designer suit joined Coates in the crumbling custody suite.

'What do you think?' Coates asked.

Sandford thought for a moment, staring through the door as though Ali had left a noxious vapour trail.

'That woman,' he said softly, 'that woman is definitely a loose cannon.'

Chapter 35

'WE WILL SUPPORT you with any story, Ali. That goes without saying.' Gordon Whitford was Irvine's boss, the Echo's Executive Editor. In trying to sound reasonable, he was coming across as insincere. 'But you seem to be on a mission with this! SO15! That's Counter Terrorist Command! Whatever you've got yourself into, you can't be taking on those boys. They thrive on collateral damage. You are putting all of our heads on the line!'

'They were after an information exchange. Off the record.'

Whitford snorted disparagingly. 'People like that are trained to extract information without you even realising. They are never off the record.'

They were in Irvine's office, Ali, Irvine and Whitford, and Ali was reporting back on her encounter with SO15. Beyond the glass walls of Irvine's office, the eyes and ears of the newsroom were straining their way. Ali knew that the glass was soundproof but she was instinctively holding her voice under.

'Nor am I,' she said softly. 'I more than held my own.'

'Who is to say?'

Irvine noticed the heat of anger spreading upwards from Ali's neck and intervened before she could cut loose.

'Good stories don't write themselves, Gordon. We all have to jump off a cliff every now and then.'

Whitford nodded like he would happily join the lemming club. 'We're not asking you to give up the story. Just play it smart. Give it the right spin.'

Ali spoke softly, her anger under control. 'What are you saying, exactly?'

'Steer clear of those people.' Whitford kept his tone reasonable, like he was trying to calm a mad woman. 'I appreciate your ability to bring in some very good stories, Ali, but the Echo Group thrives because every employee understands that they are part of the whole. If one of us has a problem, we all have a problem. You've a brilliant future. You just have to think of the big picture, play the game right.'

An involuntary scowl creased her features. Play the game right meant put up with the shortcomings of colleagues. Relish the fish-and-chip world of routine hack work. Tolerate sexism and jealousy. Back-stab peers and brown-nose superiors. And, above all, keep the stories inoffensive.

'Fine,' she said. 'You write me an outline and I'll fill it in.'

'Now, now. Don't go hysterical on me.' Whitford removed his spectacles and began polishing them furiously on his silk handkerchief. 'No investigation can be *sui generis*. Ours is a world of shrinking sales and diminishing margins. Cost-efficiency is the watchword. Administrators are running things now, kids fresh out of post-graduate Management School.'

He replaced his spectacles. If anything, they made his eyes harder. 'It would hurt your career to push on with this.'

'Gordon,' Irvine cut in, his voice hard and unyielding. 'If you are trying to kill my story, why don't you come right out and tell me!'

Whitford sat back, surprised by the tone of Irvine's intervention. 'All I'm saying is, you've painted yourself into a corner but you don't have to stay there. Just sit back, wait for the paint to dry and walk out of there.'

'This is a strong story, Gordon.' Cold fury touched Irvine's voice. 'As strong as we've ever had. I expect full backing from you and the Executive Board. If we don't write it, someone else will. Someone with a boss sporting bigger balls.'

A bitter, Siberian chill ran through the room. Whitford's head began twitching like Shifty Harry. He picked up his briefcase, came to his feet and smiled down at Ali. 'You have my full support, of course. But tread very carefully in this. Step on something that bites and you'll find yourself all alone.'

Ali watched him go, asked, 'Did I hear what I think I heard?'

Irvine nodded. 'If this goes wrong, you won't get a job writing for the parish magazine. In fact, we'll all go down. Mutually Assured Destruction in 72 font.' He grunted dismissively. 'The question is, kiddo, what are you trying to do here?'

'My job.'

'Sure. But is your priority bringing in the story or proving that you're tough enough to do it.' She glared at him, as if contemplating a particularly choice response, but she said nothing. He shook his head sadly. 'If you cooperate with nefarious people in destroying yourself, that's not integrity, kiddo. It's false pride.'

'I'm just trying to get to the truth.'

He smiled wanly. 'There's the things people want to hear, the things they want to believe, the things they want you to know, and, somewhere at the back of the line, there's the truth.'

'I'm doing what I believe in, John. It's why I sleep at night.'

'You don't sleep nights, Ali. You just haunt the dark hours in search of your next victim. It's who you are.'

Neither said anything for a while. They slipped into uneasy self-censorship until, eventually, Irvine broke their silence.

'You need hard facts. A piece based on *sources allege* will be no good for me.'

'Now you're trying to insult me.'

'No. I'm asking if you have the goods.' He paused for the reply that didn't come. 'I need a real story, Ali, gritty, with breadth and depth and names.'

'You'll have it.'

He nodded again. 'Sorry I got on your case. They want me to put a gun to your head. If you don't bring this in, and I mean quickly, they're going to make me pull the trigger.' He paused, changed tack. 'Don't let the story eat you up. Sometimes you just have to leave the bad guys to drown in their own shit.'

She maintained an injured silence.

Exasperated, he said, 'There's no point talking to you. You hear nothing I say. You're a good woman, and I love you. But you've got this fucking story in your gut like a cancer. It could mean your life!'

'It is my life.'

'What is it about being told to back off that makes you not want to back off?'

'I can't not care, John,' she told him resentfully, her voice straining as her anger rose again. 'If I stop caring, I stop being who I am. If I can't do this my way, I can't get it done. If the good old boy wants to keep the little woman in her place he's got the wrong little woman! Do what you have to do, John! Back me or sack me!'

'Ali!' His tone was soft, injured.

'What?' She almost shouted it.

'Please don't give yourself a stroke.'

She fell absolutely silent, and then she laughed. So did Irvine. Her eyes shone with a mist of tears but his eyes shone with another light, a ferocious twinkle of anger. His anger was self-directed. He bitterly regretted his decision to ask her to finish Shimmon's story. Shimmon had been his friend but Irvine the newsman could set a friend's death to one side. Ali, however, didn't have that kind of perspective. He should have known that the story would absorb her, that her obsessive determination would make her impossible to deal with until she had put the story to bed. Nothing existed for her but to find out what had happened. And, somewhere in the quest, she would take risks that, to his way of thinking, were utterly gratuitous.

He said, 'If you're even half right about these killings . . .'

'I'm *all* right!'

'Please Ali. No more crazy risks.'

'I won't even blink without a risk assessment,' she informed him gently. 'That's a promise.'

Irvine looked her in the eye for what seemed like an eternity. Then he spoke in that soft voice again. 'If you want me to swallow that, I'll swallow it. I'm behind you.'

'Fine. But how far behind?'

He ignored her jibe. 'You need some protection.'

'Now you're being absurd. I will not be hidebound by some Minder.'

'Sometimes, Ali, you break my heart.' Irvine flipped his pen back and forth in his hand. 'You keep me informed. You fucking keep me up-to-date.'

'Point taken,' she said, her voice carefully controlled. 'And I'll watch my budget.'

SHE TOOK THE stairs to the morgue. Fitch wasn't there. He had taken a day's leave. Macleod's police contact, Kaur, wasn't returning her calls. Today was going to hell.

Needing a private space to think, she took up temporary residence in a toilet cubicle. She had performed mental somersaults in an attempt to understand why so much of what she knew didn't add up. She had tried logic and free-thinking, now she was looking for some magical toilet revelation. It was time to go back to Plato's first principal of investigation: to find out what the investigation was about. She couldn't believe that she was this far in and still didn't *know*. She had read somewhere that to know that you do not know is the beginning of wisdom. Right now, she must have been the wisest human on Earth.

She had started out investigating a conspiracy to cover up the past - the British government getting into bed with the Kosovan mafia and sabotaging NATO.

Then she had moved on to the present - Figgis, money laundering, Griffin and organised crime. It seemed blindingly obvious that past and present were interlinked but where was the evidence? She had punched all the right buttons and asked good questions, yet she still had no hard leads. The more she learned the less she knew and the less she liked it.

Maybe it really was time to give it up. *You can never solve them all.* Shimmon had drummed that into her as an Intern. But she knew that he had never believed that. He had never given up on a story, convinced that, if he was intelligent and diligent and lucky enough, he would break the story open. If all else failed, he would throw stones into the pond and wait for something to happen.

She had followed Shimmon's path into the story and been led nowhere. But the story had lodged like a splinter in her mind and become her own. It was time for a new path. She could have done with an insider. Any whistle-blower would do, a backstabber, a do-gooder, a gold digger. But, as with everything else in this damn story, she was right out of luck. Intelligence and diligence had also failed her. That left her with one alternative: to throw larger stones into the pond.

Starting tonight, at the 'Age of Innocence'.

Chapter 36

THE *AGE OF* Innocence exhibition, a fund-raiser of photographic images for the Figgis' children's charity, 'Innocence', was being organised by Ciros Fine Arts Gallery. Currently the hottest gallery in town, Ciros was housed in a building of indeterminate lineage behind Cadogan Street. Its prestige and influence had been built on aggressive marketing of the most talented and prodigious artists, and it boasted exhibition rooms, bookshop, coffee shop, library, print salesroom, and a database of moneyed punters that would grace anyone's Rich List.

Ali entered the tiny reception hall and flashed her Guest ticket. The lift was up, so she took the stairs, emerging to find the Gallery awash with people. It was Godfather III without the pizza, a cameo of politicos, nouveau riche, models and actors. Another time, she might have felt self-conscious, adrift in this conspicuous display of high fashion. Dressed in white blouse and black skirt, she wasn't exactly glammed-up. But she was working and, anyway, no one was paying her any heed. The atmosphere was too sulky for that. And artisan. Yes, sulky and artisan, though the only people she could see working, apart from security and catering, were the escorts. Young women in short dresses and high heels and younger men with fuck-me-now expressions hung on every word and gesture of their benefactors without so much as a glance at anyone else. They knew the price of a meal ticket.

She spied Figgis. Tall, with a profoundly vertical and dignified carriage, he had a narrow frame, long face, prominent nose and seemingly endless jaw, all topped by a mound of greyish blue hair that matched his eyes. He wore a dark blue suit and a Guards tie. Ali noted with some distaste the regard with which he was treated, the warm handshakes, the pats on the shoulder, the smiles of goodwill from people who should have known better. Then she saw Whitford and Annie Leigh among the well-wishers. The Echo's Executive Editor was doffing his cap with the best of them. Quickly, she backed out of his line of sight.

She was here with one purpose: to get Figgis alone and put him on the spot. But she had no idea how she was going to do it. While she tried to come up with a plan, she wandered the exhibition. It was tasteful enough. There were a few images of children at play, untainted by adult rapacity, set as counterpoint to the main project, which depicted the hollow eyes and artless smiles of the exploited - the child workers, the sick and dying, the deprived, abused and prostituted. Ali couldn't fathom why or how the children managed to conjure smiles for the camera. Some viewers might have seen hope in the happy expressions, but not Ali. She read their eyes and knew that these kids were fully aware of how pathetic and hopeless they were. At some time, they must have caught a glimpse of a better life, because there could be no suffering without comparison.

Ali turned away and found herself inspecting a curious mahogany and wrought iron sculpture that defied interpretation. She studied it from all angles but couldn't decide what it was. She even tried emptying her mind, letting it wash into her. Still nothing.

A voice interrupted her reverie, sonorous, with perfect diction. 'Fascinating, eh?'

It was Figgis. He had slipped his functionaries and come to her. He clutched a glass of wine in each hand, one of which he proffered to Ali.

'Thank you but no,' she said. With some difficulty, she pulled a veil of disinterest over her eager excitement. 'Do you know what this is supposed to be?'

He spared her a little sideways glance and smile. 'If you have to ask, you'll never know.'

'Meaning you don't know either.' He didn't respond. She shrugged cynically. 'I suppose you have to give the artist credit for putting up.'

He smiled knowingly. 'Do you think any of them care about the exploitation of children? They were persuaded here by the free publicity. It's amazing what aristocracy can achieve, even in the twenty first century. How else would you gather together so many backstabbers, debauchers, and thieves whose only devotion is to themselves.'

'You shouldn't take it so seriously,' she counselled him. 'It's only art.'

'Pardon me,' he retorted, actually put out, 'but that's like dismissing sex. Art is a mind fuck - purest of sensual perceptions, the purest of pleasures.'

'Art is polite stupidity feeding on deception.' She spelt it out carefully, as though incredulous that he couldn't see it. 'How does that match up to a passionate exchange of body fluids?'

He grinned lasciviously. 'You're a strange one, Ali Feysor.' He sipped some wine and smacked his lips. 'Most people I can read like the proverbial book, but you! . . . You're a walking enigma.'

She said nothing, just smiled as though he had complimented her on her dress sense.

Lady Paula Figgis came to the dais and the hubbub in the room died down. Half the age of her husband, she was petite and slim, with an elusive, androgynous beauty. She was dressed to look vulnerable, in a teasing pink shift, yet she was glancing around the assembly like an impatient headmistress waiting for silence. Satisfied that she had the attention of her audience, she began her appeal.

Ali was not one for speeches at the best of times, and this was close to being the worst. She briefly considered grilling Figgis here and now. After all, wasn't that what she had come for? But there were too many people within earshot, people more interested in an exchange between Figgis and a journalist that they could ever be in an appeal for largesse. She groaned inwardly. Coming here was just another in the litany of inconsequential inquiries and dead ends. Frustrated, she started weighing her chances of slipping away, unseen.

As if sensing her intention, Figgis placed his arm across her shoulders. He was almost a head taller than she.

'You've got to hand it to Paula,' he whispered. 'She's bloody good at this. Do you think she should go into politics?'

'Why? Is she thinking about it?'

'Search me.' He shrugged teasingly. She stepped clear of him and he gave her that sideways smile again. 'Should I have you removed?'

'I have an invitation.'

'Not from me.' He studied her, curious. 'You're not interested in child soldiers or our friends from the glitterati. You're here in search of lies.'

'I'm here to talk to you,' she smiled sweetly, as if agreeing with his sentiment. 'Privilege of the profession.'

His eyes probed her own - icy, iniquitous, harbouring thoughts of a kind she didn't want to guess at.

He said, 'I think it's time we had a chat, you and I. Off the record, of course.' He imbued the word *chat* with all kinds of meanings, casting her as an enemy, friend, predator and victim. He added, 'Ten minutes.'

With that, he walked away.

THERE WAS A small lounge behind the gallery offices. A quirky room, with a catholic mix of leather and brocade sofas, rainbow cushions, and shaggy rugs, all chosen randomly on the simple rationale of personal preference and comfort. It was as if someone - presumably the owner of Ciros - needed a refuge from the stark minimalism of the gallery outside. All that was missing were Beatrix Potter prints on the walls and soft toys on the furniture.

Figgis was alone, standing against the window and staring out over the heart of Chelsea. They were just around the corner from Kings Road and Sloane Street, but this was rear window land, a far cry from the Village's high-roll ambience of designer fashions, bars and coffee houses. He heard Ali come in and spoke without turning.

'It's strange, but I never feel at home in London. Whenever I'm in town, I just long to be back in the country.'

Ali shrugged. 'I'm the opposite. I hate the countryside. It always seems so dead.'

Figgis turned to face her. 'In the country, death is a natural part of life. Here, life is just a part of dying.'

Ali blinked. She thought she understood. Figgis motioned her to sit down, then selected a chair opposite her. Seated, he looked even taller than his six foot four; His face transformed itself into a smiling, disingenuous countenance, the light in his eyes deliberately unfocused, the lips parted solicitously.

'I can't begin to think why an investigative reporter such as yourself would be interested in me.'

'I didn't know I was.' She tried to hold her eyes dispassionately on his and concentrated on her single objective: to leave a tangle of snakes in his head. She offered him her best professional smile. 'Should I be?'

He ignored her question. 'They tell me that you're looking into the untimely death of your colleague, Steven Shimmon.'

She shook her head. 'That's a job for the police. I'm just finishing his story.'

'Which story would that be?'

'The one involving a peer of the realm, the Kosovan mafia, arms sales and a money laundering operation.'

He responded with a fixed smile, but the ripple of anger that crossed his eyes contained a hatred so unconstrained by human conscience that Ali instinctively drew back.

He asked, 'What has that to do with me?'

She hesitated, letting him know that she was posing her next question with some personal reluctance. 'There is a rumour that you are involved, that you have used your position to forge links with the Kosovan mafia and are now wielding your considerable influence to ensure that the story doesn't see the light of day.'

He looked at her like she was the other side of sanity's coin. 'Tell me, who are your sources for this information?'

She smiled. 'You know I can't do that.'

'Anonymous sources,' he sneered. 'I suppose I should feel flattered, to be the subject of an anonymous source. It sounds so very glamorous, don't you think?'

'I take it you're denying that this peer is you.'

'There is nothing to deny,' he told her coldly. 'I have no knowledge of such matters. And, as for leverage: I might have sway over the career of anyone foolish enough to give credence to these rumours, but I have no influence whatsoever in what would be a strictly judicial matter. I had granted you enough intelligence to understood that.'

She smiled away the insult. 'I understand perfectly, thank you.'

'Good. After what happened to your friend, I would have thought that these things are best left alone. If you keep digging into other people's affairs, there is no knowing what you might stir up. You, and you alone, would be responsible for any unpleasantness.'

'It's the things *Best left alone* that most interest people in my business.'

'So I understand.' In a voice as soft as a baby's sigh, he asked, 'Do you believe in evil, Ms Feysor? I don't mean the wicked deeds we sometimes do in a weak moment. I mean evil in the darkest theological sense.'

Reason was eluding her, but Ali could manage reaction. 'Do you?'

Figgis snorted: *of course I do.* 'I've lived with it all my life.'

'What kind of evil?' Ali tried not to sound too eager for the answer.

Figgis settled back into the soft leather seat, his eyes latched securely onto her. 'I would like to say, Ms Feysor, that you can count on me for all the support you need. Anything. Just ask. I would be more than happy to sponsor your investigation.'

It seemed to Ali that she had chanced upon a black hole in human thought where nothing happened that could be explained or remembered. Helping her was not on Figgis' agenda so she could only assume that he was offering to buy her.

She asked, 'Is that why you invited me here? To offer me money?'

'Money? Of course not. It would be too crass. But you interest me. Most people would have given up after all you have been through. You didn't. A woman with your tenacity and skills is wasted at a rag like the Echo. You are relentless and smart and that combination is valuable to a lot of people. Important people. With your talent and looks you should be pursuing a career in TV. I know the right people. I can land you an important gig.'

'Is that a job offer?'

'Would you like it to be?'

She gave him a single, slow shake of the head. 'I love my job.'

'Yes. So your boss tells me. He is a personal guest of mine and a great admirer of your work.'

She rode over the implied career threat. 'If you want to support me, the most useful thing you could do would be to give me a full and frank interview, on the record.'

He fixed her with the unremitting expression that he routinely used on errant Ministers. 'I can tell you one thing for the record, Ms Feysor. I am a jealous guardian of my reputation and of the reputation of my family. There are people who would damage me but I will not countenance it. Anyone who seeks to peddle fiction about me will quickly find themselves back in the gutter where they belong.'

'Peddling lies is not what I do,' she retorted, surprised by her own calm, 'and I'm offended that you would even suggest it.'

'I'm glad to hear it.' He smiled, and at that moment the room became the coldest place in the universe. Like an arctic wind, his eyes stripped the skin off her face. 'If you continue with this, I shall be forced to muzzle you.'

He paused, waiting for some response. Ali had nothing to say to that.

'It's a terrible thing about Steven Shimmon.' Figgis' voice was soft; his regret so practiced that Ali almost laughed out loud. 'It's hard to understand why anyone would want to kill a man like that.'

'I find it hard to believe that they have.'

'Yes,' Figgis agreed. 'It is. It would be sensible to think of his death as a lesson. If you choose to live in a man's world then you must expect to be treated like a man. Now, I believe we're finished here.'

For a protracted silence they stared at each other. His threat was veiled, but it was real enough, and Ali realised that Figgis had granted her this *interview* in order to warn her off. She, in turn, seemed to have achieved nothing.

Outside in the gallery, Lady Paula had finished her appeal and was engulfed in polite applause.

Ali's mouth was dry but her palms were damp. She stood up and collected her bags. 'Thank you for your time.'

He rose and shook her hand with a surprisingly ineffectual grasp. He tried and failed for that disarming smile of his. 'I'm pleased that we understand each other.'

Close to, his breath tasted like the inside of a

cigarette pack. Sweetly stale, it was the odour of death.

Chapter 37

ALI HAD BARELY closed the door when it opened again and Burns came in. Figgis was pacing and snorting like a frustrated bull and he turned on the newcomer, his features twisted with rage.

'Feysor! The bitch is on my case and nobody thought to tell me!'

Burns glanced at him blankly, then selected a chair near the window and sank into it. After a brief hesitation, Figgis followed suit.

Figgis bit back on his anger, 'This is the Sunday fucking Echo we're talking about!'

'We have Feysor under control,' Burns said. 'She is trying to follow Shimmon's tracks but they just lead her back to where she started. She is not a serious threat.'

'Not a threat!' Figgis spat. He thumped the desk. 'The whore called my office, then she had the nerve to turn up here! I don't think she wants to talk about my charity work, do you? If she's following Shimmon! . . .' He took a deep breath. 'Shimmon, let me remind you, was writing a book on Kosovo. He had everything on our Balkans operations. Names. Dates. Ghost sites. Kill squads. More specifically, he knew about our efforts to back the Serbs, our liaisons with the mafia and

Operation Mammon. If Feysor has got hold of his story we're in deep shit. I was assured that this little episode had been dealt with! She's in a position to name names, for fuck's sake!'

'Shimmon is dead,' Burns reminded him equably. 'His story died with him. Feysor is night fishing.'

'Then how did she come to cast her line in my waters?' Figgis let his gaze drift through the window then abruptly pulled it back to Burns. 'Let us not make the mistake of being sentimental, here. Any one of us is expendable. Remove her while there is still time.'

Burns spoke slowly, pointedly avoiding euphemisms. 'Are you suggesting that we kill her?'

'There's an old saying: four men can keep a secret if three of them are dead, If you lack the balls to do it, I have contacts of my own.'

'No!' Burns masked his irritation; it took a real effort. 'Silencing her now would be counter-productive. It would arouse suspicion, draw unwanted attention. There are more effective ways, subtler ways. We have her under control.'

Figgis held his eye, his mood reckless. 'Who do you think breaks the big scandals? Watergate, political corruption, big pharma, election fixing, Is it law enforcement? Is it parliament? Of course not. It's the media! You want this story on the market to the highest bidder? I don't think so! Fuck subtle! I won't allow your indecision to compromise me.' His eyes became black dots as he said the next words. 'I will destroy anyone who threatens my position. Anyone.'

'Don't fall apart on us.' Burns spoke calmly, as though to a friend, but the underlying threat was clear. 'Our interests intertwine. We need to act together.

United front and all that. The likes of you and I must maintain distance and deniability. If you involve yourself in every little shift in the time-space continuum you will be drawn into precipitous action that will blow our whole operation wide open.' Pause. 'We are at war. It is not a conventional war. Even Jo Public knows that much. Compromise the security services and you compromise our country's security. Alpha is our last line of defence. We fight fire with fire, dirt with dirt. That's what we were set up for. We do whatever has to be done for the good of the country. Leave it to Sandford. Let him do his job.'

'You are trying to close Alpha, you quisling. You can't over-rule me on this. You're not the only one with the PM's ear.'

'He won't thank you for breathing this at him. He doesn't want to know.' Burns paused, as though considering whether to risk breaking a confidence. 'The PM asked me if we killed the journalist, Shimmon.'

Figgis widened his eyes and pursed his lips. He started to smile but took in Burns' expression and thought better of it. 'He asked you directly?'

'Off the record, of course.'

'I thought he was never going to do that.'

Burns lips twitched. 'I told the PM that we had no hand in Shimmon's death. However, following this new precedent, I have been instructed to cast adrift anyone in our team who might be that reckless.'

There was a moment of tense silence, just two brains grinding soundlessly in that testosterone-filled room.

At length, Figgis asked, 'How much does Feysor know?'

'Nothing of substance,' Burns assured him. 'Nothing she dares print. As I said, we have her under control. We have planted the seeds of disinformation and discredit. She will find what we want her to find, and no more.'

Figgis nodded. 'I will hold fire for now. But the second you look like losing control, I will step in.'

Burns had had a lifetime of dealing with people like Figgis. His Lordship might smile, he might even put on a beguiling tone, but nothing could mask the psychotic proclivity in his eyes. Here was a man who craved power so badly that, at some point in his life, he had made the Faustian pact that had unleashed his insatiable appetites, unpredictable violence and cruelty. He had an unshakeable conviction in his own importance. Burns knew that a man who could absolve himself of his own sins would never defer to lesser mortals over a matter of such importance?

Figgis, Burns knew, was not going to hold back on Feysor.

The moment he hit the street, Burns hit speed dial on his cell phone. It was answered on the second ring.

He said, 'We have a problem.'

Chapter 38

ALI WAS WIRED tight as she drove home from Chelsea. She had a nagging sensation that Figgis had let slip something important but, however many times she re-ran their conversation, she found nothing. She pulled into the back road behind her flat, opened her garage door with her remote and drove straight in. It was only when she came back out of the garage that she realised that her security flood was dead. She tried the switch. Nothing. There was no public lighting here and she was as blind as a moth. The sodium rays leaking from the Edgware Road didn't help. They merely deepened the shadows.

She sensed eyes on her, and whirled around. There was no-one in sight, no movement and no sound. She blinked hard, searching for focus, and saw a shadow flit within a shadow. Or did she? In the claustrophobic blackness, she couldn't be certain. She looked harder, shielding her eyes from the city sky. Nothing.

She was spooked. Her chest had tightened, her stomach chilled with fear. She punched her remote and, without waiting to watch the door close, she turned towards the misty lights of Sheaveshill Road. There was an urgency to her walk. A dozen paces and her fear mutated to a conviction that she was being followed. She broke into a run, not daring to glance back lest the very act of looking might attract a crazed killer from her deepest nightmare.

Then she was on Sheaveshill. Light and noise. And people. A young couple, and a woman, alone and unafraid. Feeling foolish, she slowed to a walk. But her pace remained too swift to quieten the rasping clatter of her own breathing.

She reached the tunnel-like stairwell that led up between two shops to her flat and hesitated. The lamp was out. Not usually a problem - it was broken more often than not - but her stomach was like a spitting volcano as she mounted the stairway, feeling her way up steps she couldn't see towards the rectangle of grey light at the top. There was a faint, musty smell of stale urine, and she could read the graffiti of darkness on the colourless walls.

She emerged into the open to find the walkway empty. No one was waiting to beat her, or stab her, or tip her over the waist-high wall into the rear yards below. Buoyed by a sense of reprieve, she covered the short distance to her flat, took out her key and opened the door.

It was then that she sensed him. A tiny movement in the electrical field behind her, a hole in the darkness. She half-turned and caught a flash of an eye and a mouth glistening in the dark. Instinctively, she threw herself to one side, just in time to avoid the substance of the sickly sweet halothane spray, though not the residual mist that drifted across her face.

Like a wasp hit by fly-killer, she went berserk, lashing out with fists, feet and knees. But her assailant was too fast and strong. She knocked the nebuliser from his hand but he swayed out of reach and swatted her with a single punch to the left temple. Her ear exploded, her head started spinning and her legs wobbled from under her.

Déjà vu. Flashing images of Kosovo mania.

She slumped down into her hallway, was flipped over and felt the elephant kneeling on her chest. Cruel hands pinned her down and she felt hot, acrid breath on her face. Her assailant was dressed in a black tracksuit and balaclava. Only his eyes and mouth were visible and they were deadly, like a cobra's. Terrified, she writhed in desperate, unavailing attempt to escape.

'We told you it would come to this. You should have stayed away.'

He put his hand to her throat and she fought harder. But he was too heavy and strong, and she felt her strength failing. Then, quite suddenly, he was gone. More dislocation, the scene registering pre-thought. For an instant, she seemed to levitate, then there was the sound of a brief scuffle, followed by the sickening crack of snapping bone.

She didn't want to look. She was tired of looking.

Yet she looked.

Her attacker lay deathly still, the faint grey of his unmasked face standing out from his amorphous black form. Keaton was frisking him. Ali registered no surprise at seeing her saviour from Kosovo. She watched, dazed, as he found a silenced gun, phone and car keys, which he pocketed. It didn't matter to her that her assailant had no wallet or ID.

She asked, 'Is he dead?'

Keaton said nothing. With a grunt, he manhandled the man onto his shoulders, crossed the walkway and threw him over the wall into the yard of the fast food outlet below. The body vanished into the darkness, crashing down onto the scree of general garbage and discarded food. She imagined oversized rats scurrying over the corpse.

Her phone started to ring.

Keaton pulled her to her feet, thrust her telephone at her.

'The alarm company,' he said. 'Password.'

Mechanically, she recounted the password and reassured the voice on the phone that all was well. Keaton had her reset the alarm, then he grabbed her laptop and pulled her from the flat.

She jerked free of him. 'What are you doing? Where are you taking me?'

He took her arm again, this time more firmly.

'You can't stay here. Not tonight. There's no knowing who else might be coming for you.'

Part Two

We cannot solve our problems with the same thinking we used when we created them.

Albert Einstein

Chapter 39

KEATON SPED SOUTH on the Edgware Road, indifferent to the flashing traffic cameras, eyes scanning instead for signs of pursuit. He saw none. Coming down from West Hendon towards the Staples interchange, he cut across two lanes of traffic and plunged down the slip road to the North Circular. No one followed. He slowed to a legal speed, turned east then north onto the MI and settled into a steady 75. Traffic was light enough to monitor for pursuers and he saw none. By the time they were passing the Watford interchange, he was relaxed enough to break their silence.

'You good?' he asked. 'You hurt?'

Ali seemed not to hear. She just stared ahead.

He asked again, 'Are you hurt?'

'He really wanted to kill me!'

'I won't let it happen.'

'Right.'

He reached into the glove compartment, took out a small black bag with a Velcro fastener and handed it to her.

'It's a signal blocking pouch,' he said. 'Take the battery and sim card out of your phone and keep everything in the bag. It prevents your phone talking to networks.'

'Where are we going?'

'Somewhere safe.'

She said nothing to that. She disabled her phone and stored the pieces in the black bag, then she shrank back into her seat and stared out of the windshield at oncoming nothingness. Her lips were clamped, her cheeks were sucked in and her eyes were grey-rimmed slits. Her quietude made it impossible for Keaton to speak. It was like all the thought had been sucked out of the car. Soon after, he realised that she had fallen asleep.

WHEN ALI AWOKE, she was alone in the car. There followed a moment of chest-constricting panic before she registered the petrol fumes, the petrol pump, the wrap-around light, the shop and Keaton. He was at the checkout, wearing his trademark grey training trousers, long sleeve base layer/running top, Boss bomber jacket and Merrill shoes. The clock on the car's fascia showed 00.55. When Keaton came through the automatic doors, he was carrying several bags of groceries which he put in the boot.

She asked, 'Where are we?'

'Northampton.'

Northampton. To Ali, it was just an exit sign on the motorway. She had never taken the turn, didn't know anyone who had.

'That sounds safe,' she said drily.

He pulled out onto the empty road, turned left then left again into a one-way residential street. He slowed right down, allowing his eyes to suck up all there was to see. Victorian terraces, facing each other across a street that was narrow and treeless. Desultory street lighting. Bumper to bumper kerbside parking. Tiny front gardens filled with waste bins. No sign of life. On reaching the end of the road, he drove round the block and back down the street again. Satisfied with his surveillance detection run, he repeated his circuit, this time just three legs of the block, and squeezed into a parking space.

'Wait here,' he said.

He got out of the car and disappeared round the corner. Ali had no way of knowing what he was doing. Time dragged on and she began to fear that he had run into trouble. Arrested. Or killed. Her heart began beating so hard she had to clutch the seat to stay still. Just as she was reaching for the door handle, preparing to bolt, he reappeared.

'Come on!'

He grabbed the groceries and she followed him round the corner and along the street to a house with a blue door. He didn't have a key so he used a small pick gun, like a miniature electric screwdriver, to open the lock. Once inside, he scanned the alarm pad, tapped in the code and they were in.

This was a safe house, Keaton explained, owned by his employers. It was set in a student and short-rent housing area, with a constant turnover of occupants. Transients like themselves. They could stay here for an hour or a year and never be noticed. The house itself was cold and unlived-in, all pastel paint and stripped pine, with minimal furniture. Keaton gave her the tour, at the same time double-checking the windows and exterior doors. They ended up in the kitchen. It was clean, well-equipped and unused. They unpacked the groceries in uneasy silence.

'Just remember the drill,' he told her with some gravitas. 'Don't open the door and don't call anybody. Whatever you do, don't switch on your cell phone.'

Ali realised that he was preparing to leave her. 'Just remember the drill,' she mimicked, lowering and flattening her voice. 'Don't call anyone! What the fuck is this?'

'It's no joke, Ali. The GPS in your phone is a homing beacon to these people.'

'Even I know that!' Suddenly, she felt very vulnerable and lonely. 'I'm not staying here by myself.'

'Your flat's not safe. This place is. There is no way they can know you're here. Catch some sleep. I'll come back tomorrow and we'll work out where to go from here.'

She stared helplessly at him. 'You can't leave me alone, not now.'

'There's things to do.' He paused, as though considering the complications inherent in changing his mind, but stuck to his guns. 'I can do better for you by myself.'

'No! If you go, I'm coming with you.'

They locked eyes.

'Okay,' he conceded. 'I'll stay. But tonight only. Tomorrow, we make more permanent arrangements.'

She opened her mouth as though to argue further, then nodded and turned away. She filled the kettle and searched out coffee and cups.

He sat at the table. Relaxed, defences down, he watched Ali at work, his attention drawn by the clink of metal on china and held by the tightness of her skirt and blouse which added sensuality even to the tiniest movement. For those few moments, he saw the self-contained tranquillity of the woman who refused to let others define her. But then she became aware of his scrutiny, and her countenance, which had been drawn into a puzzled frown, switched to a girlish glow.

Self-conscious, Keaton turned away. He felt dirty, like a punter in an Amsterdam porn booth. His tender, protective feelings were suddenly vain and presumptuous.

Ali placed the coffee on the table and sat opposite him. She looked unexpectedly frail, her face pale and pinched.

'Are you okay?' he asked. 'You look like hell.'

'I look like hell!' She echoed, all mock offence.

'Worse, actually.'

'I've got a headache, that's all. I've had a weird day.'

'A weird day,' he chuckled. 'You're a tough one, Ali, I'll give you that.'

She laughed, a little hysterically. 'Tough?' she echoed. 'I'm scared of being alone, scared of people, scared of the light and absolutely bloody terrified of the shadows.' A pause. 'I should go to the police now. If I wait until the morning they'll wonder why.'

'If you go to the cops, you'll have to tell them everything. They'll treat you like a criminal.'

'I've got friends in the Met.'

'So have I, people I trust. But they can't help me any more than your friends can help you.' He dismissed her perplexed look. 'By all means talk to the police. But they will want to know everything, and more besides. They will put your statements onto the system then the people hunting you will find you. Their electronic tentacles reach everywhere. Their search algorithms will flag you and then you'll get more than a visit from Thames House.'

Flashback to that empty building in Willesden Green. 'Those guys were MI5! How do you know about them? How come you were there tonight. Why are you following me?'

He responded to her questions with a stony face.

They heard a dog barking. Ali sensed the presence of people out there in the night, people who shied away from the light.

'We've been here before,' she said grimly. 'I guess now is the time for you to say *I told you so.*'

'I told you so.' He tried to smile but his face was stretched too tight. 'I'm sorry, Ali, I should have been more persuasive.'

'I'm a big girl, Chris. I make my own decisions.'

'That's what worries me. I've seen the kind of decisions you make.'

Her rejoinder was dancing, waspish, on her tongue, but she bit it back. She was all out of fight.

Keaton said, 'We have to plan our next move.'

Her eyes glistened and her face clouded with the realisation of her new reality. She had been selected as victim by people she didn't quite know for reasons she didn't quite understand. Fragmented images of Prishtina came flooding in. The tears spread to her cheeks and she squeezed her eyes shut, like she was in pain but trying to control it.

He looked at her and his expression softened. He went around the table and put an arm about her. It was a wooden, awkward gesture.

'I *will* help you, if you'll just let me.'

She relaxed into him and immediately he froze against the intimacy. He removed his arm and eased himself away, leaving Ali hot with embarrassment. Furious with herself for such a show of weakness, she clenched her teeth, concentrated on breathing and demanded:

'What were you doing at my place, tonight?'

'Looking out for you.'

She fixed her hazel eyes on him. 'Who told you to do that?' Faced with his obdurate silence, she snapped at him. 'Someone hired you to watch me. Who?'

'I don't know.'

'How could you possibly not know that?'

'It happens a lot in my business.'

Her face stretched with frustrated anger. 'Who do you report to? You must know that!'

'My boss.'

She waited but he wasn't about to elaborate.

'The guy at my flat,' she demanded. 'Was he Paul's killer? Did he kill those others?'

Keaton was shifting uncomfortably, as though her words had inflamed his haemorrhoids. 'How would I know that?'

'Of course. You're the hired muscle. No brain cells.' But, for all her sarcasm, she couldn't recall the last time she had felt so safe and protected.

'There was more than one of them, tonight,' he said. 'I thought the other guy might follow us but I guess he ran away. They won't underestimate you again.'

That should have spooked her but she couldn't believe how calm she felt. She reached for her coffee.

'Why now?' she wondered. 'Why kill me now and not before?'

'They were playing a watching game, waiting for you to give up. You didn't, and now you've become too dangerous for them. You must be getting close to whatever it is they don't want you to know.'

'Close hell! I'm no further forward than I was in Kosovo.'

'You must have learned something without realising it.'

She tightened her fists in frustration. 'But what?'

She felt as if she was being pulled in ten directions at once. Yet, somehow, all paths led to the same place. To Figgis and his shadowy associates? Could it be that simple? Had approaching Figgis precipitated the end game?

She glanced sideways at him. 'If you don't know who you're working for, you could be working for *them*.'

'Trust me, I'm not.'

'Trust you!' she echoed incredulously. Then, unexpectedly, her face transformed into an impish smile. 'You want me to trust you? Tell me the worst thing you've ever done.'

'What?'

'The very worst - if you can trust me with that! . . .'

He took in her intensity and his mouth twitched. 'That won't work.'

'That bad, huh?'

There was nothing he could say. She was brave and resilient, willing to put herself on the line for principles that meant nothing to him. Who was he to expect her trust?

'Maybe not as bad as you think.'

'Right.' She probed his eyes, trying to read him. 'You've killed a man. No that's not it, you were a soldier. You've killed a man in cold blood. Assassination. Murder. Whatever.'

He looked at her blankly.

'Worse than that?' She thought for a moment. 'Women and children. You've killed women and children.'

More inscrutability.

'Oh fuck!' she cried in mock horror. 'You killed someone's pet hamster!'

Keaton's face creased into an involuntary grin. 'Finished?'

'I'd like to be.'

Suddenly she felt drunk, drunk enough to fuck him right here, right now. She wondered if he could sense how she felt, guessed he did by the unease that entered his eyes before he turned away. She wondered what that was all about.

His voice dry, he pulled their conversation back to business. 'If these people are hunting you, they will find you. They know your habits, your likely hiding places. They'll be watching your friends and haunts. They are not going to give up. You'll have to become someone else, cloak yourself in anonymity and disappear.'

The suggestion horrified her. 'I can't do that! My life may not be perfect, but it's the only one I've got. I'm not leaving my friends or my job or my home. I will not let these bastards force me off the grid! Do that and they win. It's the worst thing they can do to me.'

He smiled. 'I'm glad you feel that way, Ali, because the cruel truth is that there is no hiding. No matter how careful you are, you will leave a trail that someone like me can follow. If you hide, you live with one eye over your shoulder until they get you. And they will find you - New Zealand, Arizona, the far side of the moon - wherever. Running guarantees one thing: you'll be all alone when they catch up with you. You can't live waiting for someone like me to turn up to tidy up some loose end you don't even know about.'

'And if I do nothing?'

'You die.'

'Wow. Stay put and die; run and die. That really makes me feel better. What's the best I can hope for?' she asked with genuine flippancy. 'Avenge my friends before the Reaper comes calling?'

He smiled; he knew she was scared and he couldn't help admiring her bravery. 'The game is survival, not revenge. The dead don't need your help, they don't care if you avenge them, and they can't thank you because they're dead. If you become blinded by revenge you will not survive. To survive you need leverage.'

'So we fight?'

'You can't fight these people, Ali.' His face looked reflective, philosophical, a pocket of air in one cheek. 'You would have to get them before they get you. You're not equipped.'

'So what do you suggest?'

'Reset your life and start again.' He saw the despair in her eyes and immediately regretted his flippancy. He smiled apologetically. 'We sleep on it.'

Chapter 40

ALI WAS DRIFTING in and out of sleep, her body growing hot and sensitive. She shifted onto her back and her nipples hardened against the duvet. Her fingers slid between her legs, caressing, rubbing and dipping. A sweet and sour perfume enveloped her. She moaned and suddenly Keaton's face appeared.

She snapped awake. Her sexual longing had gone, with it her tranquillity as she remembered where she was and why. She struggled to a sitting position, her breathing awry.

Keaton!

The man had exploded into her life. She didn't know why, yet she had accepted his presence without demur. He had told her nothing about himself, though, when he looked at her, he seemed to be inviting her into the mystery of his life. He was a killer yet she had never felt threatened by him. He had not tried to seduce her and she felt strangely ambivalent about that. Disappointed but not offended. She was attracted to him and would have been happy for him to join her in bed. Was that sex as comfort? Sex as protection? Right now she would take either. But he wasn't interested. He was Alpha male, no doubt there, but he lacked the wayward fluency in body language that afflicted so many of her colleagues. She recalled something that Shimmon had told her: *Men are kind to women for two reasons. Either they want to get inside their knickers or they don't have to prove anything.* She shrugged. Maybe he had nothing to prove. Or maybe he was gay! . . .

From somewhere below came a muffled sound. She couldn't identify it, wasn't even sure that she had heard it. It could have been Keaton but she sensed not. A glance at her watch told her that it was just before two. She sat very still, held her breath and listened intently to the night sounds.

A minute of nothing.

Then she heard the click of a door closing. The front door?

Now she was certain. Someone had just come into the house.

The events of the night came back like a slap, reawakening her paralysing terror.

Keaton was in the room down the hall, the other side of the stairway. Was he actually asleep? Was he really going to slumber on as they broke in and murdered her? Sweat was trickling, little rivulets, down her spine and the hairs on her neck were rigid. She couldn't shout a warning without revealing where she was. She had to get to him. She dared not switch on a light but the faint, bluish radiance from the window was enough for her to get her bearings. She slipped out of bed, frantically pulling on clothes as she crept across the room. She cracked the door open and listened. Nothing. She slipped into the hallway. The street lamps cast a grey, minimal light. She turned towards Keaton's room and safety, but a creaking footfall near the top of the stairs effectively blocked the way. Biting her lip, as if that would somehow silence the ancient floorboards, she crept the other way into the bathroom.

As she closed the door, a figure moved onto the landing.

Chapter 41

CONSCIOUS ONLY OF soft footfalls approaching, Ali flattened herself against the bathroom wall and tried desperately to dissolve into the shadows. Her head pounded with fear and a little voice kept demanding, over and over, *Where's Keaton?*

The door opened.

Her breath began to rattle so she stopped breathing altogether. She locked onto the grey rectangle of the doorway. The shadow deepened and a man came into the room. There was no escaping him. Her body tensed for fight and she sucked in air to scream. Then came a curious sound, like the whip of a wet towel, followed immediately by another. The intruder crumpled to the floor.

She was vaguely aware of someone – Keaton? - moving swiftly away, across the landing and down the stairs. Stunned, she slid slowly down the wall onto the floor and she was still sitting there when Keaton returned, a suppressed Glock 28 in hand.

'We can't stay here,' he said tersely. 'We have to move.'

She didn't react. He heaved her to her feet but she pulled away and stared at him, all shock and mistrust, like he was the threat.

He moved close so that they were face to face. 'We have to get away from here.'

She stared at him blankly. 'How did they find us?'

'Later,' he snapped. 'We have to go.'

She nodded.

They gathered their few belongings. Keaton switched off the lights, peered through the windows, then slipped through the front door. He stood motionless, checking the street for movement, a noise, a shadow out of place. Nothing. He crossed the street, eyes switching left and right, checking under cars and behind walls. Satisfied, he returned and led her out to the car. He didn't reset the house alarm, fearful that a chance burglar might attract the police.

She said nothing and he was glad of the silence. It helped him focus. At this time of night, the roads were all but empty. Nevertheless, he kept to a legally acceptable speed as he drove them west along the A45 then south onto the M1. At Newport Pagnell services, he pulled off the motorway and parked away from the facilities.

'Okay,' he demanded. 'How did they find us? Did you switch your phone on? Who the hell did you call?'

'Did I use my fucking phone!' she flared. 'What's wrong with using my phone? Normal people use their phones all the time! It's what we do!'

'You're right, Ali,' Keaton said, regretting his outburst. 'It's what people do. This is no place for you. There's a police office the other side of the motorway. Over the bridge. Tell them everything. Get your Paper involved. Make enough noise and you'll be safe. They'll believe you. They have to. You have the bodies. Tell them everything.'

She stared at him as though considering his suggestion, then shook her head. 'My phone is still in pieces in that bag you gave me. I haven't touched it. So how *did* they know where to find us? Nobody knows we're here. Nobody can possibly know. It's not possible. Who are they?'

'I don't know. I've never seen them before.'

'What about the house. Someone will find the bodies. The place is awash with our prints and DNA.'

'It'll be taken care of.'

She nodded. She should have known he would say that. They were silent for a long moment.

Eventually, she asked, 'So where do we go? Another *safe* house?'

He had already searched through his memory bank of fall-backs – escape routes, safe houses, trusted friends – but had found none that would fit this situation. He had just never envisaged being stuck with a female journo on the run.

'No. We have to find somewhere to rest up. A motel will do it.'

'If I use my cards they'll track us. Even I know that.'

'I'm a cash man,' he told her distractedly. His mind was working elsewhere. 'They must have bugged you somehow. Tagged your clothes, most like.' He saw her quizzical look and explained. 'RFI. *[Radio Frequency Identification]*. It was developed for tracking stock, clothing, stuff like that. The tags are thinner than a human hair and less than an inch long. The RFI readers are linked to satellite.'

'You're saying they've bugged me!'

He shrugged: how could he be sure? 'They didn't tail us, my car is clean, yet they still found us. We have to assume all your clothes are tagged. I don't have a bug detector, so we'll have to dump them.'

'Dump my clothes?' She laughed, a touch hysterically. 'You want me to drive around au naturel? *The naked journalist!* That'll fool them. They'll never find us!'

'Wait here.'

He reached into the back of the car for a cap then, keeping his face averted from the CCTV cameras, went inside the filling station shop and had a brief word with the attendant. He returned to the car.

'There's a 24-hour supermarket. Not far.'

The store was hardly designer-world, but it was just ten minutes' drive away and it was open. They kept it simple: jeans, t-shirts, sweaters, underwear, socks and trainers. In the toilets, she stripped off, combed her hair through and rubbed herself down before putting on the new clothes. She found herself thinking about Keaton doing the same thing, wondered if he was thinking of her.

They threw their old clothes into a dumpster and an hour later they were booking into a chain motel.

THEY LAY ON the double bed, close, but not close enough to touch. They had kicked off their shoes but were otherwise fully clothed, A reading lamp provided a subdued light.

Keaton clasped his hands behind his head. 'How are you doing?'

Her cheeks warmed but her smile was curt. 'Never better.'

'If it'd help to talk about it. . . .'

She shook her head. 'You don't want to talk about it.'

'On the other hand, if I don't want to talk about it. . .'

This time her smile was warmer. 'I'm fine,' she said. 'You can trust me, Ali. I want you to know that.'

'I do,' she said. 'Like a gazelle trusts a lion.'

His mouth twitched just short of a grin. 'You should get some sleep.'

She hesitated, then said, 'I was thinking about when my mother died.'

'A traffic accident, right? I couldn't imagine losing my mum that way.'

That surprised her, his knowledge, his softness of tone.

'It wasn't her death,' she explained, 'or even the way she died. It was my reaction. I didn't mourn. I carried on with my life like it didn't matter.' She had never spoken of this to anyone but her father and she revealed her secret in an agitated burst that darkened her face. 'My grief came out in other ways, of course. I did booze, drugs and sex like there was no tomorrow. A whole year of purple haze that was just a long search for rock bottom. I was lucky. When I did hit bottom, I bounced right back up again. No addictions, no disease, just a fondness for vodka and an aversion to sex. My father was still there, never judging, and that made me so guilty. I handled the guilt by feeling sorry for him. Thinking how selfish I was to leave him so lonely. It took me another ten years to realise that he was fine. I was the lonely one.'

He could think of nothing to say. Words were too trite.

Misunderstanding his silence, she turned onto her side and glared at him. 'Okay, your turn. Tell me something you don't tell other people. Something to dent that macho image.'

He pursed his lips thoughtfully, then unexpectedly responded. 'First time I was choppered into the jungle at night. It was a training exercise. We were green as hell. It was so dark you can't even see the nose on your own face! There's snakes, and millipedes and God knows what else rustling about. You can't see them but you know they're there, crawling all over you, sniffing out your crotch.' He chuckled as she recoiled in horror. 'First night, no one slept a wink. It was like a bad acid trip. Jungle's screaming like the devil himself's being tortured. We just clung together all night, firing off clips as if we had shares, shit-scared terrified!'

He paused. 'Come morning, the jungle was littered with dead howlers. Whole families of them. Poor little buggars. A species became extinct that night.'

She laughed. She didn't quite believe him but oh how she needed a moment of light-heartedness. 'So the world's elite fighting force is just a band of wimps.'

'We're at our most effective when we stay in base,' he said without irony. 'They hear the Brits are coming to get them and they shit themselves to death. Nothing more potent than a myth.' He shrugged. 'There's nothing macho about that. We're just men. *I'm* just a man.'

'Just a man?'

'You know. I lie, I drink, I cheat on my wife, I'm only happy when I'm brawling with the lads.'

'A real live Homo Inferior.' She looked off, as though bored. She could feel her suspicion of him ebbing away. 'I didn't know people like you were married?'

'I'm not.'

They lapsed into another silence.

'I was married,' he admitted unexpectedly. 'We had a little girl. Jannie. But what I do for a living – I was taking that home and damaging the most important people in the world. I haven't spoken to them in three years, haven't seen them in four.'

'I'm sorry, Chris. I can't help prying. It's what I do.'

He shrugged. '*Everything I loved was taken away, and I did not die.*'

Ali hesitated. She almost said it, almost snapped it right out. How hot pursuit of her own career had destroyed her love life. How men peeled from her like dead skin, tired of being stood up, or just plain unwilling to get involved with someone so committed to rooting around in society's detritus. But she didn't. What was the point? There was no one else to blame for her life but herself.

'At least you tried,' she said ruefully. 'I just take the easy option. If I meet somebody I might love, I back away.'

'That sounds tough.'

'Not if you do it right away, before you get to liking someone.'

Their eyes met in a moment of poignancy mixed with regret. She leaned in close to him and they kissed, briefly. There was a sense that this was how it should be. They kissed again, this time for longer and with tenderness. Suddenly he was tasting salty tears.

He eased away. 'Hey?'

'I'm sorry,' she whispered. 'I just . . . I'm freaking out. All those people dead.'

'You're the victim here, don't lose sight of that.' He put his arms around her and she nestled into him. He held her like that until he realised that she had fallen asleep.

THE PAIN FILTERED through, insinuating its way into Ali's sleep so that she spent the night somewhere between hallucination and nightmare. A succession of dreadful images assailed her: Last night's assaults, surreal, like half-remembered clips from a film; Shimmon's animated death mask; her mother, screaming in her blazing car; Stewart, his life-blood pumping from a thousand jagged holes. The dead kept her company: friends, family and a host of supporting extras. As ghouls, they were benign enough - they couldn't muster a *Boo!* between them - but the very fact that they were there was enough to keep the nightmare going.

While she slept on the bed, Keaton sat in a chair in the dark. He felt inexplicably wary of the bed and of her and of sleep. A moment of intimacy had passed between them but it couldn't last. Keaton had long since closed his life to fatal distraction.

He settled into hiatus mode, inert yet alert for any sound that might suggest that the hotel was no longer safe ground. A comfortable enough routine until, just before dawn, Ali's demons came visiting. She grunted and snarled, battled, grappled, writhed and scuffled, until the room filled with the odour of her perspiration. Keaton's first instinct was to protect her from her terror, but he decided to leave her parasomnia where it belonged: in her sleep. Why wake her and risk bringing that through?

He watched, helpless, until, eventually, she became still and her breathing relaxed.

Relieved, he settled back into his routine.

Chapter 42

WHEN ALI OPENED her eyes, Keaton placed a mug of coffee on the bedside table. It was 9.17 and a new day. She sat up stiffly and took a grateful draft of coffee. She might have been dented by her dreams but the events of the night seemed distant for all that.

'I have to make some calls.' Her voice sounded tight. She wished it didn't. 'I know, I can't use my cell. I'll find a payphone.'

'I've some calls of my own to make.' He dropped a cell phone on the bed. 'Some pay-as-you-go anonymity. No GPS. Use once then turn it off, strip it down and discard it. If you want to shower, do it now.'

He left the room and she showered and dressed. She picked up the phone and punched out a number from memory.

'It's me,' she said.

'Where the hell have you been?' Irvine was testy. She was used to that. But there was something else in his tone. A deep unease? 'I've been trying to get hold of you.'

'So now you have me.'

'I'm closing down your story.'

'You can't do that!'

'No arguments, no appeals. It's done.'

'I don't believe this!'

'Believe it, girl. Believe it like your career's hanging on a thread. The Paper's all set to drop you like a ton of hot shit. You actually did it! You confronted Figgis! Fuck, Ali! You crashed his charity do and went head to fucking head with a guy like that!'

'You were okay with it, yesterday. You supported me. Why the change of heart?'

'I was okay with professional, diplomatic, savvy, but this! . . . If you go within a hundred miles of Figgis, he will sue you and the Paper. Write a word about him and he'll sue. His lawyers have threatened to cripple both the paper and you financially. He has access to top lawyers who specialize in bringing defamation cases against journalists. Win or lose, you'd be finished. The owners will throw you to the wolves, me with you if I'm not careful. Take a vacation. Leave your bloody obstinacy on the beach along with the other garbage. You've turned it from a strength to a weakness.'

'This doesn't make sense, John,' she complained. But suddenly it did. 'You've been got at!'

'Back off, Ali!'

'You've been got at!' she yelled. 'You fucking coward! You cowardly fuck!'

Furious, she ended the call. Fatigue and disorientation had been replaced by anger and adrenaline. It took her a while to control her breathing but then her anger melted away into clear insight and she knew what to do.

She tapped out a text message for her father and Kate.

'Taking some much needed time out. Be off the grid for a day or two. Love you.

Feeling anchored and calm, she called Irvine back. He was tensed for a fight; she heard it in the way he said *Ali!* But he was a tolerant and decent man who deserved better than she had just served up.

'John,' she said sweetly. 'I'm taking your advice. A couple of weeks off.'

'Good. You need the break.' He hesitated, then told her, 'The lawyers can't get anyone at SO15 to admit they spoke to you. The two guys you name swear blind they were on another job at the time.'

'Don't worry about it.'

'I will.' There was a brief moment of silence before his final word. 'Just remember, it's more important to be alive than right. Suicide by career achieves nothing.'

By now her coffee was cold. She made another, propped herself on the bed and drank it slowly. *I've had enough of life on the run*, she thought, *and I've only just started.*

Keaton returned and she told him about her chat with Irvine.

'So they've got to your boss.'

'Irvine won't hurt me. Whoever these people are, they can't control everything. But I have to ID this Griffin.'

'Ali, you know that'll make you a target.'

'I'm already a target.'

'Then it'll make you a bigger one.'

Her stare was a grim challenge. 'If you're backing out now, tell me.'

He held her gaze. 'Fear doesn't shut you down, Ali, it wakes you up. Every time. It's fascinating.'

'Fascinating,' she echoed. 'Okay, if you're with me, we start by following the money. We unravel First Garanty.'

Keaton shook his head. 'You should be done with all this, Ali. Just drop the story.'

'And do what?'

He opened his mouth to tell her, decided that it would be a waste of words. 'You're right. It's too late for that. So! . . . Unravel First Garanty, you say. How do we do that? Break into the Bank's HQ and steal their files?' He shook his head. 'You can't hack your way in. You could try snatching data from the air, or digging underground for the fibre-optic cables. but even if you could get to the data it'd be encrypted. That means you have to fall back on HUMINT [*Human Intelligence*]. Use bribery, threat or blackmail. But who do you bribe? Where do you get the dirt for blackmail? And supposing you do find evidence of wrong-doing? These people have friends high and low. They will set up an investigation under a tame judge and sacrifice some scapegoat. They might even hold a parliamentary enquiry but that'll just trigger an epidemic of selective memory syndrome. Everyone lies to those pompous idiots on select committees with impunity.' Keaton shook his head. 'Follow the money! It's just a movie cliché.'

'So what do we do?'

'We make them want to keep you alive.'

She smiled. For the first time since they had met, she looked directly into his eyes with no defensiveness or anger or fear, but with a measure of respect that he felt was not easily won. 'I'm all for that,' she told him.

'We forget financial records and computer archives and go for the bodies. One at a time. We stir the water and create overlapping ripples, each ripple leading to the next and breaking it. We start at the bottom of the food chain and roll it right up to the top.'

She frowned. 'I thought these people insulated themselves from the dirty end.'

'They do. But I've known many men like this, even worked for some. Break down the insulation and they're there. Follow the line of least resistance.'

She gave him a conflicted, thoughtful look: this was uncertain territory for Ali the journalist. 'You're talking about hurting people. Killing people.'

'Not if I can help it.' He saw her doubt and sat on the edge of the bed. 'I don't kill for the fun of it, Ali. Sometimes, in my world, you can't avoid it. Am I supposed to stand by and let these people hurt you? I don't think so.' His voice dropped a few decibels. 'Killing comes with a price. When you kill a person, it doesn't matter how much they deserved to die, their face never goes underground with them. It stays with you forever, free to rise up at any time and torment you. It becomes your malign spirit. You can't exorcise it.'

'None of this seems real.'

'It will. Then you'll struggle to forget it.'

'That's comforting.'

Her eyes blinked and went away from his.

'Tell me, Ali, what do you do when there's no way out of a situation?'

She shrugged. 'What do *you* do?'

'If there's no way out then I go further in. It's the last thing they'd expect.' He could see that she was unconvinced. 'You're not looking for the story any more, Ali. You have that. You're looking for an answer. An answer to your question. And that's your problem because the question that drives you is the wrong question. You have the facts but you're looking at them with the wrong eyes. Start with the piece of the puzzle that doesn't fit.'

Ali looked skeptical, one eyebrow raised, though her mouth puckered open, like she was hungry for trust and answers. 'You're talking in riddles.'

'Someone made a big mistake in sending amateurs to kill you. Cut-price killers leave a trail.' He held up the phone he had taken from her assailant at the flat. 'The name of the guy at your flat was Carl Whitton. According to his phone he was in close contact with another of his kind, a guy called Craig. Craig will tell us who contracted them.'

Ali twisted her face in disbelief. 'We just ask this Craig and he tells us,' She saw the murder in Keaton's eyes and understood that he was serious. 'Right. You and me, alone against the world. That's a wrap, then.'

'We're not alone.'

WEST OF HIGH Wycombe, just past Bledlor on the A40, Keaton turned onto a country lane that wound upwards through the pastures and beech woods of the Chiltern scarp. They reached the village of Higher Welling and Ali caught a prospect of the Oxford Plain, a patchwork of green, brown and yellow that stretched far into ancient Wessex. The village itself was a linear settlement, just an elongated village green with thirteenth-century manor house and church, bordered by immaculate thatched houses. It took less than half a minute to pass through. Another five minutes and they reached their destination.

Ridge End was a late seventeenth century brick and flint house. It was isolated, secured by state-of-the-art intruder surveillance, yet retained enough period features to be listed for its special historic interest. Its six bedrooms and three receptions, stables, pool, landscaped grounds and fenced paddock were a wet dream for Home Counties estate agents. If only they knew how to pitch the brick and timber barn that had been extended and converted into an accommodation block for a dozen people,

Keaton was at home here. The electronic gates swung open in welcome and he drove straight to the front door of the house. They were greeted by a tall man, maybe six-five, who carried a broad grin and the bulk of a serious lifter.

'Chris Keaton returned from his travels,' he announced. 'Warrior monk, retard and world-class monkey killer.' He grasped Keaton in a bear hug then held out his hand to Ali. She took it and found herself staring up into the amused, deep pools of his blue eyes. 'So you're the famous Ali Feysor.'

'Infamous,' she corrected him.

'My mistake,' he chuckled.

'This is Peter Corbin,' Keaton said. 'He runs Corbin Defence Services. He's my boss.'

'His mate, first and foremost,' Corbin said. 'Come in out of the light.'

He led them through to a lounge. It was comfortable but not quite homely. There was a PC, a TV combo, a few books but no clutter. Nothing in this room was there for the sake of appearance.

Corbin nodded at Ali. 'Would you excuse us, Ms Feysor. Perhaps you would like some refreshments.'

Keaton read his meaning. 'Whatever we say, we say in front of her.'

'She's an investigative journalist,' Corbin noted without malice. 'The worst kind of hack.'

'She's not interested in you.'

'I'll remind you of those words when she betrays us with her venal lies.'

Keaton nodded. 'If that happens, you can shoot me.'

'Don't worry, I will.'

Corbin elected to sit on the sofa and he motioned them to sit in easy chairs. He looked from one to the other. 'You'd better update me.'

Keaton proceeded to do just that. Using the clipped sentences of a field report, he appraised Corbin of their up-to-the-minute status.

Corbin looked at Ali approvingly. 'You hold up well under pressure. No wonder Chris is impressed with you.'

Ali blinked. 'He is?'

She shot Keaton a knowing, crooked smile, telling him that there was nothing more he could do or say that would surprise her, affect her or impress her.

Corbin asked, 'Are the police after you?'

'No,' said Keaton. 'But these other people are not going to give up.'

'Do they know you're involved?'

'We have to assume yes.'

Corbin looked at Ali. 'So you're going into exile.'

'Am I hell!' she responded vehemently. 'Tell him, Chris, I'm going nowhere!'

A half smile crossed Keaton's face. 'She's not looking for a new life.'

'You only have to wait them out,' Corbin assured her cheerfully. 'They all go down eventually.'

Ali shook her head. 'I'll be an old woman by then.'

Corbin nodded sympathetically. 'You have a plan?'

'We keep moving,' Keaton said, 'We hide in the open. We go on the offensive.'

Corbin sucked in a deep, sceptical breath. 'Staying alive would be my priority. You don't want to go marching into the man's crosshairs?'

'No. I want him in *our* crosshairs.'

'Ah Jesus, Chris! You're going to start a war!'

'Not a war, exactly.' Keaton said carefully. 'But if you think my involvement's bad for business, cut me loose.'

'Same old Keaton,' Corbin grinned. 'You see what you see and you follow what you follow. Nothing changes. You should learn to walk away.'

'And become a dried up desk jockey like you?'

'It's where the money is. It's best to control your emotions, Chris. They can make you stupid.' He turned to Ali. 'And you? You're like the child who thinks she can banish the monsters by closing her eyes.'

She stared at him. 'My eyes are wide open.'

'Okay,' Corbin said. 'What's the plan?'

Keaton said, 'I need you to clean the Northampton safe house.'

'That's a plan?'

'The guy I killed at Ali's flat was Carl Whitton.'

'Whitton? Who would employ that roach?'

'You knew him!' Ali couldn't contain her surprise. 'Jesus! Did he work for you?'

'Not at all,' Corbin said, sounding deeply affronted. 'He runs his own operation, small, just guns for hire, at the low end of the market. His speciality was always the dirty jobs no-one else would touch.' He saw her quizzical expression, shrugged. 'He enjoyed his work. After he left the forces, he carved out a career as a mercenary. Three years ago, he was thrown out of 21st SAS. That takes some doing, a real plunge into the dark side. The reason's murky. Ostensibly, it was because he was fingered as a mercenary – the Regiment likes to pretend they don't approve - but there are rumours that he got up to things that shocked even his fellow cut-throats.'

'And his friend?'

Corbin turned to Keaton. 'Friend?'

'There was someone with him but it was dark. Who does he work with these days?'

Corbin shrugged. 'That's a very small group. He's too unpredictable for the legitimate end of the market, just as likely to turn on his friends or his master. He even failed BG training – too gung-ho. He works alone or with one of his old buddies.'

'The name Craig,' Keaton asked, 'Mean anything to you?'

'Craig Clark. He sometimes works with Whitton.'

Ali glanced at Keaton, her face light up with excitement. 'He's our man.'

Corbin studied her thoughtfully. 'Clark doesn't have too many branches on his family tree.'

Keaton nodded. 'Where do I find him?'

'I'll find out,' Corbin said with disarming self-assurance. 'You'd better stay for lunch.'

Keaton said, 'I was hoping to stay for a little longer.'

Corbin looked from one to the other. 'You're welcome.' He frowned. 'Look, I know what you're doing, mate, and I'm with you. But I don't like to see you getting involved in something you can't finish.'

'It's too late to pull out.'

'It's never too late. Negotiate.'

'They're holding all the cards.'

Corbin nodded doubtfully. He turned to Ali. 'I'll get someone to sort you a passport and papers. You know, Ali, the government took their eye off the prize with Songat and the boat people. Most illegals come in via legal routes on forged or borrowed passports. Anyone can get perfectly legit-looking papers. Now, that would be a good story for you. It's like the old second world war escape routes in reverse, only no one keeps a record of numbers.'

With that, he left the room.

Before Ali had had time to settle, a young woman came in. 'Hi Chris. Good to see you.'

'Me too.' He turned to Ali. 'Marie is the best makeover artist I know. You're in safe hands.'

Marie caught Ali's eye. 'Come with me.'

Ali threw a puzzled glance at Keaton, then followed Marie to a bathroom.

Marie indicated a chair in front of a long mirror. 'Sit here, please.' She picked up a pair of shears and lifted a handful of Ali's hair. 'Shame. You've got beautiful hair.'

Ali pictured her hair floating to the floor and tensed against the other woman's touch. After being assaulted, terrified, chased and bloodied, she wanted to protest this final indignity, But the sight of her features in the mirror, so distinctive, so unmistakeably her, brought a reality check. She would never escape detection looking like this. After all she had endured, was she really going to throw her life away over something as trivial as a haircut? She took a deep breath and slowly let it out.

'This must be where I close my eyes.'

Some time later, Ali was a short-haired blonde, her eyes were green instead of hazel, and makeup had darkened her skin, rounded her eyes and narrowed her lips. She studied herself with an interest that was surprisingly detached and nodded her approval.

Marie produced a small camera and took some shots.

'You will fool all but the most modern facial recognition software. You'd need plastic surgery for that. Just be confident. You have to be real enough to be believable, not real enough to be real. When you're being scrutinised, at an airport say, don't try to hide. Stay in the open, make yourself as obvious as possible. Use the make-up, perhaps bulk up your clothes a little, and your cheeks. I'll have your passport and driver's licence ready later.'

When Ali returned to the lounge, it was crowded with laughter and loud conversation. Keaton and Corbin were there, together with half-a-dozen other men. They were in celebratory mood and Ali noted that they were at ease with each other in a way that she had never quite understood. As individuals, they seemed very different. A random mix of genes and nurture with no common characteristic to bind them.

Yet they had the comradeship of shared experiences. Brothers in arms.

Looking at Keaton in this company, she seemed to be seeing him for the first time as he truly was. Not at all taciturn and remote but noisy and companionable. It reminded her of how little she knew of him. Unexpectedly, she felt as forlorn and out of place as a nun in a lap dancing club.

Corbin noticed her lurking in the doorway and called her in. As if by some pre-arranged signal, the others began to leave. Ali acknowledged their smiles and curious, appraising looks, but there was something else, an underlying sense of brutality, that made her uneasy.

Corbin and Keaton remained, together with a man Keaton introduced as Dave Pearce. Five ten and wiry, Pearce was early forties, though the years had treated him kindly. Very kindly. The colour had yet to fade from his face and hair, his worry lines were shallow and his jowls were still firm. In skin-tight jeans and a soft leather jacket that had seen plenty of life, he possessed an androgynous grace; a true, baby-faced killer. Pearce, Keaton informed her, would be helping them.

Corbin grinned at her and said, 'Dumb blonde suits you. You look kinda cute.'

'Cute!' Ali bridled. 'I've never been cute.' She waved her hand in the direction of Pearce. 'Your friend is cute.'

Pearce threw his arms up, mock offended. 'She called me cute!'

'You are cute,' Corbin said. 'If it wasn't a sexist remark, I'd come out and say so.'

'Be careful,' Keaton warned them. There was a broken smile at the corner of his mouth. 'I know this woman. She'll rip your arms off and beat you to death with them.'

Corbin glanced at her and grinned. She put up a blank expression and his humour deepened. 'Good news. The Met are treating the death of Clark as a misadventure, the self-inflicted consequence of a burglary gone wrong.'

Ali reacted with a little nod but her expression didn't change.

Keaton laughed. 'We have an address for Clark. Get your stuff and we'll go have a little chat.'

'Now?'

'You have something better to do?'

Chapter 43

BURNS WAITED IMPATIENTLY as the Alpha analyst gathered up her papers and locked down her laptop. He had come in person to Sandford's Gower Street office, which fact alone should have communicated criticality, and yet he had been forced to wait several minutes while Sandford brought his meet to an orderly close. It didn't help Burns' temper that he held analysts in contempt. It was a paradox of the Job, he thought sourly, that the more trivial and diverting the information the more money was spent on collecting and analysing it. More data, of course, meant more IT, and money spent on IT brought diminishing returns from the human element..

At last, the analyst left and Burns sank down onto the chair she had just vacated.

'We have a problem,' he said tersely. 'Feysor has gone to ground,'

Sandford raised a finger. 'Not here.' He led the way to the Cage where he waited for Burns to settle then raised his eyebrows:

'So, Feysor's in the wind?'

Burns nodded. 'Figgis tried to murder her and she got away.'

'Figgis!' Sandford couldn't contain his contempt. 'The crazy bastard. He should have been lobotomised at birth.'

'It might come to that.'

'I take it his madship wasn't personally involved.'

Burns pursed his lips. 'Figgis had Dumb and Dumber try to assassinate Feysor at her home. Unfortunately, she seems to have acquired a Minder. Someone good enough to kill one of his Lordship's men, chase off the other then disappear with Feysor into the night.'

'She has protection?'

'So Figgis says. This morning, Feysor called Irvine. He chewed her out and pulled her off the story. She agreed to take a vacation.'

Sandford said, 'To Mars, I hope.'

Burns scowled as Sandford missed the obvious. 'She's lying. Her phone is dead. She used a burner, for God's sake!'

Sandford nodded; now he got it. 'She won't get far, Minder or no minder. Sooner or later, she will pop up on the system: a card, a ticket, facial recognition, some other identifier. She can't fly undetected. Public transport is too dangerous. We will soon know what car they're driving. We will have them within days, if not hours.'

'And the girl? Sarah York?'

'We have no leads, no idea where she might be. We know she was warned off. A telephone call. Untraceable. The recording of the message has been processed inside out, but the voice matches no-one on record. She is having professional help.'

'Professional help! Like Feysor!' Burns stared at Sandford with unnerving hostility. 'How is it that two rag-tag girls are running rings around you, You are supposed to be the ultimate professional.' His eyes seared into Sandford. 'If Feysor has protection, it must be because she has something worth protecting. No-one seems to know what she has dug up, and, perversely, that makes it all the more urgent that it be re-interred. Feysor, it goes without saying, will have to be buried with it. The same goes for this York woman.'

Sandford shook his head. 'Figgis has torpedoed the final solution. You said yourself that we can't kill someone on the basis that she *might* know something, It just draws attention. It becomes whack-a-mole.'

'Never leave anything to chance,' Burns said. 'People who do invariably live to regret it. We've asked her nicely, offered her good incentives, threatened her, and still she comes. In the interests of self-preservation, you might think on that.'

Sandford shrugged away the irony that the two men had exchanged positions on killing Feysor. He said, 'No court will accept that our self-preservation equates with the national interest.'

'Fuck the courts!' Burns' face was crimson, his tone chilling. 'I'm not paid to trouble the courts, or to indulge in conscience, but to keep the country safe! I will kill anyone who fucks with me, do you understand?'

Sandford paused momentarily before responding. 'Of course.'

Burns told him starkly. 'Figgis is no longer one of us. That makes him a threat. We take care of him or we burn. Call in Gallacher.'

'Gallacher!' Sandford repeated, sounding rattled.
He was rattled.

In his early career, Sandford had taken it as a matter of faith that the survival of his country depended on him. He had hunted the enemies within - socialists, terrorists, and trade unionists - remorselessly prising innocent and guilty alike from their credibility and livelihood. Collateral damage, maybe, but all for a safer future. Gallacher, however, represented brutality untempered by hope. In his professional life, Sandford had come across all sorts of killers. They killed for power, for money, for revenge, for self-preservation. But Gallacher killed for pleasure. Ex-IRA, he was one of those who had crossed the line at some point in his life and declared war on humanity.

Sandford stared at Burns. For an instant, he seemed to be on the point of rebellion. 'Using that psycho usually proves fatal for the wrong man.'

'Gallacher is deniable.' Burns' eyes were dark, cold and commanding. 'You meet with him. Explain what is required.'

Sandford nodded, though he said nothing.

Burns' eyes lingered on Sandford. 'When all this is over, we are going to audit Alpha's activities. It might be that Alpha has run its course, that it needs some time in cold storage. It is imperative that we close down the Griffin link. We must never again find ourselves so exposed.'

THERE WAS TO be no immediate meet with Gallacher and no immediate hit on Figgis. Later that day, the Irishman's broker informed Sandford that his client was on another contract and the Alpha man put

Figgis' murder on hold. Gallacher's unavailability suited Sandford. Not because Figgis was being spared. People like Figgis, he reflected bleakly, were the true enemies within, with their selfishness and greed, routine dystopian lies and hunger for power. They should have been thrown in jail years ago but, in a sick twist of fate, were actually in charge of rewriting the rules and dictating the law. No, Sandford was not in favour of reprieving Figgis, but he was coming to abhor the use of psychopaths like Gallacher with their trickle-down random violence.

Still, use him he would. There was no room for doubt in Sandford's world. He might have come to a paradoxical phase of life - the closer he got to his destiny, the further he wanted to be; the further from his past, the closer to hell - but it was too late to change direction now.

Chapter 44

CRAIG CLARK LIVED on the Gladstone Estate in Cricklewood. The street was narrow, the houses identical, the gardens neat and tidy. The Clark residence stood out for its neglect, with its peeling paint and pockmarked stucco, and front yard of mud, weeds and trash. The only sign that anyone lived here was an old Ford on the drive.

Pearce drove past the house to the end of the street where he parked against a row of garages. From here, they could watch the house without being too obvious. Keaton was in the front passenger seat, Ali in the back. Young children played in and out of the gardens, but the only interest they attracted was from two youths and a girl who stared hard at the people who had dared intrude on their territory.

Pearce switched off the engine and nodded towards the youths. 'Feral kids. Their thing might be smart phones, computer games and reality TV, but they'd be happier duelling banjos and humping pigs.'

As if to prove his point, the girl stepped towards them aggressively, jaw working gum, arms folded.

Pearce chuckled. 'Here we go.'

Keaton wasn't amused. 'They'll draw attention.'

Pearce stared at the girl. 'She will.'

'Then there's no point in delay. Wait here.'

Without further word, Keaton got out of the car. The two youths sensed his lethality and took a healthy pace backwards but the girl made a sideways move into his path. He stepped around her and walked up to the house.

A woman opened the door. Mid-thirties, trim and manicured, she looked out of place in the neglect. Keaton recognized her from her file photo as Clark's wife, Stacey.

'Hi, Stacey,' Keaton said. 'I'm Chris, an old army buddy of Craig.'

She squinted at him suspiciously. 'He's not here. He's away on a job.'

'Well, that's great,' Keaton grumbled. 'We were on for a drink today.'

'He came home late last night, packed a bag and left. He said he wasn't sure how long he'd be away. No notice or anything. You know what it's like.'

Keaton nodded; he knew. 'You got a number?'

She shook her head. 'He left his mobile at home. He's incommunicado. I have to wait for him to call me.'

Another Keaton nod. 'I guess I'll catch him later.'

He returned to the car. The youths had disappeared.

'She claims he's not there and she doesn't know where he is. She's lying. Let's give her a few minutes.'

Pearce got on his cell and networked his contacts, giving out a simple message in the expectation that someone would get it through. He wanted Clark to call him as a matter of grave urgency to sort the mess with the journalist. They were just debating their next move when Stacey emerged from the house. She was carrying a toddler.

'Look at that,' Pearce said. 'Guys like Clark, they kill, they rape and butcher, then they switch off, go back to their women and spawn a pack of squalling kids as though nothing's happened. I never understood that.'

They watched as Stacey Clark strapped the child into the car, reversed onto the street and drove off. Pearce waited a moment then followed. She turned south onto the Edgware Road and they had no problem hiding in the heavy traffic as they tailed her through Cricklewood. She stopped once, in a no parking zone, leaving her child in the car to go into a tobacconist. She emerged with a pack of cigarettes, stripped the cellophane, plugged a ciggie into her mouth, then got back into her car. Heedless of honking horns, she bludgeoned her way across two lanes of heavy traffic, then executed a right turn onto Chichele Lane. Ten minutes later, she pulled into Stonebridge, a public housing development of grainy-grey concrete high rise, dumped into the triangle between two railways and a major road.

Pearce drew up a discreet distance away. Keaton made to get out but Ali gripped his arm.

'They know you.'

'They won't see me.'

Stacey was disappearing into a high rise, child wriggling under her arm, and Keaton did a scuttling jay-walk as he rushed after her.

THIRTY MINUTES LATER Stacey Clark had gone and Keaton was leading them inside. Clark had taken refuge in a tower that housed asylum seekers, foreign workers, the homeless and other inhabitants of London's underclass. The lifts were out and they walked up. Some residents had left their doors open to dispel the claustrophobia and Ali had to avert her eyes from the grey, empty adults and silent, apathetic children. She held her breath against the odour of stale cooking, fresh nappies and weed and she was sure she could hear rats squealing and squabbling.

Clark's door was firmly locked and it took several loud knocks before it opened a millimetre.

'Keaton.' A look of impending annihilation came over Clark's face. 'And Pearcy. This is a surprise.'

Keaton said, 'Let us in nicely, Clarky, and there'll be no trouble.'

'I'd like to believe that,' he said. 'I'll have to take the chain off.'

The door closed. There was an uncertain pause, then the chain rattled and the door opened.

Thirty-seven-years-old, Clark was compact, hard and mean, like an in-shape welterweight. Dressed in a baggy jogging suit, he looked as though a face scrub designed to clear away the skin's trash would pare him to the bone. He had a can of lager in one hand, an old FN Five-seveN in the other. The gun wavered between the two men.

Keaton and Pearce kept their hands clearly in sight.

'Chris!' Bewilderment and fear crossed Clark's face in waves. 'Am I glad to see you.'

'Of course you are.'

Clark glared at Ali. 'What have you brought her for?'

'She wanted to meet the guy who tried to kill her.'

'Not me! I wouldn't.'

'When she was under my protection.'

'Oh fuck!' Clark stepped back, terrified. 'Oh fuck, Chris. I didn't know it was you, I swear.'

Ali kept her surprise hidden: since when had she been under Keaton's protection?

Keaton said, 'The possibility of your ignorance, Clarky, is the reason you're still alive.'

Clark gripped his gun more firmly. He was the spectre of a man whose obsession with survival had brought an end to living. 'Are you carrying?' he demanded.

'What do you think.' Pearce said. 'Look, we're here to talk, so let's put the gun away.'

Clark shook his head. 'I know you. I know what you're capable of.'

Keaton said, 'If we wanted you dead, Clarky, you'd be dead.'

Ali ignored the boy's games and took a sly glance about her. Despite the previous occupants' strenuous, almost desperate efforts to make a home of the place - pictures on the wall, a few pot plants, some mean furniture - it was very decrepit. The carpet was worn and stained, and just a faded coat of pastel on the walls indicated that the room had ever been intended for human habitation. The present incumbent - this man with the blue eyes and shadowland skin - had imposed his personality with empty cans and the residues of abandoned takeaways that littered the room. The distinctively unpleasant smell of stale fast food mixed with the putrescent aroma stealing from the bin.

For some odd reason, Clark was distracted by her disapproval. 'It's cosier than a casket.'

Ali shrugged, indicated the room with a sweep of her hand. 'You live the life you choose.'

'What would you know,' he snapped.

There was a disturbed and disturbing edge to his voice. More vulnerability than anger, it sat well with the intensity in his eyes. He wiped his mouth on the back of his hand and studied Ali artfully. She saw the glint of vicious cruelty and stared back, hard, unprepared to let up on the man who had tried to murder her. But she had nothing to say to him and their silence dragged on until it was penetrated by external noise: the muffled sound of a door closing, a young child wailing in misery, the sound of traffic.

Eventually, Clark was driven to drop his eyes. 'I'm on the run,' he explained.

Ali shrugged, suddenly indifferent. Her anger, sincere though it was, felt detached, as if it was a social construct rather than deeply held emotion. Just as her synapses had failed to connect the threads of her investigation, so they were failing to connect emotions to experiences.

Keaton asked, 'Who from?'

'Not you,' Clark said with an ugly smile. 'I didn't know about you. From my own people. You don't fuck with people like that and get away with it.'

Ali found her voice. 'Your people being Griffin?'

Clark was genuinely puzzled. 'Who's Griffin?'

She tried again. 'How about Figgis?'

He scowled. 'I don't know who you're talking about.'

'So,' Keaton accused him, 'you'd kill your own mates for an anonymous buck?'

Clark turned a deeper shade of grey. 'Jesus, Keaton. I didn't know. This was business, that's all. I didn't even know you were involved.'

Keaton nodded as though he understood. 'Talk to us and we'll forget you exist.'

'I'm talking.'

'And pocket the gun.'

Clark hesitated momentarily, then reluctantly did as he was told. He also put down his beer. Ali frowned, wondering why a man such as Clark could be in thrall to Keaton.

Keaton asked, 'How did you get the job?'

Clark shrugged. 'Carl Whitton. He calls me when there's a job on.'

'Who contracts him?' Keaton said, adding, 'We can't ask him. He's in the mortuary.'

Clark dropped his eyes. 'It's need to know, deniable.'

'But you do know.' Keaton stepped forward menacingly, determined to obliterate Clark's residual defiance. 'When it's mates doing a job there's talk.'

Clark flinched, working his lips as he tried to read Keaton's eyes. 'I'm not supposed to know, but there's a guy called Sullivan. Frank Sullivan. He calls Whitton, Whitton calls me.'

Keaton asked, 'How do we find this Sullivan?'

'Sullivan's probably not even his real name.'

'Don't shit me.'

Clark shuffled nervously. 'I have a number. For emergencies.'

Keaton smiled grimly. 'For you, mate, this is an emergency.'

Clark nodded. He took out his phone and started scrolling through it. Pearce took it off him. Clark made to resist, thought better of it. He glowered as Pearce checked through his contacts.

Keaton said, 'Tell us about Sullivan.'

'I've never met him. I left all the organising shit to Carl.' That wasn't information enough for Keaton and Clark knew it. 'Carl did say that Sullivan isn't the boss man but I don't know anything else, Chris, I swear.'

Keaton fixed him with a mesmerising stare. 'If you're lying to me, you're a dead man.'

Clark turned appealingly to the woman in the room but Ali held herself cold and hard. His voice became a desperate whine. 'I'm a dead man whatever. I fucked up, missed my target. These people . . .'

He faltered as he realized that his target was here with him. His face screwed in pain. He went to the fridge, which was rammed so tightly with beer it contained no food. He winced as he realised that Pearce had come up behind him to check the fridge for concealed weapons, then he selected a can, opened it with practised ease, and took a swallow. He didn't offer anyone else a drink.

Keaton said, 'I have it from a reliable source that your people are running with the fucking Kosovans. Bringing drugs, guns and sex slaves into our country. Little girls, Clarky. And you're helping them.'

Clark squirmed, his eyes retreating from Keaton's stare. 'No, Chris! Not me! What do you take me for?'

He was lying. Ali saw the tell take hold in his face and a resentful light glimmer deep within his eyes.

Keaton paused, as though trying to work it out. 'These spics have a bad gene. It's their birthright. But you, Clarky, you're one of us. So I'm giving you a chance to make amends.'

'I don't know nothing!'

'Then you're nothing to me.'

Clark's agitation turned to claustrophobic panic. He went to the fridge, opened it, closed it, opened it again, took out another can, turned back to Keaton. Now he had a can in each hand but he still struggled for the right thing to say. Beads of sweat were coalescing on his face, running down into his neck. To the watching Ali, the puzzlement seemed as genuine as the terror. But she enjoyed watching him squirm.

'Look, I can't hurt you.' Clark was actually pleading for his life. 'I tell them I talked to you and I'm dead. I give you up and your people kill me. I won't say anything. Fuck it, Chris, I can't talk to anyone!'

Keaton glared at him in contempt. 'People like you make me sick. You don't want what you have and can't have what you want, so you turn on your mates.'

'No. I didn't. I wouldn't.'

'I should kill you. Right here and now. But there's a way out that will make us all happy. All you have to do is help us get to Sullivan.'

Clark threw his arms out, spilling his beer. 'How am I supposed to do that?'

'Where did Whitton do his business?'

'From home. He lives in Streatham. He's got an office there.'

'I need you to call Sullivan and tell him to meet you there.'

'How do I get him to do that? I can't tell him what to do.'

'Use your imagination,' Keaton told him. 'Tell him the hit went wrong, that you're holed up at Whitton's place. You're wounded. You need medical help, money. You need his help to get out of the country.'

'He won't come. He'll send someone.'

'Tell him if he doesn't come himself you'll go to the authorities.'

'Jesus, Chris. That's like signing my own death warrant.'

Keaton tapped the gun in his pocket. 'Already signed, mate. I'm just trying to stay the execution.'

'How fucking fair is that?'

'Fair?' Pearce chuckled. 'The only thing we're entitled to in life, Clarky, is a probability curve.'

Clark uttered a sound somewhere between a growl and a whine. 'I hope in the next life you come back a guy like me. See how you like it.'

Chapter 45

ALI DREAMED OF Prishtina and awoke with a lingering angst that drove her from her bed. She wasn't the first one up. There were voices in the kitchen. She craved a coffee but was even more desperate for some solitude. Events were moving too quickly, leaving her thoughts spinning in the slipstream and, somehow, she had to slow them down. As quietly as she could, she made her way outside. It was a crisp early morning, a watery sun in clear skies, a heavy dew just short of frost.

She wandered down herbaceous terraces and informal lawns, flanked by meticulously sited ornamental trees, and passed through an opening into a brick and flint walled garden. The garden was dominated by a Japanese folly that overlooked a carp pond. She perched on a sculpted stone bench and took out her phone. It was her own phone, the iPhone. One of Corbin's men had fitted a scrambling device that made tracing her location impossible. *'All your calls will come in,'* Corbin had told her, *'but if they try to trace you, they'll end up in North Korea or someplace.'*

'Is it safe to use?' she had asked.

Corbin had grinned. 'What part of 'untraceable' don't you understand?'

She went online and searched Corbin Defence Services.

> Corbin Defence Services, also known as CDS or Delta Securities, is a UK-based private security company that operates in government and the corporate sectors. It specialises in military activities, personal protection, specialist security and risk management. It has three divisions: Intelligence; Technical and Security. It is a registered UN contractor.

CDS seemed kosher enough. But then, so should HMG. She considered for a moment, then punched in Macleod's number.

'Hello?'

He sounded hesitant. She realized that she wasn't transmitting an ID.

'It's me.'

'So it is.'

'What do you know about Corbin Defence Services, aka Delta Securities?'

'Private military security company. It's not the biggest in the field, but it has a good rep for such a company. Why do you want to know?'

'The why doesn't matter.'

'To me, it's all important.' He waited for her reaction but there was none. 'Okay. Let's say it's a key defence contractor rather than a main contractor. It's not involved in the murkier end of the market, or so I'm told. Is this Steven's story?'

'How does Figgis stay free from investigation?'

'As long as the criminals investigate themselves, people like Figgis will always be free.'

'I need specifics.'

'Do you know what kind of spot you're putting me in?'

'No, because I have no idea what you know.' Silence. 'Don't lie to me, Malci. By all means, refuse to talk to me, but don't lie. '

'Okay,' he said. 'I've tried to protect you. . . .'

'It's too late for that.'

' . . . but since you insist. A faction within the security services has been covering up his Lordship's criminal dealings.' Macleod abruptly stopped himself. 'I'm not too happy talking about this on the phone. If it came out that I told you this, I'd end up in some Egyptian gaol. Let's meet. Today. Usual time and place.'

'I'm not in London at the moment.'

'Ah. Then we'll do it when you get back.'

'I can't . . .' She paused; she needed this meet. 'Okay. Tomorrow.'

With that, he cut her off.

She was suddenly aware of someone settling in beside her. Keaton. She hadn't heard him approach, hadn't seen him, and she wondered how long he had been there. She felt as though she should be afraid, yet she sensed no threat.

She frowned. 'How is it I never hear you coming?'

'You don't know how to listen.'

He was dressed in shorts and t-shirt, fresh from a morning run. Though hardly fresh. His skin glistened, his shirt was damp and his sweat was already turning stale.

He said, 'You're abroad early.'

There was something in his tone that said he was checking up on her. She snapped at him. 'Since when has that been a crime?'

He held up his palms, unoffended

'How did you know I was here?' she demanded,

'You've tripped so many security devices they're expecting a full-scale invasion up at the house.'

She looked at him sceptically. 'The only security I've seen is the boundary fence. I haven't been near it.'

'I thought journalists were supposed to be observant.'

'I'm a people person,' she told him drily. 'I don't do inanimate. It's why you and I don't get on.'

He grinned, genuinely amused. He glanced upwards, guiding her eyes to a drone that hovered silent and all-seeing.

'This placed is ringed with intruder alarms,' he informed her cheerfully. 'You can't move without triggering something - TI cameras, CCTV, geophones. You leave the house and the world rattles. That's you trying to get out. Anyone trying to break in! . . .' He made a throat-slitting gesture with his hand. 'Our host likes to live free of fear of criminals, terrorists and madmen.'

'But they let you in.' She managed a half-smile. 'At what stage does a fortress become a prison?'

'Try leaving without me. You'll soon find out.'

She shook her head. 'Won't you boys ever grow up?'

He stood and offered a helping hand. 'We've found Sullivan, by the way. I thought you'd like to be in on it.'

A brief but pointed hesitation, then she allowed him to pull her to her feet.

Chapter 46

WITH ITS PHONEY, diffused light, Heckstall Gardens resembled the ghost of a film set - lonely, deserted and with all the colour sucked out. They arrived three hours before the meet with Sullivan, and a pale blue glow was already peeking over Streatham Common. It wouldn't be long before this part of South London was awake.

There were four of them in the car, Ali, Keaton, Pearce, and Clark. Pearce was driving and he cruised slowly by Sullivan's house. A prim, three-story Edwardian building close to the Common, it was double-fronted and immaculately preserved. Even its original stained glass and ornate veranda were intact. It was the lone remnant of a street torn apart for apartments and bedsits. And, just as last season's stable citizens had moved on, so their place had been taken by the defenceless, the predatory and the downright dangerous – citizens too preoccupied with their own survival to care who lived in their midst. It was an ideal lay-up for a criminal fixer like Whitton.

The house looked empty. It should have been empty. The plan was to get inside and wait for Sullivan. Keaton acted as pathfinder, slipping from the car and disappearing into the garden. Minutes later,

Pearce's cell phone rang and he led the others through the gateway, past the crumbling little walls of the flower beds, and up the path to the entrance.

The door was open and Keaton was waiting inside. He had disarmed the alarm panel and he was holding his favoured Beretta 84 down by his thigh. Pearce took out his gun and they froze into the listening stance. The house was all dark gloom. No sounds, apart from the distant hum of traffic on the High Road and the gentle click as Clark closed the door. The air was heavy and musty, and there was a pervasive aroma of furniture polish. The ground floor was fitted out like a retro Welsh farmhouse, with antique dressers, '60s Ercol furniture and a huge pine table. Rugs covered the wooden floor, old prints of the Principality the walls, and Mr Sheen every exposed piece of wood. Ali could almost smell the sheep.

In silence, they cleared the farmhouse level. There was no sign that the house had been lived in for years.

Pearce tested his foot on the first stair, using hand signals to tell Keaton to leave a gap then follow.

Keaton chose that moment to say, 'House is clear.'

Pearce heard the smile in Keaton's voice, turned and punched him non too gently on the shoulder. 'Bastard!'

Ali was slow to catch on. 'Are you saying no one's here?'

Pearce said, 'Keaton thinks he's funny.'

Ali turned to Keaton. 'So you do jokes now.'

Keaton shrugged modestly. 'I'm practicing.'

He switched on the lights then followed Pearce upstairs. Clark came next and Ali trailed behind.

Pearce reached the landing and stopped so abruptly that the others crashed into him. There was a moment of cussing before the others could see what had checked him, then they fell into open-mouthed silence. They had just climbed out of a claustrophobic Dickensian underworld into an expansive AI designer world of light gray walls and white-oiled pine floor. The dissonance was enough to confound even these cynics. There was an open-plan living room and kitchen area, a boutique bedroom, a bathroom featuring an elliptical sunken bathtub and state-of-the-art tech throughout, There was no flatpack furniture, just beautiful woodwork and black electrical outlets. Natural light flooded in from picture windows that offered unobstructed views of the Common. The one incongruity was the tiny, purely functional home office.

It was Pearce who broke their silence. 'The guy must be schizoid.'

'Maybe,' Keaton nodded. 'But we're not playing celebrity fantasy homes. Let's focus on what we came for.'

Without another word, they set about tossing the place. Leaving the others to search the living area, Ali made her way into the office. It was little more than a broom cupboard, with desk, PC and phone and a few shelves of dusty files and papers. This was not the office of a man with a penchant for admin. Ali, who had been hoping for a gold mine, felt like a pauper who'd just been given a Gold Card without the pin number.

Keaton appeared at her side. 'What do the dead have to say?'

Ali shrugged. 'Short answer: not a lot.'

They sifted through the jumble of paperwork: invoices, letters, bank statements, military and gun magazines. There was nothing that connected to Sullivan, Shimmon or anyone else of interest.

Ali sat at the PC and turned it on. It booted to the Desktop without demanding a password. A bad sign. It was the work of moments to discover that the computer held just a handful of docs and pictures. No accounts, client lists or spreadsheets. A search of Whitton's browsing history was just as fruitless. It went back months, undeleted, but was intermittent and took in mostly military- and travel-related sites. He obviously didn't use the computer much. Clark confirmed that this reflected the Whitton he knew. Ali briefly considered the possibility that the artless clutter might conceal a hidden drive but concluded that Whitton had no mind for order and administration. Nevertheless, they would take the computer's drive for forensic analysis.

The milk in the fridge was usable so Pearce made coffee and they settled in the lounge to wait. No-one felt like talking. The house lights were off but the spreading dawn lit them up through the windows. Pearce briefly left the room and Ali thought she could hear the bath filling. She was too listless to ask why. They maintained a low-pressure silence right up to the moment when the doorbell rang.

Clark went to the door while Pearce followed him downstairs and watched over him from the shadows. Sullivan immediately started venting at Clark about protocols and never meeting face-to-face and he kept his diatribe going right up to the moment that he reached the living room and saw Keaton waiting for him. Sullivan's face displayed a range of emotions - surprise, recognition, fear, aggression and panic – before he turned to flee. Too late. Pearce was blocking the doorway, gun in hand. Sullivan instinctively stopped moving, holding out his palms as the fight-or-flight instinct left him. Pearce prodded him and he moved into the room and sat down on a white leather sofa.

Sullivan was in his late forties and the same height as Keaton. But whereas Keaton was lean meat, Sullivan was mere sinew. Even age and a sedentary lifestyle couldn't turn him to fat. He had pale skin with a shaved head and dark stubble. He was dressed in a black suit and pink shirt, no tie, and he carried a Fendi shoulder bag.

'Who are you?' he demanded. 'What the hell are you doing here?'

Keaton said, 'You know who we are.'

Pearce took the Fendi and tossed it to Keaton, then fastened Sullivan's wrists behind him with plasticuffs.

Sullivan didn't resist but he warned them, 'You're in big trouble. You don't know who you're dealing with.'

In reply, Pearce punched him on the side of his head.

Sullivan was momentarily stunned. His slumped sideways on the sofa, tried to put his hand to his head, found he couldn't and hunched miserably into the cushions. His face had turned a sickly grey. He showed no response as Pearce told him:

'You speak when we tell you to.'

Keaton was already searching the shoulder bag. It contained just three items: a smartphone, wallet and an iPad Pro. He did a preliminary check of the wallet and phone and found nothing blindingly obvious. The iPad was password protected. He looked at Sullivan.

'What's the password?'

Sullivan stared back, a mix of perplexity and defiance, and said nothing.

Keaton moved closer and stood over him. 'Password.'

More silence. Sullivan struggled up to a sitting position, a sickly expression on his face.

Keaton made a show of studying his watch then nodded at Pearce. 'That's us out of time.'

Abruptly, Pearce grabbed Sullivan by the hair and dragged him off the sofa and into the bathroom. At first, Sullivan was too shocked and hurt to resist. But, when he saw the bath full of water, he began to struggle so violently that it took all three men to hold him.

'No!' Sullivan pleaded. 'You don't have to do this!'

'But I want to.' Pearce forced Sullivan's face down into the water, muffling the scream that was forming on his lips. The three men held him steady until the desperate heaving slowed and the stream of bubbles terminated. At this stage, Ali, who had been stunned immobile by the sudden violence, come into the room. She saw what was happening and made to intervene, but Pearce was already lifting Sullivan's head out of the water.

'Don't you try and hold out on me,' Pearce said mildly. 'There's nothing I'd like better than to watch you drown.'

'Let me up,' Sullivan spluttered, his words coming as desperate sobs. 'I'll talk. Let me talk.'

Pearce plunged Sullivan back under.

This time the kicking and thrashing was more vigorous but it died away so quickly that Ali stepped forward to intercede. Keaton held up his hand like a traffic cop.

'If you can't take it,' he hissed, 'go wait in the lounge.'

Ali faltered, momentarily paralysed with indecision. It would be so easy to close her eyes to this, to slip away and hide in the other room. But they were torturing Sullivan in her name. Just as they had killed Whitton and the Kosovars. Whichever way she looked, her hands would still drip red with blood, What they were doing was so wrong but so was the threat to her own life. If Keaton was doing this to keep her alive, the least she could do was stay and watch.

Pearce lifted Sullivan's head and waited while the man coughed and heaved back to life. Sullivan tried to talk but his windpipe was squeezed against the edge of the sink. Then the hands that held him pulled him upright and let him go. He keeled over, arms cuffed uselessly behind him, and crashed to the floor. Instinctively, he curled into a ball. Unable to speak, or fight, or focus, he was helpless. He knew that he couldn't survive another ducking so he stayed down, afraid that these precious seconds of respite would end if he dared to look up.

A voice told him, 'Get up.'

Sullivan unraveled from his foetal position, peering up at the figures looming over him. His face streamed water, tears and mucous. Somehow, he managed to arrange himself into a sitting position.

'Password,' Keaton intoned.

This time, Sullivan told him. Keaton unlocked the iPad and was astonished to find what appeared to be Sullivan's entire business database. Page after page of jobs with initials for client, contractor, job and place, fees paid and commission. The entries were abbreviated but unencrypted.

He glanced at Ali. 'This is the motherload.'

Ali crowded him as he scrolled through the data.

'Here we go,' he said. 'AF must be you. Contractor is W for Whitton. Client is V.' He looked at Sullivan. 'Who is V?'

'V?' Speaking induced a coughing fit as Sullivan vented more water. 'Vanavasam.'

'He set you on Feysor.' Keaton registered the little nod. 'Who is he?'

'A client.' Every utterance was accompanied by the cough and wipe routine. 'He puts a lot of work my way.'

'What kind of work?'

'Security. Body guarding. Enforcement. That kind of thing.'

'Murder,' Ali added icily.

Sullivan pretended not to hear. 'He tells me what he needs and I find the right contractor for the job.'

'Whitton?'

'And others like him.'

'But you gave this job to Whitton?'

Sullivan nodded. He was still sitting on the bathroom floor though he was breathing more easily now.

Pearce said, 'You must be crazy to carry this with you. Unencrypted! Your friends will be queuing up to slice and dice you.'

'You'll all be dead before that happens,' Sullivan said, his voice thick and broken.

Keaton asked, 'Where do I find this V?'

'I don't know.' Sullivan saw Keaton glance at Pearce and almost hyperventilated. 'He works for someone called Crain but I only have dealings with V.'

'How do you contact them?'

'Secure email. The address is in V's file.' Sullivan had another wracking coughing fit. 'I've never had direct contact with Crain. I'm not supposed to know about him. V let the name slip once, when negotiating fees. He said Crain wouldn't pay that much. I tried to check on this Crain, thinking I might cut V out, but I came up blank.'

'So Crain is the main man.'

'The man with the money. The accountant. I think he's high up in their organization.'

Ali picked up Sullivan's phone and checked the directory and call history.

'This number for V,' she said. '0041. Switzerland.'

'The number is+ discontinued.' Sullivan managed to stifle a cough. 'I no longer have a phone number.' He read Keaton's scepticism and said, 'At one time, I contacted V by telephone. It was a Swiss number. Then he changed the procedure. He contacts me. Via email. The phone is gone. I just haven't got around to erasing the number.'

An uneasy silence filled the room. Sullivan coughed again and spat a few droplets of water onto the floor.

Ali asked, 'Who is Griffin?'

'I don't know a Griffin.'

Ali took in the man's fear and believed him.

'Figgis?'

Sullivan shook his head.

'How about First Garanty Bank?'

A hesitation betrayed Sullivan's knowledge and a thoughtful little frown appeared on his face. 'The money comes through First Garanty. How did you know that?'

Ali hadn't.

Keaton crouched down, took hold of Sullivan's chin and stared him in the eye. 'What will happen to you if V knows you've talked to us?'

Sullivan's eyes became wild. 'You can't do that! He'll kill me! The man's an animal.'

'And if you convince him that you told us nothing?'

'He'll kill me anyway.'

Keaton nodded cheerfully. 'So we'd best forget this little chat happened. If you don't tell anyone, neither will we. But mention it to someone else and we'll be leading the queue to murder you.' Keaton smiled mirthlessly. 'Consider this your lucky day. You carry on as if nothing's happened and you'll have all the life you deserve.'

Chapter 47

WHILE KEATON AND Pearce headed back to Ridge End, Ali set out for Covent Garden to meet with Macleod. She had almost reached Streatham Tube station when her phone rang.

It was Macleod. 'I'm afraid I have to rain-check.'

There was tension in his voice, a feature so uncharacteristic that she knew another lead was dying on her.

'Don't let me down, Malci.'

'That's why I'm calling. To put it right, to put you right.'

She said, 'Put what right?'

'Steven was set up,' he said. 'There is no story.'

'Bollocks there isn't.'

Macleod ignored her reaction and ploughed on. He sounded like a cold caller reading from a script. 'His source told him that Figgis had been dealing with the mafia in the Yugoslavia wars, on behalf of HMG. Supposedly, Figgis channelled money through First Garanty for weapons deals. The source seemed genuine enough. He even had documentation to back up his story.'

'Don't tell me,' Ali said, her voice thick with sarcasm, 'the source was fake.'

'From beginning to end. He was clever. He wrapped enough truth inside the lie to be convincing. He gave Shimmon *independent* sources who confirmed the story. Unfortunately, the documents were skilful forgeries.'

'That is unfortunate.'

'In hindsight it was very easy to see how Shimmon was manipulated. The story seemed airtight. But it was pure bullshit.'

'This is pure bullshit. Why didn't you tell me this the other day?'

'I didn't know the other day.'

'But you do now.' Ali let the anger flow. 'Nice people you work with. And they're listening in now, aren't they. Ready to give you a pat on the back!'

Furious, Ali cut him off. She called Keaton and had the guys turn around and pick her up. Once in the car, she told them what had happened with Macleod.

Keaton's face drew tight with concern. 'So they got to the old boy.'

It took a moment for Keaton's words to sink in, then Ali went hot with shame. She had put Macleod in harm's way and now she was throwing a tantrum because he had chosen life over truth. Why shouldn't he? What kind of person had she become, expecting everyone to sacrifice themselves on the altar of her story? She fell silent and spent the rest of the journey staring sightlessly out of the car window.

At Ridge End, Corbin greeted them with some positive news.

'There is just one Crain with accountancy offices in London and Zurich. The man himself is in Zurich. We have feet on the ground – and brains - but one of you should get over there to assess the situation.'

'That'll be me,' Pearce volunteered cheerfully. 'I've been to Zurich. I like it there. I know people. I dig clocks.'

Keaton smiled. 'Get a flight.'

Pearce left the room. Ali made to follow but Corbin motioned her to stay. He sat on a sofa and she selected a chair across from him.

He said, 'You want to know about Mammon?'

She stared at him, her eyes now bright and focused with a strange intensity.

'Yes.'

'I've been talking to an old buddy.' He paused for effect. 'This is deep background. You don't use this without my say-so, you don't use my name, and you must find another source, a source willing to go on the record. Oh, and there's one other stipulation: I retain control over copy. People's lives are at stake here.'

Ali didn't hesitate. 'You have my word.'

Corbin looked at Keaton who gave him a firm nod. Corbin hesitated further, as though wondering where to start.

'Towards the end of the Balkan wars, the allies compiled a wanted list of paramilitary leaders and other war criminals. It was said that special forces black units were hunting them down.'

She nodded. 'The UN investigated rumours of extrajudicial killings and found no evidence.'

'They wouldn't.' Corbin's mouth twitched in a cynical smile. 'Some on the list cut deals. Lucca was one of them. Cue Operation Mammon. It was an SAS op. Contrary to rumour, they didn't watch his own people kill him, or help them do it, or even kill him themselves. The team actually spirited the man away into a new life.'

That would explain the secrecy, the decades of unbroken conspiracy. But Ali couldn't quite bring herself to believe it. 'Why would they do that?'

Corbin shrugged. 'He gave up a truckload of his own. Why hold one trial when you can have twenty?'

'It was a numbers game?' Ali's brow wrinkled. 'So Lucca might still be alive?'

'Doubtful. Too many people wanted him dead. All I do know is that his handlers lost track of him.'

'Why are you telling me?'

'To make sure you understand the kind of people you're dealing with. If you get them, they kill you. If you don't get them, they kill you. This is a zero sum game. You're playing a game you already lost.'

'So why are you helping me?'

'People like me, and Chris, and Pearce, we do our job, we kill enemy soldiers or we die. It's the nature of the game. But the rape and slaughter of civilians? Women and children? The freeing of mass murderers for political gain! . . .'

Ali turned to Keaton. 'Did you know?'

'No.'

FOR THE NEXT few days, Ali felt redundant. She knew that it was a temporary inactivity, one that would end as soon as Pearce had gathered intel on Crain and Vanavasam. Nevertheless, she was in limbo and she fretted unhappily. As a child she had learned the three catechisms: effort was prayer; commitment was faith; trust in herself the creed. She had to do something!

Corbin's techs had cloned Sullivan's tablet and she spent days methodically working through it for leads. But the constraints of her situation were too big. She couldn't communicate with outside data sources, electronic or human, and she couldn't go anywhere.

The longer she achieved nothing, the worse she felt. A variety of apparently unrelated facts all came together in her brain, each a piece of the puzzle. But she couldn't fit it together. Her mind had been racing on single track for so long that she was coming up empty. There was something right in front of her nose that she was not seeing. She was so close that she could sense shapes, but when she stepped back to bring the picture into focus the shapes disappeared.

The summons from Switzerland couldn't come quickly enough.

Chapter 48

BY THE TIME Ali drove north to East Midlands airport, Pearce had been in Switzerland for six days. She boarded her flight to Zurich knowing that Keaton was already flying from Luton to the same destination. It was the first time they had been apart for over a week and part of her was relieved to have some alone time. The other part couldn't help but feel vulnerable.

She was traveling under the name of Elaine Morgam. This was a cover not a legend. She was still answering to her own name. At Kloten, She was met by a sallow-faced man of about forty who greeted her with a smile and perfect English. He guided her to his car, parked amongst the taxis outside the arrivals hall, and within thirty minutes they were pulling up at a CDS safe house on Loorenstrasse.

The building was a spacious, split-level design, set on the edge of the hilly woodlands that encroached into the east of the city. Sunlight streamed through the windows, painting a blush sheen on the waxed wooden floors and refracting off the frosted white walls. Bland prints hung in cold metal frames, complementing the modern Danish-style chairs and long, pristine white sofa. There was an overpowering neatness, a Germanic cleanliness.

Ali dumped her bag in her bedroom and returned to the living room. Keaton was on the balcony with Pearce and another man. Ali joined them and was surprised to find that the balcony was heated. There was a jug of coffee on the table and she helped herself before sitting down. Another day, she might have remarked on the view, looking out over the pool, patio and garden to the forest and mountains beyond. Today, she didn't even notice it.

Keaton introduced the newcomer as Kurt Kopke, a Swiss national and freelance intelligence officer. He was lightly-built and his suit looked hungry on him. The fact that he had spent the last few days working without a break had left him looking grey and skeletal.

Pearce cleared his throat. 'While you guys have been on vacation, we've been working all hours.' He responded to their insults with a wide grin. 'Crain's real name is Kurt Olsen. He's a Danish accountant and lawyer. Pays his taxes in Denmark and keeps offices in London and Zurich. He operates as Crain so we'll stick to that name. According to Kopke, here, he's a kind of consigliore to a guy who calls himself Michael Ashe.'

Pearce paused to check that everyone was focused. 'Crain has oversight of Ashe's business empire. His key talent is not so much his ability to launder money but his skill in laundering reputations. He loses the old, unwanted rep under layers of facts and fiction and he creates a new, more palatable truth to replace it. For people like Ashe, creating their own truth is all important in avoiding investigation, competition or murder.'

Keaton nodded. 'What do we know about this Ashe.'

Kopke glanced at Pearce who gestured for him to proceed. 'He is the CEO of Leke Corporation, one of the biggest private equity companies in the world. The company is registered in the British Virgin Islands, while Ashe himself is registered as a non-dom in the UK, where he pays nominal tax. He is somewhat reclusive. He has homes all over and he moves between them by private jet and helicopter. At any given time, you can't be sure where he is, where he's come from or where he's going. When in Switzerland, he stays at his schloss near Zug. This schloss is registered to Otwell Metals Inc., which is an off-shore holding company. We've been unable to trace its real ownership but Ashe will be in there, hiding behind a chain of dummy companies.'

'And he's at his schloss now?'

Kopke grimaced regretfully. 'According to my sources, he left there three days ago. They don't know where he went. Crain has stayed behind, presumably to tidy up some business or other. But he won't be there for long.'

Ali asked, 'What about Ashe's background?'

Kopke pursed his lips. 'We know very little. I traced him back to South Africa in the late nineties. Before that he is a blank. He had a series of business ventures that went wrong, then he founded Leke in 1998. He moved to the UK in 2001, since when his wealth has expanded exponentially. He was the subject of a joint Swiss-German investigation into his finances but that was called off.'

Ali frowned. 'Why?'

'According to my source in the FDF [*Swiss Federal Department of Finance*], Leke was suspected of involvement in organized crime and money laundering. The authorities could find no hard evidence.' Kopke paused. 'The investigation team lost two agents – they just disappeared – but they could prove no links to Leke. In the end, they closed the inquiry down.'

Keaton was disgusted. 'They've had agents disappear and they stopped investigating?'

'Three years of audits and surveillance, electronic and humint, produced nothing. Apparently, the decision to close down came from the higher-ups in the law enforcement and political spectrum. My source believes that the investigation was a sham. A means of deflecting then killing off interest in Ashe.'

Ali was sceptical. 'Why did they investigate him in the first place?'

'Because he's dirty,' Kopke said sourly. 'Leke was established by a South African private equity consortium whose background and finance were opaque. Leke specialises in private equity investments, using leveraged buyouts to acquire operating companies generating big cash flows. Suspicions were aroused because this consortium consisted of a network of companies - legitimate, dodgy and dummy - all controlled by Ashe. He uses clean and dirty money to purchase legitimate companies in financial services, healthcare, oil, power & gas, media and technology. There are too many companies within his empire to keep count. Some are legitimate, others less so.'

'I don't get it,' Ali said. 'If you know this why don't the authorities?'

'Knowledge isn't proof. Also, the authorities in many countries choose to look the other way. Money makes everything easier. Ashe buys the media, politicians and judges. He hires former special forces soldiers as a bodyguard. If people get close, he buys them off or scares them off. If that doesn't work, he disappears them.'

Ali exchanged an uneasy glance with Keaton.

She asked, 'Have you come across the name Griffin?'

Kopke smiled ruefully. 'The invisible man.'

'Griffin,' she breathed. How could she have missed it? 'The Invisible Man. H G Wells would turn in his grave.'

Pearce grinned. 'Seems our man has a sense of humour.'

'Sure,' Ali responded. 'Monty Python with a death rattle.'

Kopke said, 'The myth has grown up that there is a secret entity, a force. An evil force, if you like. It moves against anything that it perceives to be a threat, using bribery, intimidation and murder. All this is carried out in a businesslike manner, like closing down an unprofitable operation. But there is no evil force. Just an evil man.'

'Griffin?'

'That is the name given, yes. Only, in Switzerland, he is known as Frief. Frief is German for Griffin. He is also known as Grifo in Spanish, Grifone in Italian and Griffin in French.'

Ali said, 'We have linked this with First Garanty Bank. And Lord Figgis?'

'These names are in there, yes.'

Ali felt a rush of excitement as pieces began to fall into place. 'Is Ashe Griffin?'

'It is possible.' Kopke shrugged. 'His business empire operates like a terrorist cell structure. Each activity is separate from and unknowing of the others. He thrives on secrecy; very few people have knowledge of his activities.'

'Forget secret empires,' Keaton said. 'It doesn't matter who Ashe is. We stick to the plan. One step at a time. We came here for Crain. He's the next link to finding out who ordered the hit on you.'

Ali nodded. 'What's the next move?'

Pearce said, 'We've got taps on Crain's phones. Kopke's friends are handling the land line. A bit of grease, a few key strokes and we're in business. We're using a Stingray on his cell phone.'

[The Stingray is an IMSI-catcher, a device that pretends to be a legitimate base station for a cell phone network. When the mobile phone authenticates itself to the network, the IMSI-catcher handles the call.]

Keaton asked, 'What about surveillance?'

Pearce said, 'I had a look at the schloss. It's a big house surrounded by a very high wall, with extensive grounds beyond. They even land helicopters in there. There are armed guards. I asked around, discreetly, of course, and was told that the place has been mothballed for the time being. Crain is still there. We're watching the house but I can tell you now, it's too well protected to be a snatch point.'

Keaton glanced at Ali. 'Let's go take a look.'

Ali went to her room to change. When she returned to the balcony, the others weren't there so she sat and waited. A melee of children passed by, kicking and chasing a football. The woods echoed with their laughter. There was not a mechanized sound on the street, only the swaying of the breeze and the rustling of leaves on the pavement. Ali didn't want the moment to end.

But it did. Keaton appeared, then Pearce. The latter dropped a SwissAir flight bag on the table, took out two Glock 22s in clip-on holsters, passed one to Keaton and kept the other for himself. He placed a box of ammunition on the table. The bag contained additional ammunition. The two men then began to strip, inspect and re-assemble the weapons.

KOPKE DROVE THEM in a grey Audi. First stop was Crain's office. They parked down the street.

'He goes there maybe twice a week,' Pearce told them. 'His name's on the brass plate, the receptionist is a hot piece of work, and the practice still functions. But without him. He needs a legitimate front, hence his chain of accountancy firms.'

Keaton nodded. 'So we won't snatch him here. Let's see where the man lives.'

Kopke drove them out of Zurich on Route 4, then turned east onto the N4A motorway into the gentle hills of Canton Zug. They by-passed the ancient walled city of Zug and took the Lucerne road towards Cham. For a moment, the full nine mile stretch of the Zuger See lay before them, enclosed at its southern end by the steep scarps of the Rossberg and Rigi. Then they swung south-eastwards from Cham, taking the N4 towards the Gotthard tunnel before coming off the motorway at junction 35 and picking up the Holzhausernstrasse. They drove through Buonas and

Risch and continued along the western edge of the Zuger See. Ali was just beginning to wonder how much further when they saw a compact schloss off to their left. They passed its narrow access road and, some five hundred metres later, pulled into a layby.

They got out of the car and pretended to stretch. Kopke actually took a piss. Ali leaned on the roof of the car, energising on the pure air and enjoying the view down the rolling parkland to the schloss, the lakeside and beyond. The schloss itself was renaissance, dominated by its tall entrance tower and topped with coloured roof tiles arranged non-com that were offset by the burnt magnolia render of its walls. It was surrounded by a high wall, outside of which was a moat. She could also see a rosarium, stables and other outbuildings. A boathouse, half-timbered, with steep-gabled tiled roof, dominated the near shoreline while, a hazy three mile distance across the water, set against the backdrop of dark green patches of woodland on the gentle plateau of the Zugerberg, she could make out the whitish, linear spread of Zug.

Next to her, Keaton was eyeing a different world. Instead of renaissance beauty, he saw only advanced hardware, cameras and geophones and boundary wires, and, the ultimate in security, even in the twenty-first century, a flock of geese.

Pearce said, 'Our man's on the hillside behind us, armed with bins and a radio.'

Keaton nodded. 'You're right. There's no way in, not with all that surveillance. You'd have to walk in through the gate or lead a Pagoda squad. Neither is an option. We need a contact inside. Someone who can move around without drawing attention to himself.'

Kopke shook his head discouragingly. 'Only a handful of people are that close to Ashe and they've been with him for years. Even if we got someone inside, and they had a year to establish themselves, they would never gain a position of trust.'

'This needs some thought,' Keaton said. 'Keep that man of yours on the hill for tonight.'

'That'll please him.'

'So what's the plan,' Ali asked. 'Snatch him off the street?'

'Pretty much,' said Keaton, feeding off her sarcasm. 'We're looking for an opportunity. A few seconds is all it takes. It sounds half-cocked, I know. Even if we can detach him from his people, there must be no witnesses or they will be looking for him straight away.'

Pearce said, 'Be easier to hit him.'

'Dead men don't talk.' Keaton bumped his fist against his friend's arm. 'He's a gateway target, remember. A means to his boss.'

Kopke stretched and slowly got into the car. Pearce followed. Ali opened the door to get in. As she did so, she noticed that Keaton was still watching the building, his face wistful and hungry, as if he was hoping to devour its secrets.

Chapter 49

KOPKE'S PEOPLE HAD been watching Crain for almost a week, during which time their target had followed no routine that might expose him. On two occasions, the accountant had been driven into his Zurich office, where he had stayed for less than half an hour before returning to the schloss. Another time, he had visited an apartment block in the east of the City. On each excursion, he had been accompanied by at least two BGs. He could have been snatched but not without a very public skirmish.

The pressure was on. Crain was preparing to relocate and they didn't know where, when or for how long. His fortified home and the lack of identifiable pattern to his behavior made it near impossible to devise an effective plan to snatch him. They talked through as many scenarios as they could imagine, planning action, fallbacks and escape routes. In the end, they opted for Keaton's random opportunity strategy. This involved following Crain whenever he left the Schloss and waiting for a chance to take him unobserved. They would have to shadow him without detection for an indeterminate period of time, a task made difficult by the presence of his trained bodyguards. Their window, if they recognized it in time, would be tiny. Ali didn't think it a plan at all but what did she know? Keaton just grinned and told her that, as contingency plans went, it was good.

They kept a spotter on the hillside above the schloss and put a car on each of the two routes that led away from it.

ON THE THIRD morning, they were in place by six-thirty, eyes sticky after only a few hours' sleep. Keaton and Ali were covering the northern route along Holzhausernstrasse, parked up a mile-and-a-half from the schloss. Pearce and Kopke had the southern route. Each had a local operative as a guide. Two other cars were available as back up.

Ali and Keaton had relaxed into the dormancy of the watcher. Each was an expert in waiting. Neither required chatter, music, smartphone or reading material. They were content to do nothing, think nothing and burn no energy. But the success of this stakeout didn't require silence and, from time to time, Ali tried to coax Keaton into conversation.

'You've done bodyguarding work, right?' she said. 'Who was your worst client.'

To her surprise, he answered. 'There was a guy, Hollywood actor.' He gave her the name of an action movie star which she knew very well. 'He was a total arsehole to work for, showed you nothing but contempt. You'd be somewhere and he'd suddenly look at you and say *Piss!* and you'd have to immediately check and clear the toilets.'

'Did you have to hold his teensy little penis?'

'I'd have sliced it off.'

She smiled. 'You shouldn't have told me that. I'm a journalist.'

'I'd deny it.'

They lapsed back into silence.

It was almost eleven o'clock when the spotter saw the Mercedes turn out of the schloss. It was headed north. The car had darkened windows and they couldn't be sure that Crain was inside. Keaton decided to assume that he was.

The Mercedes passed them and they fell in behind. Whilst on Holzhausernstrasse, they maintained a safe distance, even losing eye contact from time to time. Their target accessed the N4 northbound and they could afford to keep distance and several cars between them. North of the Lucerne turn, Pearce and the back up cars joined them and the four cars rotated obs until they reached Zurich.

The Mercedes crossed the Limmat over the Bahnhofbrucke and threaded its way through local streets, eventually stopping at a small but exclusive-looking restaurant. Keaton slipped into a parking spot that gave him eyes on. Crain was exposed for a matter of seconds between car and restaurant. He had a thick briefcase in his hand.

'We can't take him here,' Keaton said into his mic. 'It's too public. Stay out of sight.'

A little under an hour later, Crain was on the move again.

The watchers stayed with him, dropping back when they could, getting tighter when there was a chance of losing him. On Gloriastrasse, they held back as their target drove through Fluntern so they had time to react tactically when the Mercedes turned into an upmarket apartment house on Kurhausstrasse. Keaton parked up in a spot that gave them eyes on but was out of range of the CCTV cameras. The other cars drove on out of sight.

The block was on an exclusive development, with underground parking, a swimming pool and golf course. According to the discrete notice outside, it had been recently renovated to offer stylishly furnished, spacious accommodation with large balconies. There was a secure entry system and manned security.

Ali and Keaton watched as Crain emerged from his vehicle. He wasn't alone. His companion was fortyish, conditioned and watchful.

'BG,' Keaton said into the radio. 'Armed.'

Pearce acknowledged, then informed them, alert and hopeful. 'This is the apartment block he visited last week.'

Judging by Crain's demeanor, it did seem to be a routine visit, one that he had made many times before. The BG waited until Crain had been buzzed into the building then returned to the car and drove off. Pearce followed discreetly.

Ali asked. 'Why don't we go in after him?'

'We don't know what we'd be walking into. He might be visiting a mistress or inspecting the troops. Plus, we have no idea which apartment he's in. We can't knock on every door without arousing suspicion.' Keaton pointed out the cameras. 'We won't take him without a fight and there's security and CCTV everywhere. If we try to snatch him here the cops'll be all over us in minutes. Killing him would be easy enough but the whole point of this is to talk to him. He's a gateway target, don't lose sight of that.'

'So we wait?'

'We wait,' Keaton agreed. He thumbed his cell phone and called Pearce. 'You on the Mercedes?'

'It's parked up by a supermarket.'

'Could you take it?'

Brief assessing pause. 'Yes.'

'You remember Belfast? The 'One Way Ride'?'

Chapter 50

ARMED MEN SURROUNDED the wooden barn, some in uniform, some not, all members of the same rag-tag paramilitary mob. A hurricane of yellow fire reached into the night sky, roaring and crackling with destruction and terrible death. Intermittent laughter from the mob accompanied the bursts of gunfire from the village behind them as terrified folk were dragged from their hiding places. The screams of the women and children inside the barn were beginning to die away when, all of a sudden, a young girl escaped the inferno and ran down the street. She was on fire. The man who pursued her was laughing so hard that he was losing ground. They came closer and then Rachel could see it all.

The laughing man was her father.

The running child was Rachel herself.

The child Rachel screamed, snapping her adult self awake and propelling her from bed to window. She stood there, gasping for air, until she could breathe more or less easily. The atmosphere in the room was sweaty, gloomy and airless. Below her, street lamps penetrated the shadows, though their feeble aureoles of light couldn't reach up to where she was standing.

Above her, a scattering of stars penetrated the artificial glow of the New York sky.

She had always been afraid of the night sky, with its pinpricks of deadly attraction, afraid of its emptiness and deadness. Even now, in the safety of her bedroom, she stepped back lest she be sucked up through the broken cloud to infinity.

She became aware that his smell was with her. The choking, foul breath of stale alcohol. The acrid, sweaty excitement. She shivered and pulled her nightdress tighter. He wasn't here, of course. She knew that. Nevertheless, she switched on the main light before climbing back into the comfort and warmth of her bed.

But there was to be no more sleep this night. She had been cast into a black hole - less nightmare, more cosmic joke - and no matter how hard she tried she couldn't find a way out. If she were different she would turn her angst into something holy. A jihad, perhaps. Maybe then she wouldn't be so afraid.

She had suffered enough to be a martyr. Not as much as her mother, of course, but she had endured her share of suffering. Endured it alone. She didn't want to think any more about other victims, didn't want to think about their terror and the helplessness as they were lined up and murdered. She wanted to unburden herself of her own victimhood. Confide in someone. Ease her memories by sharing them.

She pulled on her robe, and made her way into Nadia's room. Her new friend was sprawled, dead asleep. Rachel hesitated, but decided not to wake her. Instead, she sat on the edge of the bed. She was silent for several minutes, then she spoke softly.

'How could he do that? How could he kill his own family then lie to me for so many years. How could he pretend to love me when he planned to kill me?'

She clenched her hands as if afraid of falling apart, digging her nails into her palms so that the spasm of pain brought tears to her cheeks and made her feel better.

'For a long time, I wanted to kill him,' she told Nadia softly. 'I lived for revenge. I wanted to wash my hands in his blood. But now I think it would hurt him more for everyone to know the truth. Only the dead are free of pain. Why kill him and set him free?'

She stood, her eyes coming to rest on the window. Both drapes and blind were open.

'At my mother's funeral, there were no mourners.' Hot tears teased her eyes. 'I can't even remember her face.'

She paused to recover herself.

She realized that first light was percolating the cold morning, backlighting the mist of dried raindrops on the window.

'*Only the dead are free of pain!*' she repeated, her words infused with self-mockery. 'What's that all about?'

Chapter 51

Crain emerged from the apartment block just as the Mercedes pulled up by the entrance canopy. He walked the few paces to the car, opened the rear door and slumped into his seat. He was sated, a fine meal followed by even finer sex, and it took him a few minutes to realise that they were travelling northwards, away from Fluntern and towards the forest. Something stirred deep inside of him, a hint of danger, but he couldn't quite believe it.

'Hey!' he managed to call out. 'Where are we going?'
Silence.

For the first time since getting in the car, he looked at the driver. The eyes that stared back from the mirror were blue, not brown. It wasn't Henning. And the driver was alone. Where the hell was his BG?

Then Keaton rose from a crouch in the front passenger seat, a shaft of amused hostility in his eyes and a gun straight out of Star Wars. Crain struggled to sit up but he knew that he was lost even before Keaton fired the Taser.

CRAIN WAS MANHANDLED into the room by two of Kopke's team who stripped him of his jacket and taped him to an upright chair. The puncture wounds and bruising from the taser were clearly visible through his open shirt though the soreness had yet to kick in. When Keaton came in, closely followed by Pearce and Ali, Kopke's men left. They were in a holiday chalet in the Naturpark Sudschwarzwalk, an isolated, one-roomed house with two small bedrooms overhead. It had a flag floor and black leather couch, with matching easy chairs on either side of a granite fireplace, and the walls were decorated with art from a depression ward, random strokes of black paint on canvas that made Munch seem like a comic genius. A video camera was recording events. The Mercedes was in the garage. Ali had no idea what had happened to Crain's driver and BG.

Crain was grey and twitchy, and looked to have aged ten years, but his body was beginning to function again, He had a cultured, patrician air and a face to be trusted. Try as she might, Ali couldn't map his laughter lines onto her mental image of evil.

As if reading her thoughts, Crain stared straight at her. 'Ms Feysor,' he said in perfectly enunciated English. 'I see that reports of your demise were greatly exaggerated. Please don't think that these gentlemen represent a guarantee of your safety.'

'You're the one who's tied up,' she responded acidly.

He gave her a thin, pained smile.

Keaton glowered down at him. 'Forget the small talk. Tell us what we want to know and we'll be out of your life.'

Crain hesitated, like he was hurting too much to speak. He wasn't that damaged, just hell-bent on survival, and his mind was working furiously.

'If I talk to you, I'm a dead man,' he said. 'You don't know who you're dealing with.'

'I *don't* know who I'm dealing with,' Keaton told him softly. 'That's why you're here. Tell me, who are we dealing with?'

Crain said nothing.

Keaton jabbed out his right fist and hit Crain in the nose. The accountant rocked back on his chair, blood trickling from his nose. Involuntary tears pooled in his eyes, but he made no sound.

Pearce grasped Crain's hair and jerked his head back. Pearce's face was distorted, cruel and hateful. 'You think the taser hurt? Just wait until I get started.'

Keaton said, 'Tell us about Ashe.'

'Ashe?' Crain actually laughed, a pained, hysterical cackle. 'This is about Ashe!'

Pearce disconnected Crain's laughter by digging his fingers beneath the accountant's collarbone and crushing the brachial plexus nerves into the bone. An instant of silence then Crain emitted a thin screech that became a gasp of air as the pain intensified. He was completely disabled. Silent tears spilled over his face.

Pearce released the pressure and Crain flopped forward, his face twisted and bloodless.

'Stop! Please!' Crain's words were fractured, disembodied. 'Please! . . . Don't hurt me again!'

Ali was stunned by the suddenness of Crain's collapse. She had steeled herself for another session of water treatment, but this? *Horses for courses, Keaton told her later. No need to be clever. Just use the quickest and most effective method, depending on your subject.* In truth, Ali was more troubled by her own dispassionate reaction. It was as if her moral core had been sucked out, to be replaced by a dark, pitiless emptiness. She didn't have to like what they were doing, of course, provided that she could justify it to herself. And, at this moment, she could. Her own survival, and that of her companions, depended on getting Crain to talk. People like him lied as a matter of course and, if it took a bit of coercion to get to the truth, she told herself, then so be it.

Keaton regarded Crain impassively. 'Okay. We've stopped. Talk to us and we won't need to hurt you again.'

Crain lifted his head and stared back at him, his mouth wide with shock, his eyes sunken and out of focus. 'I'm just an accountant,' he gasped. 'What can I tell you?'

'Understand this,' Keaton told him softly. 'I admire courage in a man but too much courage will just prolong the pain. My friend here enjoys inflicting pain. And me: I enjoy killing people. You have this one chance to survive. Stall, or lie, and you will experience pain beyond your imaginings. Then you will talk and, believe me, your subsequent death will be rapture. But if you answer our questions now, without further persuasion, we won't hurt you again. Understand?'

Crain's eyes slid from contact and his voice was barely a whisper. 'I understand.'

'Fine. So dredge your memory and don't waste any more of our time.'

With that, Keaton stepped aside and nodded to Ali.

She shrugged aside her own doubts and said, 'We want the inside deal on Ashe's business and financial affairs.'

Crain reacted with consternation. 'I can't! . . . He would! . . . Give me your gun and I'll shoot myself!'

Pearce stepped closer. 'What did you think we wanted? The name of his cat?'

'You can't touch him!' Crain was terrified by the thought that his own life depended on these people taking down Ashe. 'They've all tried. Law enforcement. Financial authorities. Journalists. None of them came close.'

Keaton asked, 'Did any of them have you by the balls?'

Crain flinched but managed to keep his focus on Ali. 'Ashe has more than two thousand business holdings world-wide, and as many bank accounts. Legal and illegal, real and dummy, separate yet tied together. And it keeps changing. Constantly. It's almost beyond understanding. Even I would struggle to audit it.'

Ali smiled. 'You're saying we're too ignorant to understand it?'

'No offence.'

'None taken,' Ali said. 'We don't want to audit him. We're not even interested in his business empire. We want the man himself. Give us a way in and we can help you out.'

'Help me?' Crain laughed mockingly. 'The establishment protects people like Ashe. Too many people rely on him. Bankers, industrialists, politicians, intelligence agencies, terrorists, drug cartels! They can't operate without people like Ashe. You want justice? The justice system *protects* him. Even if you gathered the evidence, you would never reach a court of law.'

Keaton curled his lip. 'Who said anything about a court of law? We recognise no authority and we don't care about evidence. We already know the man is guilty and he will pay. That, my friend, is life under a black flag.'

Crain shook his head. 'Do you have any idea what they will do to me?'

Pearce rested his hand on Crain's shoulder. 'No, but you know what we will do.'

Crain's eyes opened in terror, beads of sweat appeared on his temple and his legs started shaking, as if his software no longer controlled him. Muscle memory can be an unpleasant thing. Pearce removed his hand.

There was a long moment of narcosis, when no-one moved or spoke. Then Crain cleared his throat.

'Ashe is not the boss man,' he said, his tone and demeanor calmer. 'He answers to a man called Bowman. David Bowman.'

Ali couldn't conceal her surprise. 'Bowman?'

'Bowman. You might have heard him called Griffin.'

'Griffin?' Ali was turning into an echo. 'So Griffin is real.'

'Very real.'

'What can you tell us about him?'

'Precious little. I have only met him on two occasions. Ours is a purely business relationship, conducted through Ashe.'

'You must have some background.'

A little shake of the head. 'Bowman told me never to look and I haven't. He said he would know if I did and I believed him.'

'You run his empire but you don't get to meet him?' Ali smiled scornfully. 'How does that work?'

'He came to me at the end of the Balkan wars. South-east Europe was in total chaos at the time but we managed to retrieve and launder tens of millions of dollars. I created shell companies and intermediary companies – all opaque operations whose ownership was untraceable – and set up the financial systems. When Lucca fled Kosovo, I helped him expand his business worldwide. I started to launder his money into legitimate businesses, initially real estate, casinos, restaurants, hotels. At the same time, his illicit businesses were growing so quickly that we could hardly keep up. At this stage he started working through Ashe. Ashe wasn't interested in the mechanics, but I introduced him to the *legitimate* white collar professional world of bent lawyers, bankers, stockbrokers, accountants and realtors. Before long, the business was growing exponentially. Now I oversee a virtually integrated world-wide corporate empire.'

'You still work through Ashe?'

'Yes.'

'And it was Ashe who had you hire the men who tried to kill me.'

'I don't hire contractors. I pay them. I told Ashe to insulate us, to channel these activities via an untraceable dormant company, but Bowman has trust issues. I do my best to conceal the payments, but you found me nevertheless.'

Keaton cut in. 'Tell us what you know about Bowman.'

Crain sucked in a deep breath. 'He keeps himself invisible. The world is not permitted to know that he exists. That is difficult in the age of the internet but we manage it quite well. Only a handful of people can put a face to the name and they are close, long-time associates. He is a citizen of everywhere and nowhere. He lives through cutouts. You won't read about him in society or business papers or on Wikipedia. He employs me to keep his name out of the public domain and I use a team of PR wizards, lobbyists and lawyers to make it happen. When all else fails, he uses bribery, intimidation and worse to secure his privacy.'

Ali glared at him, her voice thick with fury. 'You arranged the murder of Steven Shimmon and Paul Stewart.'

'No!' Crain was indignant. 'Never. I arrange payments on the instructions of Ashe. That is my only involvement. I don't ask what the money is for.'

'But you do know.' Ali sneered. 'Just because you didn't sign off an invoice: *For murder services rendered*. You know!'

Crain said nothing. Despite Ali's anger, the atmosphere in the room was losing its charge, as if the air filters were sucking out all the testosterone.

Ali resumed. 'So Bowman controls Ashe. Does that mean he owns Leke.'

'Ultimately, yes.'

'And your role in all this?'

He shrugged. 'It's twofold. I maintain his privacy and I macro-manage his money.'

'How does the money side work?' Ali wondered. 'Keep it simple.'

'I oversee the creation of false financial records for his holdings. He presents these to his public accountants as genuine. They then draw up the official company accounts - balance sheets, P&L and so on - and file the appropriate tax returns. And I set up the companies and transactions to obscure the source, movement and destination of the monies. First Garanty Bank is the primary conduit.'

Ali nodded. She was back to the money. She was not sure that she would ever understand how these connections fitted together but she didn't need to. She had found a trail to Griffin.

'So you control Bowman's financial records for all his operations, both legal and illegal?'

He nodded. 'Yes. Not even Bowman has the kind of overview I have. The genuine companies stand up to public scrutiny and audit. They are incredibly profitable but, like all moguls, Bowman is never satisfied. He uses them, in conjunction with a network of dormant companies, to launder the hundreds of millions of dollars generated by his illegal activities.'

'Dormant companies?'

'They are fronts for a range of activities.' Pause. 'Let me give you an example. Kiera Industries was a big name in footwear back in the day, with a reputation for being an honourable, old-fashioned company. In 2006, it was dying on its feet. Then it acquired M.P.A. Imports plc, a dormant company registered in the UK, since when its fortunes have taken a dramatic upturn. M.P.A.'s chairman is Michael Ashe.'

Ali gave him *so what?*

'If you follow the paper trail back and forth across the globe, you would find that M.P.A. actually owns

Kiera Industries, not the other way round. Kiera is now used as a clearing house for many of Bowman's illegitimate activities. It's how Bowman operates. How he built his empire.'

'I assume you keep records of your activities.'

For an instant, Crain considered holding out. But he sensed Pearce behind him and he knew that he was beaten. 'In my office at the Schloss. Don't ask me to go back. If I turn up without my driver and BG, they will know. I would never get out again.'

'Without the records, you are of no value to us.' Keaton told him.

'I have copies.' Crain hesitated to cross the line but this was his life they were talking about. He had to deal with this threat now and worry about Ashe later. 'In a bank deposit box, here, in Zurich. I can retrieve them for you.' Another pause as he registered their scepticism. 'What can I do? You have the video of our little chat. Even without that, I am finished. Like I said, Bowman has serious trust issues. If I was seen giving Ms Feysor directions in the street, he would kill me.'

Keaton was unsympathetic. 'How do you contact him?'

'Bowman? I don't. I deal exclusively through Ashe. Ashe is his right hand, a barbarian. A fucking Kosovar.'

Ali took a moment to make sense of this. She was full circle back to Kosovo. Ask one question and another was thrown back at her. The deeper she ventured into the maze, the more impossible it became. But it didn't matter. Keaton was right: the time for analysis was past. Just go with the flow.

'Is Bowman a front for the Kosovan mafia?'

'Bowman? A front?' Crain managed a pained chuckle. 'He *is* Leke. A true Napoleon of the multinationals.'

'What about Lord Figgis? Is he involved?'

'Figgis? Yes. But he is nothing. A gofer.'

'Where is Bowman now?'

'New York. At his Long Island home.'

They paused to absorb what Crain had told them.

Keaton said, 'Is it true that you have a mole inside your organization.'

'You don't know?'

'No.'

Crain laughed, a slightly hysterical cackle. 'You are truly blundering about in the dark.' He quickly controlled himself. 'There is a mole, as you call him. His identity is unknown but he talked with Shimmon and he helped the girl. Ashe's people are turning the world over to find them, the girl and the mole both. The British security services are helping him.'

'The British?' Keaton echoed. 'Helping Ashe? Are you sure?'

'Yes.'

'Who?'

'That, I don't know.'

'You said a girl,' Ali demanded. 'What girl?'

'I believe that she is Bowman's daughter. She has run away and taken with her a memory stick. I am told that this stick contains financial data concerning assets in tax havens, secret agreements with the British government, and other damning documents. Its loss has created a crisis big enough to involve Bowman himself.'

Ali asked, 'Do you know where she is?'

Crain stopped laughing but there was a manic glint in his eye. 'She's close. I can sense that. But I'm not quite there. Wait a moment. Let me tune my telepathic powers.'

Keaton snapped, 'Cut it out.'

Crain turned grim. 'If I knew where she was, she wouldn't be missing.'

Ali asked, 'How can she have got that kind of data?'

'She copied files from his personal computer.'

Ali scowled. 'Only a retard keeps everything on his PC for some girl to copy.'

'A very rich and very dangerous retard.' Crain told her. 'The kind of man who thinks he is invincible, who kills without compunction to protect his privacy. Even a journalist should not look into the darkness of this man's soul.'

Ali almost nodded her agreement, but it was much too late for her.

Crain's words seemed to have affected Crain himself. A concern worked into his eyes, a worry, a fear that had nothing to do with his captors or the pain and humiliation that had been inflicted upon him. It was the fear that came with the realisation that he was now dealing with forces that were cruel and unchecked by morality. His chest moved up and down with his breathing.

'Bowman,' he said.

'What about him?'

'He lives by the vendetta. You may not have pulled the trigger but you have just killed me.'

Pearce said, 'You chose the life.'

Crain seemed not to hear him. 'You have to help me.'

'Why?'

Pause.

'I can help you,' Crain said earnestly. 'Quid quo pro.'

Silence, They just looked at him.

'I can steal his money for you.'

Ali couldn't conceal her surprise. 'You can do that?'

'Of course. I could drain his accounts. Though it might be better to be less greedy and more subtle. It would take longer for them to realise what's happening.'

He fielded their dubious stares.

'Threatening his money is the best way to hurt him.' He read their continued cynicism. 'I have full control of all accounts. He would not know until it was done.'

Ali could see the glimmer of an opening here. Extort Bowman's co-operation. But she wasn't convinced. 'We're talking millions. Somebody would notice that amount of cash shifting.'

'Billions,' Crain corrected her. 'London holds trillions of pounds in offshore accounts. A billion is nothing.'

Keaton asked, 'How would it work?'

Crain paused to gather his thoughts. 'I contact Baker at First Garanty Bank. Baker arranges the activation of dormant non-published accounts. The accounts are opened, used for the transaction, then closed. All in the blink of an eye. They don't show on the accounts list so no investigator or auditor would ever know of their existence. Which means that neither Ashe nor Bowman would know.'

Keaton said, 'The banker would tell them.'

'Baker?' Crain shrugged. 'It would be after the fact. And they would kill him.'

Ali could see another problem. 'They have your accounts at the schloss. They would set an army of accountants on finding the money.'

'I use my own system for the felonious accounts. Ostensibly to keep the authorities at bay but also to make myself indispensable to Bowman and Ashe. There are shell companies and dormant accounts that only I know about. It would take them months to unravel the systems and codes to trace which money has gone, let alone where it has gone. That's if they succeed in doing so. If the authorities can't fathom what I do, what chance Ashe or Bowman? I'm just too far ahead of the game.'

'You've got it all worked out,' Keaton said approvingly. 'How long have you been planning this?'

Crain permitted himself a weak smile. 'I lacked the courage to do it. Now, of course, it would take courage not to do it.'

'Okay,' Keaton said. 'We'll think about it. But first, we go with you to your bank. We need to put your records in a safe place.'

'First,' Crain corrected him, 'I must call the Schloss. They will need the code that tells them I am staying out overnight and that I am safe.'

Chapter 52

THE EARLY MORNING sun pierced the departures hall of Madrid Airport, a tiny disc centred in broadening pastel bands of mauve and pink. A miracle of colour but a harsh light to the eyes of a woman who hadn't slept.

Ali had flown overnight from Kloten with Keaton and Pearce. They had been met by a middle-aged woman who exchanged their false passports for documents drawn up for new fake identities. From Madrid, they were to make their separate ways to New York, Ali via Berlin, Keaton via Paris and Pearce by way of Helsinki. Meanwhile, two men and a woman were flying on to London using passports almost identical – the photos were different - to those that Ali and the two men had just surrendered. All courtesy of Corbin.

Ali was losing count of the number of passports they had used. Each was a genuine British passport made out to a false identity. Maybe her colleagues at the Echo were right: British passports were as freely available as travellers cheques. It was certainly a safer way to travel for illegals than clinging to an overcrowded boat or suffocating in the back of a container.

Not that she felt safe. From now on, it was a case of us looking for them looking for us looking for them.

Part Three

The winner plots one step ahead of the opposition. And plays her trump card just after they play theirs. It's about making sure you surprise them. And they don't surprise you.

Miss Sloane

Chapter 53

Somehow Ali managed to carry the malodour of violent death across the Atlantic. Animal decay, coppery blood and charred flesh. No-one else could smell it, no-one else was aware of it. But it hung on her like death clung to the old buffalo hunters as she passed through JFK immigration.

The three of them - Ali, Keaton and Pearce - had arrived within hours of each other. Pearce, who was experienced enough to drive like a New Yorker, collected a Ford Edge, pre-hired by one of Corbin's New York associates. He rolled into the pick-up area by the terminal and Keaton settled into the front while Ali climbed into the back.

A distant glimpse of Queens and Brooklyn briefly stirred Ali. She was back in her beloved Big Apple, a city with which she had enjoyed a romantic attachment since her teens, when she had embarked on a celluloid affair with De Niro, Scorsese and the Goodfellas. But the buzz didn't last. All too soon, she recalled that she was here for a different kind of made guy. Disenchanted, she hunkered down into a haze of micro-sleeps and troubled melancholy as they crawled along the I-678 N, picked up speed on Grand Central Parkway and slowed again on the Cross Island

Parkway. They followed FDR Drive south to Yorkville, by the East River, where Pearce turned into East78 Street and stopped the car.

'Give me fifteen minutes,' Keaton said. 'Come around and pick me up. If I'm not here, go.'

He got out of the car, put on his shades and tapped the roof. Pearce took off along East78 Street and Keaton walked in his exhaust trail before turning left along York Avenue and left again into East73 Street. The apartment block that contained their *safe house* dominated the skyline, fifty stories of black and gray glass. Keaton approached at a leisurely pace, his demeanour relaxed, his eyes busy behind his darkened lenses. He couldn't pick out a watcher, which was hardly a surprise. He wasn't expecting one and why should he? No-one knew that they were here. But he had been trained to expect the unexpected. He couldn't be sure that he was surveillance-free - you can't prove a negative - and he maintained his vigilance as he approached the apartment block, turned past the gatehouse and strolled up the private driveway. He exchanged a brief word with the doorman guarding the porte cochere, then showed his paperwork to the concierge in the lobby and was politely waved through.

He ignored the lift and slow-jogged up the staircase to the twelfth floor. He came out into a wide, air conditioned corridor with extensive city views. He approached their apartment and listened at the door. Hearing nothing, he rapped hard. No-one answered. He put the key in the lock and, standing to one side, pushed the door open. The place was empty. He entered a comfortable foyer, with en-suite bedrooms right and left. Ahead of him was the living room, complete with granite kitchenette and dining alcove. A picture window took up much of the east wall with panoramic views of the East River. The apartment itself was minimalist, with functional furniture and rugs scattered over polished oak floors.

Satisfied with his inspection, he took the lift down to the parking garage. Roughly half of the spaces were occupied, one by an Eco Green Jeep Cherokee which was their change car. He retrieved a small metal box attached to the underside of the Jeep and extracted two sets of car keys. He returned to the lobby and made his way out to the street. He stood for a moment, as though gaining his bearings, eyes working overtime behind his shades. Pretty sure that he was unobserved, he made his way to the rendezvous point. Pearce picked him up and, moments later, they were bumping down the ramp to the car park.

Once inside the apartment, Ali claimed a bedroom and a moment of solitude. She dropped her bag on the floor and went to the window where she was greeted by a vertiginous view of the East River that prompted her to take a step back. To the north, clouds scudded through the blue sky over the Triborough Bridge. Below her, the tree-lined basin reminded her that the East River was no river. It was a tidal reach. A 55 metre ocean-going yacht cruised smoothly past, leaving a small sail yacht trailing in its wake. Two old barges spluttered seaward, loaded with the ghosts of railway carriages. Beyond the boats, occupying the middle of the River, was the detached finger of Roosevelt Island. Google Earth come to life. She was looking down on the Coler Memorial Hospital, with the old power station and high rise beyond, and the Southern Construction, an array of apartment blocks clustered together against the South Queensborough Bridge.

She dragged herself away from the window and switched on her iPhone. Plenty of emails and messages dropped in. Only a few days ago, that would have confirmed how important she was. But not now. Just a single item grabbed her attention. Shimmon's funeral had been fixed for tomorrow. That put her in a classic double bind. Stay in New York or attend Shimmon's funeral. She couldn't do both, she couldn't give up on either. And what was happening about Stewart's funeral?

She started to tremble. There was a rush of heat to her head and her extremities turned to ice. She eyed the bed, expecting to collapse, but then all was normal again. It was as though a spike of emotion had blown her fuse. It wasn't the first time it had happened, nor the last. It was a useful defence mechanism to have, but one day her whole damn system was going to shut down. For now, it was enough to realise that missing Stewart's funeral was not the end of the world, not like his death had been. Given the circumstances, she knew that he wouldn't mind.

She became aware of movement and voices. She opened her bedroom door and the smell of freshly brewed coffee wafted over her. The others were in the kitchen. Keaton glanced up as she entered the room and put a finger to his lips.

'I was just about to fetch you,' he said.

A pulse of silence.

'Are you ready, now?' Corbin asked.

Ali realised that they had him on speakerphone.

'Fire away.'

Corbin said, 'I have some background on Ashe, though, to be honest, it doesn't tell us much more than we already knew. He was born in Harrow in 1960, went to a Grammar School in Edgware, studied Engineering at Manchester University where he spent some time as social secretary. He went to South Africa in '84 to work as a mining engineer. As a chartered engineer, he had a good reputation. His South African phase is a bit of a black box. One report has him suddenly resigning from his mining job - no notice, no explanation - and disappearing. He resurfaced in 2001 in the UK, by which time he was head of a multinational conglomeration and mega-rich. He had also become a recluse. Now, that is some transformation, one that I cannot explain.'

Ali asked, 'What about family?'

'From what I can find, his parents are dead and he has no siblings. He is not married and I can find no evidence of children. In the UK, he is registered as a non-dom. As such, he pays nominal taxes. To be honest, I can't find anywhere he does pay taxes. It's beginning to look as if he really is a citizen of everywhere and nowhere.'

Ali sighed. A rich guy who doesn't pay tax and values his privacy. They already knew that. Yet there was something else. According to Corbin, Ashe was a Brit with maybe a hint of South African. Crain, however, had told them that Ashe was a Kosovar. Could that explain why Ashe had changed so much in South Africa? Had a different guy returned to the UK? Had someone taken Ashe's identity?

'I need pictures,' she said urgently. 'Before he went to South Africa and when he came back.'

Corbin caught on immediately. 'You think he's two different people?'

'According to Crain, Ashe is a Kosovar. And he should know. I think some Kosovan gangster killed Ashe in South Africa, took his identity and used Leke to legitimise his criminality.'

'And had Crain redact his identity,' Keaton said.

'Sounds plausible,' Corbin said. 'It's well known in security circles that you don't document an Illegal as a national of the country he is infiltrating. You would need a history that is virtually impossible to create and sustain. Better to present yourself as an alien, say a South African Brit, who has come to live in the country. I'll have a closer look. And I'll check in with the guys holding Crain.'

The phone went dead.

Keaton considered for a moment. 'Whatever Corbin comes up with, we need to keep to the strategy. Crain reported to Ashe. Ashe is now the target.'

Ali nodded as if that was the easiest task in the world, 'What about this girl, Sarah. And Shimmon's Deepthroat.'

'We don't have the resources to search for them. Let's not get distracted. We stay with Ashe.'

Pearce said, 'Maybe Ashe is Bowman is Griffin. It could be that simple.'

There was a knock on the front door. Pearce went and, just as in Switzerland, returned carrying a sports bag. Ali didn't need to look inside to know that the two men had rearmed themselves.

Keaton started checking a hand gun. 'Our local contacts have come up with addresses for Ashe's private residence on Long Island and for Leke Corporation HQ. Let's get to work. We're leaking time, here, and that's just leaking blood.'

THEY TOOK THE Jeep through the Queens Midtown Tunnel and followed the Long Island Expressway eastwards onto the Island. While they drove, Ali searched for Ashe's house on her iPhone.

'Fifteen bedroom mansion,' she announced, 'set in 86 acres and costing $28 million. Who says crime doesn't pay?'

'Something that size:' Pearce ventured, 'the security will be full of holes.'

Keaton grunted sceptically. 'Let's wait and see.'

Ali switched to Satellite image. 'Half of the estate is farmland, fenced into fields. The main house is set towards the south of the estate and seems to be surrounded by ornamental gardens and a cluster of outbuildings. Looks like stables and houses and a couple of biggish buildings. I can't quite make them out. The rest is open parkland. It's a sizable area, stretching from the house to the Sound. The farm seems to be a separate entity from the rest of the estate. There's a boathouse and jetty on the waterside, and a narrow passageway to the Sound between two fingers of rock.' She looked up. 'I'm surprised the property isn't obscured. Surely they have enough clout to have the image pixelized?'

'I'm sure they do.' Keaton shrugged. 'Those kinds of restrictions have lapsed. Pixelization image downgrades are pointless when high-res photos and aerial surveys are available elsewhere on the Internet.'

They by-passed Huntingdon and turned off the Expressway, taking the Knight's Highway along the Gold Coast. This was the kind of landscape that looked great in summer, bleak in winter. The ocean was iron grey, the trees had been stunted by salt winds and the beaches had been scoured away by gales and storm tides. Here, amid scenic bluffs, rocky inlets and quaint harbours, colonial New England mixed with the grand, high society estates of early 1900's tycoons.

It was five in the afternoon, when they reached their destination. Pearce turned north onto a narrow road that had been cut through a thickly wooded headland. The leafy canopy was tunnel-like and it reminded Ali of probing the badlands near Prishtina with Donylla. After a hundred metres or so the canopy thinned and they burst out of the trees into the open. Two hundred metres ahead of them, there was a steel gate with gatehouse that would have graced any military installation. The road led straight to the gateway and nowhere else. There were no deviations and no turn-offs. Pearce cursed and brought the vehicle to an abrupt stop. To either side of the gate, an eight foot high boundary wall stretched away out of sight. It was topped with coils of razor wire. The zone between the woods and the wall had been laid waste to create a security buffer zone that seemed to extend all the way round the wall. Beyond the gate, a long driveway led to a brick colonial-revival mansion. It was U-shaped, and a large central courtyard faced the gate. The house stood on a knoll overlooking its estate. From their restricted vantage point, they couldn't see any outbuildings, or the farm. They could just make out the avenue of 80-foot beech trees that swept from gateway to house.

Keaton saw activity at the gatehouse and knew that they had been spotted. The last thing they wanted was to be identified.

'Turn around,' he said. There was urgency but no need to panic. 'Slowly, like you're lost. We don't want to alert them by running away.'

Pearce performed a slow and deliberately clumsy three point turn. As they drove slowly away, Keaton saw what looked like a tiny helicopter appear above the gatehouse. It bristled with antennae and electronics.

'Drone!' he said.

Pearce waited the few seconds until they were in the canopy then he hit the gas. They reached the highway and started west for the City. The drone had been launched to inspect them but its operator seemed content to have seen them off. On reaching the main road, the drone turned back, leaving them to drive on towards New York in empty, defeated silence.

They stopped in Port Jefferson for a toilet break and a meal. In no mood for exploring the town, they settled for the first restaurant they came across. It offered gourmet burger, avocado fries and beer which kept them happy enough. While they waited for their food, Ali, hyper as ever, opened her laptop and searched for satellite images of the estate.

She said, 'The wall doesn't extend north of the house. That leaves it wide open.'

Keaton pulled his chair closer and looked with her. 'The wall is window-dressing. The whole estate is secured like some secret government establishment. State-of-the-art security, way over-the-top, just how I like it.' He pointed out various features, some of which were just tiny splodges to Ali. 'There's boundary fences, probably electrified. They've got every kind of intruder alert. You can even make out armed security personnel in the grounds. We'll not be joining them for tea, not without an invitation embossed in gold. The place is a locked box.'

Ali visibly deflated. 'So we're fucked.'

'Not at all.' Keaton was cheerfully undeterred. 'The house was always going to be beyond our capabilities.'

Despite his optimism, Ali felt beaten down. For a brief while, every little thing became a problem. She watched Keaton pay for their meals and began to worry that they would soon run out of cash, She couldn't access her accounts and Keaton, though he claimed to be a cash man, couldn't be carrying unlimited funds. Money – or the lack of it – was going to vaporize their investigation. If she could still call it an investigation. Subdued by the mission impossible of Ashe's twenty-first century fortress, and by their complete and absolute lack of a plan, her morale was sinking fast. The drive back to New York was going to be a foul end to a foul day that she knew would end in a sleepless night.

But once they hit Queens, little thoughts started popping up, pointlessly optimistic, like the suggestions of a child trying to cheer up a depressed parent. All were useless. But eventually she caught on and started thinking for herself.

Cash might be short, she reasoned, but money wasn't the problem. It was still the solution. Keaton was right. Keep to the plan. The next guy in the money chain was Ashe. And even if Ashe was beyond their reach in Suffolk County, he could be found at Leke Corporation and elsewhere.

Chapter 54

DAVID BOWMAN STOOD by the living room window of his Suffolk County home. It was a misty day and he was mesmerised by the red oaks shifting like wraiths against the soft infinity of the Sound. He could never fall out of love with this bewitching landscape, could never quite believe that he actually owned this private park that undulated down from his designer gardens to his wooded beach. This, he reflected with a dread of the hereafter that was growing with age, was the closest a crude and violent man such as himself could ever hope to get to heaven. He knew of no other place where he was so at peace with himself.

Not today, however. He had the prickling sense of an approaching cataclysm, as unpredictable as it was dangerous. The journalist Feysor had tracked him down and, if she exposed him, the jackals would gather at the gates. He had so many enemies. None would have forgotten or forgiven. That didn't happen in his world. *The past is a dead hand on the face of the living.* The myth of his power and invulnerability would not save him. His only real protection was that the world thought he was dead and Feysor was close to changing that. The FBI and the International Criminal Court he could handle. His lawyers would keep them at bay until long after his death. Vengeful clansmen, government assassins and mafia hitmen were something else.

Barring a Reaper drone strike, he was safe enough here. Over the past two decades, he had spent many millions on security. The house had been structurally reinforced, fitted with bullet-proof glass and refurbished to the highest specifications. He had installed a security suite, with banks of surveillance screens and monitoring equipment to control the anti-intruder systems. Outside, a small barracks housed the mercenaries who watched over him, and there were guest cottages, a gymnasium, and a music theatre-cum-movie house. If the only consideration was his personal security, he need never leave the place. But did he really want to transform his haven into his prison?

Bowman turned to those behind him. Ashe and Vanavasam, his two close confidantes and friends from his childhood whom he trusted with his life. And Thomas Suzman, leader of his mercenary force whose professional skills were unimpeachable but whose loyalty was to the money.

'I want security tightened.'

'Couldn't be tighter,' Suzman told him with a confident smile. 'Nothing can get in – or out. Not even a mouse.'

'If you think mice are the problem,' Bowman told him testily, 'perhaps I need another security consultant.'

Suzman lost the smile. 'I will conduct a full review.' He took his cue and left the room.

'So,' Bowman said, 'Crain has disappeared.'

'With his bodyguard and driver,' Ashe said. 'We have him on CCTV getting into his car outside the apartment of his mistress, then heading north out of the city. After that, nothing. No more cameras. His mistress knows nothing. She says he was his usual, enthusiastic self. Earlier, he had dined alone. Our people at the Schloss noticed nothing out of the ordinary. Security was normal. Everything was normal.'

'Far from normal,' Bowman corrected him, 'Someone was careless. Do the authorities have him?'

Ashe shook his head. 'He would have surfaced by now. Contacted our lawyers.'

'And if he contacted lawyers of his own?'

'He would be a dead man.'

'What about our enemies?'

Vanavasam shrugged. 'They might kill him. If they knew how much difficulty that would cause us.'

Ashe rubbed his chin thoughtfully. 'I think not. Killing Crain would be a declaration of war. No one is that stupid. No-one has the power to move against you.'

'There are many,' Bowman told him. 'The past is all the power they need. Family honour. Blood.'

'Crain is not blood,' Ashe pointed out. 'He has either stolen from you or he has been taken into custody.'

Vanavasam was doubtful. 'He would not dare steal. He has no need. And I am assured by our friends in the Swiss police that he is not in custody.'

Ashe said, 'The journalist Feysor was in Zurich when he disappeared.'

Vanavasam snorted, genuinely amused. 'You think she kidnapped him?'

'No,' Ashe responded. 'I think she made him an offer.'

Bowman dismissed the idea. 'She has nothing to interest a man like Crain. Except maybe her cunt. If Crain has betrayed us, it is an inconvenience, no more. He will never get to testify. We will find him and silence him. Just as we will find and silence Feysor.' He stared at Ashe. 'Who should replace him?'

Ashe had a ready answer. 'Crain has two associates, one in London, the other in Zurich. Both are tainted by association. The best qualified person to replace him, the one with the necessary combination of ability, knowledge, ruthlessness and trustworthiness, is here, in New York. In Leke.'

'And who is this superman?'

'Superman is a superwoman,' Ashe said with a confidence he didn't feel. 'Victoria Ramey.'

There was an ominous, watchful silence in the room. Bowman was an unashamed misogynist and racist. There were no non-whites and no women in his entourage and his response to Ashe's suggestion was entirely unpredictable.

Bowman turned his dead eyes on Ashe. 'I cannot believe that you can find no-one else. How hard did you look?'

'Replacing Crain is the most important decision we have made in many years,' Ashe said earnestly. 'Ramey is the one person in our world who comes close to matching his talents.'

'You can guarantee this?'

'I guarantee this.'

Bowman gave his approval with a little nod. 'How soon before we know the extent of the damage?'

Ashe could give no definitive answer. 'We will have to audit every account. It could take weeks. Months! We might never know.'

'Then we have to recover Crain and persuade him to help us. In the meantime, tell this Ramey that her life depends on the speed of her audit.'

Bowman waited for Ashe's nod then turned back to the window. He looked as if he was thinking hard but, in truth, he was angry with himself for trusting someone like Crain. He had survived for so long because he refused to trust his associates. Certainly not associates in the business, political or security worlds. He had made a mistake with Crain but, having survived this long on his cold, calculating ruthlessness, he knew that he would roll that back.

He turned back to the others in the room.

'The past is dead and buried,' he said. 'There is no connection to us. No one can touch us, We have too many friends.'

'And Sarah?' Ashe said cautiously. 'If she intended to harm us she would have done it by now. Our friends in London believe that she has come to New York. Perhaps she wants to come home.'

'Home!' The frustrated anger inside Bowman boiled over into hatred. Powerful, unconscionable hatred that emanated from the hindbrain and over-rode the instinct to protect his own. His daughter had betrayed him and, blood on blood, it was his duty to kill her. 'She has no home. She is dead to us.'

Ashe persisted. 'Let her come home before it's too late.'

Bowman wasn't listening. 'Secrets never stay secret,' he said, as though to himself. 'Even our own people cannot be trusted to keep ours. The trick is not to limit the damage but to ensure that its impact lies elsewhere.'

Chapter 55

EARLY AFTERNOON FOUND Ali in a Greek Tavern on 6th Avenue, just south of West Houston. She had already dubbed this part of the city Schizo-ville. It *felt* Village, with its easy-going ambience of rebellion, bizarre fashions and informal bars and coffee houses, but it *looked* Downtown, with its spillover of businesses and transactions confined to a desolate world of screen, keyboard and fibre-optics. It was the kind of place tourists passed by on the way to somewhere more interesting.

Ali was no tourist. She was here to watch the comings and goings at Leke Tower, headquarters of Leke Corporation. Her cover was simple enough - a journalist in search of vox pop. For each of the past four mornings, she had arrived with the commuters and divided her day between the street and the string of bars and cafes that gave eyes on the Tower. The Tower had been a surprise. She had been expecting a cloud buster, some ostentatious monument to excessive wealth and stunted manhood, but had instead been dealt a nondescript little block of grey, concrete cladding.

After the rush of London and Zurich, Ali was finding it difficult to adjust to the inaction. Her reliance on industrial quantities of caffeine didn't help. On top of the jet lag and long, slow adrenaline burn, it was distorting her perception. She was desperate for something to happen, dreading that it would yet knowing that it wouldn't. In all likelihood, Ashe never came near Leke Tower. If he did, he could have been tripping in and out of that building all day and she would never know. He wouldn't be on foot, he would be in one of the tinted gas-guzzlers running back and forth into the underground car park. She was wasting her time here. It didn't help that Keaton and Pearce were also striking out. For all their covert skills, they had been unable to find a lay-up that offered eyes on the Long Island mansion.

Not for the first time, she cursed her own impulsive nature. She should have reined herself in when she first encountered the Kosovan mafia. She should have buried her head in the sand when faced with the parallel universe of money laundering, people trafficking and arms dealing. And she should have admitted defeat when the bodies started to drop. Instead, she had clung on in there, compulsive and hopeless like OCD Woman, only to find herself up against the invisible man, the head of a multi-national empire of criminal enterprises who was also a psychopathic killer. To survive, she had begun to crisscross the line between good and evil, turning herself into something she despised, someone not only inured to the violence and hatred but an active participant. She had lost free will and become just another random particle.

A random particle!

The thought was just taking hold when a man who looked remarkably like the photo of Ashe emerged from Leke House. He was with a woman. Ali grabbed her bag, abandoned the vantage of the window seat, thrust some notes at the startled waitress and scuttled out of the Tavern into the street.

The man she thought was Ashe was walking north on 6th Avenue. Ali ran to close the gap then slowed to a walk. She was less than twenty metres behind them. She took out her phone and called Keaton.

'I think I have Ashe.'

'Where are you?'

'6th Avenue, going north.'

Ashe and his companion headed through the wedge-shaped plaza of Father Fagan Park and reached the confluence of 6th, Spring Street, and Prince Street.

'He's crossing Prince Street and going into Macdougal Street. . . . He's going into a restaurant. Hold on. . . . The Hundred Acres. . . . He's with a woman. Looks like business rather than pleasure.'

'Keep me updated. I'm on my way.'

Ali looked for an observation point. Macdougal was one way and narrow, with trees in iron cages, cars parked bumper to bumper and Citi Bike cycles chained to anything that didn't move. There were offices and retail businesses but no handy café. If she loitered here, she decided, she would be too conspicuous. She crossed back over to Father Fagan Park and selected a bench built around one of the park's Callery Pear trees. From here, she could just see the entrance to the Hundred Acres. She had a clear view of the pavement outside.

She brought Keaton up to date, then amused herself playing with her phone while she watched the restaurant. She had no sense of passing time, just a continuous dull ache in her head as her mind revolved endlessly.

'You look worried to death.' The voice at her shoulder belonged to Keaton. He had arrived without her noticing.

She raised her eyebrows mockingly. 'I'm trying to shake off the waking impulse to file my nightmares.'

'Gonzo made a living doing just that.'

'Hunter Thompson! You've read him.'

'I saw the film.' Keaton smiled, a rare expression of sympathy. 'You're in a bind, Ali. You can't run, you can't hide, you can't fight. You'd have to be crazy not to be crazy.'

'So you think I'm crazy.'

'Crazy as a mother.'

She grunted, mock affront.

Keaton had brought a camera bag and tripod and he set up his equipment while he talked, pointing his long lens along Macdougal.

'Pay no attention to me,' he said. 'I'm just some photography nut with a thing for cityscapes.'

'Make sure you get the woman, too.'

'That's the idea,' he smiled.

'Just checking.'

'Latest from Corbin,' Keaton continued conversationally, 'is that Bowman has no tax account, bank account, credit card or phone in his name. Maybe he's joined a cult and renounced his name. Maybe he's given over all earthly wealth to a higher being named

Leke, and in return been granted eternal bliss and immunity from snoopy journalists.'

'Does Corbin have anything useful?'

Keaton grinned. 'Oh yes. The Ashe who runs Leke is not the man who went to South Africa. You were right. There is a likeness, but the software draws clear distinctions around the ears and the nose. As for his ID, we have a probable hit. Stane Syla, a Kosovan Serb. His family was decimated in the Yugoslav wars. He was reputedly a member of a paramilitary group, actually a Serb kill squad, but that's just a rumour and he is not on any wanted list. His career is a little sketchy. Most UDBA [*the Yugoslav secret police*] files from the time were destroyed. However, he had a close association with Lucca, in whom you also have an interest. Syla disappeared just before the end of the war.'

'And HMG protected him?'

'Actually, he was not one of the protected. He literally vanished. A couple of things of note here. Leke comes from the Book of Leke, an ancient Albanian codification of an eye for an eye. Can you believe these people?'

'You said two things.'

'Syla, or Ashe, had a sister who was married to Lucca.'

'So Ashe was Lucca's brother-in-law.' Ali's headache was getting worse.

A man and a woman emerged from the restaurant and started walking towards them. Keaton squinted into the lens.

'It's him,' he confirmed between clicks. 'I wonder who she is.'

THEY TRAILED ASHE and the woman back to Leke Tower and that was the last they saw of them that day. Mid-evening, they returned to their apartment. Keaton checked his computer and Ali watched disinterestedly as Pearce flicked through TV channels. Eventually, Pearce gave up, tossed the remote onto a chair and began playing a game on his phone.

'American TV,' he grumbled. 'For kids and morons.'

'That's what they say about computer games,' Ali said.

'You wouldn't understand,' Pearce growled. 'You're a woman.'

Ali smiled. 'Is it true you *boys* are a macho brotherhood?'

'You boys?' Pearce echoed.

'*Special* forces. The impenetrable brotherhood. All that fierce loyalty.'

'Can't speak for our friend here,' Pearce told her, throwing a mischievous glint in Keaton's direction. 'But I am definitely impenetrable.'

Keaton glanced at her. 'It's the brotherhood of the lone wolf. You're an honorary member.'

She sucked in her cheeks. 'I've never liked the self-image of a loner.'

Keaton shrugged. 'Most people are so afraid of being alone they have a cell phone grafted onto their ear. But I like being alone. It's just a question of finding something about yourself that you like. Me? I trust myself.'

'The thinking soldier,' she grunted. 'Next, you'll be telling me about the ethical war.'

Keaton shrugged. 'Do you run ethical investigations?'

They had been here before. On their first night back from Kosovo. Now she answered truthfully. 'Yes and no. I have to live.'

'So there's not much difference between you and me, is there?'

'I wouldn't go that far.'

Keaton's jaw flexed. 'You became a crusading journalist to redeem humankind from evil, only you discovered that life is not as black and white as you thought. There's a little bit of evil out there but a lot more human frailty. We can't get to the evil ones so we start lying to ourselves and to those around us. We say, if the law can't touch the bad men they can't be so bad after all. They must be innocent. The powerful and privileged are always innocent. They have the law on their side. They have a clear conscience because they can afford to buy it from others. Like buying carbon credits. Another lie. You can't undo your bad deeds so you put them on someone weaker. That's the law of nature.'

'I'm confused. Are you saying we can't touch Bowman?'

'Not legally.'

'But illegally?'

'That's the part you should never bring up.' He shrugged. 'Never think about it before you do it, never think about it after it's over.'

'How is that supposed to help?'

'Do what has to be done. Don't be weak or you'll be dead.'

'Don't be weak.' She paused for thought. 'Are you the kind of man who keeps his promises?'

'Not always.'

'You don't believe in God,' she ragged him. 'And you don't believe in your own word. What's left?'

'I believe in the next promise,' he said. He turned to squint through the window at the broad avenue of traffic below. 'People can keep the next promise even if they broke their last one.'

Keaton turned back to his laptop and twisted it around so that the others could see the screen.

'Corbin confirms that the guy we photographed is Ashe. The woman with him is Victoria Ramey. Forty. Accountancy background. High up in Leke New York. It occurs to me that Crain's disappearance has created problems we hadn't really considered. They have to plug potential leaks and keep Leke functioning. Maybe that's why Ashe is going into the office. Why he's lunching a senior accountant. If this Ramey is any good, we have to wonder how much time we have before they discover that Crain is deep into Leke's accounts.'

'Talking of money,' Ali said. 'What are we going to do about cash? I'm all out and I can't access my accounts.'

Keaton frowned. 'I thought I told you. Crain has opened a new account for us and transferred in some of Bowman's money. We have more than enough.'

They fell into reflective silence. Ali went to the window and stared out at the Queens' night sky, a brand new world of fragmented illumination. A nearby office block created a black hole, visible only because of the broken array of lights that surrounded it. To its left, a chimney thrust into the sky, tall and narrow. The river was flat, dull and lifeless, sparked only by reflections from Roosevelt Island and the Triborough bridge beyond.

Suddenly, Ali wanted some of that outside world.

She turned, snatched up her jacket and headed for the door. 'I'm just popping out.'

Surprised, Keaton reacted swiftly to grab her arm. 'Where are you going?'

Ali stiffened as if someone had thrown a switch. She stared hard at his hand without moving.

Keaton said, 'What?'

Ali's eyes flicked up from the hand to Keaton's eye and locked on.

He gave her embarrassed and let go. 'Sorry.'

She said, 'I won't be long.'

'I'll come with you.'

'Like hell you will.'

'You don't know what's out there.'

'Nor do you.'

SHE HAD BEEN drawn out by the lure of the water, yet she turned west, away from the river, towards York Avenue. After a couple of blocks, she went into a D'Agostino store where she bought a bottle of vodka, some chocolate and snacks. She didn't particularly want them; she just needed to do something normal. She decided to return to the apartment via the river and she turned into East 80 Street.

Suddenly the streets were deserted. There followed one of those strange moments of sudden silence, when the city caught its collective breath. There was no reassuring rumble of distant traffic. No forced laughter or loud conversation. Just the echo of her own footsteps on the paving. Quick and light.

The echo kept pace but followed a different rhythm from her own. Fractionally slower. Three-four to her four-four. Because the strides were longer. Because they weren't an echo.

She walked on, keeping her pace steady. She felt safe enough. The guy behind - for she was sure it was a man - was coming no closer. She forced everything from her mind except the distant footsteps behind her. She zoomed in on them. Concentrated on them. They were there, faint but perceptible.

If she was being followed, they must have found her!

How could they have known that she was here?

She turned right into East End Avenue and increased her pace. She heard him speed up to match her. She fancied that she heard a faint sibilant whispering, forty yards behind her. He was on his cell phone. *Who are you talking to?*

She turned left into East79 Street then right onto the riverside walk. Then she ran. Five paces, ten, fifteen, twenty, fast and silent. But she was no athlete. The apartment was too far. Momentarily panicked, she turned into East78. She thought about hiding in John Jay Park, opted instead to run another thirty metres and dive into the first alley she came to. It was very dark in there. She felt her way along the wall and slipped behind a recess. She crouched back in the shadows, trying to choke off her harsh breathing. Her eyes quickly began to adjust – amazing what fear will do - and she ducked behind a refuse bin.

Something moved in the shadows behind her. Some animal, a monster crouching in the darkness of a doorway. Her heart stopped then lurched into motion. Fear brought a fleeting image. A flash. A young boy and girl. Lying beneath an unzipped sleeping bag, safe in love, masters of the art of fully-clothed ecstasy.

The image vanished in a blink, leaving Ali with the girl's smile. A young soul in need, not of ecstasy, or sexing up, but of human warmth, consolation and protection. Needing a certain and gentle affection for life. A soul-mate.

Ali moved back to the recess and waited. Senses heightened, she heard footsteps on the opposite sidewalk. Coming closer. Closer still. Then she saw him. Knew him. He was on the other sidewalk. Against the fence to John Jay Park. He was on the hunt, prowling slowly. But there was uncertainty there. His eyes were darting from the shadowy darkness of the Park to the street-side trees and parked cars that might conceal her.

He had spooked her into running and now he was reaping the worry.

He studied her alley, stared straight at her without seeing her.

She would rag him about that.

She waited for him to pass from view then stepped out behind him and shouted:

'I thought you people could see in the dark!'

Keaton turned, saw her, and a broad smile of relief creased his features.

Chapter 56

FROM THE WINDOW of the Greek tavern, Ali watched the police car scream to a halt outside Meyer's Bank. Two officers rushed into the building, leaving their car slewed across the road, doors open, engine running, gyro flashing. A small crowd gathered to watch, and it maintained a discreet distance lest it become involved in the excitement.

Indifferent to the melodrama, Ali turned her eye back to Leke Tower. It was several days since they had first spotted Ashe and they had yet to agree a plan of action. Ali was in favour of approaching Ashe directly and negotiating a mutually assured survival pact. The others had pretended to discuss the idea but, when they thought she wasn't watching, they had looked at each other and smiled paternally.

Pearce was in favour of taking him off the street. Each day Ashe walked out to lunch with Victoria Ramey which made him an easy mark. Pearce would thrust a pocket gun into his ribs – a Glock 42 would do it – and guide him to their car. But he had to accept that the street was too busy, always too busy, and that Ramey was always there. Too much could go wrong.

Keaton's preferred option was to ambush Ashe's car somewhere in the quiet Long Island roads beyond the

Knight's Highway. By cross-matching license plates, they had established that two cars made the daily trip between Long Island and Leke Tower. Unfortunately, they had no idea which car Ashe would use, if either, and jacking the wrong car would spook their prey.

They had even considered taking Ramey. Ali was convinced that she was Crain's replacement and this theory was backed up by Pearce when he opened up and inspected her apartment. But, as a gateway target, Ramey would take them a step backwards.

Today, Keaton had joined Ali for a late lunch. He finished ordering and took over surveillance while Ali spoke to the waitress at her shoulder. The woman was of uncertain ethnic origin, some kind of Hispanic-Asian mix with English to match. She made a careful note of Ali's lunch order, then asked with a friendly smile:

'What are you doing here every time?'

Ali noted her eagerness and groaned inwardly. The curiosity was hardly surprising - Ali had been in and out of the cafe for days, like some frantic bulimic. Maybe it was time to use another, less comfortable vantage point.

In a conspiratorial whisper, Ali told her, 'I'm watching this man. He's an international criminal.'

The waitress smiled politely. 'What are you really doing here?'

Ali held the woman's eye and told her, 'I'm looking for illegals. Ethnics who've overstayed their visitor's permit and taken jobs.'

'There are no illegals here!' the waitress protested. Her face mirrored her sudden confusion and resentment, and she was looking at Ali as though for reassurance.

'Then you've nothing to fear.'

The waitress backed away hesitantly.

'Cruel and unusual,' Keaton muttered.

Ali shrugged. Feeling calm and anchored, she settled back to wait. The tavern, at this late lunch hour, was all but deserted. Outside, the street was still. The waitress leaned against the counter, studiously ignoring the journalist yet stealing an occasional glance as though she were some kind of monster. The chef, hot and sweating, was more interested in his glass of Stella than cooking, but the two Brits were in no hurry.

Through the window, the street had come to life. The police officers were returning to their car, laughing, almost euphoric. Testing their response target, cut fine in this moneyed zone, they had shaded it by seconds. The shadowy group of watching figures started to break up and a man detached himself, heading north-west. It took a double-take to register, then Ali realized that it was Ashe. Sporting a dark blue business suit, white shirt and patterned tie, he was coming from the direction of Leke's underground garage. He was alone.

She felt a surge of adrenaline. 'We're up.'

Keaton dropped some cash on the table and they went outside. Ashe was walking north up 6th Avenue and they hung back as he crossed West Houston and turned into Bleecker Street but, when he entered Cornelia Street, they hurried to close the gap. They needn't have worried. He stopped beneath the red awning of the Cornelia Street Café and joined a young woman sitting at a table. Ali and Keaton continued past on the opposite sidewalk and stopped in the shadows of a tree. From here, they had eyes on Ashe. Ashe didn't order. Instead, he sat stiffly, as though the woman was a stranger and he was waiting for someone else. The woman finished her coffee and started to walk up Cornelia Street. Moments later, Ashe rose and followed, quickening his stride to catch her. On reaching West4 Street, they stopped for a brief, close conversation. Keaton took advantage of the clear sight-line to photograph them.

'They're separating.' Keaton said. 'I'll take Ashe. You follow the woman.'

Without hesitation, Ali trailed the woman towards 7th Avenue. She hung back just a little too far, so that, when the woman entered the subway at Christopher Street, she had to break into a run. By the time she reached the station concourse, the woman had vanished.

Ali used her Metro-card and, ignoring angry protests, pushed her way onto the crowded stairs. A little jostling and buffeting and her quarry came within range. She was on the northbound platform, squeezed tightly among the tourists and students. The train, when it came, was standing room only, but Ali had no difficulty observing the woman from a discreet distance. She appeared fit, tanned and self-possessed. She also seemed to be lost in thought, with no real suspicion that she was being followed.

Ali, too, was losing concentration as lack of sleep caught up with her. By the time they reached Penn her concentration had dissipated on the warm, rhythmic rocking of the train. She found herself thinking of

Keaton. Tall, lithe and strongly built, with a handsome face that dimpled into a reluctant smile, he carried the aura of a man who knew more about his own strengths than his weaknesses. The kind of man who would dominate her dreams, re-created in teasing humour by some unseen Power: the unobtainable, returning again and again to confront and discompose her.

Ali's reverie was disrupted at 86th Street, when the woman got off the train. As circumspectly as she was able, Ali shadowed her out onto Amsterdam Avenue. Had she been Keaton, she would have taken precautions, concealed her presence, marked her surroundings, identified escape routes, but she was focused on one thing: not losing her prey. The woman turned into West89 Street. Ali did likewise, but not before she had crossed to the other side of the road. A third of the way into the street, the woman stopped at a town house. She tried her key, found the door locked and rang the bell. Ali slowed her walk and snapped a mental picture of the girl who opened the door. The girl and woman hugged briefly then the door closed on them.

Ali's thoughts leapt back to the interrogation of Crain, in Zurich, and his mention of the runaway girl. She took out her phone, scrolled through her gallery and found the photograph he had given them. The hair was different, now, lighter and shorter. The eyes, too, had lightened, but the shape was consistent. There were other differences, particularly around the mouth and eyes. But that was just make-up. The shape of her face was unaltered, as was her beauty. And the real giveaway: her ears were a perfect match.

She shuddered as the realisation seeped down her spine.

She had found the missing girl.

She turned away and punched in Keaton's number. No signal. She cursed. The middle of New York and it might as well have been the Hells Canyon Wilderness.

She hurried further down the street and tried again. Still no signal. She drafted a text message and set her phone to send and retry.

If you find something, do nothing, Keaton had instructed her. *Call and I'm on my way. If something happens and I haven't got there, hit the panic button.*

Ali froze in indecision. Should she loiter and watch, or retreat and wait. She didn't know. All she knew was that the girl was being hunted by the bad guys because she knew too much and had in her possession a flash drive worth killing for.

Then it struck her.

Ashe knew where the girl was!

He had just met with the woman who had come straight here to the girl. Who was this woman? Why had the girl hugged her? What had the woman been doing with Ashe? What the hell was going on?

Suddenly the woman came out of the house and turned towards Broadway, a route that would take her past Ali. Without hesitation, Ali entered into a fake conversation on her phone, eyes flipping as casually as possible between the pavement at her feet and the houses opposite, Somehow, she resisted a glance as the woman hurried past her and rounded the corner into Broadway. Acting on pure impulse, Ali walked swiftly back to the Brownstone and rang the bell. The door began to open and, too late, she wondered if the girl was alone in there.

Sarah had the appearance of one just dragged out of bed. She squinted out at Ali as though the apathetic light hurt her eyes. She didn't want to talk, that much was obvious from her reluctance to remove the security chain, but she was too polite to slam the door in the face of a well-heeled stranger.

'Sarah? I'm Ali Feysor. A journalist from London. A friend and colleague of Steven Shimmon. I'd like to talk to you, if that's okay.'

A range of emotions crossed the girl's face - surprise, fear, anger, tightness, uncertainty - and Ali waited for the expected denial. It didn't come. Sarah removed the chain and stood aside.

'You'd better come in.'

The girl led the way into the living room, where she invited Ali to sit then slumped into the chair opposite. The muted TV was showing some chat show. The girl's clothes were a mismatch, as though she had expected to spend the day alone. To the casual eye, she could have been described as child-like, yet she gazed out on the world from eyes grown tired and old before their time. She said nothing, just perched on the settee and stared at Ali. She seemed all out of words. The stale air of the house pressed against her and squeezed her lungs. Ali sat patiently, giving her time to compose herself.

'It's okay,' the girl said at last. 'I'm not a ghost.'

'Sorry. I didn't mean to stare.'

'I'm no longer Sarah,' the girl explained. 'Rachel. I'm Rachel now.'

'Okay, Rachel. I'm glad I've found you at last.'

'They told me you were looking for me. How did you find me?'

'We were watching Ashe.'

'My uncle!' The colour drained from Rachel's face. 'But he hasn't been near this place.'

Uncle! Ali concealed her surprise. 'He met with a woman and I followed her here.'

'Nadia!'

There was a difficult silence.

Rachel said, 'If you can track them, anyone can.'

Ali went cold at the thought. 'Who are they? Who are you hiding from?'

Rachel's face wrinkled in distress. 'I need time to think. Please, let me think.'

Ali offered her a smile but didn't want to run the risk of her shutting down. 'Why disappear like this? What are you running from?'

'The past.'

'We all run from our past,' Ali pointed out reasonably. 'But not many of us are so scared by it that we turn into someone else.'

'It's not *my* past I'm running from,' the girl told her. 'The secrets in my head are the secrets of others. They are the kind of secrets that must stay secret.'

They heard a key in the front door and Ali suddenly felt vulnerable. Had Sarah been keeping her here until help arrived? If so, what were they going to do to her? She jumped to her feet. She must have looked alarmed, because Rachel said:

'It's okay. It's only Nadia. She's a friend.'

When Nadia came into the room, she exhibited no surprise but her stance became watchful and aggressive.

'Who the hell are you?' she demanded. 'What are you doing here?'

Rachel said, 'This is Ali Feysor. She's a journalist.'

'It's okay,' Ali said, 'I'm on your side. I'm not going to betray you.'

'That's for sure.' Nadia took a step towards Ali. 'How did you find her?'

'We were watching Ashe and saw you.'

Nadia flinched at her own carelessness She turned to Rachel. 'What have you told her?'

'Nothing.'

Nadia took out her cell, punched a preset, said, *The journalist is here*, listened momentarily then closed her phone. She stepped forward, just a pace, but with enough threat for Ali to realise that she meant what she said and had the strength to enforce her words:

'I'd like you to leave now.'

Rachel tried to interject. 'Nadia!'

Nadia took Ali by the arm. 'Stay out of this, Rachel. Your safety depends on not talking to people like this.'

Rachel's anguish was turning to mistrust as though all her certainty was seeping away. 'What are you doing, meeting with my uncle?'

Nadia looked at her.

Rachel's face was flushed and tight. 'You're working for my father!'

'No,' Nadia told her forcefully. 'I am your friend. Your uncle is your friend. The journalist is not.'

Ali looked at Rachel. 'We're both on the run from these people, you and me. The only way out of this mess is to work together.'

Rachel shrugged helplessly. She didn't know what to think.

By this time, Nadia had guided Ali to the front door. She turned the latch, cracked the door and suddenly all hell broke loose. Two men barged through the door and both women went flying. Ali was grabbed, bundled into the lounge and thrown into a heap with Rachel. Nadia was manhandled and pinned to the wall. The arms that held her were strong and cruel. None of the women fought back. The two men were big and muscled, though that would never have daunted Nadia. But there was no resisting their suppressed Glock 22s.

Ali untangled herself from Rachel but stayed on her haunches. The lack of sound was eerie. No-one had groaned or protested or screamed. Nobody had uttered a word. What do you say when you open the door to death? A death, as Ali knew only too well, she had brought with her.

Nadia knew it, too. She caught Ali's eye and hissed, 'What have you done?'

Chapter 57

ASHE DIDN'T GO back to his office. Instead, he made his way to Sixth Avenue and crossed into West 4 Street and Washington Square Park. He stopped by the Parisian arch where a small crowd had gathered to watch a mime and juggling show. A tiny part of Keaton's brain considered the possibility that Ashe was here for a meet or a drop. A crazy, paranoid notion that he had no choice but to run with. Ashe joined a small crowd gathered to watch some mime artists and Keaton backed away. He took out his camera and wandered randomly among the park's students, tourists, street performers, bums and vendors. Just another tourist angling for a photograph, Only this one moved with veiled purpose: to keep Ashe under observation and record anyone he encountered.

After a minute or so, Ashe took out his cell phone and moved away from the crowd. An incoming call. He listened, spoke briefly, then rang off and made a short call of his own. A worried frown settled on his face, He turned his back on the melee, hunched down into the collar of his jacket and quickly left the park by the Washington Arch.

Keaton followed, conceding distance in the open space. In so doing, he made the rare mistake of allowing his quarry too much lead. By the time he turned into MacDougal Street, an unexpected shaft of sunshine was lending an exotic air to this urban oasis and Ashe had vanished. Keaton sprinted down the road, glancing left and right, until he reached 3rd Street. Mayhem. An RTA towards 6th Avenue had brought traffic to a standstill and the pedestrians had halted in sympathy. To Keaton, it seemed that all of New York's children were on the street, determined to conceal his quarry in their dull, lifeless hurrying to nowhere. Only Keaton himself was animated, his eyes darting everywhere, searching every face, every car, every building. But Ashe wasn't waiting around.

Ashe hadn't clocked him, Keaton was sure of that. He must have got into a vehicle, perhaps one summoned by his outgoing call. Alternatively, he could have gone into any one of a dozen buildings. But which one? Keaton could trawl the reception desks, or wait for Ashe to emerge, but that would run the risk of being exposed. There was urgency in the situation, but it fell some way short of panic.

His cell phone vibrated in his pocket. An SMS from Ali. Timed some minutes ago. She had located the girl. He tried to call Ali back but her phone was switched off.

That wasn't so good.

He called Pearce. 'I need you, now. Ali has found the girl and God knows what else.'

Chapter 58

UNDER THE WATCHFUL eye of his companion, the younger of the two men pinned Nadia into a holding position against the wall, feet spread back and apart, weight on her outstretched fingers. He frisked her and tossed her Glock 29 onto an armchair. Neither Ali nor Rachel moved. Nobody bothered to search them. These men understood the who's who of this scenario.

The older man studied Rachel, a humourless smile on his face. 'Daddy's rather disappointed in you, young lady.'

Rachel's face twisted in contempt. 'I have no *daddy*.''

He shrugged indifferently. 'Daddy or not, he wants to know who has been helping you?'

'Helping me do what?'

'Play your little game of hide and go seek. What else?' He waited for her reply but none was forthcoming. 'No matter. You will tell me soon enough. Why don't you start by handing over the flash drive you stole?'

'I have stolen nothing.'

That mirthless smile again. 'I would guess it's here. It won't take us long to find it but search and destroy is such a devastating undertaking. Why don't you hand over the drive before we tear apart this beautiful home.'

Rachel's poker face was beginning to crumble. Ali decided on a little distraction, 'I'm Ali Feysor. A British journalist.'

The older man smirked; he knew who she was. 'I'm David Sandford. British security service. And this is my friend, Faulk. You've been leading us a merry little dance, Ms Feysor, and I'm pleased to meet you, at last. Behave yourself and you might even get to walk out of here.'

Nadia glanced over her shoulder. 'You're a dead man, Mr British security service. If you sold your soul to Bowman, he will claim it soon enough, your body with it.'

The man named Faulk slapped her head. He was a Latino, five ten with broad, muscular shoulders and tapered waist. The blow was sharp and painful. 'Shut up, dyke.'

Nadia didn't flinch. 'Damned if I will.'

'And damned if you won't.'

Faulk rammed his gun into her ribs. Nadia buckled with pain but she didn't fall or cry out. Instead, she fixed a recriminating eye on Ali.

'You brought them here.'

'No, I swear.'

'Then they were watching you.'

'That's impossible. I was careful.'

'You weren't careful enough.'

'We're here,' Sandford told them caustically. 'That's all you need to know.' He kept his blue-grey eyes locked on Ali, his expression unreadable. In a conversational voice, he asked, 'These stories of yours

– Lucca, HMG, the Leke Corporation - where do they come from?'

'They're not my stories,' Ali glared defiantly at him. 'You have me confused with someone else. If you had done your homework you would know that I haven't published a single word on those subjects.'

Sandford continued as if she hadn't spoken. 'Someone's blown a little whistle in your ear. Give me a name and I'm out of here.'

'I'm a journalist not a clairvoyant,' she told him. 'I work for my stories. That means accruing information by the byte. Tips, interviews, research, legwork, guesswork. If I'd had insider help, I would have known about you.'

Sandford glanced at Faulk. 'A journalist without a rat? Can you believe that?'

Faulk said nothing. Instead, he stared at Ali and rocked back and forth on his feet, like a vampire on his perch, starved of blood and sizing up his next meal. Ali stared back. Fear was trickling down her neck, but she couldn't hold back her contempt.

'This is a guessing game, right! Guess what the nutter's thinking?'

Faulk's face didn't budge but the light behind it flickered a little.

Sandford chuckled. 'I wouldn't upset my friend here. He's a master of torture techniques. His subjects don't whistle, they sing. All we want is a name or two.'

Ali had no way of knowing if Sandford was who he said he was but, British intelligence or not, neither he nor Faulk seemed the type to count empathy and remorse amongst their character traits. Her mind flipped to water torture and brachial plexus neuropathy and she knew that she would break at the very mention of a wet towel.

'They don't pay me to sit on stories,' she said stiffly. 'If I had one, I would have written it.'

'Yet here you are,' he scoffed. 'You've spoken to all those people - Macleod, Figgis, Kooper, Connolly, Uncle Tom Cobley - and still you know nothing. I am frankly astonished that you are still in the job.'

'Outsiders,' she said. 'Each and every one of them. There is no insider. I have no Deep throat! You know that. You know everything I've done. You've even run interference so I can't trust anyone.'

'And what has little Sarah told you?'

'The girl?' Ali reacted as though she had never heard the name Sarah before. 'What's to tell? Until a few minutes ago, I didn't even know she existed.'

Sandford glanced at Rachel who shrugged and said:

'She just appeared on the doorstep. I thought she was with my father.'

'Bitch followed me,' added Nadia.

Sandford was growing impatient. 'Don't play me for a fool.'

'We don't have to!' Ali was exasperated. 'When did you stop listening and turn into this mindless zombie?'

Moving with unexpected speed, Sandford clamped his hand about her neck. His eyes were lit by a cold sun and he was close enough for an intimate exchange of gases. She dare not breathe. It felt as though the tiniest exhalation would allow the python to strengthen his death grip.

'I want answers,' he told her. His expression should have been cruel, distorted, hateful, but it was friendly and agreeable, and all the more scary for that. 'We can be civilised or not. It's all the same to me.'

Okay, she blinked. She was aware that he had withdrawn his hand from her neck, but she could still feel it there, like an amputated limb. His limb! She shuddered, despite herself.

Sandford smiled that curious, leery smile of his. 'You've brought this upon yourself, Ali. You were warned to leave it alone. What did you expect us to do, jerk off in a corner and watch while you destroy us?'

Ali's response stuck in her throat. She coughed, found some moisture from somewhere, and managed to say, 'I don't know what you think I know.'

'What happened to the data Shimmon gave you?'

'He didn't. . . .' She had almost forgotten about that. It had happened in a different life. 'Shimmon didn't give me anything. He was dead before I inherited his story. All his work had been destroyed, lost or stolen. But you know that already. You did it.'

Ali saw a mask of callous detachment spread over Sandford's face and knew that she had made a big mistake. He was beginning to think that she didn't know what he wanted to know. That made her expendable. But what else could she do? If she told him what she knew, he would kill her; if she kept silent he would torture her and then kill her. There was no way she was going to walk away from this. She would die here. She had known it before, of course, only she hadn't *known* it.

Nadia sensed the change in atmosphere. She twisted her stance and fixed Faulk with a look of utter contempt.

'You Muscle Marys are only good for two things: beating off into a gym mirror and beating up on defenceless women.'

Faulk stepped closer. Having already taken her down with ease, he was confident, open, relaxed. He read her compliance as weakness. He didn't see her shift her weight from her fingers to her toes.

'Keep your mouth shut, bitch.'

'Or what? . . .'

He went to slap her again.

The next moment was a blur. Nadia drove her elbow back and upwards, smashing it into his trachea. His knees buckled, he dropped his gun as his hands clutched at his throat and he gasped for air. She turned swiftly and kneed him in his groin. He groaned and doubled up, and she snapped his head to one side with a haymaker. She had disabled him but hadn't yet stopped him. He lunged at her like a punchy and she stepped to one side and hit him again. This time she cracked his nose and he went down. She adjusted her feet and administered a fiercesome kick to the head. He slumped over and lay still,

Adrenalin flowing, Nadia turned towards Sandford. He had already moved out of range to a position from which he could cover all three women, and his gun was pointing steadily at Nadia. Undeterred, she faced him down with a mask of hatred and determination. Her intention was clear to all.

Sandford snarled. 'Don't be a fucking idiot!'

Rachel cried, 'Nadia! Nooo!'

Ali shouted, 'Don't do it!'.

For an instant, their eyes locked, Nadia and Sandford's, then she launched herself. A nano-second later came the whup of Sandford's gun, painfully loud, despite the suppression.

One instant, Nadia was flying like Wonder Woman, the next she had crashed onto the floor. A thin red mist hovered above her. The bullet had entered by her sternum, exploded down through her heart and other vital organs and exited by the lumber vertebrae. Her body twitched horribly then succumbed to the numbness that was spreading quickly through her. The expression on her face was one of shock and anger. Her eyeballs rolled upwards until only the whites showed. She shuddered one last time then was still.

With a yelping scream, Rachel went for Sandford. He swatted her away and had trained his gun on Ali even before Rachel had hit the floor.

Ali raised her hands. 'There's no need for that,' she said.

'Sit down and shut the fuck up!' he snarled. 'Make a sound or twitch a muscle, and I will kill you.'

Ali ignored him and went to help Rachel to her feet. Under Sandford's watchful eye, the two women struggled to the sofa. Rachel's head was bleeding but she seemed oblivious as she stared in horror at Nadia. There was a gaping wound in her friend's back, and there was more blood seeping out from beneath her. A shocked silence filled the room, deafening in its impact, and it seemed to drag on and on. Then Faulk broke the spell by groaning and struggling to his knees.

Rachel spoke first, in a voice that was surprisingly calm and steady. 'Only Nadia knew who was helping me and you killed her. Why would you do that?'

Sandford said nothing. The fight and subsequent shooting seemed to have shifted him to another place. Gun in hand, he exuded an extreme lethality, a capacity for inflicting hurt and pain that at one time would have been beyond Ali's comprehension.

Hell-bent on taunting him, Ali said, 'Kill me and your schoolboy secrets will go viral within minutes.' An inner voice cautioned her, *calm down! don't antagonise him!*, but her indignant rage had overridden her impulse control. 'It will hit the world's press and the internet. You will be all over social media!' She broke into a near-hysterical giggle as she saw it at last. 'I might have led you here, *Mr British security service*. but the joke's on you.. You kill me, you kill yourself and you finish off Bowman. How's that for a result? Me, the bringer of death. The Grim Reaper on tour!'

Sandford gripped his gun with renewed focus. 'I think we're all finished here.'

'Not yet, arsehole!' The voice from the door had an unreal clarity. It was Pearce. Hard-faced and purposeful, he was pointing his Sig Sauer P230 at Sandford. 'Don't you twitch a fucking muscle!'

Sandford turned towards him, his eyes dark, bottomless pools of ice. Keaton appeared beside Pearce and Sandford acknowledged defeat by lowering his gun.

'Pity,' Pearce said. 'I've always wanted to kill myself a spook.'

Keaton stepped into the room and Pearce followed. Ali almost screamed with relief. Somehow, she resisted the impulse to leap into Keaton's arms. Instead, she watched as Pearce had Sandford place his gun on the floor and kick it to one side, then lie face-down with his hands behind his head.

'No harm done,' Sandford said into the rug. He seemed unfazed. 'Nothing personal. We're on the same side, here.'

Sandford's words triggered an interlude of vicious mayhem. With a screech of rage, Rachel leaped at him. She kicked and stomped him repeatedly, screaming barely-recognisable words of pure hatred, then leant in and began punching him on the head and tearing at his face and neck with her nails. Sandford did his best to protect himself though he made no attempt to fight back, not with two guns trained on him. Eventually, Pearce intervened but it took all his strength to subdue Rachel and pull her away. She fought against him, flushed and shaking, her teeth bared. Ali moved to help but it was several minutes before Rachel came back to their reality.

Sandford was a mess of incipient bruises, scuff marks and bloody gouges, yet he seemed unaffected by the battering. He glanced over at Rachel and said, 'You know, I had my doubts about your lineage, but I can see now that you're carrying your father's genes.'

Rachel lost it again, ripping free from the others and throwing herself down on Sandford, raining blows and tearing at his face. This time, Pearce was quicker to pull her away. He half-dragged half-carried her to the other side of the room where he held her tight and murmured soothing words until her breathing slowed, her clenched jaw relaxed and her flushed face and neck turned mottled white.

Keaton placed a heavy foot between Sandford's shoulders. 'Still think we're on the same side?' He glanced at Nadia, lying in a pool of blood. 'No. Don't answer that.'

'I'd rather have recruited her,' Sandford said of Nadia. 'She took on Delta Boy and nearly killed him with her bare hands. Tried to do the same to me. Went up against my gun. Didn't even flinch. Made us both look like pussycats.'

'So you killed her?' Pearce scoffed as he leaned over Sandford to search him, 'You *are* a pussy.' He extracted Sandford's wallet and cell phone, then grinned up at Keaton. 'He's even brought his ID. That's very nice of him. David Sandford. British security services.' Pearce whistled. 'British security services and US Delta in bed together. Now we're in for some fun.'

'Delta?' Keaton stared at Faulk who was still dazed on his knees. 'These boys bring top dollar.'

By now, Ali was wired tight. She did her best not to react but she was close to snapping. The room hummed with duplicity and no one spoke as they contemplated what had just happened and what to do next.

'What a fuck-up!' Keaton looked at Ali. His face was sad in a way she found confusing. 'What you did could have got us all killed. Acting on your own like that. Without back-up or communication. Do you want to die? Is that what this is all about?'

Furious, she grabbed his shirt. 'That's stupid! . . .'

'What you did is stupid. Don't do it again. Think it through.'

'Think it! . . .!' She clutched his shirt so tightly it ripped. That brought her short. There it was again. That image of herself that was not right, a tiny tumour of viciousness and ill-will that was mutating inside her and spreading. That frightened her. She uttered an involuntary sob, though it emerged like a laugh. 'This can't get any worse!'

'Of course it can. Do you have any notion of how crazy you are?'

Keaton caught her eye then glanced away, as if the weight of her gaze was too personal. Surprised, Ali realised that he was angry for her, not with her, because all of this was so much worse than he had imagined. He was hiding his feelings for her as he hid everything else.

He suddenly grinned. 'The grim reaper on tour? Where does that come from?'

She smiled, shrugged.

The sound of the shot, even suppressed, was startling in its suddenness and mind-numbing in its loudness. Keaton and Pearce reacted with practiced speed but there was no danger. Faulk was slumped lifeless on the floor and Sandford was kneeling, holding Faulk's gun above his head, his finger off the trigger to indicate that he was no threat. In an exaggerated show of submission, Sandford allowed Pearce to take the gun from him.

Keaton was furious. They had taken their eyes off the ball and he had lost the chance to interrogate Faulk. Worse, if Sandford had kept shooting, he would have killed them all. Keaton felt no gratitude, or reprieve, His impulse was to finish it now, put a double-tap in Sandford's brain. And why not? Men like Sandford were truly malignant. They were highly intelligent, highly educated and highly trained, but their real strength lay in their deranged egotism, their lack of conscience, and their capacity for manipulation and cruelty. They were imbued with the narrow-minded certainty that they were untouchable. Sandford had no need of denial, or justification or refusal to answer. It was enough to rationalise himself as a protector of the state. The guy who carried out the ops too black for his own government to acknowledge. Keaton knew that death was the only cure for this kind of psychopathology but he sensed Ali's recriminating eye on him and he stayed his hand.

Pearce cuffed Sandford, mouth twisted with anger. 'I should have done this before.'

'Hell of a CV, Delta Boy,' Sandford said, looking at Faulk with feigned regret. 'Airborne, ranger, special forces. He had a rep for being permanently armed and extremely dangerous but the woman took him out like he was the class weakling. He'd never have lived with that. I did the poor bastard a favour.'

Keaton was still struggling with his own murderous rage and contempt but Pearce had other matters on his mind.

'We have to go.' he said urgently. 'We're all out of time. Two shots is sure to bring the cops.'

Sandford spoke up, like he was part of the team. 'At this time of day, the houses on both side of us are empty. The shots might have seemed loud to us but they won't have carried. New York's finest won't be coming. Best to wait it out until dark.'

'And if they do come? How do we get out?'

Rachel knew. 'Nadia had an escape route, out back.'

'Do you know it?' Keaton asked.

'She made me practice it.'

'Show me.'

Rachel led Keaton into the kitchen. A back door opened onto a small yard from which a wooden gate led into a communal space. From here, there was egress between two houses to the next street and safety. Keaton took a moment to consider their options. They should go now, while they still had time, but he was worried about leaving behind the bodies and all that forensic trace. They had to make the time to clean up. He returned to the others.

'Okay,' he said. 'Sandford's right. We stay. The cops should have been here by now. If they do come, we slide out the back way.'

Pearce took that as his cue and aimed his gun at a point between Sandford's eyes. 'Okay. Get to your feet.'

A hint of doubt crossed Sandford's face. 'Why?'

Pearce's gaze burned into him and his voice was hard and fierce. 'Do it.'

With two guns on him, Sandford came gingerly to his feet. 'We're on the same side here,'

'I'm glad you think so,' Pearce said, pushing forward into Sandford's space, 'because I'm going to search you.'

'What? You already did that. You have my gun and wallet.'

Pearce cut off Sandford's cuffs. 'Take off your jacket.'

'You think I'm wearing a wire? Don't be dumb.'

'I'd just as soon shoot you.'

Sandford hesitated, then felt the muzzle of Keaton's gun against his spine. Slowly, he removed his jacket and handed it to Pearce, who went through it, found nothing and had Sandford strip to his underpants.

After a thorough search, he nodded at Keaton. *All clear.*

Without warning, Keaton grabbed the semi-naked Sandford by the hair and forced him down and backwards. Sandford's surprise was real, as was his fear when he felt the point of a black steel blade threatening his carotid.

'What are you?' Keaton demanded. 'Five? Six?'

With an effort, Sandford managed to sound matter-of-fact confident. 'Five-ish.'

'What are you doing here?'

'Protecting the girl.'

'Liar!' Keaton spat. He pressed the knife into the skin until blood trickled. 'You have one more try.'

'I'm here to offer protection for the girl.'

'You killed her bodyguard! How is that protection?'

'The woman went crazy and tried to kill me.' Sandford's tone was resigned, self-deprecating. 'She left me no choice.'

'What's the girl to you?'

'We want to bring Bowman down. She can help with that. He wants her dead, we want her alive.'

'How can she help you?'

'She's carrying something that belongs to HMG.'

'The flash drive.'

'Yes.'

Keaton glanced at Rachel who was using tissues to clean Sandford's blood and skin from her nails. 'She's also carrying a pound of your flesh. What makes you think she would want to help you?'

Sandford touched his face with a rueful smile. 'As you say, she's had her pound of flesh.'

'How did you know where to find us?' Keaton demanded. 'Have you been following us?'

'I was given the address.'

'When?'

'Two days ago.'

'Who by?'

'My London office. That's all I can tell you.'

'Two days ago? Why wait until now to act?'

'We were watching. Waiting to see who came. I saw Ms Feysor enter. It forced my hand.'

Keaton's eyes narrowed. 'Who are you working for?'

Sandford seemed surprised by the question. 'HMG, of course.'

'Not Bowman?'

'Getting this mess cleaned up is the mission. Bowman is the mess.'

Keaton removed the knife and let him up to his feet. 'Okay. Get dressed.'

Pearce watched Sandford pull on his clothes. 'What do we do with this pussy?'

'We can't leave him here,' Keaton said.

'Then don't leave him here.' Sandford said, joining the third party narrative with more than a hint of self-deprecation. 'By all means, take him with you. It'll save him the trouble of following you.'

'Secure him,' Keaton said to Pearce. 'Leave him for Bowman.'

Sandford said, 'Mine is the better idea. Take him with you.'

At last, Keaton acknowledged him, 'Now why would we do that?'

'Because we want the same thing.

'And what would that be?'

'This cluster fuck to go away. I can make that happen.' Faced with their open scepticism, Sandford continued. 'We have a common enemy. Bowman. He's out there planning how to get you. He won't rest until you're all dead.'

'How do you know that if you're not working with him?'

'It's what I would be doing. And now he'll be coming after me, too. We have no choice: get the guy before he gets us.'

Keaton looked at him without sympathy. 'Why should we trust a man who just murdered his partner?'

'Faulk was Bowman's man. His brief was to get the flash drive and kill the girl. He thought I shared his mission. If he knew otherwise he would have killed me. Listen, I'm off the books here. Which means I'm putting my head on the block.'

'Then why do it?'

'Because I don't want to live my life looking over my shoulder,' he said, 'Just give me the flash drive and this is over. Guaranteed.'

Ali said, 'The drive is in safer hands than yours.'

'I doubt that,' he said. 'I want this wound closed whereas you want to open it further. Trust me, you're the kind of complication we could have done without.'

Ali shook her head. 'Trust *me*. We want this story suppressed, same as you. That puts us on the same page. This is about self-preservation. I drop the story or die. I die and the story will come out. You won't be able to stop it. It'll be your very own doomsday virus. Death by social media. You can work out the rest. The

Government falls out of trust with its allies and the Muslim world. And with the voters. Then there's the war crimes tribunal. And your own trip to gaol.'

Sandford kept his face neutral. 'So you do have the information.'

'We have what we need.'

Sandford stood silently for a moment in a pretence of deliberation. 'Like I said, we're on the same side. I can wipe your slate.'

'And in return?'

'Cut me in on the disk.'

Keaton said, 'Let's see you deliver first.'

'Keaton!' Ali flared. 'You can't!'

Sandford looked at Ali. 'We're making progress here. You could at least try looking happy about that.'

'This is me looking happy.' Ali responded with an icy stare. 'Don't go thinking I want to be here. It makes me sick just being this close to someone like you.'

Sandford gave her mild affront. 'You're travelling with a killer for hire, remember? Don't go all judgemental on me.'

While he was speaking, a cell phone rang out. They all looked at each other then Ali bent to Nadia's shoulder bag. She extracted the phone and glanced at the caller ID.

'Ashe,' she said and killed the call.

The call renewed Pearce's urgency. 'Chris, We have to go.'

'Okay,' Keaton said. He held Sandford's eye. 'But we cuff this bastard and keep a gun on him.'

Nadia's phone started to ring again.

'I'd expect nothing less,' Sandford said. 'But you be careful in the car. New York's a bumpy town. Hardly the place for a heavy trigger finger.'

Ali looked at Rachel, her thumb poised over the screen. 'Ashe is your uncle, right?' A nod. 'The guy who's been helping you.'

'Wait!' Keaton cried. 'Ali, No!'

Ali took in Rachel's ambivalent nod then accepted the call.

'This is Ali Feysor. We have to talk.'

Ashe hesitated. 'Where is Nadia?'

'She's dead.'

A beat. 'And Sarah?'

'She's fine. Let's meet.'

Chapter 59

BY THE TIME they were ready to leave the house, darkness had fallen and the rush hour traffic was beginning to ease. They had plenty of enemies in the city and their priority was to exfiltrate undetected by watchers or worse. Their best driver was Pearce, and he elected himself for the surveillance detection run. While his companions watched from inside the house, he went out alone, reached the Jeep without incident and started the engine. He paused, saw no sign of a surveillance or kill team, and listened as Keaton reported the same from his vantage inside the house. Pearce took several deep, calming breaths, then drove down West 89th Street, turned left onto Riverside Drive, left again after four blocks, and made his way back into West 89th Street. It was a soft run. He did another lap, again without reaction. This time, he pulled up outside the Brownstone. He double-parked, engine running, while the others joined him. Rachel settled in next to him and the others sat in the back. Pearce accelerated smoothly to Riverside Drive and they were home free. Sandford kept entreating Keaton to be careful but the latter, not wanting to be distracted from the business of counter-surveillance, pressed his gun hard enough into the other's ribs to leave a contusion.

They stopped by the East78 apartment to pick up their gear. They had to assume that the safe house was blown, so Pearce parked down the block while Keaton went in alone. The street, building and apartment were clear. Their gear was pre-packed and ready to go, and it took but a moment to grab it and return to the Jeep.

The lack of opposition gave them an opportunity to abandon the Jeep. They wiped it clean and left it in the apartment car park. The plan was to travel in two groups, using relays of cabs to reach an area of brownstones and small hotels in the Upper West Side. Pearce started out north with Rachel. Keaton, Sandford and Ali took a cab west. Sandford seemed happy enough to go along with them and Ali was too pre-occupied to speculate on his agenda. Random choice, the two groups met up at the Norton Hotel and booked a couple of rooms.

They gathered in the women's room, a double en-suite with two beds and a rear window view. The two women sat on one bed while Pearce and Keaton bracketed Sandford on the other. Sandford was using a dampened towel to soothe his battered face and neck.

Ali turned to Rachel. 'Do you still have the drive?'

Rachel nodded. She retrieved it from her backpack and gave it to the journalist. 'You'll know what to do with it.'

Ali fingered it like the Holy Grail. 'How do we access it? My laptop doesn't have the software or processing power to break an encryption.'

'It's not encrypted,' Rachel told her. 'There's not even a password. I just copied the files. My father was in the habit of leaving his computer on when he went out of the room. He had no reason not to trust me. I just copied what I could and waited for him to confront me. He never did.'

Sandford laughed. 'You're carrying a drive that people would kill for – have killed for – and you haven't even protected it!'

Rachel threw him a hate-filled glare. 'Nadia was my protection.'

Sandford seemed on the verge of some clever retort but sensed hostile eyes on him and thought better of it.

Ali's mouth was dry and her heart raced as she plugged the USB drive into her computer. This wouldn't compensate for the dead but it would go some way.

'Ok,' she said, 'let's see what we have.'

A list of folders filled the screen, each carefully labelled in a system that might have been compiled by a child. Ali clicked on a folder labelled <ID documents>. It contained what it said: birth certificates, passports, driving licenses and a range of other documents, some fake, some real, though Ali couldn't tell which was which. Among them were documents for Lucca, Bowman and Ashe. Another file contained financial statements and spreadsheets, the secret in-house accounts of illegal businesses.

Ali blew out a deep breath. 'He had all this on his home PC, completely unprotected?'

'The computer was protected, I think. He just didn't see me coming.'

'First rule of the dark side,' Sandford remarked. 'Never piss off a family member.'

Ali shifted the cursor onto photo and video folders. Before she could open them, Rachel stood up and rested a hand on the journalist's shoulder.

'Please, do not continue.' There was unmistakable anguish in her voice. 'Not yet. I am not ready. The pictures, they are. . . . Perhaps if we ate first.'

Pearce was quick to support her. 'I think we could all do with a break. I'll go for a takeout.'

Ali made to object then swallowed her exasperation. She had seen enough to verify her story. She could wait a few more minutes. 'Okay.'

Pearce looked around at the others. 'What do we want.'

Keaton shrugged. 'You choose.'

Rachel said, 'I'll come with you.'

Pearce glanced at Keaton who nodded.

Rachel and Pearce headed out.

Ali watched them go then poked a finger at the screen and asked, 'How do we use this stuff?'

Keaton shrugged his uncertainty and Sandford stepped in.

'Email Bowman a short sampler,' he said, 'enough to let him know that you have him by the balls. Follow up with a meet. By that time, you will have everything ready to put out there. You don't have to catalogue it. Raw data would be enough. As long as it's *all* out there. I can arrange that. You show him what's waiting for him and then you force him to deal.'

Ali glanced at Keaton who nodded a tentative acceptance. Ali, too, could see how the plan might work. But there was a committee of voices in her head warning her to beware. In dealing with Sandford, she was dealing with a player who was far more intelligent, brutal, and politically connected than the kind of psychotics and losers she usually investigated. She felt sure that Sandford's proposal was designed to somehow ensnare her. But he could only spring a trap if he stayed involved in their little operation. They could adopt the plan without accepting the man.

'Okay,' she told Keaton, her voice unexpectedly harsh with mistrust. 'We go with the plan but we don't use him, He arranges nothing.'

'Ouch,' said Sandford, as though his feelings were being trampled on. 'I thought we were on the same side here yet I offer you the benefit of my expertise and you cut me out. That's no basis for trust, Ali?'

'Trust!' Ali uttered a soft cackle that might have been a laugh.

'Pearce has the contacts,' Keaton said. 'He can arrange matters so that none of us knows who's handling it. That way we can't tell anyone, however persuasively they ask.'

They set about selecting samples of data to use. Ali felt compelled to find the best examples, those that would be certain to make Bowman sweat blood, and she dutifully clicked through every page, reading each document until they ran one into another. Before long, her eyes were sore from screen burn and lack of sleep, and all she could think about was room service and a pot of strong coffee. It was a relief when Pearce and Rachel returned with lamb, falafel wraps and beers.

While they sorted and ate the food, Keaton explained the plan. Pearce reacted enthusiastically.

Ali looked at Pearce with open scepticism, 'Are you set up for secure email?'

Pearce smiled. 'End to end encryption. My phone has the same encryption algorithm and key as my contact. Only he can unscramble it.'

Keaton noticed that Ali's food was untouched. The reporter looked grey and wiped out.

'Take a break, ladies,' he said. 'We'll go next door and let Pearcey do what Pearcey does.'

He picked up the laptop, waited for Ali's assenting nod, then led the men next door.

Rachel switched on the TV for company then sat cross-legged on her bed. Ali stretched out on her bed, hands behind her head, eyes closed. But she was too wired to eat or sleep.

She sat up and asked, 'Why are you in hiding?'

'My father is afraid I'll talk. He wants me dead.'

'Talk about what?'

'Who he is. What he has done.'

'What has he done?'

Rachel didn't answer directly. 'When my family was murdered, I was told it was the Muslims. I wanted revenge. I wanted blood. I was going to kill all Muslims, then dig them up and kill them again! It became my mission. My reason for living.'

Ali nodded; she understood that kind of commitment. *Kill those who killed people you loved!* The thought caressed her like a cold, loveless hand. She shook herself free, took a deep breath and placed a halter on her runaway thoughts.

'And did you?' Ali asked. 'Kill Muslims?'

Rachel stared ahead, unseeing, like an arthritic resting from pain. When she spoke, her voice hobbled along, wounded and shrinking.

'Before the war, our village was a good place to live. Serb and Albanian lived together as neighbours. Christian and Muslim as one. Then the Serb militia came to our village. They came to kill Muslims and many villagers joined them. These people murdered their own neighbours, their friends, my friends! Men, women, children. It was too terrible for words. I saw a man cut his neighbour's throat. This man, he had always wanted his neighbour's fields by the stream, and his greed overcame his humanity. I knew them both as goodhearted men. I could do nothing. They shot any Christians who tried to stop it. They pushed the Muslims into a barn. They locked the barn and set fire to it. They shot those who tried to escape. I still hear the screams.' She paused. 'The Serbs killed my people. I am a Serb but I wanted all Serbs dead. I wanted the Serbs dead, I wanted Muslims dead. I vowed to kill everyone!'

'I would have done the same.'

Rachel acknowledged that with a little nod. 'About a year ago, I had to take a day off uni. A stomach upset, I think. I woke at midday and went downstairs for a glass of water. I heard voices from the kitchen. My father and Vanavasam. For some reason I didn't join them but waited in the hallway. They were talking about a journalist who was interested in what had happened in Kosovo. Vanavasam said it would be easy enough to stop him and keep it secret. My father agreed but said the big disaster would be if my mother's brother found out. I realised they were talking about the death of my family. There was something about the way they were talking that made me suspicious.. I found out the name of this journalist and talked to him.'

'Steven Shimmon?'

A nod. 'He told me that my father had murdered my mother and siblings before fleeing the country with me and my uncle. At first, I refused to accept it. Steven was very kind and said it was better for me if I didn't believe him and then I knew he was telling the truth. My own father! He murdered everyone I loved! He cut the throats of his own children! What kind of man does that?' Rachel paused to regain her composure. 'I want him to suffer. I want him dead but I can't do it. I can't kill him. I've known that all along, somehow, but seeing Nadia like that - I can't do it.'

Ali nodded. 'You're not like him. That's a good thing.'

Rachel reached for her bag and produced a Ruger LC9. 'I am not so pure. Pearcey gave me this. I would use it on Sandford without a second thought.' She paused long enough to fix a child-like obduracy on her face. 'It is fortunate that God forgives liars and fools. He has to, he made so many of us. I wanted my father punished but he is untouchable. I knew it was up to me but I lacked the courage to kill him myself. I thought about telling my uncle. He would have been obliged to take revenge. It's *our* way: blood for blood. But they are so close, my uncle and my father. I feared he would simply warn my father. I thought about telling the authorities, but there are so many in the pay of my father. After my father's people killed Stephen Shimmon, I realised what a long reach he has. I knew he would discover that I knew. And he knows only one language for solving problems, the language of violence and death. I became frightened and decided to run away. Peter Jackson, my driver, helped me. And my uncle. I know that now. I needed some insurance so I copied some of my father's precious files. It scares him to know that I have them.'

Before Ali could reply, there was a knock on the door. Keaton was there. He studied Rachel for her reaction as he said:

'Ashe is on his way here. If that's a problem for you we can go next door.'

'No problem for me.' Rachel shrugged. 'For my father, maybe.'

'Your father being Bowman?'

'Bowman.' A nod. 'In Kosovo he was known as Lucca. Mergim Lucca.'

Chapter 60

BOWMAN WAS LUCCA!

Before they had time to process the information, Ashe came into the room. He had an evasive and calculating look about him but, when Rachel stepped forward, eager to greet him, a warm smile brightened his face. Then he saw Sandford and his smile froze. For an instant, he was thrown off balance. But only for an instant. Brusquely, he shrugged Rachel aside and set himself for the fight, eyes darting from face to face like a cornered fox until they settled back on Sandford.

'What is he doing here?' he demanded.

'It's okay,' Keaton reassured him. 'He's with us.'

'What kind of trick is this?'

'It's no trick,' Rachel said. She knew only too well her uncle's volatility and was imploring him to understand. 'They defended me. My father sent someone to kill me and they saved me. They want to help me and I want to help them.'

'So they're on your side,' Ashe snorted, his eyes locked on to Sandford. 'Is that what this man told you? And you believe him?'

'We all want the same thing,' Keaton said. 'We want to survive Bowman.'

'So we do,' Ashe said harshly. His malevolence put the East European back into his voice. 'But you can't trust a man like this. He will tell you what you want to hear but he will do what serves his own interests. His idea of survival is to give Sarah up to her father as soon as he can.'

Keaton shook his head. 'He wants Lucca buried.'

'He wants the truth buried, of course he does, but he is Lucca's man. He knows that the only way to survive is to kill all of you. I am sure that you are finding him very helpful, very friendly. But you cannot trust him.'

'Talking of trust,' Sandford spoke up, 'aren't you the man whom Lucca trusts most in this world? Funny you should turn out to be the quisling in his tribe of monsters. And still talking of trust,' he continued, turning to face Rachel, 'has your uncle told you how he personally pummelled your friend into oblivion?'

Rachel was puzzled, 'What friend?'

'Jackson. Your minder. The man who helped you disappear.'

'Martin? What have you done to him?.'

'Martin is dead, dear girl. Uncle Ashe killed him with his bare hands.'

Rachel turned to Ashe. 'Is it true, Martin is dead?'

Ashe ignored her and spoke directly to Keaton, 'Sandford is following his own agenda here. Disrupt, divide and destroy. You've brought him into your camp and now you've exposed me. If he speaks to Lucca before we are ready, we will all die. This is Lucca's country. This is Lucca's man. If you do not kill him you will regret it. If you lack the stomach then kindly permit me to do it.'

Amused by the open discussion of his fate, Sandford said, 'If Ashe killed everybody he doesn't trust, there would be a sixth mass extinction.'

Ashe and Sandford were staring at each other, unblinking. The atmosphere in the room was murderous. Ali couldn't help noticing how similar the two men were. Gaunt, middle-aged and grey. Doers used to having things their own way. Proven killers, cold-blooded and unremorseful.

'Is it true.' Rachel's tone said it all; she believed it. 'Did you kill Martin?'

Ashe said, 'He would have betrayed you.'

'Never.'

'Your father would have made him talk. There was nothing else to do.'

'You could have let him live! He was the one person who was always kind to me. And loyal. Without question. He would do anything for me. He was my big brother and you murdered him. Why would you do that?'

'He was happy to die for you.'

'He didn't have to. I would have come home.'

'And your father would have murdered you. Be reasonable.'

Rachel choked and turned away.

'Be reasonable!' Ali snapped. 'Since when has murder been reasonable? What kind of psycho could think that? Talking is reasonable. Negotiation is reasonable!'

'Then let us negotiate,' Ashe said. 'But I will not talk if Sandford is in the room. If Lucca learns of our plans, we are dead. Either he goes or I go.'

Unexpectedly, Sandford said: 'I'll leave. We'll get nowhere otherwise.'

Ashe was still not happy, 'You can't let him leave. He will return with Lucca and a posse of gunmen.'

Pearce looked at Keaton who nodded. Wordlessly, Pearce led the smirking Sandford outside. Ali sat on her bed. Rachel joined her, pointedly avoiding Ashe who sat on the other bed. Keaton stood by the door until Pearce returned.

Pearce spoke softly into Keaton's ear. 'Ashe has a point, Chris, Sandford is insinuating himself and I don't trust him.'

'Nor do I, mate,' Keaton whispered. 'Nor do I.'

'Ashe is unarmed. I didn't see anyone with him. I'm pretty sure he came alone.' He raised his voice for all to hear. 'I've cuffed Sandford to a bed. He won't be contacting anyone.'

Keaton sat next to Ashe while Pearce stood by the door.

Ashe glanced at the others in turn. 'Where would you like me to start?'

Ali had been thinking about this and she replied without hesitation. 'Operation Mammon.'

Ashe was silent for a while, as though wondering where to begin. 'The British SAS had been sent to assassinate Lucca, who was on the run from civil authorities, NATO and the War Crimes Tribunal. But the British didn't want him in court. He knew much that was embarrassing to them and they wanted to silence him. Fortunately for Lucca, he had gathered incriminating evidence of their involvement together and he used this to gain a reprieve.'

'He blackmailed the British Government?' Ali couldn't keep the surprise from her voice; it made her feel like an ingénue.

Ashe shrugged, 'Figgis, yes. You cannot blackmail the innocent. Lucca persuaded them to put him in their special protection programme.' He uttered the latter phrase with real invective. 'At the last minute, the assassination was called off. The SAS was instructed to help him escape and disappear.'

'Where were you when this was happening?'

'I was running the business. I had no part in his paramilitary operation. I am no saint, but this I could not do. At one time, we had maybe a thousand men engaged in drug trafficking, arms trafficking, extortion, prostitution and other activities. It kept me too busy to concern myself with other people's wars. At the time of his escape, I was in Bucharest, arranging some business with the Bulgarians. It was there that I was told that my sister and her family had been murdered. At the time, I thought Lucca and Sarah were dead, too.'

'When did you discover otherwise?'

'I went home to bury them and he contacted me. He said he had already avenged their deaths. He wanted me to go direct to London to consult with Crain. . . .'

'Crain!' Ali cut in. 'He was involved that far back?'

Ashe nodded. 'At that time, he was a consultant. He came to work for us much later. First, I had to collect Sarah, or Elena as she was then known. She was at school in Belgrade. After all those years of slaughter, she is my only blood. I had to make her safe. I took her with me to London. There, my job was to help Crain create a network of businesses around the world to re-launder and invest our money. This was a very complex operation. I worked with Crain for nearly six months before I was satisfied that he was progressing in the right way. Then I took Sarah to her father in Johannesburg. Needless to say, he was surprised to see her.'

'He didn't know that she was alive?'

'I thought it best not to tell him.'

'Why?' Ali was finding it difficult to take this in. 'Did you think he would kill her? His daughter? That's it, isn't it. You suspected him of killing his own family?'

'He had to run. He couldn't take them with him, he couldn't leave them behind. So, yes.'

'If he killed your sister, why didn't you kill him? What happened to your precious blood for blood?'

Ashe paused to fix a difficult smile on his face. 'I had no proof. And I had to protect Sarah. Vengeance is no reason for watching your loved ones die. It was time to break the chain.'

At this point, Sarah reached out and took his hand in hers.

Ashe offered her a wan smile. 'It was only a matter of time before someone cracked open our world. Your friend Shimmon came close. You, I believe, are closer.'

'Close as death,' Ali said grimly.

Ashe said, 'I will help you.'

'Okay,' Keaton said. 'But the question is, help us do what?'

'Neutralise him.'

'Lucca? Kill him, you mean?'

'Killing him is not enough. Lucca lives by the feud. He will reach out even after his death. First, we must make him want to keep you alive. Second we must eliminate the threat that will follow his death. Then we kill him. The timing is all important.'

'The timing,' Ali echoed sceptically.

Ashe nodded. 'You start by cutting a deal with him. He blackmailed your government to stay alive. You do the same to him. Convince him that you know everything about him and will use it if he doesn't deal.'

Ali explained that they had already planned to do just that.

Ashe nodded approval. 'You have to convince Lucca that he cannot control what you know. It would help if we could find Crain. He has everything on file. He has disappeared. Lucca is very worried.'

Keaton permitted himself a smile. 'He should be. We have Crain and his files.'

Ashe was genuinely shocked. 'You abducted Crain!'

'Let's say we persuaded him to change sides.'

Ashe considered for a moment. 'Lucca thinks that he has stolen from him and run. That will give us an edge. Unfortunately, Crain's disappearance has put him on alert. We have lost the element of surprise. We have to hope that Lucca doesn't discover that you are here.'

Pearce said, 'Maybe Sandford's already told him?'

Ashe shook his head. 'Lucca would have told me.'

Pearce was still troubled. 'We have to assume that Sandford's playing all sides. His type always does. In which case, everyone knows we're here, including Lucca,'

Keaton nodded. 'Then we're in for a difficult time.'

'I can't believe I'm asking this out loud,' Ali said, 'but how do we kill Lucca? You said it yourself. He's protected better than the President. You'd need an army.'

Keaton smiled. 'Getting in is never the problem, It's getting out.'

'If you can't get out you're not going in,' Ali said, an edge of panic in her voice. 'You're not on a fucking Jihad, Chris. Don't think you can exchange a Kevlar vest for a suicide vest. I won't let you. I'm not losing anyone else.'

'Afraid I'll come back and haunt you?'

'No.' She concealed her concern with sarcasm. 'I'm worried you'll start a blood feud.'

'There is no more blood,' Keaton said. ' We're the end of the line, Lucca and me both.'

'So you kill each other,' Ali snorted. 'Great plan.'

'I wouldn't call it a plan,' Keaton responded, mock offended. 'Not yet.'

Ashe interrupted them. 'Lucca has a private army, it is true. But these are mercenaries. They will take the side of the highest bidder.'

'So we outbid Lucca?' Keaton smiled. 'I suppose I could cash in my pension.'

'We have Lucca's money,' Ali said. 'Let's put it to good use.'

Keaton's smile became broader.

'Lucca has a small inner circle of people he trusts,' Ashe told them, 'people who have been with him since Kosovo. Perhaps five people, including me and Vanavasam. You need only eliminate this group. Money will take care of the rest. The leader of the mercenaries is Thomas Suzman. I will speak with him.'

Pearce said, 'I know Suzman. He's a good man. We've done ops together. This could work.'

'First priority,' Ashe said, 'is to show Lucca that you mean business. Prevent him from killing you first. What do you have?'

Ali told him, somewhat reluctantly, like the trust wasn't quite there. 'Incriminating documents on his criminal activities, including how he launders the money. There's a list of dummy companies. We have his agreement with the UK government, and his false identity documents, and photos and video that we haven't yet watched.'

'Don't view the videos,' Sarah said, her voice dull and angry. 'Believe me, you will not be the same person after watching them. It is enough to know what is on them. My father raping and torturing people. He enjoyed watching himself at work. Trust me when I say it is good evidence for a court.'

'He claims that watching them helps him sleep,' Ashe added. 'He used to joke that his brain is just a life support system for his testicles.' He remembered Sarah. 'I am sorry Sarah. Forgive me.'

Sarah shrugged. She was very subdued, her face red and hot. Despite her entreaty not to watch, Keaton couldn't accept an unseen video as evidence. He made to slot the USB drive into the laptop.

Ali stopped him. 'There's more to believing than seeing.'

Chapter 61

BOWMAN READ THE contents of the email with growing fury. The attempt to silence Feysor and her friends had backfired. Somehow the journalist knew everything about him and she was threatening to put it out there for all to see. *Just a sampler,* her email said, *a little teaser.* Some sampler! Birth certificates, driving licenses, financial statements, spreadsheets, names, photos and a video clip from his time in the Balkans. The journalist was demanding a meet to negotiate a solution that would let them both walk away from this. The alternative was that she would expose him.

The email was proxy-this and proxy-that untraceable. But the real issue was how she had got hold of his data? Her informant had to be someone close to him. Only a handful of people had that kind of access.

And, of course, only one had a stolen memory stick. Sarah.

Sarah Bowman. Born Elena Lucca. Fruit of his loins turned blood enemy.

Somehow his daughter had got together with the journalist, Feysor. Which would explain how the journalist knew so much. She knew that he was Mergim Lucca. She knew his identity trail from

Kosovo via South Africa right up to the present day. She had details of his business empire, legit and criminal. She knew which politicians, law enforcement, legal and other establishment figures he was bankrolling. Her information was good. Too good. He had to get to Feysor and his daughter both, then extract and eliminate their sources. That was the priority. Then he would kill the women. Slowly and painfully.

First, he had to limit the damage. What was the worst someone like Feysor could do? Give him up to the British Secret Service, or maybe the FBI? He had good friends in those agencies, though he didn't make the mistake of believing that he could rely on them. He had once made the error of thinking that these western agencies were soft. Not any more. Even now, they might charge in through his gates, mob handed, a convoy of agents driving gangsta SUVs. And they would want him dead, not alive and talking.

He would accept a meet. That would ensure her silence until he could get to her. And he would get to her, he was supremely confident of that. He had never failed to deal with a problem. No one had come close to identifying or apprehending him. He had made himself untouchable. The bitch journalist had dared to threaten him with full exposure but he knew which one of them would survive. After all, half the world was in his debt and the other half didn't care.

His skin was crawling with the need to kill. His mind was racing uncontrollably in a dozen haphazard directions, all of them lethal. He just had to kill somebody. It had been this way with him for a long time, and that had been his dirty little secret. He truly loved the feeling of power that killing gave him. Some depersonalised the act. Thought of it as business. But where was the fun in that?

Perhaps he didn't have to meet with Feysor. Perhaps there was another way.

He called London. 'What's going on? You told me the story was dead.'

'This is not a clean phone.'

'Clean? Dirty? Who gives a fuck? Feysor is here and she has it all.'

'No names! I can't have this coming back to me. The Sandman will clean it up. And, if the op goes south, we will roll it up, put it around his neck and start all over again.'

The phone went dead.

The snub infuriated him. Now he knew that there had to be another way.

Chapter 62

THEY HAD ARRANGED to meet in Love, one of NYC's hottest dance clubs. Intuitively, it was a quirky choice of venue, but Ashe had soft-sold it as neutral ground with hundreds of disinterested witnesses. It was raining when Ali arrived with Keaton and Pearce, and security was struggling to maintain control over the restless lines of clubbers. The crowd at the nearby VIP entrance was almost as big, professional celeb-watchers and the merely curious. The three Brits attracted barely a glance.

The club was a huge multi-room space with black walls and three main tiers. They came in on the mezzanine level, mezzanine being designer speak for the wide interior balcony that circled the inside of the club. The balcony was taken up by black leather booths and a number of small bars. Food was served at this level, mostly with fries to judge by the ineluctable odor, and the booths were full. A glass balustrade overlooked the main dance floor below, which was jumping: solid music, booze, drugs, understated fashion, overstated dancing and a light show to rival the old Tate Modern experience. Giant screens showed indie clips, film tributes, music videos and ads. The aerialists were on a break but the DJ booth was pulsing and there were magicians and dancers on the small stage. Adjacent areas housed a massive square bar and party rooms which boasted their own DJ systems.

Keaton looked for cameras. There were none on this level. Above them, he could make out a smaller mezzanine floor over which there appeared to be an illuminated glass atrium. No cameras in view up there so he wondered about hidden cameras. He had no way of knowing but this was a CCTV-intrusion-free club. The celebs wouldn't have been here otherwise.

As arranged, they were picked up by a young woman from Love hospitality. She led them upstairs to the higher mezzanine level which turned out to be the VIP room, all red sofas and tiny bars. The lights were up and the music down but, though the temperature soared with the body heat of the Beautiful People, there was no wild dancing. In fact, there was no dancing at all. Everywhere Ali looked, there was a face from a magazine or film or TV but, despite the absence of busies taking photos, no-one was prepared to let their hair down. Ecstasy generation this was not.

To judge by the air-kissing, everyone seemed to know everyone else. Ali was no gatecrasher but she couldn't shake off the growing expectation that these people would soon turn, hissing with venom, on this gross nonentity of an interloper. Even her clothes felt wrong. She had spent all that money - she could just imagine Helm in accounts: 'Expenses! 400 quid for a fucking t-shirt! What planet are you on?' - and the clothes didn't even feel right!

Not that she would be claiming expenses. She wasn't even working. It was crazy. She couldn't fix the exact moment when Shimmon's story had taken over her life, or when it had begun to crush the life out of her, but it was breaking open before her with exponential speed. A scoop this size, one that carried its own momentum, was a hack's dream. But, for Ali, it had become a nightmare. If she brought the story in she would die. On the other hand, if she didn't bring the story in, it would bring her in and the end result would be the same! Lose-lose. Her mind just wasn't configured to redact a story.

The girl led on, out of the VIP room into a brightly lit corridor. A length of red carpet stretched past two doors to a lift which took them up into the Sanctum, a kind of VVIP room that was a large glass box cantilevered over the club below. The crystal-clear floor seemed to quake to the thumping music and Ali braced herself against the vertiginous views of the dancers far below.

The girl took them directly to a booth where a silver-haired man was holding court to a circle of women and other flunkeys squeezed onto red sofas.

'Mr Bowman,' the girl announced before abruptly disappearing. 'Your guests.'

Bowman looked to be in his fifties, with a full head of hair brushed back and a smooth, patrician face. He was fashionably dressed in a black double breasted blazer and blue jeans with a high-collared, open necked gainsboro-grey shirt. He waved away his people and sipped his drink while they were jostled out of earshot by a couple of club bouncers. That's when Ali noticed Bowman's own security. Four men standing close quarters. Conspicuous by their dark suits, shiny shirts and white skin.

One man stood close to Bowman. He was fortyish, a gym monkey with a big neck and a challenging expression that he fixed on Keaton. Three men moved in behind Ali's group, locking them in. Two matched the age and bulk of the gym monkey. A younger man, was less bulky but lithe and manoeuvrable, Their loose-fitting jackets and strategic bulges indicated that they were armed. They settled into maintenance mode a comfortable distance from Keaton and Pearce. Their relaxed demeanour told Keaton that they thought they were in charge. They were acting like amateurs but Keaton didn't kid himself. These guys might not have been the best but they only had to be good enough.

'Please, Ms Feysor, take a seat,' said the man with the silver hair. 'Can I order you a drink?'

Ali ignored the overture. Instead, she made a show of studying him. The photo she had seen of Lucca had been decades old, so old that she hadn't even thought to bring it with her. But the image that stuck in her mind was rough and brambly. Add decades to that and she should have been looking at an ancient man as gnarled and ground down as a bristlecone Pine. This guy certainly could have been Bowman but, if he was, the years had brought him unexpected refinement.

Pointedly, she said, 'You're younger than I expected.'

'And you are more attractive than your pictures suggest.'

Touché, she thought. 'Let's keep this brief, shall we? You know what we're offering. You know what we want.'

He waved off her opening gambit like it was a buzzing wasp. He stood and stepped around the table towards her, piercing her with his pale, washed eyes, and she felt as if he was going to hit her. Instead, he beamed a smile and indicated a door at the back of the room,

'We should go somewhere a little more private.'

Ali hesitated. *Somewhere a little more private* suggested that they leave this neutral ground, relinquish the safety of all these witnesses and expose themselves to who-knew-what risk lay beyond that door. She glanced at Keaton whose facial expression told her that he would support whatever decision she made but that it was her decision. She took a deep breath then allowed it to slide out slowly. They had come here to negotiate, she reasoned, Ali and Bowman both, and she reckoned that neither of them could afford to pass up the chance to deal.

Ali smiled, 'Lead the way.'

Bowman set off for the door. Ali followed, then came Keaton with three of the minders. Pearce made to follow but the fourth minder, the slim one, put up his hand to stop him.

'Not you.'

Pearce glanced at Keaton who nodded and said, 'Ten minutes.'

Pearce watched them until they were out of sight, then sat down in the booth. The wiry minder sat with him, careful to stay out of reach.

Bowman led the way out of the Sanctum, past the lift and through a door into a short, empty corridor. An anonymous entrance opened into another, equally void and gloomy corridor with a fire exit some fifteen metres away. Lighting was dim and yellow. If she had been thinking about it, Ali might have expected something more glamorous than this fifties film set, but she had more pressing things on her mind. They walked halfway down the passageway and stopped at a green wooden door. No-one spoke as they waited for a minder to jiggle the key in the lock. Behind them, they could hear music and the subliminal hum of the city. The door opened and they went through into a disused office.

It was a windowless room, with a table and a single upright chair. The space was airless and quickly filled with the odours of stale sweat and deodorant. There was a camera on the wall and one of the minders made sure it was off.

Bowman leaned against the table and addressed them. 'Let me be clear about this since you seem to be under the illusion that we are equal parties in some sort of negotiation. There is no deal on the table. The fact is, I can make you disappear at any time of my choosing. No trace, no mess, no fuss.' His smile was naturally at ease, his manner one of complete control. 'Let me tell you what *I* want. I want all of your files, notes and scribblings. Without exception. I also want the heads of the people who have been helping you. Once I am satisfied that I have all that I want, then I can begin to consider an arrangement.'

'Arrangement?'

'I will call a truce.'

Ali scoffed. 'Truce's never last. I'd rather have a war and get it over with.'

Bowman misinterpreted her belligerent stance as bravado. 'We don't want to kill you, Ms Feysor. Do that and someone else will step into your shoes. Just as you did with Mr Shimmon. We survive by learning from our mistakes.' He paused. 'So tell me, how did you find me? Who helped you?'

'Finding you was child's play. A few days on your case and I knew all about you and Leke. I touch down in New York and here I am talking to you.'

'For which fact, I am grateful. Perhaps, while we are talking, you can explain what happened to Mr Crain?'

She hesitated. If she could have done, she would have called a time-out. There was something wrong about this man who called himself Bowman. An incongruity that couldn't be explained away by the ageing process or cultural assimilation. It wasn't just his soft physical appearance, though that had sown the first seed of doubt. It was his speech. The accent was too cultivated, too New England, too ingrained. There was just too much WASP about this man and literally none of the Balkans that had suffused Ashe's words with unrounded vowels and misplaced umlauts. This man was not Bowman. She tried to keep the realisation to herself but she could see that he had already read her tell. He knew that she knew that he was a proxy. He knew that she knew that he had no intention of negotiating a deal. Bowman didn't believe they could expose him. Ashe had suckered them and drawn them into a trap.

She glanced at Keaton, 'I think it's time we left.'

Too late. Bowman's minders had produced their guns, all Glock 27 9mm weapons, like they were official issue, and were pointing them with intent. Keaton offered her an impish, reassuringly confident smile.

'I am sorry to disappoint you, Ms Feysor.' The man calling himself Bowman smiled. 'As I said, there is a disjunction between what you think you can do and what you can do.'

Ali nodded. 'Then help us out. We know you're not Bowman. So who are you?'

'That doesn't matter. But please, if it helps you, you may continue to call me Bowman. Now, would you please take a seat.'

'I'd rather stand.'

One of the minders prodded her in the back. She sensed movement and a rise in tension as Keaton shifted in reaction to the threat,

'Be very careful,' Keaton said mildly.

'Don't try anything melodramatic,' Bowman said, as though bored of the prospect. 'We would hate to have to shoot you in front of your friend here.'

'Kill any one of us,' Ali said with a confidence she didn't feel, 'and you set in motion the destruction of your empire. Keep us alive and you stay in business.'

'Ah yes, your Mutually Assured Destruction fantasy.' Bowman didn't move for a long moment and his eyes stayed with her. The smart bomb acquiring its target. 'You will tell me everything I want to know. It is merely a question of time and I have that in abundance.'

Keaton cursed himself. He knew well enough that plans rarely stay in place once the action starts and this wasn't going to plan. Bowman was not interested in an accommodation for the future. He had the upper hand in the here and now. Against his better judgement, Keaton had allowed Ali to cheerlead him into the jaws of hell. But he couldn't blame her for his own stupidity. His mind worked furiously through his options and found none that would guarantee Ali's safety. His instinct was to attack, unleash instant and devastating aggression, but he was unarmed and his priority had to be to protect Ali from threats to front and rear.

His hesitation was but a nano-second but it was enough. There was a flash of something metallic coming towards him. He twisted away but the object connected with the side of his head. It was more than a glancing blow. Pain shot through his body. His legs turned to rubber, like those of an overextended marathon runner, and he crumpled to the floor. The room blurred, he could taste blood and he felt himself drifting.

Instinctively, Ali went for Bowman, clawing at his eyes. He twisted away but she caught him on the cheek and neck. She heard him cry out but she was already turning to help Keaton. The nearest minder made a grab for her but her momentum allowed her to rip free. He swung his fist at her and she ducked, slipped and fell.

Keaton was lying on the wooden floor, blood pouring from his split head. He felt surprisingly self-assured. His wound might have appeared disabling but it was superficial. They hadn't killed him so maybe they wanted him alive for now. That gave him an edge, as did their over-confidence. Feigning weakness and vulnerability, he struggled slowly to his feet. He kept his back to his adversaries, creating an inviting target. One stepped closer, intending to put him down again, and swung his gun like a baton.

Keaton backstepped into him, twisting around with a speed that took the minder by surprise, and elbowed him in the throat. Winded, the man clawed at his neck, gasping for air. Keaton twisted his gun from his hand and stabbed the muzzle into his neck. Hard. The minder collapsed, clasping the wound in his neck.

The minder watching Ali turned towards Keaton, gun coming up for the kill. Keaton used the Glock in his own hand to put him down with a single shot. It wasn't a kill shot. The man stood for several seconds, peering down at his bleeding chest, as though puzzled by it, before slumping to his knees. Keaton had already turned to Bowman and his BG. Somehow they had tangled up. The BG fired at Keaton but missed and Keaton put a double tap into him before turning the gun back to the man with the chest wound and shooting him in the forehead. By now, the minder with the injured neck was struggling to his feet, his breathing shallow as he clutched his bruised and torn throat. Keaton killed him with a single shot.

Which left Bowman.

Keaton turned towards him, gun already seeking its target. But Bowman had Ali in a neck lock, knife pressed against her throat, and he was using her as a human shield. Keaton had no target.

PEARCE HAD WAITED for much less than ten minutes when he decided to move. His every instinct told him that his friends were in trouble and that even seconds counted. The time for waiting was over.

He stood and stared at the minder assigned to watch him. 'I'm out of here. If you decide to murder me in front of all these people, go ahead. My guess is you don't want to do that.'

With that, he started threading his way through the VIPs and flunkeys to the exit. None of the club bouncers showed the slightest interest in his move. But when he hurried past the lift and went through the door to follow Keaton and Ali, the minder tasked with watching him suddenly woke up and ran after him. In the short corridor, Pearce heard muffled gunshots from round the corner. That pulled him up short. He counted six rounds. At the same time, the door banged open behind him as the pursuing minder came through.

IN TRYING TO avoid the blade, Ali had thrust herself up and back so that her right cheek was close as a lover's to Bowman's. From somewhere, she had found the courage for silent self-control, but all the youth had been sucked from her eyes, and her cold, white lips were distorted with fear.

Keaton knew how many rounds he had fired but had no idea how many rounds he had left. Keeping his gun trained on Bowman, he picked up a fallen Glock with his left hand. He checked the magazine. It was full. He fired a shot into the ceiling to verify that the gun was working then transferred it to his right hand.

Bowman was staring fixedly at Keaton, his face a mask, eyes aimed carelessly at his chest. A crawling sensation started in Keaton's nape; he'd seen that expression before. Icy fear prickled at his spine. He tried to aim his gun at Bowman but it pointed straight at Ali. He jerked the weapon a fraction left and right. It still pointed at Ali. He had no clear shot. Bowman was shifting her around, making himself a moving target, and he had edged them sidewards so that the table stood between them.

Trying not to look at Ali's face, Keaton said, 'Put the knife down.'

Bowman said, 'Drop the gun and we'll talk about it.'

It was a stalemate. Even if Keaton could fire first, Bowman might be able to use the knife. A pulse of death would do it. It was too much to risk. Keaton kept the gun in place and said:

'We should talk.'

'We're past that.'

From outside came the sound of a gunshot. Ali sensed Bowman relax his grip as he turned his head towards the door. She grabbed his knife hand and suddenly she was bouncing and wrestling and stamping and kicking. Bowman staggered against her energy and Keaton started forward. Bowman saw him coming and shoved Ali away. She crashed into Keaton and slumped down, silently fingering her neck and sucking in deep drafts of air.

TRAINING HONED TO instinct, Pearce turned and caught the surprised minder with a vicious jab to the solar plexus. The man crumpled in agony and Pearce relieved him of his gun. A Glock 27. He racked the slide and headed for the corner. He heard a curse from behind him and turned to see the minder coming to his feet with a blade in his hand. Without conscious thought, he shot the man in the forehead,

There was another gunshot from inside one of the rooms and Pearce threw caution to the wind and ran towards the sound.

WITH A ROAR, Bowman charged at Keaton, twisting his body sideways so that Keaton's bullet struck him a creasing blow across his chest and passed through his right bicep. Bowman kept coming, scrambling through chair and table and bundling Keaton across the room. They crashed into the wall and collapsed in a heap onto the floor. Gun and blade clattered free. Keaton hit his head again and the room blurred. He was struggling for focus when Bowman's hands found his throat. Desperation and adrenaline gave Keaton some strength but not enough. He was heaving left and right, furiously using his knees, his nails, his teeth but still Bowman maintained his throttling grip. Then Ali was there, her voice a screaming yell as she tried to wrestle Bowman off. Unfortunately for the weakening Keaton, all she achieved was to add her mass to Bowman's, putting Keaton so far out of weight that he began to lose the struggle.

Then it was over. Bowman collapsed abruptly into a lifeless mass, pinning Keaton with his dead weight. Keaton fought for air as he struggled to extricate himself and it wasn't until he had crawled free of Bowman that he saw the blood, the stab wounds on Bowman's neck, and the knife in Ali's hand.

Pearce appeared, stared down at Keaton and Ali, both heaving for breath, and glanced at the scratches and bite marks on Bowman's face.

'Keaton! You gouged him! And bit him! Oh my God! You fight like a fucking rugby player.'

Keaton managed to say, 'What kept you?'

Ali realised that she was holding the knife. Her hands were bloody. Horrified, she dropped the blade then allowed Pearce to help her to her feet. He saw how deathly white she had turned and assumed that she was in shock. She seemed to twitch as a thought struck her.

'It's okay,' he said. 'You've just exterminated a rat. Think of all the people you're saved.'

Ali shook her head. Killing Bowman didn't bother her. Not yet anyway. Her expression neutral, her eyes unblinking, she fished out her cell phone and called Rachel's number. She was diverted to voicemail. She tried again with the same result. She had no number for Sandford. She called their hotel but there was no reply from their rooms. She stared at Keaton, her face distraught, and, when she spoke, it was to say just one word.

'Rachel!'

Chapter 63

KEATON LED THEM from the abandoned office, through the fire door and down three flights of stairs to the fire exit. He waited a moment while Pearce killed the lights, then he opened the door and scoped the rear access road. It was little more than a dark alleyway with dumpsters, parked cars and an accumulation of random trash. The rain had eased but the single lamp gave minimal illumination and plenty of shadow. The streetlights were some fifty metres away.

Keaton stepped outside and suddenly felt like a drunk hitting cold air. His vision burred, the world shifted and he fell to his knees. It had stopped raining but the ground was wet. Not that he cared. He knew where he was but he couldn't see the alley anymore. Desperate for an anchor, he pressed his forehead to the concrete ground.

Thinking that Keaton had been shot, Pearce pushed Ali to the ground and crouched over her, gun sweeping the alley. As soon as he realised that there was no gunman, he scrambled over to Keaton.

'Watch the exit,' he hissed, and Ali turned to scan the door. Her heart was pounding in her ears.

Pearce hauled Keaton to his feet and hustled him towards the road. Ali followed, her eyes fixed firmly over her shoulder at the door behind. By the time they reached the street, Keaton was able to move unaided but that did nothing to assuage the bleak, hopeless air that underpinned their urgency. There were plenty of cabs. Ali wanted to go direct to their hotel but the men insisted on following basic counter-surveillance measures. The first cab took them east to Gramercy Park. En-route, Ali tried Sarah's phone again. It went to voicemail. She called their hotel but there was no reply from their rooms. Somehow, she managed to control her panic. Another cab took them north through Murray Hill and Midtown East, and a third cab carried them to the Upper West Side within a couple of blocks of their hotel. By now, Keaton was able to walk unaided. They approached the hotel and stopped in the shadow of a large Hornbeam. There followed a brief argument when Pearce insisted that Keaton stay with Ali while he checked the hotel alone. Keaton refused point blank.

Pearce was adamant. 'You're concussed.'

'Am I hell. I'm A1.'

'I can't take that chance. Head trauma can affect judgment, reflexes, coordination. If I take you into a hot zone. I'd be looking out for you. Fatal distraction.'

Frustrated, Keaton blew air through his nose. He conceded with a reluctant nod.

Pearce went into the hotel, chose the stairs over the lift and reached his room without seeing anybody. The place was empty. He retrieved his gun and went next door. A moment to listen then he gave the prearranged knock, used his key card to crack the door and announced himself.

'It's Pearce!'

There was no reply. He went in, closed the door behind him and called out again. No answer. The room was empty and ominously silent. There was a backpack, case and laptop bag, all packed to go, but no personal items, no shopping bags, no overt sign of occupation except the dents on the beds where people had sat. His pulse started to rise. He moved silently around the bed to the bathroom door and hesitated. He had a horrible feeling about what he was going to see inside. His stomach tight, he stepped to one side, took a deep breath and turned the handle back-handed.

Wet towels were strewn on the floor but the shower stall was dry. There was a faint trace of Rachel's perfume. There was no one hiding, no one waiting.

No one alive anyway.

Rachel was on the floor. Lying on her front, her head twisted so that he could see the side of her face. An ugly patch of red trickled from the bullet hole in the back of her head, a larger patch had spread onto the tiled floor from the exit wound in her forehead. There was no sign of Sandford.

For the first time in his adult life, Pearce choked up. In the short time that he had known Rachel, he had grown really fond of her. As had the others. Such a sweet girl. Kind and decent. An angel sprung from the devil. Worth saving. Worth dying for.

He squatted down next to her. He knew it was pointless, but he checked her pulse anyway. Her skin was still warm. She seemed to be looking at him, reproachful: *where were you?* He reached out a hand

and gently closed her eyelids. Now she looked asleep, peaceful.

There were no defensive wounds, no evidence of a fight of any kind, Pearce knew that the girl would never have died without a struggle. She had been taken by surprise. Taken from behind. The handiwork of a coward who couldn't look his victim in the eye. A coward like Sandford.

He stood up, his knuckles white. He felt sick. He left the bathroom with cold anger in his eyes.

He took out his cell and called Keaton. 'The girl's down. No sign of Sandford. Come up but stay frosty.'

While he waited, he rechecked the room. Then he did the same for his own room. Nothing unexpected. There were signs that Sandford had turned the place over looking for the flash drive. But the drive was in Keaton's pocket and a copy had already gone to Pearce's IT friends.

Pearce heard the others arrive and followed them into the girl's room. Just in time to see Ali headed straight for the bathroom. Too late, Pearce tried to stop her. Ali reached the door and froze. Déjà vu, a flashing image of Stewart dead in his bathroom. Rachel and Stewart, innocents both, murdered because they might know too much. All at once, events caught up with her. She clamped her hand over her mouth to muffle her scream but she couldn't stop the sobs. She felt an intense pain in her stomach and she dry retched.

She sensed Keaton's hands on her shoulders. She wanted the comfort but was too overcome with guilt and remorse. She had caused this! If only she had listened, left well alone. Everyone had warned her off, friend and foe, but, of course, she knew best. And now look what she had done.

'This is all my fault,' she said, her voice thick with guilty sorrow.

'Suck it up Ali,' Keaton told her, a little more brutishly than he had intended. 'You didn't cause any of it. You're just a spectator.'

Stung by his words, she shook herself free and glared round at him. 'There's no show if no one watches.'

'Bastards like Lucca and Sandford are bred to kill. They didn't invent death, they just live for it. You can't take the blame for that.' He shrugged wearily. 'We're here then we're gone, Ali, It's a random thing. The universal truth. '

'I should have finished him when I had the chance,' said Pearce, his voice cracked.

The room stayed quiet for a long moment. Just muted city sounds from the window and the hum of the bathroom extractor fan.

At length, Pearce said, 'We can't stay here. Rachel's not their only target. And if the cops come we are in deep shit.'

'What do we do?' Ali asked.

'We find Sandford,' Keaton said grimly, 'and we kill the bastard. We get Lucca off our backs then I kill him and I kill his people. He thinks he's an expert on *Blood*? Well, now he's crossed the flaming sword!'

A few short weeks ago, Ali would have flinched at Keaton's' vengeful fury. Now she understood it. She shivered as something snapped inside. Her mind flashed back to the struggle in the club when she had gone at the fake Bowman like the Springwood Slasher, and she knew that she had gone into the darkness and the darkness had gone into her. She was about to add her voice to the cries for vengeance when her phone rang. It was Ashe. She accepted the call and put it on speaker. Then she left him hanging.

'Feysor?' he asked. A moment of silence, then, 'My boss would like to meet.'

She said nothing. She just didn't trust her voice.

'Hello,' Ashe demanded. 'Are you there?'

'We've tried meeting,' she told him flatly. 'You sent your fake Bowman to kill us.'

'Not kill you. That was never on the agenda. You passed Mr Bowman's test and now he would like to meet with you in person.'

'Mr Bowman's Test? You betrayed us, you fuck!'

'No,' Ashe persisted. 'I set up a deal.'

Ali asked, 'Where is Sandford?'

'At a guess, I would say thirty six thousand feet over the Atlantic.'

She killed the call. It was an impulsive gesture as if his words had made her finger twitch.

'Fuck!' Pearce said. 'Sandford's gone already!'

The phone rang almost immediately. Ali ignored it.

Keaton said, 'He's just a plane ride away.'

After five rings the phone fell silent.

'When he calls again,' Keaton said, 'insist on naming the place and time. That way we can force them to improvise. Give us an edge of sorts.'

The phone started ringing.

Keaton nodded encouragingly as she took the call.

'We must talk,' Ashe said, 'for the sake of the girl.'

'The girl?' Ali shot back, her emotions snapping into wild fury. 'Sarah! She's dead! You know that! You murdered her!'

'You're lying,' Ashe said.

Ashe's breathing had become unexpectedly harsh and Keaton took that as a tell: Ashe hadn't known! He decided at once that there was an advantage to be gained and he took the phone from Ali.

'We meet in the morning,' he said. 'In the city. I'll text you one hour beforehand with the location. If you're late, or if Bowman himself is a no show, or if he brings more than one guy, we're gone and his life is out there for the world to see.'

Ashe started to speak but Keaton clicked off.

'This place is blown,' he said. 'We have to get out now.'

Chapter 64

TO SAVE PRECIOUS time, and to keep Bowman guessing, they decided to abandon their hotel without checking out. They left a *Do Not Disturb* sign on the door to keep the cleaners from Rachel then made their way down the back stairs. The alleyway was clear. Two parked cars, both empty, and no people. They walked to West93 from where a relay of yellow cabs took them to West42 Street on the edge of Midtown Manhattan's Hell's Kitchen. Once a bastion of poor and working-class Irish Americans, the area had been undergoing gentrification since the 1990s and it now boasted a number of boutique hotels.

It was the hotels they had come for. After the near-miss at Love, they knew that they had to meet Bowman on their own ground where they could monitor threat, record and control the meet, and prepare fallbacks. In a foreign country, without time or a safe house, what better place than a hotel room? They selected the building that seemed to best fit their needs and booked adjacent double rooms. They had to show photo ID and credit card, but would be long gone by the time they were compromised. The only real problem was their lack of numbers. Which was why Keaton's first move on booking in was to call a friend, a local CDS contact.

'I need to borrow some surveillance and communications equipment,' he said. 'Plus eyes on the ground. And I need them now.'

'Don't tell me,' his contact responded sardonically. 'Life and death.'

'That's the one.'

'Jesus, Keaton. Why don't you just dial 911.' There was a brief, thinking pause. 'I can loan you a couple of WMs from the office. They're good, guaranteed, but they're watchers only. These are not, repeat not, action women.'

'Perfect. I just need an early warning system.'

They exchanged details and Pearce left to collect the gear. He estimated a round trip of some ninety minutes. That left Keaton alone to worry. He had been on the sharp end of enough debacles to understand that even the best laid plans can fall apart, but this enterprise didn't even have a plan. It was a genuine snafu. Serendipity had brought them this far but he doubted it could take them further. After all, they had just fled a crime scene that was covered in their prints in order to meet with a killer who possessed a private army and wanted them dead.

Some time later, there was a gentle tap on the door. It was Ali. Keaton explained where Pearce had gone. She nodded then sat on a bed, legs curled up beneath her. He stood, restless, thinking.

'What are our chances?' she asked.

'The odds lie with Bowman,' he said. 'Which means you get murdered in some sadistic, painful way.'

'That's reassuring,' she smiled. 'I wish I could say something flip to show that I'm not scared. But I can't. I see the man in my head all the time, when I sleep, when I wake. I feel as if I can't live while he's still breathing.'

'It's not too late,' he said. 'You just walk out the door and keep going.

She smiled wryly. 'It's hardly an option. He'll find me and kill me.'

'Not if you do it properly. I've always been ready to walk away and I'm confident I can do it. All you need is money, and you have plenty of that, courtesy of friend Crain. I can whistle up driving licences, credit cards, passports, any kind of documentation. There's no shame in running away.'

'Would you run?'

He didn't answer. He could say *yes* but she would see through the lie and he didn't want to let her down like that. Seeing her face, pale and pinched, he understood that she never did anything without believing in it. She might have been tenacious and hard but there was nothing hard-bitten or cynical or calculating about her. Even now, after everything that had happened, she was still able to hope. She still wanted to believe in justice, in good defeating evil.

'There's nothing to stop you walking away,' Ali persisted. 'Why are you still here?'

He shrugged, unable to admit that it was for her. 'I didn't sign up for Black Ops, or Mammon. I don't do business with terrorists, drug dealers or dictators, and I don't associate with anyone who does. It's not that I'm a saint. I've done plenty that's outside the law. But these people are inhuman. Reprehensible. Beyond morality.'

'You won't admit it, Chris, but you're a good man.'

On impulse, he sat on the bed and took her hand. Surprised, she looked at him but said nothing.

ALI WAS ASLEEP when Pearce returned. His backpack was loaded with tech. Miniature US military cameras, Russian pinhead mics, high-end recording equipment and two-way voice communication. He laid them out on the bed and the two men set about placing the recording devices. They were in a typical boutique hotel room, with two king-sized beds, neutral carpet and curtain to offset the red and yellow bedding, TV and sound system, furniture and en-suite. Plenty of concealment points. They positioned the mikes and cameras then set up the recording equipment next door in Ali's room. They assumed that Bowman would bring a scanner so, after checking the system, Keaton deactivated it.

At that stage, they woke Ali.

AN HOUR LATER, Pearce was seated at a table beneath the green, gold and black façade of the Pig and Whistle, another Irish theme pub on Third Avenue. He was fidgeting impatiently, as if he was waiting for someone. Which he was, of course, though he wasn't expecting Bowman just yet. The boss of Leke had yet to receive his invitation and that wouldn't happen until Pearce was satisfied with his recon.

At this point, Third Avenue was one way, six lanes wide and rush hour manic. Bowman would arrive by car which meant that he would have to come from the south, Pearce's right. Pearce glanced at his watch, as if growing exasperated, then strolled south, ostensibly to kill time. He was looking for threat points, where Bowman might hide a back-up, and fall-backs for his own egress. He walked a couple of blocks then crossed the road and came back north. A pug of a police officer stood in the middle of the road facing oncoming traffic as if daring anyone to hit him. No one did. Pearce passed the black and grey Chase building on his right and continued along Third until he was sure of his bearings. Satisfied, he backtracked to the traffic island, crossed the road and went on into the pub.

The 'Pig' was bigger than it looked. Long and deep, and wider than the average New York bar. There was space for tables along the side and at the back and, best of all, elbow room at the bar. The interior had recently been made over, with ornate ceilings, antique mirrors and glass cabinets overflowing with Guinness memorabilia. Pride of place was the snug, an intimate semi-private bar-room modelled on those found in traditional pubs in Ireland.

Pearce picked a bar stool close to the entrance and adopted a hide-in-plain-sight strategy. The 'Pig' was quiet but sociable, the clientele mostly male and mostly young. Pearce was dressed for the part, sporting glasses with photochromatic reactive lenses, white open neck shirt, black blazer, black and white plaid pants, black leather shoes, shoulder bag and a Capas lambskin newsboy cap. The cap was the thing. He had long wanted to own a newsboy. It was a cherished vanity that said, look at me, I have an interesting hat. It was attention seeking. Insecure. Not like an operative. And that was the point.

He let Keaton know that he was in place then messaged Ashe's cell phone with the location. He ordered a classic-bar burger, which came quickly, with a dark char on tender meat, and he sipped delicately at a cold glass of Guinness. Keeping his attention on events outside, he chatted with the bar-huggers and pretended to watch the TV – an English Premier League football match.

The SUV arrived after some fifteen minutes and stopped outside. A *gangsta* vehicle, black, brutal and dark tinted. Three men got out. Pearce could tell by the way they checked the street that they were close protection trained. A step up from the enforcers at Love. Satisfied that the way was clear, they guided their boss from car to pub. Pearce was ninety per cent certain that this was Bowman. He tensed up, unsure if his disguise would hold. Another guy, whom Pearce recognized as Vanavasam, alighted from a second SUV and joined Bowman. Two more BGs accompanied him, making four in all. Two stayed with Bowman, eying with quiet suspicion anyone who moved, while the others surreptitiously searched the pub.

A young couple left the bar and Pearce tagged along. Bowman's cars were illegally parked but the cop on traffic duty showed no interest. Pearce could pick out no obvious backup, not on the sidewalks, not in vehicles. Just the two SUVs. He turned south and walked past the art gallery, coming to a halt against the Magazine and Cigar store. He phoned Keaton to confirm that Bowman had arrived with Vanavasam and at least seven men, counting drivers. Then he called Ashe's phone.

He said, 'Bowman was told to bring one man. He's mob-handed.'

Vanavasam answered, not Ashe. 'He doesn't trust you.'

Pearce laughed cynically. 'What has trust got to do with it? This is your territory and you have the advantage of numbers. What more do you want?'

'Oh, we can swat you any time, but you might get lucky with Mr Bowman.'

'If we wanted him dead, he would be dead. If we wanted him in the War Crimes Court he would be on a plane. Lose the meatheads and give Bowman your phone. We'll be watching. If your boys don't disappear back to the gym, consider us gone and you splashed all over the internet. I'll call in 30 minutes.'

Pearce rang off. By the time Bowman and his party were back on Third, he was on East55 and away.

THE TWO MILES from pub to hotel took thirty minutes. Pearce couldn't see the CDS operatives though he knew that they were there. He stepped backwards into the darkened entrance to the hotel car park and connected his earpiece and sleeve microphone to his two-way radio. The system was an upgrade on that used by the Secret Service, less vulnerable to monitoring and jamming. He made contact with the two watchers then moved outside to refresh his take on the territory. The hotel and its environs was supposed to be a DMZ but he surveyed it as he would a combat zone. They were in a mini-basin of low-rise in NYC's canyon city, a mixed area of upmarket retail outlets and luxury apartments, nightclubs, even a male strip club. The glass fronted building opposite reflected the hotel façade behind him. Just down the road was the 4 storey brownstone remnant that housed the Manhattan SRG1 (*The NYPD's Strategic Response Group, set up for advanced disorder control and counterterrorism protection*). Opposite the SRG1 was the Midtown Emergency Care Centre. It made Pearce wonder if Keaton was planning a war.

He returned to the car park entryway and let Keaton know that he was on station, then he called Ashe's phone and insisted that Bowman come with just one man. He gave him twenty-five minutes.

Twenty-eight minutes later, the SUV dropped Bowman and a single companion whom Pearce recognised as Vanavasam. The Englishman waited but could see nothing untoward so he sent Keaton the text signal. Moments later, he saw Bowman take a call and knew that Keaton was telling him to wait in the lobby and not use his phone.

Pearce watched the two men go inside and the car drive off. He could see no sign that Bowman had brought back-up. No soldiers on the street, no vehicles circling. He didn't doubt that there were people close by, but they were not operative, not yet. He waited ten minutes. No-one had come in before Bowman, or with him, or after him. Nothing was happening. Just the regular ebb and flow of a busy mid-town street. It looked as if Bowman hadn't brought a crew but, of course, there was no way of being certain.

Decision time. There was little else Pearce could do. Without back up of their own they were desperately short of numbers and options. He had done as much risk analysis as he was going to do. Time to leave the early warning to CDS.

He called the watchers in. Both were women, both were mid-thirties, but there the similarity ended. The operative who took Pearce's place wore scuffed denims and a plain grey coat while the woman who followed him into the hotel to take up position in the lobby was more formally dressed in suit and white blouse. Pearce disconnected and pocketed his radio system then, with one last look about him, entered the hotel. Bowman was seated in a plush armchair near the centre of the lobby. He was in a navy suit with a white shirt and a red tie, and he appeared as calm as a Buddha. He also looked tanned, rich, powerful, and full of energy and charisma. Vanavasam was sitting to one side, suspicious gaze flitting between entrance door, stairs and lifts.

As Pearce approached them, he noted with concealed pleasure the curious looks that his attire attracted.

He said, 'Mirësevini në Ferr, Z. Lucca.' *[Welcome to hell, Mr Lucca}*

Chapter 65

NO-ONE SPOKE as the lift crawled upwards, though the men took the opportunity to size each other up. What Pearce saw reassured him. Two men in their early sixties, each as mean as hell but slowed by age. Trust issues had forced agreement that both sides could be armed and Pearce picked out Vanavasam's shoulder rig and the smaller gun nestled in Bowman's jacket pocket. Both shoulder holster and pocket were slow-draw options in an OK Corral scenario. Pearce carried his gun at the hip, as did Keaton.

They disembarked at the second floor. Pearce led them along the empty corridor to the hotel room where Keaton invited them to scan for bugs. With a kind of clumsy thoroughness, Vanavasam ran his scanner over the three Brits. Ali objected to the intimacy but Vanavasam ignored her protests. The Kosovar found nothing, not even Pearce's radio. Inexperienced in using the scanner, but meticulous to a fault, he walked it around the room. He even tested the flowers on the coffee table. Satisfied at last, he nodded to Bowman and put his scanner away. Pearce then waved his wand over the two slavs. There was nothing. Scanners off, Keaton squeezed the coin-shaped remote in his pocket, once to activate the surveillance equipment, again to trigger it.

Pearce went outside to take up watch by the door. He re-connected his radio and listened in turn to events in the room and to the monosyllabic reports from the watchers.

With four people crammed inside the room, it seemed tiny, swamped with testosterone and mute hostility. They used the two beds as sofas, sitting in pairs opposite each other. Bowman stared at Ali who held his gaze without flinching. She couldn't help thinking how ordinary he looked, with his craggy face, grey hair, immaculate suit and the ghost of a friendly smile. He might have been anybody's father or grandfather.

Bowman it was who spoke first. 'You've been asking a lot of questions about me, Miss Feysor. Why are you so interested in David Bowman, a simple businessman?'

She smiled patiently. 'You are Mergim Lucca. Mafia gangster and war criminal. We have incontrovertible evidence of your involvement in genocide, the trafficking of arms, drugs and people, money laundering and, of real interest to me, the murders of Steven Shimmon and Paul Stewart.'

Bowman smiled in return. 'Are you sure you're not confusing me with someone else?'

'Many years ago,' she went on, ignoring his intervention, 'with the assistance of the British Government, you faked your own death and created a new life for yourself. In the process, you killed your own wife and children. The gentleman with you is

Upandar Vanavasam, your long-time lieutenant, also wanted by criminal and war crime investigators.'

Bowman leaned forward, his face indifferent. 'I'll make things easy for you, Ms Feysor. I confess to everything. And much more besides.'

That threw her. Her senses jangled with incoming danger signals. Suddenly he was no longer ordinary. She felt his strength, his rage, his capacity to inflict pain and hurt. It seemed to radiate from him so that even sounds, smells and colours had become threatening. She shuddered and she felt the fear creeping up on her again, this time colder and more threatening than before. Her eyes dropped. She couldn't help it. The situation seemed to be going out of kilter. She could feel him sucking her in.

Bowman's face twitched into another smile. But his eyes stayed cold and unyielding, like they wanted nothing to do with what the rest of his face was doing.

He said, 'I am told you have a proposition for me.'

She avoided his gaze by reaching for her Mac. 'Less a proposition,' she informed him, 'more a demonstration. You saw our email.'

She brought her computer out of sleep and turned it so that all present could see the screen. For a few moments, it stayed blank and grey, and it seemed that she had glitched up. Then a website appeared. It had a simple, almost crude design. Yellow background with red lettering centre-page that read: *Mergim Lucca, David Bowman and Leke Corporation*. Beneath the title was a menu, also in red. Ali selected an item and a page of Leke accounts appeared, the secret in-house accounts of an illegal business. Ali scrolled through a couple more pages.

'Just a sampler,' she said. 'The rest is ready to go live. Hundreds of pages.'

'That fucking Crain,' Bowman spat. 'I will peel his skin.'

'That fucking Crain,' Ali lied, 'is dead.'

She noted with satisfaction the flicker of troubled surprise that crossed Bowman's face.

She selected another page, which showed some of Bowman's fake ID documents, then moved on to a clip of one of the videos Sarah had stolen. A young girl, naked and terrified in a darkened room. Then, as suddenly as it had appeared, the website dissolved into blank greyness.

'I'm sure you would have liked to have seen more,' Ali said, unable to keep the smug from her voice, 'but I have no control over the technical side. Others are managing that for me. Even I don't know who they are so it isn't even worth your while asking me. Once the information is out there, of course, you will be free to read it all. Along with the rest of the world.'

At that moment, Bowman's loathing for Ali had an intensity that burned like a black star. He was going to kill her. He would make her grovel at his feet and beg for mercy. He would choke her with his bare hands until she was all out of air. He would release his grasp but only so that she was alive to experience the violation and penetration. Finally, he would gouge out her eyes. Not now, of course. He would have to wait. But it would be worth the wait. As a connoisseur of vengeance, he knew only too well that it matured like wine.

He smiled, not a happy smile, rather anticipation of what he intended doing to her. 'Insignificant lives,' he said, 'call for ignominious death.'

She felt the bed shift as Keaton set himself for action. Vanavasam touched Bowman on the arm and his anger seemed to switch off. Ali noted that Keaton didn't relax.

'The information will run through the web like spider cancer,' she continued. 'It will infect social media like a doomsday virus, trending the in-boxes of the world's media, politicians and busy-bodies The internet can spread and magnify the big lie. It can also magnify big truth. You can't stop it. You might think you can close it down but, for every site you close, ten will pop up. Once this particular little genie is out it will stay out. And if you're thinking that your friends in high places will bail you out, forget it. People will believe what they see! Do you know why? Because the people who matter already know all about you. They do nothing because they have no definitive proof and because they're scared of the expensive, amoral crooks you call lawyers. Now they'll have their proof.'

Bowman stared at her, his eyes full of murder. 'I would need guarantees that your information is destroyed?'

'Why would I ever destroy it?' Ali smiled coldly, 'If I do that you will kill me without hesitation. Keeping me alive and allowing me to live a normal life is your only guarantee of my silence. We live or die together. Accept that or the truth will out.'

'Truth? Is there such a thing?' He gave a little Gallic shrug. 'Surely there are just agreements. Agreements that can be entered into, kept or broken.'

'So, we have an agreement. Don't ask to shake hands.'

Bowman nodded at Vanavasam who took out his smart phone, opened an app and offered it to Ali.

Ali took the phone tentatively, as if it were an IED. 'What is this?'

Lucca said nothing, just studied her expression. Ali was looking at a paused MP4 file. Ashe was sitting on a chair and Lucca was standing beside him holding a smart phone. Ashe was looking at Lucca's screen, Lucca at Ashe. Ali pressed play and watched Ashe's face as recognition dawned, an unguarded but fleeting range of emotions - surprise, horror, loss, loathing. Ashe's eyes shifted to Lucca and his face filled with hateful contempt.

'You killed her,' he said. 'Your own daughter. Why?'

'She betrayed me.'

It dawned on Ali that Ashe was watching a video of Sarah's murder. The room around her filled with foreboding. Ali was glad of Keaton. Keaton would not be distracted by a video clip. His focus was on the enemy.

On-screen, Ashe suddenly saw his own fate. He tried to stand and it was then that Ali realised that he was tied to his chair. Lucca laughed then stepped forward and plunged a blade into Ashe's neck, thrusting it all the way in and severing everything in its path. He pulled the weapon free and Ashe collapsed, trying with desperate futility to close the wound by hunching a shoulder.

Lucca leaned over his dying brother-in-law. 'It's what happens when you sell me out.'

Grey faced, Ali stopped the video and handed the phone back. She understood now that Ashe had not betrayed them after all.

'Your own family,' she said softly. 'Why?'

'To remind people what happens if they cross me,' he said. 'I never forget a betrayal, Ms Feysor, or an insult, Many people have believed that they bested me but I bided my time, waited until I was in a position of strength, then I struck back. Even when I no longer needed to.'

Ali realized that he was vowing to avenge himself for this humiliation, telling her that he would come for her at some unspecified time in the future. She recoiled inwardly at the thought. She was beginning to feel sick with anger and fear. The cold-blooded indifference that oozed from this man went beyond anything she had encountered before.

'We're not negotiating, here,' she said. 'Don't get that idea. This is a straightforward extortion. You have no choice but to keep your end of the agreement. Anything happens to me, the information comes out. I die in an accident, the information comes out. You even *think* about harming me, the information comes out.'

'Bide all the time you like, Lucca,' Keaton said evenly. 'There is no time limit. The moment anything happens to Ms Feysor, you will be the walking dead. We die, you die. If you're lucky. The alternative is eking out your days being humiliated at The Hague.'

Bowman's face was a mask, showing no hint of the seething rage inside. Yet Ali sensed his mood spike with a malignancy and ferocity that made the small room smaller. All at once, she understood. This was

Bowman's world, *his* domain, the place where *his* hands, whitened with distilled evil, had busily dealt death to so much innocence. Here, Bowman truly was the Lord of Darkness, feudal, all-powerful, unfettered by civilised mores, free to treat people as his playthings, ready and all too willing to do with them as he wished.

Watching him, Keaton read his rage and murderous intent. He smiled and, for an instant, both men knew. One of them was a dead man. They were locked in an old-fashioned duel. Man on man. They hadn't chosen the weapons yet, or their seconds, or their location. But they had just agreed that one of them had no future.

The unspoken exchange seemed to take all of the belligerence from the room.

Keaton said, 'We have some . . . ethical . . . concerns about the police investigation into the deaths of your people and others, including your daughter. I'd hate to see some poor innocent hauled up on murder charges. You have the resources to clean it up.'

'I will see to it.'

Keaton nodded. 'Then we're good?'

Bowman nodded in return. 'You leave well alone, I leave well alone, and we never have to cross paths again.'

Ali pasted a neutral smile on her face but her mind was already planning how to make him pay for Sarah.

Part Four

Unless there's been a reaction, there's been no journalism

Hunter S Thompson

Chapter 66

THE AFTERNOON WAS bleak beneath grey, watertight clouds, so bleak it felt as though heaven itself was in mourning. The houses by Handsworth cemetery were lighting up early as Ali parked her car, and a cold, empty wind bit through her coat as she made her way into the consecrated zone.

She checked her hand-drawn map and found Stewart's grave without difficulty. She placed a rose and read his epitaph then was suddenly at a loss. What was she supposed to do next? Pray? She had no belief. Talk to the stone? That was for crazy people. Lay a wreath? Why avenge his death by killing all those flowers? Meditate on his life? That made sense but she couldn't summon up a remembrance. Stewart had been a true friend, a man so full of life and laughter and sex that, even dead, he was more alive than she could ever be. Yet, she couldn't retrieve even one of those happy memories.

All at once, hot tears were trickling down her face. She couldn't help herself. She was benumbed, unable to think or see or hear. She was aware of crying, but there was no sobbing or gasping. It was as if someone else was silently weeping and she was the guilty watcher.

She shivered against the wind and the desolation that was Stewart's little patch of Birmingham. Several people had offered to accompany her pilgrimage from London – among them her father, Keaton, Kate and Prisha - but she had insisted that this was something she had to do by herself. The guilt of Stephen's death was her guilt alone. She had come to atone, to ask his forgiveness. But he wasn't here and her inability to sense his presence piled more shame onto her guilt. The guilt of causing his death, Of missing his funeral. Of allowing his killer to go free while the case went cold.

Stephen would never have justice!

She was guilty of that!

These crippling attacks of conscience would always be with her.

She deserved nothing less.

But that didn't mean that she could wallow in self-pity. There was always a premium for life. It was time to front up. Accept the injustice and the bitterness and the sorrow and the regret. She couldn't have anticipated the nightmare of the past few weeks so why claim all the blame for herself? Life was going to be tricky enough avoiding Lucca without casting herself adrift in a void of regret and loneliness and self-denial.

Bottom line, she had lost loved ones but she wasn't alone. In the week since returning from New York, she had enjoyed a brief, sheltered retreat with her father and experienced the joyful reunion with friends who had almost given her up for dead.

Good memories, real enough to put a dent in her pathos.

Little by little, the world came back into focus. The sweeping lawns and sculptured pathways, the deciduous trees that whipped, leafless, in the wind. And the chapel, tall, slender and gothic, fronted with two pointed spires. With focus came an epiphany of sorts. Coming here had cracked open old, half-healed sorrows: Stewart, Rachel, Shimmon, her mum. Which was okay because her kind of grief, she now realized, was the catch-all, catch-up variety. Delayed grief they called it. She was not built for the kind of wailing, self-mutilating, public grief that brought closure. Hers was the long goodbye, a self-suffering, simmering grief that every now and then just had to boil over.

She stared off over Stewart's grave into the forest of headstones and the death and mystery they contained. Suddenly, for a reason that she could not explain, it became the most comforting of visions, It was almost enough to make her finger the rosary.

Chapter 67

SANDFORD AND FIGGIS were nursing coffees when Burns entered the Cage. He acknowledged their greetings with a cursory wave of the hand, perched on a chair and declined the offer of refreshment.

'I don't have a lot of time,' he said. 'It is rumoured that we have ruffled the feathers of our American friends. That hasn't gone down so well in Downing Street. So do please reassure me that all is well.'

'Couldn't be better,' Sandford said. 'Feysor met with Lucca in New York and struck a Faustian pact that guarantees their silence. The transaction involved a number of corpora delicti, but nothing that can be traced back to us.'

'This pact?'

'The journalist suffers a memory loss in exchange for her life. If she breaks the deal he kills her. If he breaks the deal, he dies the death of a billion social media cuts.'

'What does she know?'

'Everything. It was all on the stolen memory stick. Lucca's identity and history, his business interests and the role we played in setting him up and protecting him.'

'And this couldn't be better?' A small frown of contempt betrayed Burns' displeasure. 'What about the girl?'

'Dead.'

Burns paused his cross-examination to process Sandford's words. 'Lucca will never keep his end of the deal,' he concluded. 'Feysor is as good as dead. And, if she is true to her word, the information will then surface for all to see.'

'He is one crazy bastard,' Sandford said. 'We should have taken him out years ago.'

Figgis wasn't happy. 'We can't rely on either one of them to keep this quiet. If the Cabinet Office whisper about closing Alpha is true, we will be left exposed. *I* will be exposed! And if I go down, I can promise you, the whole pack of cards will go down with me,'

'Get a grip of yourself,' Burns told him. 'I have it under control.'

'Don't tell me to get a grip!' Figgis snapped. 'You're nothing but a jumped up clerk! If you had any balls, you would have eliminated Feysor and Lucca when I suggested it.'

Pointedly, Burns said nothing. Entirely self-possessed, he would not be drawn into a fight by mere insult. Sandford, however, had something else on his mind.

'I've heard nothing about closing Alpha.'

'Nothing is settled.' Burns assured him. 'Recent events have all but exposed the Unit and it has been mooted that we place it in temporary shutdown. Better that than leave it open to the vultures.'

Sandford was shaking his head, perplexed. 'Now is not the time. So much needs to be done. Killing Alpha would leave the country exposed at a time when we are most needed.'

'If the PM is seriously considering this,' Figgis added, 'he is clearly out of his mind. With that kind of stupefying ignorance, he is frankly unfit for office.'

'We are talking about a temporary closure,' Burns said smoothly. 'We will always need Alpha, but a fundamental component of any such unit is resilience. From time to time, it must be obliterated then reincarnated.'

'Last time this happened,' Sandford pointed out, 'we simply closed the unit and opened it the following day under a different name.'

'Different times, different narrative,' said Burns. His voice was liquid. 'Our lawyer in the attorney general's office warns us that Alpha is illegal and that its operatives would be subject to prosecution. There is a great deal of back channel manoeuvring going on. Everybody in the know is attempting to insulate themselves from what's coming. We must take pre-emptive action and remove all traces of Alpha. There must be nothing to expose. The cryonics solution will see us through. Once this little crisis blows over, we cut away the necrotic tissue and revive it.'

'Necrotic tissue,' Sandford repeated, his tone dripping with sarcasm. 'Who would that be?'

Burns screwed his eyes as though he didn't understand.

Sensing betrayal, Sandford held nothing back. 'I will oppose any form of closure. We are not some cabal of rogue officers. We must act together, put up a united front, remind our political masters that we are at war: terrorists, rogue states, Russia, China, the whole damn world. Who will run covert action, special access programmes, lethal authority? If we let them equate clandestine with illegal, no one will be able to do what is necessary. Now is not the time for you to turn craven, Burns. Kill Alpha and you compromise the security of the nation.'

Figgis had a solution. 'We cannot permit Lucca to surface. He knows too much. He would fatally damage anyone associated with him, and that includes me, you and your friends in Downing Street. Rather than let Alpha go down, we must eliminate the underlying problems: Feysor and Lucca.'

Burns shrugged, as if Figgis' decision was a matter of indifference. 'I would advise you to leave it to the professionals. As for me, I am deniable. This is the last time I talk about it.'

Abruptly, Figgis came to his feet. 'There will be no washing of hands,' he erupted. 'You don't get way that easily. I will not let you. The PM will hear of this. I have friends!'

He stormed out.

'His Lordship has always been a loose cannon,' Burns said with almost casual indifference. 'Now he has made himself an outright liability.'

Chapter 68

ALI WAS OPENING her front door when Keaton appeared at her side. She hadn't seen him for a week and she didn't bother to conceal her delight. She hugged him, clinging on for longer than he found comfortable and eventually he eased her away. While she made coffee, they caught up, exchanging more gossip in minutes than they had in weeks. They took their drinks into the living room and sat on the sofa. Keaton listened silently for a while, then he interrupted her flow.

'Lucca is coming to England so I'll be under the radar for a while. Pearcey will check in on you.'

'You're going after Lucca! That's crazy. He's untouchable!'

'You will never be safe as long as he breathes.'

'You think I'll be safer when you're dead? '

'Well, there's a vote of confidence.'

'Don't commit suicide on my account,' she exclaimed. 'Don't you dare put that on me!'

'Don't worry,' he said. 'There'll be no comeback.'

'No comeback! That's like saying Russian roulette is safe because no one knows when the bullet's in the chamber.'

'I haven't come to fight you.'

'Of course not. Reticent muttonhead like you would never win a war of words.'

'Ouch,' he grinned.

Neither spoke for the next minute or two as they let the tension drain from the room.

'Make sure you hurt him,' she said at last. 'You hurt him for Sarah and Stewart and all those others.'

He raised an eyebrow. 'What happened to that nice liberal pacifist I once knew.'

'She's more worldly,' Ali laced her voice with more than a little irony. 'I can't say I'm proud of what I've learned but I'm sure of one thing: it's worth knowing.'

'And worth telling?'

She shrugged: she no longer felt qualified to judge. 'I've dug out the story and there's been a reaction. That's good journalism. Action and reaction. It's not always necessary to write it.'

'Maybe not.'

She held his eye, 'What if I wanted to go with you?'

'I'd say no.'

'And if I insisted?'

Keaton grinned. They both knew that there was nothing she could do or say to force the issue. 'I'd insist back.'

On impulse, she moved closer. He put his arm about her and she snuggled close. She lifted her head to talk to his throat, pressing her body closer for emphasis.

'How are you going to do it?' She asked in her most sceptical voice. 'You'll never get near him. They'll cut you to pieces. I don't want you to die.' She felt herself tearing up and paused until she had regained control of her voice. 'What are you going to do?'

'It wouldn't be good for you to know.'

'Need to know,' she smiled wanly. 'The story of my life.'

'What I will tell you is that I'm not doing this alone.'

She shifted so that she was lying across him, head on his chest, eyes closed, arms loosely embracing him. Her fragrance was an intoxicating mix of coffee, perfume, sweat and sex, and Keaton was all too conscious of the way her breasts were pressing against him.

He reached down and stroked her back, gently exploring the incurvation, enjoying the smooth, sliding sensation of her skin through the blouse.

'Mmm,' she murmured, 'don't stop! That's just right. You should take this up.'

She crushed up against him, rubbed against him, and he traced round the bottom of her rib cage, feeling the involuntary tightening as he worked his way upwards, rib by rib. She arched ever so slightly, giving him room. He leant down and kissed her head. She smiled and he kissed the hot lobe of her ear, then the corner of her parted lips.

They were still for a moment, then her hands were probing his body, ferreting and caressing. Opening his shirt, she ran her tongue over his chest, burning his skin and sending a warm rush rippling through his body. His heart was thumping, about to jump out of his mouth, and he couldn't trust himself to speak.

But the time for talking had gone.

SHE WOKE TO an empty bed. He was sitting across the room, dressed, watching her sleep.

She jerked upright. 'You're going?'

'Yes.'

'I thought you might change your mind,' she said softly. 'So what just happened here?'

'I wanted some sex to remember you by. Last request of the condemned man.'

She threw a pillow at him.

Keaton grinned. 'Listen. . . . I . . .'

Ali interrupted, 'No, you listen.'

They paused, both unable to say what they wanted. She had the chance to tell him how she felt but she wouldn't let herself do it. Nothing would come of it. He was a wilful man; she was a wilful woman. There was no meeting point.

Keaton said, 'In another life, eh?'

Ali nodded. 'Sometimes, I wonder if God will forgive us for what we do to each other. Then I remember that God left this place a long time ago.'

'Forget God. You find yourself a good man, Ali Feysor.'

She wanted to say *I've found one*, couldn't get the words out. 'I know people who've found a good man. I prefer my life.'

There was a difficult pause.

She said, 'You call me when you get back. Promise?'

'Promise.'

'Because if you don't, I'll come looking for you. And that is a promise.'

Chapter 69

THE SKY WAS on the back edge of rain, exposing a horizon that could have been the first glimmer of dawn. A false, grey, moonlit dawn. The weather might have been clearing in this Edwardian enclave in South Woodford, but the temperature was plummeting and a loose drizzle drifted across the gravel drive. Motionless among the shrubs and conifers of the front garden, Sandford watched the Bentley swing onto the drive. He caught a glimpse of Figgis's face at the rain-smeared windscreen, white, featureless and inhuman, as if the maggots had already been at his treacherous smile.

Head down, Figgis hurried into the house. He didn't bother to set the alarm. This wasn't one of his homes and, anyway, security was for servants. It was a bad habit but Figgis was an amateur in a pro's game.

Lights flickered on upstairs. Figgis and his mistress were wasting no time. With unhurried speed, Sandford put on latex gloves and clicked a suppressor onto his Sig-Sauer pistol. He pulled the hood of his black jogging suit over his face and walked to the front door. No hesitant glance to betray him, he popped the door with a simple lock tool and slipped inside.

Glittering eyes on the stairs, he ghosted upwards. The landing was empty. He paused to listen by the bedroom door and suddenly it started going wrong.

The toilet flushed from down the hallway. Katie Brewer, Figgis's mistress of twenty years, emerged only to stop dead in her tracks. She was naked. Her breasts tensed and swelled with fear but it was her eyes that thralled. She wanted to scream, Sandford could see that. His brain put a brake on time, slowing events to a near halt so that he registered every nuance of the next instant: the woman's dry, crinkled, already-dead lips; her terminal eyes, open and unflinching; her chest heaving as she fought for words.

Then her sound burst through, ululation for them both, and his finger twitched on the trigger.

The force of the bullet twisted her around and threw her sideways against the wall. Her eyes popped open, she gasped, then coughed. There was the briefest moment, then she slithered silently down to the floor, an expression of startled surprise etched onto her face. The shot left a whiff of powder, a thin, red trail of lifeblood on the wall.

Sandford cursed. He hadn't come here to kill a forty year old woman. He should have been in and out before the echoes faded. The noise was sure to have alerted Figgis who would be on his phone calling for help.

Moving swiftly, he opened the bedroom door. It was then that everything went to hell.

Figgis launched himself at the Alpha man, swinging the golf club that Katie Brewer kept by the bed and hoped never to use. Surprised, Sandford diverted the blow with his arm and swatted the other man away.

His arm felt broken but there was no time to dwell on it as Figgis came again. Sandford had virtually lost the use of one arm but, with his superior skill and fitness, it was an easy enough task for him to disarm the old man. Yet Figgis came at him once more, all flailing fists, fingernails and curses, slashing him across the face and neck. Sandford swore. He had come to interrogate then kill Figgis but he couldn't even subdue him. He sidestepped and pistol-whipped the peer to the floor. Blood poured from Figgis's gaping head wound but he wasn't done yet. He made a clawing grab for Sandford's legs. For the first time in his life, Sandford experienced a sensation close to panic. This guy wasn't human; he was the undead. He managed to kick free of the grasping creature and stepped quickly away. Still Figgis came, his mouth opened, his teeth bared, saliva mixing with the blood as he screamed:

'You fucking traitor! I'll kill you!'

Sandford tapped two bullets into Figgis's head and watched as he crashed to the floor. For a long moment, he stood there, breathing hard, pistol still aimed, half expecting the dead man to rise again.

'I've got to hand it to you, old man,' he muttered with grudging admiration. 'You're as tough as any soldier I've come across.'

SANDFORD REACHED THE front door, heard a vehicle pass outside and paused. This job had proved unexpectedly tricky but it was a loose end successfully eliminated. From here, it was just a short walk to his stolen car, a steady thirty miles drive to Berkhamsted Common and an off-road ride into the veiled woodland. He would dump his fibreless polyester jog suit onto the rear seat, throw trainers, overshoes and gloves after it, and torch the lot.

Just another joyrider.

The street was quiet now. Nursing his injured arm, he inched the door open and slipped out of the house. He turned to close the door.

It was then that he felt the muzzle of a gun placed directly against the base of his skull. With sharpened perception, he noticed pointlessly how the attached suppressor almost doubled the barrel length of the compact 9mm.

He caught a glimpse of Pearce's bright eyes staring at him.

'You!' he said.

His absolute shock lasted barely a second, just long enough to know that Alpha was another loose end safer.

Chapter 70

FOLLOWING KEATON'S DEPARTURE, Ali's apartment was quiet in a way that made the emptiness seem larger. Her home was no longer her refuge. It wasn't the cosy nest she had made for herself. She had to admit that she was more frightened now than when cruel men had had her in their grasp. They were still out there and Keaton had gone. She couldn't shake the chilling sensation that they were watching her, that they prowled her home whenever she went out. She hated that feeling. She wanted this madness to stop but how could it?

When she heard that Figgis had been murdered, she didn't know what to think. Aggravated burglary, they said, and even her own paper carried that version of the story. There was a media outcry focused on statistics that showed crime rising in direct proportion to the fall in police budgets and boots on the ground. But Ali had the inside story. Convinced that the murder was connected to her story, she showered, changed and went into the office.

The Echo building felt like the location of a half-forgotten dream, familiar yet alien. The newsroom was sparsely populated and she negotiated the greetings, banter and small talk without difficulty. It was only when she reached the sanctuary of her cube that she realised that she had come to work without her MacBook. Odd that she should forget that. Odder still that she didn't miss it. Or maybe not odd at all. It fit well with this feeling of dislocation. She had come in expecting it to feel like a homecoming, and in a way it was. The people were welcoming enough. It was just that she wasn't convinced that she belonged here.

Irvine saw her from his office and came out to fetch her. He led her back to his office and looked her up and down, face beaming broadly, body twitching as if he longed to hug her.

'Glad to see you back,' he said warmly. 'Did you have a good vacation? Where did you go? Did you meet anyone exciting?'

She smiled at his enthusiasm. 'Here and there. A bit of travelling. Nothing and no-one to get excited about.'

'Nothing like a few weeks of hedonism to get this place out of your system. No need to be ashamed, kiddo. I take it you heard about his Lordship. Time to cash in on your story before someone else does.'

She fixed him with a disingenuous expression. 'There's a problem with that, John. There is no story.'

'Bollocks there isn't' He studied her quizzically. 'You're serious. So what happened to the story of a lifetime? You took some mind-altering drug on vacation?'

'I discovered I was being played. There was no story.'

'So Stephen was played too? That's the two best investigative reporters I've ever known both conned into believing in a non-story.' He shook his head in knowing disbelief. 'Before you went away, you asked if I'd been got at. Well, now it's my turn. Have *you* been got at.'

Ali gave him peeved. 'You bang on endlessly about my unique and priceless insight yet you don't even trust my judgement.'

'Last time we met got me thinking. If you and Steven both believed it was such a big story, there had to be something in it. And, of course, there was all that pressure to drop the story. So I did some checking of my own. You were close to unearthing a scandal of epic proportions. The story's got more legs than an African Giant Millipede.'

'And can be squashed just as readily.'

'So all this has been for nothing. Fuck it, Ali, last time I saw you, you were going to war over your right to pursue a story you now say doesn't exist. We seem to have changed positions here. Why? You owe me that explanation, at least.'

'I don't know if I can write it. I'm not sure that I want to go back to that life.'

'So you admit there is a story.' Irvine eyed her sombrely. 'There's a scramble of hacks poking away at the Figgis murder. I can't ignore it, not when I have a journalist who has the real goods. Tell me, do you think the murder of Figgis has anything to do with your story? Yes, I can see you do. You can't let someone else have it. Give it to me and I'll get it written. Your by-line. If you're worried, we can leave your name out of it. That's it, isn't it. You have been got at. Someone's threatened you. Who? With what? Tell me and we'll get it sorted.'

'You can't finesse your way through this, John. I am truly sorry to have put us in this situation. I can't write the story. I can't even talk about it. I'll resign if you want.'

He looked at her with fresh eyes. 'We'll figure it out.'

Ali nodded, then shivered as someone stepped on her grave. For her, this affair would never be over. In this post truth world, she had a duty to tell the truth, if she was going to be haughty about it. A duty to Shimmon and Stewart, and those little girls on the video. Kids leaking time, withered old ladies in children's bodies. She had the power to release them all by telling their story to the world. But the prospect filled her with a holding dread. She would have to unlock her mind, go over the past, re-acquaint herself with so many ghosts and expose herself to the devil Lucca. The sensible thing would be to cut herself loose, sever the ties of a story that had consumed her like an abusive lover. But she couldn't. Poor, defeated cow, she couldn't let go!

She tried for a smile. 'Okay. I'll write it. But you don't publish until I say so. You can't print the story, not yet. You wait until you get the go-ahead.'

'Ali! My instincts are telling me . . . '

'For God's sake, John!' she snapped. 'You don't have instincts. You've not been running around the world getting shot at. You will hold the fucking story until I tell you otherwise. If you screw me, I will come to your house and rip your face off. You trust me in this or you get nothing! Capishe?'

'Capishe,' he echoed, his tone conciliatory. 'Now tell me what's going on. Off the record.'

'I will. But not now, John.'

With that, she left him hanging and made her way to her cube, She was surprised to find Fitch sitting in her chair clutching a thin file. He stood and allowed her to hug him.

'Fitchy,' she said warmly. 'You never leave your dungeon. What brings you above ground?'

'I heard a rumour that you were back. I thought I'd better check for myself. To tell the truth, I was beginning to think that Irvine had buried you under his patio.'

'No such luck, Fitchy. It's good to see you.'

'How was your holiday?'

'Windsurfing off the Somali coast? On the hot side.'

'Foolish girl. No-one, but no-one would pay your ransom. Tell me, are you still working on that story of Shimmon's?'

'Nope.'

'So what are you doing?'

'Writing Irvine's biography?'

'Autobiography,' he corrected her. 'He'd never let anyone else's name on the cover.'

'Then meet the ghost.'

He smiled, played along. 'Dynamite, right.'

'Fucking dynamite,' she grinned. 'I've got a sweet tooth for this kind of shit.'

They stood without speaking for a long moment.

'Anyway,' he said, 'that story of Shimmon's that you're not writing. Our friend Macleod asked me to give you this.'

He pulled a photograph from his file and passed it to her.'

Four smiling men stared out at her, all clad in the kind of informal gear worn by special forces soldiers. She picked out Pearce, Moorhouse and a stranger. And there, right in the middle, his face alight with a broad, beaming grin, was Chris Keaton.

She glanced up at Fitch.

He said, 'The official version of events was that Mammon never existed. But it did. There was an SAS team. Dave Pearce, Bryan Wright, Kenny Moorhouse and Chris Keaton.'

Ali stared at Keaton, her eyes bright and focused with a strange intensity while her limbs were freezing over with a glacial, numbing fear.

'On the night in question,' Fitch told her, 'Keaton wasn't there. Thanks to some admin balls-up he was stuck in Hereford on his annual Refresher. He had completed fitness and weapons requirements. and a three-day seminar at Bramhill Staff College updating surveillance, communication, sabotage and Det skills, He was at the Regiment's Counter Revolutionary Warfare Wing when Mammon came up. For some reason, he didn't get the call. That meant he didn't go to Kosovo with his patrol. They went operational without him. A cock-up rather than a conspiracy, I believe. Macleod couldn't find the name of the guy who took his place.'

'Keaton always denied knowing about Mammon.'

'What else could he do?'

He could have told me! She thought bitterly. *He could have trusted me with the truth! After all we've been through, he should have trusted me! Why lie to me? And if he lied about Mammon, what else has he lied about?*

Ali found herself struggling for explanation. For understanding. But her mind was racing on single track and coming up with just one question:

Had everything about the Shimmon affair been a lie?

Chapter 71

LUCCA LIVED HIS life by history and tradition, yet his first act on buying a West Oxfordshire country estate had been to tear down its stately pile. Crumbling ruins and their bottomless sink funds represented a tradition beyond his understanding. His own heritage - clan, fic and blood – was tied to people, not place. It was entirely logical for him to illegally demolish the listed buildings, pay the nominal fine and bribe, and construct a house and outbuildings in contemporary Palladian style.

Regardless of all the money invested, this was the least favoured of his homes. Lucca rarely stayed here. For that reason alone, it was a convenient refuge while the New York mess was being cleaned. And if New York was beyond cleansing, if he had to disappear again, it would be a good jumping off point.

Ashe's betrayal had hurt him. It was not just the loss of his closest friend and confidante. Without Ashe's expertise, how was he to find Crain and the money? Without Crain and the money, how was he to manage his business empire? The people close to him lacked the requisite skills; those who possessed the skills were not close enough to be trusted.

Lucca wasn't worried about a slump into penury. He had multiple accounts and assets hidden even from Crain. The money Crain had syphoned from his accounts was Monopoly money. Numbers without meaning. Lucca was not the kind of man to spend his days in the counting house. He had more money than he could hope to use and he could always cash in a few assets. His West Oxfordshire estate alone was valued in excess of ten million sterling. Realising the asset would be far from straightforward since he had no idea which of his companies and personae actually owned it, but that kind of problem was easily greased. He would never be too poor for the rich list. It wasn't the loss of money that troubled him; it was the betrayal.

Ten million sterling. Keaton had spent twice that amount buying Lucca's mercenaries. Purchasing their fealty, intelligence and practical help with Lucca's own money. Suzman, quiet and unassuming, was a natural leader and experienced soldier, trained, like all US special forces, in combat, diplomacy and nation-building. He had confirmed to Keaton that Lucca's inner circle of trusted people amounted to between four and six men, including Vanavasam, and that maybe another three or four might stay loyal. The loyalists would have to be eliminated.

Ten days ago, Suzman had informed Keaton that Lucca was coming to his Oxfordshire estate. That had afforded Keaton plenty of time to undertake a close recce of the house and its secluded woodland setting, to obtain detailed plans of the buildings and to devise his strategy. Four days prior to Lucca's arrival, Suzman had turned up with an advanced guard of six men. Men he had carefully chosen himself. Their assigned task was to secure the house, take control of the custodians minding the house and estate, and vet the newly-employed domestic staff. Their other, unofficial, task was to arrange for Keaton to move in to the annex above the garage.

As a live-in ghost, Keaton continued to prepare meticulously. He installed anti-intruder alerts and fixed the curtains so that no light would shine. He hardly moved lest he be discovered. It was slow time waiting but, as lay-ups go, this was comfortable and easy. No wild-life or weather or crotchrot. At night, he carried out dummy runs, learning 'assault' routes via the underground link to the house, thence to all parts of the main building. On one run, he even oiled locks and hinges. He also practised exfil and escape routes.

When Lucca's Airbus H155 touched down on the heli-pad, Keaton counted Lucca, Vanavasam and six men. Some were suited up, others more casual, but mostly they looked to be what they were, experienced and grizzled paramilitaries. There were also two hungry looking Rottweillers, the kind that might turn on their own handlers. The newcomers hurried inside and that was the last Keaton saw of his target for two days. This, for Keaton, was the critical moment. Cautious and suspicious, he trusted no-one, and he readied himself for Suzman or one of his men to betray him. It didn't happen but Keaton couldn't afford to take anything for granted.

The problem Keaton hadn't foreseen was Lucca's dogs. Two large, blocky Rottweilers, 50 to 60 kgs of black and tan. Belligerent, distrustful killers with massive heads and square muzzles. One seemed to stay in the house. The other patrolled the grounds with Lucca's people and became keenly interested in the garage and its annex. Whenever it came near, it lunged, whined and barked as if it sensed the provocative presence of Keaton, until, eventually, its handler decided to investigate. Keaton heard him try the annex door. It was locked. He peered through the curtains and saw the dog standing rigid, eyes fixed on the door. It refused to move away and that really got its handler's attention. Keaton saw him inspecting the lock and knew that he was in trouble. The door opened directly onto the steep flight of stairs that led straight to him. He had tampered with the lock to slow down anyone trying to get in but it wouldn't stop them.

With discovery moments away, Keaton had to think quickly. This was no mere fight or flight situation. It was fight or die. He couldn't avoid the fighting. The big question was: could he avoid the dying? For once, Keaton was ambivalent. He didn't know where Lucca's men were. He didn't know if Suzman would join him or cut his losses and kill him. All he knew for certain was that the dog handler was about to drive him from cover and that there were at least fifteen men out there. He could let the dog and handler inside then kill them. That might buy a few more minutes to come up with a plan. But what sort of plan? His choice was attack or escape. Covert action was out of the question. He half-smiled at the image of himself tiptoeing across the broad lawns. He would inevitably be seen and then he would be on the back foot, fighting on their terms. Better to use controlled aggression from the start. A one man assault into the unknowable.

But which way? The house or the outside world?

It wasn't a real choice. Deep down, he knew that his decision was already made. He was here. He had come to protect Ali's future. That meant eliminating Lucca. He would probably be cut down trying. Better that than being cut down trying to run away.

He abruptly changed his mind set. No more worrying that he was being compelled into action before he was ready. He was ready. He knew what to do. He had to fight his way into the house, find Lucca and kill him. After that, he would get out if he could. An interesting prospect but there was no point in feeling sorry for himself. He had the advantages of surprise and extreme aggression, and he would use them to the maximum. He strapped on his combat belt. It was already loaded with ammo, HE grenades and flash bangs. He clipped his holstered pistol to his belt and picked up his MP5, He heard the dog handler working the lock and peeked through the curtains. The dog must have sensed him because it began snarling, snapping and muzzle-punching the door. That prompted Keaton to clip a spare gun onto his belt. He might have been a one man blitzkrieg in the making but he was definitely not looking forward to meeting this monster.

He concealed himself near the top of the stairs and tensed as the Kosovar opened the door. The dog leaped forward eagerly but, instead of letting the dog go ahead and do the dirty work, the handler held on and kept it under control. Perhaps he wanted the dog to protect him; or maybe he was worried that the dog might go blue on blue. That made it easier for Keaton. He didn't want them to separate. He could hear them on the stairs, the dog thirsty for blood, the handler struggling for control. Keaton grew in confidence. The handler was focused on his dog and he hadn't even called for backup.

Keaton waited calmly, controlling his breathing and keeping his heart rate down. The dog's muzzle appeared first, mouth drooling, teeth bared, then its grotesque head and ears. Its eyes were rabid with hate and, the instant they located Keaton, the animal uttered a killing growl from deep in its throat and strained forward. Keaton fingered the trigger of his MP5 but he didn't fire. Not yet. He was waiting until the handler reached the landing. The last thing he wanted was bodies tumbling back down the stairs through the open door.

Just then a voice roared from below. 'What the fuck are you doing?'

The Kosovar yanked his dog back under control. 'Something is wrong. The dog! Someone is here!'

'Of course something's wrong, you moron!' yelled Suzman. '*You're* here, you fucking pussy! These are my quarters so get the fuck out.'

'I am told you sleep with your men. My orders are to check the annex.'

'Your orders are to get out now before I shoot your fucking dog!'

'You will not do that. I must check.'

Suzman lifted his gun and fired into the stair riser just below the dog.

The dog turned to meet this new threat, instantly forgetting Keaton and setting itself to attack Suzman.

The mercenary aimed his gun at the dog. 'You've had your warning.'

Understanding that Suzman wouldn't hesitate to kill his dog, the handler made a show of bringing the Rottweiler under control. In truth, it took all his alpha skills, plus some brute force, to persuade the dog down the stairs and keep it from attacking Suzman. The mercenary had shuffled back outside and to one side and was pointing his gun unwaveringly at the snarling animal.

The handler said, 'Lucca will hear of this.'

'You tell Lucca, if I see this fucking dog anywhere near the garage again I will kill it and feed its heart to the crows. If I see you here, I will do the same to you.'

'You will regret this, English.'

'I'm American.'

Suzman watched him go, then went inside, closed the door and climbed the stairs. He threw a huge grin at Keaton. 'For a moment there, I thought he was going to play.'

Keaton managed a rueful smile. 'You cut it close.'

'You look ready enough.'

KEATON HAD PLANNED to move on Lucca's second night but his target had a couple of girls brought in and that forced Keaton to abort. He wanted no witnesses or collateral damage.

Just before two o'clock on the third night, Keaton donned dark training trousers, hoodie, tactical belt and soft shoes, checked his gun and ammo clips and clicked on the silencer. Suzman collected him, tested his ear bud and transmitter and led him from the annex to the pool complex. Keaton knew the route and the routine by heart, only this time he was psyched up for an ambush. He moved cautiously through the underground link from the pool to the lower ground floor of the main house. He had heard no gunfire so he was surprised when they came across the first body. It was the dog handler from the day before. His Rottweiler was stretched out close by, its body torn and bloodied by a burst of automatic fire. Its killer had taken no chances.

Keaton slipped into the security suite, located between the gymnasium and the cinema and featuring a state-of-the art intelligent building management system. Suzman's men had taken control and Keaton was able to study the AV client interface which showed gate entry and CCTV. He could see what looked like two more bodies at strategic points in the building. There were no signs of life, friendly or otherwise. The guard monitoring the screens confirmed that Lucca's men had all been taken out. Keaton hoped so but it all sounded too neat and slick, and he made sure not to drop his vigilance. He had known too many guys who had died from a microsecond of carelessness. He checked his radio and moved on.

The lower ground floor was empty, as were the stairs up to the ground floor. Suzman sensed Keaton's suspicion and showed him his back by leading the way upstairs to the main reception hall. Subtle LED down-lighting illuminated marble flooring and six reception rooms. Another guard lay dead. The voice in Keaton's ear told him all was clear. At the same time, one of Suzman's men appeared and nodded him onwards. Cautiously, Keaton mounted the sweeping galleried staircase. Suzman came with him and Keaton's senses were on ultra-alert. He still didn't quite trust his new allies – can you ever trust a bought man?

He emerged onto the first floor with its quality velvet carpeting. He knew that there were five en-suite bedrooms on this level, three of them occupied, together with a master suite. Two of Suzman's men were waiting. They indicated by sign that three of the bedrooms contained dead men. There were no women. Families weren't due to arrive for another week. Vanavasam was in the master bedroom.

'Okay,' Suzman whispered. 'We have your six.'

Keaton nodded but, as he crossed the landing, he maintained vigilant watch on the five closed doors and two flights of stairs. He reached the master bedroom without incident and he stopped to listen. The voice in his ear told him that it was clear but there was only one person he trusted in this house.

Hearing nothing, he checked his gun, stepped to one side of the door and turned the handle. The door opened soundlessly. Keaton could hear someone snoring loudly. He slipped into the room and stood motionless against the wall.

Vanavasam was on his back, mouth open, snorting and snuffling. With Sarah in mind, Keaton wanted him to suffer but he couldn't risk waking Lucca.

He moved swiftly over the velvet carpet and put a double tap into the man's forehead. Vanavasam died peacefully in his sleep, an end he didn't deserve. It was then that Keaton noticed that the man was sporting ear plugs. He couldn't believe that kind of self-confidence.

As agreed, Suzman didn't accompany Keaton up the stairs to the second floor. By now, Keaton was prepared to place some trust in the voice in his ear, which told him that Lucca was asleep. Without hesitation, he slipped into the bedroom. The bed was to his right, facing the curved sliding doors of the Juliet balcony. The adjacent dressing area and luxury bathroom were empty. The far wall was made up with French windows, beyond which was a spacious and private roof terrace enjoying far-reaching views.

Keaton took out his phone and tapped a brief message:

In. Snatch or kill?

He pressed Send.

Chapter 72

BURNS WAS IN bed when the call came through. It was one of his encrypted phones, so he left his sleeping wife and padded naked through his Belgravia mews house into the privacy of his study. He was fond of this room. Pride of place was his Italian walnut desk and office chairs, handmade in America, with a Marc Freeman painting behind. Twin Gael armchairs stood by a fireplace with open gas fire bounded by bookshelves and topped by a large Blake Daniels painting. The windows overlooked a roof garden carefully crafted for maximum privacy.

'Keaton's in place,' the voice said. 'Does he snatch or kill. I suggest the former. We should put him on trial.'

Burns settled into the Gael chair that offered a view of the garden. 'The last thing we need is a high profile trial. It would be emblematic of causes and issues far greater in importance than Lucca. A show trial would expose us all.'

'So we kill him?'

'It would be an object lesson to others in his position. More importantly, this whole damn business will be put to bed. Lucca, Figgis his recruiter, Sandford his handler – all dead, Alpha vanished without trace.'

'If we kill Lucca, Feysor will be free to publish.'

'What if she does?' Burns' dulcet tones were a parody of his words. 'No one will care. The Great British Public worries more about the price of a bottle of wine than the fate of people they don't know. Brutes like Lucca, they even respect. They give out Peace Prizes to warmongers, never to men of peace. Once we put it out there that he killed his own wife and children, people will see the righteousness.'

'I wish I had your faith. We're talking state sponsored murder.'

'Everybody has to believe in something. It's what makes us human. Even atheism is an act of faith. If nothing else, you can believe that no one will want to resurrect Lucca.'

'Lucca is just the tip of the iceberg.'

'Then get Keaton to silence the journalist.'

'I can't do that. Keaton is fond of the woman.'

'And he is your friend.' Burns chuckled. 'I didn't take you for a sentimental man.'

'You call it sentiment. I call it loyalty.'

The phone was silent for a long time.

'With Figgis and Sandford gone,' Burns said, 'we are both in the clear. Feysor doesn't know of our involvement. I will arrange for pre-emptive stories to be posted, spinning Feysor as a good, well-intentioned reporter who happens to be a conspiracy nut. I will also arrange for 'experts' to go on TV to discredit her story. No need to mention her by name. Just rubbish her story before she can tell it and no-one will listen to her. The ADHD mentality of the twittering generation will do the rest. If she persists with her story she will be dismissed as a bitter, spiteful crank.'

'What do I tell Keaton?'

'Kill Lucca,' said Burns, untroubled by self-doubt. 'Murder the bastard. Then let Feysor know he has succeeded and that, providing she keeps quiet, her beloved will return home safely. Tell her to show some gratitude.'

Corbin chuckled. 'You old romantic, you.'

Chapter 73

MERGIM LUCCA, AKA Bowman, aka Griffiths was lying on his bed stark naked. His eyes were closed and his chest rose and fell in time with his rasping snores. He was alone. A lamp shone softly on his bedside table, rendering him grey and gaunt, if not quite frail and helpless. The room smelled of decay, rancid piss and sweat. There was a glass on the nightstand and Keaton leaned over to sniff it. Whisky.

He stood for a moment, taking in the rot, the aloneness, the alcohol, the night light.

What's wrong, Lucca? Afraid of dying?

He probably was. And who could blame him? He wouldn't be the first old man to be terrified that there might, after all, be an afterlife. But Keaton felt no trace of sympathy. The man on the bed was a mass murderer and Keaton had first-hand experience of the gut-wrenching results. A man like that deserved nothing but merciless hatred.

Lucca opened his eyes. He didn't start or panic to find someone in his room. He displayed no surprise at all that Keaton stood over him with a gun in one hand and a phone in the other.

'How did you get in here?'

'You should pay your men more.'

Lucca squeezed his eyes shut in atonement for his oversight. 'I have done nothing to you. You have no reason to die here. Why have you come?'

'All those bodies,' Keaton said. He lifted Lucca's phone from the table and tossed it away. 'Someone has to pay.'

'Then let me pay you. Whatever you are being paid, I will double it.'

Keaton was suddenly aware that the second Rottweiler was standing on the floor across the bed, staring him down. It was deadly still, its mouth moving as though to control Keaton from a distance. In a smooth, unhurried movement, Keaton brought his gun up and aimed it at the dog.

'No!' Lucca said in a voice that was both commanding and pleading. 'He will not harm you. He is like me. Too old for the fight.'

Something stayed Keaton's hand. He had no idea what. He certainly wasn't sentimental about dogs, or about Lucca's pathetic concern for his *pet*. He watched with one eye as the Rottweiler walked slowly around the bed to within a metre of him. It seemed to have difficulty walking and Keaton realised that it was suffering from old age. It was clearly arthritic and in pain, and, by the looks of its eyes, near-blind. It made a half-hearted show of aggression, lunging its head forward, making a guttural growl and showing its teeth, but that was just muscle memory, It didn't attack. Satisfied that Lucca and Keaton were talking quietly, it settled down chunk by chunk into a comfortable, drooling but watchful pose. To Keaton's astonishment, it even twitched its tail.

Lucca's eyes went to the silenced Steyr though his mind was on the touchpad alarm under his bedside table. If he could only reach it! 'How do you expect to get out of here alive?'

Keaton smiled a knowing, contemptuous smile. 'Your men are going to drive me out in your own car. I might even borrow your heli.'

Lucca reached out towards the bedside table, picked up the glass and took a long drink, spilling some of it on himself. His hands were trembling. He set the glass down and spoke again.

'We have an agreement.' Lucca's mouth was still dry and his voice crackled.

'You made an agreement with Ali Feysor, not me. One that you have no intention of keeping.'

Lucca sat up and snarled. 'Nobody breaks a deal with David Bowman!'

Keaton smiled. 'You're not David Bowman, You're Mervin Lucca and he's a dead man.'

'Killing me will not save your journalist bitch. Or you. My death will be avenged. You will live a brief life of terror then you will die a thousand deaths.'

'And who have you tasked with that little pleasure?'

'My people are everywhere.'

'Your people are all in hell.'

Doubt entered Lucca's eyes for the first time. 'Vanavasam will tear you apart, limb by limb.'

'Vanavasam has a neat double tap in the forehead. The rest of your people are similarly afflicted.'

Lucca didn't believe him. He started playing for time. 'Name your price. Anything.'

'Anything?' Keaton smiled. 'One day, long ago, you made a choice and that choice set you on your path. The path brought you here and here it ends.'

'You can't do this,' Lucca was inching his way towards that touchpad.

Keaton's phone vibrated in his hand. He glanced at the screen. There was just one word.

Kill.

Keaton's distracted glance was almost enough for Lucca. The Kosovar suddenly had a gun in his hand, a Ruger SR9c, but his gnarled fingers were fumbling his grip. Keaton dropped his phone, grasped the older man's gun and twisted the weapon from his hand. The dog stirred but stayed down.

'Fuck you,' Lucca hissed.

'Go ahead,' Keaton said, nodding towards the table as though granting a last request. 'Sound the alarm.'

Lucca hesitated, then scrambled for the pad and pressed it, over and over again. No-one came.

'Like I said,' Keaton told him callously, 'your people are dead.'

'You have cut the wire,' Lucca sneered knowingly. 'They will come.'

Keaton smiled. 'Your little gizmo is wireless. No wires to cut. No one is coming.'

Lucca stared at his dog, his face sly and calculating. His voice dripped with contempt for Keaton's softness, 'You spared the dog. You won't shoot me in cold blood.'

Without hesitation, Keaton adjusted Lucca's unsuppressed Ruger in his hand and shot the dog twice in the head. The noise of the gunfire was deafening. The Rottweiler's head bumped heavily to the floor. There was no other sound. It was as though someone had pressed pause.

It was Lucca who broke the silence. 'You should not have done that.' His voice was thick with venom. 'He would not have harmed you.'

Keaton glanced at the door. 'They must have heard the shots in London. Where are your people?'

At last, Lucca understood that no-one was coming. He reacted instinctively, swivelling his body upwards with surprising speed and lunging towards Keaton with clawing hands. Keaton was quicker and stronger. He stepped forward, grabbed Lucca's arm and twisted him back down again. To Keaton's astonishment, the older man gave up without a fight. He just slumped into the mattress as though his strength and power had drained away.

'I have done nothing to you,' Lucca said. 'Why are you doing this?'

'You're a butcher, A canker on the lives of decent people.'

'A man like you has no right to judge me.'

'True enough,' Keaton nodded. 'I'm Lucifer's child, much as you. I just happen to be holding the gun.'

'You don't have to use it. We are the same, you and me. Put the gun away and I can make you rich beyond your dreams. I can give you anything!'

'I already have your money, and your soldiers, and your life.' Keaton wanted to smile triumphantly but it wouldn't come. 'If you can give me Kenny Moorhouse, I will let you live.'

'Who?'

'Precisely.'

Keaton tossed the Ruger across the room and gripped his own gun.

'Wait!' A shaft of desperate hope lit up the Kosovar. 'I have to confess! You must allow me to confess my sins! I am a Catholic, I cannot die without the Viaticum.'

'When did you last confess? Where would I find a priest with the time to listen to your litany of sins?' Keaton chuckled cruelly. 'You want to die in a state of grace? I understand that. But you'll have to be satisfied with a Life Review. You know, when your whole life flashes before you as you die. Think of all those juicy murders. Or maybe you'd prefer your rapes? Whatever. You can't postpone the inevitable. Just lie back, close your eyes and enjoy the movie.'

'No! Please! It would be monstrous to deny me the confessional of the Viaticum!'

'You want your all-seeing God to forgive you?' Keaton gave him scorn and incredulity in equal measure. 'How is that fair? He was complicit in your every sin. To forgive you he would have to forgive himself. Now, that can't be right. Forgive himself, and you, and leave the tortured tortured and the murdered murdered? I don't think so. If a priest walked through that door to give you absolution, I would shoot him dead.'

Lucca started to protest but Keaton turned a deaf ear. 'This one is for Kenny Moorhouse.'

He shot Lucca in the right knee. He was hardly aware of the scream of pain.

'This one is for your daughter.'

Another shot, another knee, another scream.

'I'd like to throw you into a burning barn,' Keaton said. 'But you'd probably slither into a hole and survive.'

He shot Lucca in the gut, not once but twice.

Lucca howled softly, his hands clasped across his abdomen as if he could heal himself. His face was opened up in disbelief. Keaton thought about leaving him to bleed out but he had to be sure. It was no regal salute that sent Lucca on his way. Just a double phut. Lucca twitched and levitated several inches above the bed before sinking back down.

Moving unhurriedly, Keaton reached for Lucca's neck. No pulse. He hadn't expected one but he wanted to be sure that Mergim Lucca, the great death-cheater, really was dead. It certainly wasn't the way Keaton would choose to go: old, alone and terrified with only a crippled dog for companionship.

'You die the death you deserve,' Keaton murmured. At the same time, he couldn't help resolving to deserve a better dying for himself.

Time to go.

Not knowing what awaited him outside the room, he refreshed his gun with a full clip and made sure a round was chambered. The voice in his ear reassured him that the house was clear. But could he trust it? There were no guarantees in this world. Men had been known to take the cash and murder the money-man. The mercs worked for money but Keaton had none on him. Their second payment depended on him getting out and authorising the bank transfer. Reason enough for them to keep him safe. But life wasn't reasonable.

He opened the door with extreme caution, gun in hand and ready for anything. There was no-one on the landing or the stairs, and only Suzman waited on the first floor landing.

The two men exchanged nods. No need for words. Both were content with mission outcome. Both knew that it was over. Both knew that Suzman's second payment would be made. Suzman accompanied Keaton downstairs.

When they reached the lower ground floor, Keaton was suddenly aware of men standing in the shadows. The dead had gone but not the living. All exits were blocked, the doors were covered and the lethal menace of Suzman's men was tangible. Some instinct told Keaton to keep still, to wait, watch and listen. Nothing was happening and nothing was going to happen. But he was a man of positive action. Wired to get his retaliation in first. It was the only way he knew how to survive.

Suzman sensed Keaton's tension building to action and moved quickly to reassure him. 'We're good, Chris. We're good.' To his men, he said, 'Stand down fellas. We're done here!'

There followed the welcome metallic clacking of weapons being made safe and the buzz of men talking softly. A job well done. Suzman turned to Keaton, his arms and fingers outstretched and empty, as if to emphasise his buddy-buddy intentions. Suzman's men began to gather in the entrance hall while the man himself nudged Keaton towards the front door. No one blocked their way. A dark SUV waited outside by the fountain. Keaton's gear was already in the boot. As he got into the passenger seat, Suzman gripped his arm and gave him one last message. Then the car swept down the driveway, past the heli, through the opened electric gates and onto the Oxford Road.

Keaton settled back to enjoy the ride. Lucca could indulge in no more blood killing, not even from beyond the grave. Suzman's last words had confirmed that Lucca's people in New York were dead. The man and his fic were extinct.

Ali Feysor was safe at last.

Keaton's face creased into a cold, wintry smile. For once, just for this once, the killing had been personal and he had enjoyed it.

THE END

Printed in Poland
by Amazon Fulfillment
Poland Sp. z o.o., Wrocław